PRAISE FOR

SEAL's Honor

"Megan Crane's mix of tortured ex–special ops heroes, their dangerous missions, and the rugged Alaskan wilderness is a sexy, breathtaking ride!"

—*New York Times* bestselling author Karen Rose

DELTA FORCE
Defender

AN ALASKA FORCE NOVEL

MEGAN CRANE

JOVE
New York

A JOVE BOOK
Published by Berkley
An imprint of Penguin Random House LLC
penguinrandomhouse.com

Copyright © 2020 by Megan Crane
Excerpt from *Special Ops Seduction* copyright © 2020 by Megan Crane
Penguin Random House supports copyright. Copyright fuels creativity, encourages
diverse voices, promotes free speech, and creates a vibrant culture. Thank you for buying
an authorized edition of this book and for complying with copyright laws by not
reproducing, scanning, or distributing any part of it in any form without permission.
You are supporting writers and allowing Penguin Random House to continue to
publish books for every reader.

A JOVE BOOK, BERKLEY, and the BERKLEY & B colophon
are registered trademarks of Penguin Random House LLC.

ISBN: 9781984805522

First Edition: July 2020

Printed in the United States of America
1   3   5   7   9   10   8   6   4   2

Cover image of the couple by Claudio Marinesco
Cover art: Figures © Claudio Marinesco; Sitka, Alaska © Alex Sava / Getty Images;
Dock © Neta Degany / Getty Images; Alaskan Mountains © FloridaStock / Shutterstock
Cover design by Sarah Oberrender
Book design by Tiffany Estreicher

To all the readers who are as excited for Isaac and Caradine's story as I was, this is for you.

And for Nicole. For obvious reasons.

Prologue

BOSTON
TEN YEARS EARLIER

Julia had already ignored her father's summons as many times as she could. It was time to go back home or face the consequences.

Or, knowing her father, both.

Twenty-two-year-olds about to graduate from college *should* assert their independence. Or, anyway, that was the excuse she planned to use when he lit into her about it, assuming he was in a mood to listen to excuses. Because he was going to be furious—there was no getting around that.

No one was suicidal enough to ignore Mickey Sheeran for too long.

Julia was one of the few people who dared pretend otherwise, and—filled with bravado while safely on campus and protected by university security—she'd decided to prove it.

She was already feeling sick with regret about that as she turned onto her parents' street in their unpretentious neighborhood outside of Boston proper, which was filled with the regular Joes her dad claimed he admired as true American heroes. Julia knew that what he really meant by that was that all their neighbors were as in awe of him as they were afraid of him. Just the way he liked it.

Most people were just plain old afraid of him, Julia included.

More so the closer she got to the house she'd grown up in and hadn't been able to leave fast enough. And never seemed to be able to put behind her, whether she lived there or not.

There wasn't a single part of her that wanted to go back. Ever. And particularly not when she'd deliberately provoked him.

Sure, all she'd actually done was ignore a couple of phone messages ordering her to leave her dormitory and come home. But she knew her father would view the delay between the messages he'd left and her appearance as nothing short of traitorous. She was expected to leap to obey him almost before he issued a command, as she well knew. He didn't care that she had exams. He probably didn't know she had exams.

But Julia knew it was foolish to imagine her father was dumb. He wasn't. It was far more likely that he knew full well it was her exam period and had waited until this, her final semester of college, to force her to take incompletes and fail to graduate. He was nothing if not a master at revenge served cold.

Mickey hadn't been on board with the college thing, something he made perfectly clear every time he sneered about Julia's "ambitions." He'd also refused to pay for it and had gone ballistic when Julia had found her own loans and a job in a restaurant to help with costs.

She still thought it was worth the bruises.

Her sister, Lindsay, was fifteen months younger and

had never made it out from under their father's thumb. She still lived at home, grimly obeying his every command in the respectful silence he demanded, because females were to be seen, never heard.

She'd even started dating one of Mickey's younger associates.

You know where that's going to lead, Julia had muttered under her breath when she'd been forced to put in an appearance on Easter Sunday. *Straight to an entire life exactly like Mom's. Is that really what you want?*

You're the only one who thinks there's another choice, Lindsay had snapped right back, her gaze dark and her mouth set in a mulish line. *There's not.*

Julia had looked across the crowded church, filled with the people who came to Mass one other time each year, and stared at the back of Lindsay's boyfriend's head. She wished her gaze could punch holes in him.

I don't accept that, she'd said quietly. *I refuse to accept that.*

Next to her, her sister had sighed, something weary and practical on her face. Julia had recognized the look. Their mother wore it often. Soon it would start to fade and crack around it turned into beaten-down resignation.

He's not a nice guy, but at least it gets me out of the house and away from Dad every now and again, she'd said. *That's not nothing.*

Their brother Jimmy, the meanest of their three older brothers, had turned around from the pew in front of them. He looked more and more like Dad by the day, and the nasty look he'd thrown the two of them had shut them both up. Instantly.

Sometimes Julia lay in her narrow cot in the dorm, squeezed her eyes shut so tight she expected all her blood vessels to pop, and *wished*. For something to save her. For some way out. For the limitless, oversized life her college friends had waiting for them, with no boundaries in sight. No rules. Nothing but their imagination to lead them wherever they wanted to go.

Maybe she'd always known that she wasn't going to get any of that.

And maybe her father had been right to oppose her going off to college, because all it was going to do was break her heart. Worse than if she'd been a good girl like Lindsay and done what was expected of her.

Hopelessness only hurt if you were dumb enough to hope for something different.

Julia couldn't remember, now, when she'd first realized that her father was . . . unusual. That he was the reason the other children kept their distance from the Sheeran family. But she could remember, distinctly, the first time she'd Googled her father's name and found a wealth of information about him. Just right there, online. For anyone to see.

She'd always known her father was a bad man.

Still, it was something else to find all those articles detailing the criminal acts he'd been accused of over the course of his long career. She thought sometimes that a good daughter would have been appalled, disbelieving.

But she'd looked at her father's mug shot in an article from the front page of the *Boston Globe*, and she'd believed. She'd known. He was exactly as bad as they claimed he was, and probably worse, and that likely meant she was bad, too. Deep in her blood and bones, no matter what she did.

Every year they failed to catch him in the act, the bolder and more vicious he became. And the more she accepted that his DNA lived in her, too.

Because if Julia were as brave as she pretended she was when she was across town on a pretty campus where she could squint her eyes and imagine she was someone else's daughter, she would have called the FBI herself.

But she wasn't brave. She didn't point the car in some other direction, drive for days, and disappear. Instead, she was obediently driving home to face her father's rage. And the back of his hand. And whatever other treats he had in store for her.

Her throat might be dry with fear and her heart might be pounding, but she was still doing what he wanted. In the end, she always did.

All things considered, maybe Lindsay's grim acceptance was the better path. Julia liked to put on a good show, but they were both going to end up in the same place.

Her stomach was killing her. Knots upon knots.

She eased her car to the curb and cut the headlights, then forced herself to get out into the cool night air. It was a force of habit to park a ways down the block. There were always flat-eyed men coming and going from the house, and it would go badly for her if she inconvenienced any of them. And Mickey was never satisfied with small displays of strength when bigger ones could cow more people and show off his cruelty to greater effect.

In his circles, the crueler he was—especially to his own family—the more people feared him. And fear was what made Mickey come alive.

She leaned against the closed car door and pulled her phone out of her pocket. It was cold enough that she wished she'd worn more than a T-shirt, but there was a part of her that liked the chill that ran along her arms. It would keep her awake. Aware.

You couldn't really dodge one of Mickey's blows, but there were ways of taking it, and falling, that lessened the damage.

She'd learned that lesson early.

She pulled up Lindsay's number and texted her, announcing that she'd parked and was about to walk in to face the music.

Don't come in, her sister texted back almost instantly. *It's weird in here.*

A different sort of prickle worked its way down the back of Julia's neck and started winding down her spine. Her hair felt as if it were standing on end in the breeze, except there wasn't a breeze.

I'm coming out, Lindsay texted.

Julia found herself holding her breath, though she couldn't have said why. The night felt thick and dark, suddenly, though she could see the streetlights with her own eyes. Something about that caught at her, and she moved away from the nearest pool of light to the shade of a big tree. She stood there, keeping still. She put her back to the trunk, hoping that if anyone were looking, they wouldn't see her.

And she tried really hard to convince herself that she was just being paranoid.

But when her sister appeared out of nowhere and grabbed her arm, she bit her own tongue so hard to keep from screaming that she tasted copper.

"What are you doing?" she whispered fiercely at Lindsay. "You scared the—"

"You should go back to your dorm," Lindsay said, and this time, there was something stark in her gaze. Too much knowledge, maybe. Something unflinching that made the knots inside Julia's belly sharpen into spikes. "And stay there."

And all the things they never talked about directly seemed to swell in the cool spring night. The truths that no one spoke, for fear of what it might unleash. Not just because they were afraid of Mickey and his friends, whom he often called his brothers but treated with far more respect than he gave the members of his actual family, but because acknowledging a thing made it real.

It had never occurred to Julia before this very moment how deeply and desperately she'd clung to the tattered shreds of her denial.

She and her sister stared at each other in the inky

black shadows of the ominous night, and she couldn't tell anymore if it was the dark that threatened her, or if it was the truth.

Whatever was coming, there was no escaping it. Had she always known that? Whether it was this night or another night or twenty years down a road that ended up with her seeing her mother's tired, fearful face in the mirror, this life she'd been so determined to imagine as a path she could choose had only ever been a downward spiral. To one single destination.

Sooner or later, they were all going to hell. Or hell was coming for them. It didn't matter which. She was going to burn either way.

Julia wanted to throw up.

But at the same time, a heady sort of giddiness swept over her, and it took her a second to realize what it was. Freedom, of a sort. Or relief, which amounted to the same thing.

She reached out and laced her fingers through her sister's, the way she used to do when they were little. Back when it was easier to pretend.

"Come with me," she said fiercely.

And Lindsay looked as if she wanted to cry.

"It's too late," she replied. Her voice was soft. Painful. "He asked me to marry him."

"You don't have to say yes."

"I love that you think it matters what I say."

"All the more reason to come with me," Julia said stoutly. "We can figure it out. We can . . . do something."

Lindsay's smile pained Julia, like someone had prized her ribs apart.

"Julia," she began.

But when hell came, it came out of nowhere.

A bright, hot, terrible flash of horror.

They were both on the ground, dazed and stunned, and Julia lifted a hand to her temple, where she felt something sticky. But she couldn't find her way to caring about it much. Something was wrong with her ears, her head. Something was *wrong*.

Car alarms were going off up and down the street, there was a siren in the distance, and she couldn't remember how she'd gotten to the ground. She pulled herself to her hands and knees, grabbing for Lindsay as she went.

And they knelt there, hugging each other even though it hurt, and stared at the roaring fire where their childhood home had been.

Their mother. Their brothers. Even their father—

Julia couldn't take it in.

Lindsay made a shocked, low sort of sound, like a sob.

And somehow, that crystallized things, with a wrenching, vicious jolt inside of Julia. Half panic, half resolve.

She turned to her sister and took her shoulders in her hands, ignoring the stinging in her palms.

"This is the other choice, Lindsay," Julia said, her voice harsh and thick and not her own at all. But she would get used to it. She would grow into it. If she survived. And she had every intention of surviving. "But we have to choose it. Now."

One

The call came in at 2:47 A.M.

Isaac Gentry wasn't asleep because Isaac rarely slept, especially when Alaska Force was running active missions.

And Alaska Force always had active missions.

As the owner and leader of the most elite group of ex–special forces operatives in the world—the kind of individuals who didn't think it was particularly heroic to save the world, because it was simply their job, in and out of active military service—Isaac had long since accepted that monitoring ongoing situations came with the territory. His cabin in Fool's Cove, a remote and hard-to-reach spot on the back side of a distant, isolated island in the Alaskan Panhandle, was outfitted with enough tech to track his people wherever they found themselves on the globe.

"Report," he said into his comm unit by way of an answer, the way he always did when a member of his team called in.

"There's a fire," Griffin Cisneros, known ice man and almost supernaturally self-possessed marine sniper, belted out. Sounding in no way self-possessed or icy or really like himself at all.

Isaac's gut twisted. Because Griffin wasn't on a mission. Griffin was supposed to be at home in his cute little house on the other side of the island in picturesque Grizzly Harbor, tucked up with his woman and enjoying the relatively mild June weather.

"Report," he said again, though he already knew it was going to be bad. And worse, local. "Is it happening again?"

The tiny fishing village of Grizzly Harbor was supposed to be too far away from anything to attract attention. It was on a small island in a little-traveled part of Southeast Alaska's Inside Passage, where nothing ever happened. Something Isaac knew personally and well, having grown up here.

But the past couple of years there'd been a little too much excitement in the middle of nowhere. It had even drawn down the attention of the Alaska State Troopers, who'd needed convincing that Alaska Force were the good guys. There'd been deaths, a mad preacher with a boatload of explosives, actual deployed explosives onshore and off, two kidnappings and a cult, plus acts of criminal mischief ranging from annoying to life-threatening.

Not exactly what Isaac had in mind. He'd chosen Grizzly Harbor as his base when he'd started Alaska Force because the only danger around was the great Alaskan wilderness and weather. He'd imagined it would serve as an excellent barrier between Alaska Force and the rest of the world, because that was what the great and glorious state of Alaska did by virtue of its location. Alaska was the Last Frontier and the ultimate geographic cure.

All outside shenanigans were supposed to be over

now, six months after the last bout of excitement that had involved a high-stakes helicopter rescue of a boat on the cold Alaskan seas. On Christmas Day.

But he let that go. If it wasn't over, they'd handle it. That was what Alaska Force did.

"Isaac."

Once again, Griffin sounded completely unlike himself. It might have been terrifying if Isaac had been in possession of all the necessary information and could allow himself a response. Until then, he couldn't let himself react.

But when his border collie, Horatio, sat up from his bed in front of the fire and whined softly, Isaac suspected that maybe he was already reacting.

"Isaac. It's Caradine. Her place . . . the Water's Edge Café blew up."

Everything inside Isaac stopped.

Dead.

But he was entirely too well trained to surrender to it. Or to blank out or freeze as worst-case scenarios swamped him, one after the next, each more horrible than the last.

Griffin made a sound. It took Isaac a moment to understand it was his name.

"I'm on my way," he said, and he sounded calm. Controlled and even, as befitted a man of his rank and position.

Good to know he could still make that happen when the world was ending.

Might have already ended, with him sitting out here monitoring things he didn't care about across the planet while she—

But he locked that line of thought down, hard.

He went wide on the comm unit, barking out orders and rousing anyone who was on the island instead of out on a job. He was already moving, shoving his feet into his boots and then tossing himself out into the late-night blue of the June night. He was glad he was from Southeast Alaska, where the summer nights weren't that full-on white midnight sun they got farther north, because the eerie half-light was more than enough to make him feel restless.

Though possibly that wasn't what was clawing at him tonight.

The helicopter was already waiting for him when he made it to the launchpad, a ten-minute hike up from his family's former fishing lodge, which currently served as Alaska Force's base of operations. Tonight Isaac made the climb in approximately three minutes.

He nodded at Rory, the former Green Beret who was piloting tonight, and he was distantly aware that there were other people in the helicopter, but he didn't speak.

Instead, he stared out at the dark, inky water and the lights from the lodge and the cabins as they rose into the air over Fool's Cove. And he tried to keep his head productively blank, the way he always did before a mission. Free of his personal thoughts, open to focus on what cropped up.

But all he could see was her face. Caradine's *face*.

He had to grit his teeth to make himself stop. And all told, twenty minutes elapsed between Griffin's initial call and Isaac's arrival in Grizzly Harbor, but to Isaac every minute was a lifetime.

Rory set down near the docks, where there was a stretch of even ground when the tide was low. Isaac knew he'd jumped out when his boots hit the ground, but his focus was already up the hill, into the cluster of buildings that made up the village, and the knot of people and smoke where Caradine's café was supposed to be.

Then he was moving automatically, trying to assess the damage as he went. The fire looked to be contained to the lower part of the building where the café was. Not the living quarters up above, which was something. Then again, he couldn't see what had happened around back.

He had a flash of her, dark eyebrows raised and that belligerent *I dare you* look on her face—

But he couldn't.

He couldn't go there until he knew, one way or the other.

And he was trained for this. He was trained to gather information first, then react.

No matter the circumstances.

Isaac realized he'd been running when he stopped. He'd reached the semicircle of villagers and Alaska Force members who'd formed a perimeter around the fire. All were engaged in fighting what looked like the last of it, some of them half-dressed or in their pajamas, because this really was the middle of nowhere. If they didn't put the fire out, it could sweep through the whole town.

That was when he realized he'd showed up in nothing but the T-shirt and cargo pants he'd been wearing while not sleeping back in his cabin. Not exactly his tactical best.

Isaac nodded at the Grizzly Harbor residents he knew, which was most of them. His brain filed away the rest into a mental file marked SUMMER TOURISTS. But when his gaze found Griffin, it stayed on him. Hard.

He didn't ask the question.

"It's a garden-variety Molotov cocktail," Griffin told Isaac immediately when he came over to him, sounding cold and assessing again. Which was precisely how Isaac wanted his favorite sniper. "It went through the front window of the café. And it was a weak one, because all it did was blow out the windows and make a mess of the front room. The structure appears sound, and the living quarters upstairs are undamaged."

"Undamaged," Isaac repeated, while everything in him that had stopped still clicked over, an engine starting up again. His heart, maybe.

"But empty."

"Empty?" There was a thud inside him, like a mortar shell hitting its target, but he refused to acknowledge it. "Signs of a struggle?"

"None." Isaac recognized the voice before he glanced to the side to find Jonas Crow had materialized from the ether, or the night itself. Because Isaac hadn't seen him in his initial sweep of the area. As one of the few men still alive who knew exactly what Jonas had done in the service, Isaac shouldn't have been surprised that the man still managed to make like a ghost. Yet he always was. "If I had to guess, my take would be that there was an attempt to flush her out, but she didn't go down the back stairs. There are tracks leading away from that side window, but they disappear at the hot springs. One set of tracks, moving fast."

Isaac tried to take the information in, and everything it meant, but he was stuck on the most critical part. She was alive.

She was alive.

"This is good news, right?" Rory asked, on Isaac's six.

Former SEAL Blue Hendricks, who had caught the helicopter with Isaac, was closer to the fire perimeter. He shook his head. "Caradine in the woods? I don't see it. She doesn't even like the hot springs."

"She likes them fine," Isaac retorted without thinking.

It was a measure of how completely he'd lost his cool tonight. Since when did he show his hand? Since when did he fail to think everything through and strategize before speaking? He needed to pull himself together.

Meanwhile, he thanked whatever deities still bothered to check in on a man like him that Templeton Cross—his best friend and brother since they'd survived the six-month hellscape called the Operator Qualification Course for what was known in some circles as Delta Force—wasn't around to witness his slip. Isaac could hear Templeton's booming laugh anyway, the way he was sure he would in real time once Templeton heard what Isaac had inadvertently admitted.

Someone was probably texting him right now to tell him.

She's alive, Isaac reminded himself as the silence dragged on around him, because no one dared actually get in his face. Jonas could have, but wouldn't. That was Templeton's job.

He concentrated on the fact they hadn't found her body and not the fact he'd just contributed to the endless gossip concerning what was or wasn't happening between him and Caradine. She was alive. She'd understood what was happening and extricated herself from the situation. Then she'd taken off.

And had yet to return, though the fire looked contained and most of the village was milling around on the wooden boardwalks that served as streets.

That told him a whole lot.

Isaac scanned the scene. The one official firefighter in the village, Chris Tanaka, was barking out orders to the rest. Most of whom he'd trained at one point or another, whether they were part of the official crew or not. No one wanted Grizzly Harbor, with its boardwalks and huddled-together houses, to go up in flames. Their one truck, parked on an angle in front of the blackened, smoky front of the café, pumped water up from the harbor while a few men were supplementing with buckets. The fire was down to a smolder now, which supported Griffin's theory that it had been a weak firebomb in the first place. It had been about damage, not death.

Which meant Jonas was right, too. They'd been trying to flush her out.

He had a flash of her then, bright and hot, lighting up all the parts of him that had stopped still when he'd gotten that call. Caradine Scott, mouthy and bad-tempered and beautiful. Prickly and stubborn and wedged deep beneath his skin since the day she'd arrived here. That chipped black nail polish she always had on her fingernails. Those too-blue eyes. The baggy clothes she wore, like that could fool anyone into overlooking her toned, fit body beneath. Her astonishingly good cooking, which he'd told her once was basically her true heart on display.

That had been the first time she'd thrown him out of the Water's Edge Café. It wasn't the last time. Not to mention the many times she'd thrown him out of her bed upstairs, too, then slammed the door in his face—and locked it—in case he'd missed her point.

He felt that mortar shell hit him again. Artillery fire rained down inside him, pummeling him.

Isaac had seen her scowl at him a thousand times. He'd kissed her silly. He'd even made her laugh—though she'd told him he was mistaken and it had simply been a coughing fit gone wrong. He'd seen her stare down drunken locals three times her size, and he'd seen her intimidate tourists with a single arched brow.

What he couldn't imagine Caradine doing, ever, was running scared.

The very idea made him want to tear apart the world with his own two hands.

"I want to know who threw the bomb," Isaac said tersely to the suspiciously silent group around him. "Now. And then I want to know why, once again, people are rolling up into Grizzly Harbor and getting bomb-happy without us seeing them coming. I thought we were done with this."

"On it, boss," Blue said, in a way that had Isaac looking at him sharply. Sure enough, the ex-SEAL was exchanging a glance with Griffin that Isaac knew was as good as that text to Templeton.

He ignored that, too, because he could. Because Templeton wasn't here. Templeton was tending to his family issues in the Lower 48 and wasn't on hand to call Isaac out.

That meant Isaac could deliver another spate of orders without receiving so much as a raised eyebrow in return. Once he was done, he turned away, realizing as he did that Alaska Force was one thing. His fellow citizens, friends, and neighbors were another.

And it took him more effort than it should have to pull out that genial smile he usually wore for the public.

"You keep bringing your messes into this town, Isaac," growled Otis Taggert, who ran the Bait & Tackle. He'd always made his dislike of the Gentry family well known, even way back when Isaac had been a kid here. Whether he disliked Isaac personally or lumped him in with Gentrys past was hard to figure. And tonight, Isaac cared even less than usual. "Where's it going to end?"

"Thanks for your concern, Otis," Isaac replied, managing to keep his voice amiable. He couldn't say the same about his expression. "It looks like Caradine made it out."

The scrum of locals got a little loud at that obvious slap, but Isaac didn't take it back. Neither did the older man. And Isaac had to order himself to shift his weight, get out of a fighting stance, and run a hand over his face like he was a mere mortal instead of a highly trained piece of weaponry meant for war, not social interactions like these.

"Hero status can only go so far," Otis said, not even pretending to keep it beneath his breath.

"I never pretended to be a hero," Isaac retorted, another clue that he was maybe not operating on all cylinders, the way he would have been if this hadn't involved Caradine. Since he'd been confounding Otis with a bland smile and no reaction for years now. "But I am a resident and a local business owner. So maybe don't talk to me like I'm the enemy."

"Gentrys have been here since the gold rush," Madeleine Yazzie chimed in then, her red beehive trembling the way it usually did, even if tonight she was in her pajamas. Next to her, her on-again, off-again husband, Jaco, stood with his arms crossed, his usually dour expression aimed directly at the Bait & Tackle owner. "They weren't Johnny-come-latelies like you, Otis, swanning in and acting like you own the place."

"It's not a competition," old Ernie Tatlelik growled.

"It is to Otis," Nellie Oberlin retorted in the same brisk voice she used to keep the rowdy patrons in line at the Fairweather, the only bar in town.

"If you'll excuse me, I thought maybe I'd go look for Caradine," Isaac heard himself say with far too much edginess and not enough of that *boy next door, aw shucks* thing he'd been cultivating since moving back here. Something he'd probably regret when he recovered from this night and that call. But he'd worry about that when he found her. "Who's missing? In case that part wasn't clear."

"You're too much like your uncle Theo," Otis complained, glaring at him as if he'd said he was off to take a nap. "Always more important than everyone else in the room."

"What room is that, Otis?" Madeleine snapped at him. "That tiny little cabin in the woods where Theo lives, all alone, with nothing but his thoughts? Or that store of yours where you hold court over a kingdom of worms and flies?"

And as they all started sniping at one another the way only people with usually buried small-town grudges could, Isaac melted away, skirting around the destroyed café. He took a look at that side window and the tracks in the dirt two stories beneath it. Then he headed for the path that wound up the hill, leading away from town. Toward the hot springs where Jonas had lost Caradine's trail.

As if summoned by the thought of him—which wasn't outside the realm of the possible—Jonas materialized beside Isaac.

"Are you okay?" he asked. As if the question pained him.

And later, maybe, Isaac would think about the state he must have been in for his brother-in-arms to ask him a question like that. When they'd been neck-deep in just about every slice of hell this planet had to offer and Jonas had never inquired into his well-being. Because he'd always assumed that Isaac had himself handled.

Isaac didn't respond.

Jonas nodded, as if that was answer enough.

"Rory located a boat out in the sound," he said instead, his voice sounding the way it always did. Dark and rusty. "No sign of Caradine, but we have eyes on her perpetrators."

Isaac jerked his chin to indicate he'd heard. Inside him, the artillery fire shifted, turning into something like an earthquake.

He had another flash of her, naked and smiling, her clever face alight with mockery aimed straight at him. *Listen up, Gentry,* she'd said, with all that scornful haughtiness only she could make so hot. *If you can't pull it together, I'll throw you out in the cold.*

That had been their first night together.

Your problem, she'd told him a long time later, *is that you like it when I'm mean to you.*

But he'd been inside her, the only time she let him talk to her, and he'd pressed his advantage, the only way he could, until she'd shuddered and come apart.

Your problem, he'd replied, his mouth at her ear, *is you don't want to be.*

He'd believed that until tonight.

"Keep me informed," he told Jonas, who nodded again, then vanished.

Isaac kept going. He took the trail out of town, and he didn't look over at the house he'd grown up in, because he didn't torture himself like that anymore. He'd been a commissioned marine officer. Then he'd been Force Recon. And then he'd gone deep into a far darker hell. If he started counting up ghosts, he'd be too haunted to take a breath.

Caradine had taken care of haunting him for years now.

He listened to Blue's conversation with the hired guns Rory had rounded up over his comm unit and wasn't surprised the two of them had nothing productive to say about who had contracted them. Only that it had happened in Juneau.

And when Jonas returned and started trailing him again, he was aware of it by the prickle on the back of his neck—but that was the beauty of his silent, infinitely lethal friend. Jonas was never going to feel the need to make idle conversation.

Together, they followed Caradine's tracks to the collection of little huts that functioned as the community baths and sauna, taking advantage of the island's natural hot springs. Beyond the hot springs, the trail wound out toward the far point of Grizzly Harbor proper. Isaac stood there, ignoring interior mortar shells and tectonic shifts alike. He was aware that he was holding himself funny, stiff and furious as he glared out at what he could see of the trail in the strange summer night.

"She jumped out her side window." It wasn't a question.

Jonas made an affirmative noise. "She climbed down. Fast."

Isaac nodded, because that was how he'd interpreted the tracks, too. Enough of a depression in the dirt beneath the window to suggest a jump from a height, but not too much of one, and then she'd taken off running. Until she got here. The baths were a great place to switch out whatever shoes she'd been wearing, he figured. For a pair of hiking boots, maybe, that looked like every other shoe impression in the dirt trail.

It was June. There were a lot of tracks on the island's most accessible trail. Tourists and locals alike, this time of year.

He could picture Caradine here too easily. And as he did, separate threads he'd gone out of his way not to knit together braided up tight.

He saw her face perfectly, as if she were standing before him with her arms crossed belligerently, the way she liked to do. That smirk that drove him wild. The cool, challenging way she stared him down, as if he'd never torn her up and never would again, when they both knew better.

Isaac was done being haunted.

It was time to drag the ghost that was Caradine Scott out into the light, no matter what happened.

"You have command," he told Jonas shortly. "If I'm not back before Templeton, you can argue it out with him."

"I don't argue," Jonas replied coolly. He paused. "Are you thinking she hired those fools?"

"Caradine doesn't suffer fools, Jonas. I doubt she'd hire a couple."

Isaac stared down the trail. Follow it long enough up into the trees that covered the side of the mountain, and it branched out. The official trail carried on toward the summit of what the locals called Hard Ass Pass and were rarely dumb enough to test, because it got dangerous, fast, up there. Other paths wound around as they pleased. Many led out to the farthest, most off-grid homesteads and cabins.

Like the one where Isaac's grumpy, people-hating uncle Theo lived. With his thoughts, like Madeleine had said. That, and his own personal arsenal.

Isaac highly doubted Caradine had headed there.

But beyond the various, little-traveled trails that led to all the survivalist enthusiasts who called this island home was another path that dead-ended in a tiny inlet. Where Theo and some of the other locals who preferred not to deal with people in town—or having agents of *the man*, like the Grizzly Harbor harbormaster, knowing their business—kept their boats.

If Isaac was going to sneak out of Grizzly Harbor and then off the island, without being seen and without access to the various toys he had at his disposal thanks to Alaska Force, that was how he'd do it.

He'd steal a boat, but unlike the idiots who'd thrown that pipe bomb through Caradine's window, he wouldn't hit the open water. He'd stick to the rugged coast, find a hidden cove on a neighboring island, and hunker down until daylight. When there would be enough fishing vessels out there that it was worth the gamble that Alaska Force wouldn't catch him before he made it to a better boat. Like the Alaska Marine Highway ferry that could take him out of here and all the way down to the Lower 48, if he liked.

"I don't think Caradine lit her own restaurant on fire," he said to Jonas now. "But she sure was prepared for it to happen. Practiced for it, even, if that climb down two stories is any indication."

"Looks that way."

And those threads braided up tight inside him seemed to ignite.

There were the things he knew about her. The things he'd long suspected. This long, maddening dance of theirs had already gone on for what felt to him like too many lifetimes.

"Bring her back safe," Jonas said gruffly when Isaac started down the trail to confirm his first set of suspicions.

"I will," Isaac promised him.

He'd bring her back, all right.

But how safe she stayed while he did it was going to be entirely up to her.

Because as far as Isaac was concerned, it was high time for an overdue reckoning.

Two

Running for her life was a lot like riding a bicycle.

It came back to her that easily. Like muscle memory the moment she heard the noise outside that night. The unmistakable sound of breaking glass followed by the ominous rush of flames igniting.

She'd been asleep, then awake and alert in an instant. She knew exactly what she had to do.

What she'd always known she would have to do, sooner or later.

Even if this time, she'd gotten complacent. She'd let herself imagine that she could be Caradine Scott forever. She'd started thinking of herself as Caradine and had assured herself that was a good thing. That she was well and truly in character. That it would be that much easier to hide the more fully she embraced her made-up life.

She'd done a lot more than *embrace* it—but Caradine couldn't let herself think about Isaac Gentry. Not now, while her world was literally on fire. Again. When she'd known better all along. From her very first night in Grizzly Harbor, when she'd walked down what passed for a road in the most remote and unlikely place that she'd been able to find, located the only bar on the island, and seen him.

Only him, though the bar had been full of locals making merry on that chilly fall night.

Caradine's breath still deserted her in a rush every time she remembered it. Even now, in these crucial moments, when she should have been focused on other things. Like staying alive.

She'd pushed open the heavy door to the Fairweather, then found her way in out of the cold. And she'd gotten tangled up in Isaac Gentry when he looked up from the bar as surely as if he'd set a trap for her.

His gray eyes had found hers and held, like he'd been waiting for her all along.

And she'd known better. She'd always known how her time in Alaska—or anywhere, forever, until they finally caught her the way she knew they would—would end.

"It was always going to be exactly like this," she muttered at herself as she rolled out of her bed.

Caradine was all too aware of what she needed to do now, no matter how gray Isaac Gentry's freaking eyes were.

His *eyes* never should have mattered in the first place.

She took nothing but the bag she kept packed and ready for precisely this purpose. She'd practiced a hundred times a year, at least. More, probably. The getting out of bed at the first sound, no matter when she'd gotten in it. The dressing in deliberate layers for any weather in less than ten seconds. Then out the window immediately, scrabbling down the side of her house the way she'd also practiced. Over and over again, night and day, in all kinds of weather and regardless of whether she felt like it, making use of the fact the café stood over the board-walk and the water, but the rest of the building was set back into the hill. And though the town was built on an incline, there was nothing directly behind her.

That meant that no one could happen by and see who was at her back stairs. Or how many times she climbed out of her side window. A person would have to deliberately walk around to the back of the building to see her, and no one did. This was Alaska, where people respected one another's privacy. Because that privacy often came heavily armed.

It was nice that it was summer, she thought, as she hit the ground twenty seconds after waking up. Cool, but not cold, and that weird almost-light she'd never quite gotten used to. She froze when she landed and assessed the situation. Half hoping it had been nothing but another bad dream—but no, she could see the glow of a real, honest-to-God fire flickering in the gloom, from the front of the restaurant.

There was no time to mourn her life here. There was no time to grieve for what she was losing in those flames. *It was never your life in the first place,* she reminded herself fiercely. Not out loud, because she had to assume that whoever had started the fire was still here. Waiting for her to reveal herself.

She executed her plan, the way she'd practiced and plotted so many times. She slunk up the hill, trying to blend in with the shadows and make as little noise as possible, then caught the trail out to the community hot springs. She changed her shoes when she hit the cabin that made the hot springs accessible and comfortable all year round, grabbing the hiking boots she kept there for precisely this purpose, then kept going.

And she didn't look back.

She told herself she didn't *want* to look back, because the next step was all that mattered.

Caradine had worked out a lot of contingency plans over the years. If they came when it was winter and too cold to risk prolonged exposure outside. If an assailant broke into her apartment and attacked her, leaving her injured but still needing to disappear. If they got the drop on her and incapacitated her. If they reverted to type and used a fire—either meant to lure her out or meant to kill her.

They'd gone with the fire. Downstairs, in the middle of the night. That suggested they wanted to give her the chance to live long enough to be killed in a more personally upsetting fashion. And they weren't chasing her out of town now, meaning whoever had started the fire probably figured she was still inside. They'd have to look for her body before they decided to look for her, and she could use that.

She would use everything she had, the way she always did.

The minute she was in the woods again on the trail that led away from town, she ran. Flat out. And she was grateful that she'd trained so hard all this time. So relentlessly, year after year, without any contact, because she'd known that sooner or later, it would come to this.

It would have been so easy to get soft. To let herself imagine she was safe, here on a faraway island with its very own collection of commandos. To shift over into complacency about this, too.

That was what they'd been banking on. Caradine had no doubt.

A brutal and vertical forty-five minutes after she'd been woken up by the sound of shattering glass, Caradine made it to the inlet she'd found by accident her first year in Grizzly Harbor. When she'd done the same hike at a reasonable pace and it had taken hours. She was more breathless than she liked, sure, but that was as much to do with adrenaline-fueled trail running in the half dark as it was the fact she'd heard the Alaska Force helicopter overhead.

Another thing she couldn't let herself focus on. Not now.

Not until she found a place she could hole up in, assess the scope of the damage, then figure out her next steps. Caradine knew there was no point succumbing to emotion when she couldn't contain it—and when she couldn't tell if she was blundering into a wider trap.

And maybe by that time she could forget that when she'd heard the helicopter overhead, her first reaction had been *relief.* As if they were coming to save her.

As if she could be saved.

She climbed down the sharp ravine and found a boat that looked like the one she'd practiced on, pretending for years that she truly wanted to learn how to fish and wasn't scoping out escape routes. She checked the fuel gauge, started it up, and headed out fast. Straight out across the choppy water to the neighboring island she'd explored years ago. She left the boat in another isolated cove, nicely tied up so it would find its way back to its owner eventually, once someone stumbled upon it—but not soon. Then she set out on another grueling trail run into more dense, wet woods, too aware that she had two sets of highly motivated individuals after her now.

One set wanted to kill her—if not today, eventually. The other was Isaac and his friends, and that wasn't much better.

Because he'd want to save her.

And that was the one thing no one could do.

She hadn't looked back. She'd left her café burning and she'd loved that place, against her better judgment. She didn't have time to think about Isaac Gentry or his hero complex. Or the way he said her name.

"It isn't your name," she snapped at herself, alone in the woods on a cold island with only the wild, unsettled sea below to hear her. "You picked two surnames out of a phone book in Sioux City five years ago."

But she couldn't seem to dislodge the weight of it from her chest. The name. The life.

And if something yawned open inside of her, hollow and raw like an ache, she would ignore it. Eventually, she knew from experience, she could make herself ignore anything.

It took her well into the morning to hike to the outskirts of the main village on the island. Caradine knew the town, having visited a number of times over the years—also supposedly because she was so interested in fishing. And she had her first stroke of luck, because it was ferry day. She didn't have to camp out in the woods for half a week to wait for the ferry to Juneau to come or, in a pinch, steal another boat and hope the Troopers—or, worse, Alaska Force—didn't run her to ground out in the channel.

When she walked on board the Alaska Marine Highway vessel later that same morning, she no longer looked much like Caradine Scott, famously grumpy owner and proprietor of the Water's Edge Café over in Grizzly Harbor. She'd pulled out the first of her two carefully selected wigs, this one blond, and styled it into two cute braids. Something Caradine would never, ever do, because Caradine was never, ever *cute*. She mimicked her friend—not her *friend*, she corrected herself sternly, because she didn't have friends when her life was a lie—Mariah McKenna's thick Southern accent as she smiled and blessed hearts all the way to Juneau and then down to Bellingham.

Where, thirty-eight hours later, she dropped the Southern accent, exchanged the blond hair for bright pink, and used cash to buy a junky car from a used-car lot.

It turned out that driving was another thing that came back to a person, even if they hadn't done it in a while. Because there were no real roads in Grizzly Harbor, so there was no need for cars. People came over in them on the ferries, then left them parked down at the bottom of town.

"Stop thinking about Grizzly Harbor," she ordered herself, her voice loud in the car as she drove it out of Bellingham, then south to Seattle, where she headed west.

She drove until she reached Spokane, then found a motel there. Inside the room that smelled too strongly of cleaning fluid, she readied herself for a war and . . . waited.

But no one showed up.

No one burst through the door to confront her, or worse, kill her. She curled up on top of the thin, scratchy motel bedspread, ordered herself not to think too hard about the hygiene in a place she wouldn't want to look at in any bright light, and tried to sleep.

It was a fitful, restless night. Caradine got to work on ignoring things when she woke up with moisture on her cheeks. And again in the shower, where a casual observer might have suggested she was sobbing.

But she didn't sob. Because she wasn't observed, so it didn't happen. She hadn't let herself cry in a long while, maybe a whole decade, and this was no time to start.

"You had five years," she reminded herself once she crept back out to her car and started it up while it was still dark. "That's a lifetime. And it's much better than before."

But *before* was another thing she didn't like to think about. All that running. The panic. That first month, scrabbling to make money and find food, then another middle-of-the-night race to get away. Another few months somewhere new, then the terror of a potentially familiar face in a crowd.

The near-disaster in Phoenix that she still didn't know how she'd survived.

Five years in one place had been a gift. Wishing she could have had more than that was greedy.

Caradine twisted her hair up wet and shoved it beneath a trucker hat that dwarfed her face, added knock-off Ray-Bans she'd found in a truck stop, and drove south. Out of the cities where people gathered and watched and made calls back East. Into the country, where there were more cows and fields than curious human eyes.

She wound her way through the undulating hills of eastern Washington, then down into Oregon. She crossed the Columbia River and kept on south, following a twisty road that cut down the heart of Central Oregon. Hours later, she found herself crossing the high desert of southeastern Oregon, eventually dipping down into Nevada. Once she hit I-80, she kept going east all the way to Salt Lake City.

Caradine stopped only for gas and more caffeine, as much sugar as she could consume, and let that same adrenaline keep her going out there on one deserted highway after another. She kept heading south and east, through Albuquerque and on through Lubbock, Texas.

Some forty or so hours after she'd left Spokane and still hadn't seen anyone coming for her, she bought a cell phone from a convenience store in Galveston, Texas. She punched in a number she knew by heart and waited to get kicked into voice mail. She typed in the code and held her breath—but there was no message.

No message didn't necessarily mean anything.

Then again, it could mean the worst had already happened.

By this point, Caradine was rocking her blond wig again. She'd taken the time to curl her hair, Texas style, in a truck stop near Waco with a water bottle and a hand dryer. And she'd traded one junker car for another in Houston. Still, she felt ridiculously exposed and obvious, out there on the Historic Pleasure Pier on Galveston Island. She shoved the cell phone into her pocket and headed back toward the parking lot where she'd left her car, forcing herself to slow down to an unmemorable amble in the oppressive heat and humidity, the way some-one who wasn't afraid for her life would walk.

When she reached her car, she climbed back in, drove back onto the mainland, and headed west. Four hours in, she was too delirious to make sense of the road, so she crashed in a motel near San Antonio. Eight hours of dreamless sleep later, she felt like a new person and celebrated with pink hair again. Then she settled in for a hot, arid twenty-hour drive west.

She found another motel in Riverside, California, and called the same number again when she was barricaded in her room with the AC set up to a dull roar. This time, she left a message. One word.

The next morning, she left the cell phone in pieces in the Dumpster behind her motel, got back in her junky car, and drove north. And east. For three thousand miles, give or take.

One very long week after her life in Alaska had gone up in flames, Caradine staggered out of her car in a picturesque tourist town on the coast of Maine. The kind of place no version of her would ever go, for any reason.

The lovely seaside town of Camden was three hours or so from Boston, but might as well have been on another planet from the life she remembered there. And it was June. A town on any stretch of the Atlantic coast was filled with tourists this time of year. A whole lot more tourists than ever showed up on a Southeast Alaskan island set off the Inside Passage cruise ship route. There was always the chance that someone might come for her on a busy, happy street or along the much-photographed waterfront, but she thought it was a small one. Along the same lines, she paid too much for a room with bay windows overlooking the harbor, in an adorable bed-and-breakfast that reminded her of the Blue Bear Inn in Grizzly Harbor—

"For God's sake," she snapped at herself, staring

around the fussy room done up in overt blues, yellows, and whites. "Let it go."

Something she'd been telling herself for three thousand miles.

She took care of a few practical considerations, almost by rote. She checked the windows and took care to memorize what she could see from them. Then she crawled into the center of the full bed, curled herself in a ball on the floral bedspread, and slept for a long, long time.

When Caradine woke, she was disoriented.

It was night. And it took her several beats to remember where she was. How she'd gotten here, zigzagging this way and that, driving like a maniac on very little sleep and entirely too much caffeine and sugared-up anxiety, all over the country.

She was still a little bit addled from the road. That had to be why her heart was cartwheeling around and slamming against her ribs.

But in the next breath, she knew better.

Because a shadow detached itself from the wall at the foot of her bed.

Caradine launched herself up and onto her feet, grabbing for the .45 she kept beneath her pillow while her body readied itself—

But she recognized him almost as quickly.

"Isaac."

She sucked in the breath that had nearly been a scream, but she didn't drop her gun. Because it was Isaac, all right, but that didn't make him safe.

He had never been safe.

"Put the gun down," he advised her, in that genial way of his that she'd never believed. And didn't now.

"I'll pass on that, thank you."

She reached behind her, not dumb enough to shift her gaze from him, and found the lamp beside the bed. And glared at him when all the buttery light did was make him look even more dangerous and powerful than usual. Shadowed and gleaming and, damn him, gorgeous.

"I could have taken it while you were blinking, Caradine."

She believed him, but she sniffed. "Yet you didn't."

"Consider it a courtesy."

His eyes were still that mysterious, impossible gray, and something about them looked silver tonight. His features had *predator* stamped all over them, and though he wore that beard to hide the truth of who he was, it had never fooled her. She'd never trusted his easy smile or the general amiable demeanor he played at whenever he was in public, because she knew exactly who he was. She always had.

From that very first night, that very first look, she'd known.

The look he aimed at her was feral enough to raise every hair on her body. And she hated that even here, her body reacted to him the way it always did.

Isaac Gentry was a spectacular betrayal of herself in male form, and her curse was, that form was beautiful. More than simply beautiful—he was a perfectly honed, marvelously constructed specimen. She knew, and had soundly mocked, his dedication to keeping himself in peak physical condition, but the woman in her wanted to cheer every time she saw what a T-shirt like the one he was wearing now did to those pectoral muscles of his. To say nothing of that mouthwateringly ridged abdomen.

He had been her doom from the start. She'd known it, and she'd done it all anyway, like a moth on a kamikaze trip straight into the bluest part of the flame.

"When did you pick up my trail?" she asked, studying his grim, gorgeous face.

He had always been a threat, and she'd always understood that, but this was different. This wasn't their usual tug-of-war in Grizzly Harbor. They were on the other side of a very large continent.

He must have followed her.

She knew this was the kind of thing he and his commando buddies did for a living, but that didn't make the panic clawing at her subside any. It almost made it worse.

"I thought you were dead," Isaac gritted out, and he no longer sounded remotely pleasant.

He moved closer in that way of his that was almost as if he weren't moving. As if he were a part of the shadows, not a man at all, except she knew perfectly well that he was flesh and blood.

She knew it far too well.

"When, Gentry? Spokane?"

He moved closer, and her eyes were fully adjusted now. She could see that wild thing in his gaze. That furious glitter.

"I thought you were *dead*," he said again, emphasizing each word in a guttural sort of way that she could feel, like separate kicks.

Each one hurt, whether she admitted it or not. Especially the last.

"Obviously not," she threw back at him, because what she knew how to do was fight. On and on and on, as long as it took, because it was all she had. "And you couldn't have thought I was dead very long, or you'd be back in Alaska planning my funeral. Not lurking in hotel rooms in Maine."

"I got a call." His voice was . . . terrible. As furious as that half-wild glittering thing in his eyes, but there was something much, much worse than simply *furious* about it. Caradine shuddered. "There was a fire. *In your home.* Where I had every reason to believe you were."

"When did you pick up my trail?" she bit out, because he wasn't the only one who could use anger like a tool.

"I never lost your trail." He was too close now. Right there on the other side of her gun. She refused to waver. But then, she doubted he knew the meaning of that word.

"I watched you board the ferry to Juneau. And I watched you get off the ferry in Bellingham."

The smirk toppled off her face, and she couldn't seem to do anything about it. She compensated by keeping her gun trained on him, aimed directly at his heart.

"You really shouldn't have done that." She hated the weakness in her. The catch in her throat, the humming thing low in her belly. The ache that had been there from the start. "I know this is what you do for a living, but I didn't hire you, Isaac. I don't need you to save me. You need to let me go."

"I thought you were dead, Caradine."

She let out a sound she hoped was scornful and not a sob. "That's not even my name."

"It is when you're with me," Isaac growled.

Then he did two things so fast she didn't see either one. She couldn't react. She couldn't *resist*.

He took the gun from her like she hadn't been gripping it in the first place. As if he'd plucked it from the air.

And with his other hand he hooked her around the neck, yanked her close, and slammed his mouth to hers.

Three

Isaac had spent the last week assuring himself that what he wanted from her was a frank conversation, for a change. That a conversation was all he wanted.

But nothing with Caradine ever went as planned.

The familiar taste of her exploded through him, messing him up like a sucker punch.

The way it always did.

She was smoke and fire, need and longing, and the way they fit together was like a new religion. Every time.

He clicked the safety into place, then tossed her gun aside. And for the moment, he indulged himself.

Isaac angled his jaw, taking the kiss deeper. Pouring all the panic and dread and grief-streaked fury he'd kept locked up inside into her. Making it heat and desire.

That call. That terrible helicopter ride.

He couldn't forget any of it.

But she was here. She was alive. She was flesh and blood and kissing him back the way she always did, as if it were all her idea.

As if she were in control.

And for the moment, that was all that mattered.

She was impatient, as always. She surged against him, wrapping her arms around his neck and pressing her body against his.

Isaac let his hands travel, proving to himself that she really was all in one piece. And because he liked his hands on her. She'd been sleeping with her clothes on, and not the kinds of clothes she wore at the Water's Edge Café while she was cooking only what she felt like cooking, insulting the customers, and throwing out anyone who annoyed her.

And everyone annoyed her, sooner or later. She issued bans like parking citations in big cities, and it always took a lot of wheedling to get back into her good graces.

But there was no oversized novelty T-shirt here. Tonight she wore a formfitting white T-shirt with cute little sleeves that flirted with those biceps she pretended she didn't have. And a pair of cargo pants that whispered when she moved, telling him before he'd even laid a hand on her that they were made of tactical material.

It was all part and parcel of the same lie she'd been telling all this time, and he would get to that, but for the moment he lost himself a little—okay, a lot—in the sheer joy of kissing her again.

There was a simmering anger, sure. And all that emotion they never talked about. Lust and desire, and loss in there, too, because this never lasted. Every time he kissed her could be the last time he kissed her, and he was never okay with that, no matter what he told himself.

Isaac poured it all into her.

Caradine took it, met it, and gave it right back to him.

And since his hands were on her already, he let them trail down her body wherever they pleased, reminding himself how sleek and sexy she was. Not that he needed reminding when she was burned into him like a brand.

He also helped himself to the weapons she kept

stashed away on her person. The knife strapped to her leg. The box cutter in one cargo pocket.

He liked that she was lethal. He'd watched her extricate herself from restraints, easily disarm attackers, and escape all manner of harm in the self-defense class she took in Grizzly Harbor. But that didn't mean he wanted to give her an easy target.

She jerked her head back when he fished the box cutter out of her pocket, and he had the satisfaction of seeing that her pupils were dilated and her eyes had gone glassy. Those pretty blue eyes that she could never quite wipe clear of her true feelings, no matter how ferociously she scowled.

The way she did now. "Are you trying to distract me while you pat me down?"

"Not *trying* to distract you. Just distracting you."

She pushed away from him, harder than necessary. Isaac didn't move, but she did, and probably would have staggered back a few feet if she hadn't caught herself. He watched her glance toward the bed, where the three weapons he'd found so far lay, then look back at him, gauging her chances.

"I wouldn't." He didn't quite grin. Though he thought about it. "But you can always give it a shot. See what happens."

Some people would admit defeat. But this was Caradine, defiant beyond reason and sense, who would probably die first. Her eyes narrowed, she crossed her arms, and she glared back at him like she had some control here.

But just because he'd always given her control didn't mean she had it or could keep it. A critical distinction. One he intended to make crystal clear to her.

"If you've been tracking me since the ferry, you sure have come a long way for that good-bye kiss. I hope it was worth it." She nodded toward the door to her room that he'd jimmied in about two silent seconds. "Don't let me keep you."

"Hilarious, as ever. You should think about a stand-up routine."

"I'm not trying to be funny. You need to go. You shouldn't have followed me in the first place."

Isaac grinned then, but not in the genial, good-ol'-boy way he'd perfected for residents of Grizzly Harbor who'd known his parents, ignored his uncle, and really, truly wanted to see him as cuddly. "At what point in the five years you've known me did you get the impression that I'm the kind of man who would watch a building blow up in Grizzly Harbor and not dedicate myself to figuring out why? Or who did it?"

"Gas leak," she offered blandly. "You can go home now."

"Try again. We caught two clowns in a fishing boat who were only too happy to admit that they threw a weak Molotov cocktail through your front window."

"Youths today. *Millennials*. Am I right?"

She wanted him to rage at her, he had no doubt, so he kept his expression as even as his tone. "Some people think you hired them to light your own café on fire."

"For the supposed insurance money?" Her head tipped to one side as she considered it, the smirk that alternately infuriated and intoxicated him playing with her mouth. That didn't help anything. "Sure. That sounds like me. Shifty straight on through."

Isaac eyed the small weapons collection on her bed, pointedly, then looked back at her. "You figure you need all that to fight off the Allstate agent?"

"Isaac." She shook her head at him, managing to look world-weary and pitying all at once. "What makes you think you get to know why I left? Maybe I just left. Maybe I don't want to stand around handing out explanations to anyone. Especially you."

They were standing maybe five inches apart in a tiny, prissy room that made him feel like more than a bull in a china shop—more like a herd of bulls three seconds away from crashing through a glass wall. The double bed took up most of the floor space, and he should have been thinking strategically, but this was Caradine. So what he was really busy doing was picturing the numerous uses he could make of the bed. Not big enough for him to get all that comfortable, it was true, but certainly big enough to cause a little trouble. And adjust her attitude, as he'd done more than once.

But he'd thought she was dead.

And this was supposed to be a reckoning. Not a retread of every other encounter they'd ever had.

"These are the facts," he said coolly, the way he would if he were briefing his team back in Fool's Cove. "You arrived in Grizzly Harbor five years ago out of thin air."

"Or, you know, off the ferry like everyone else. But sure. Make it dramatic if you must."

"Caradine Scott doesn't exist," Isaac continued as if she hadn't spoken, and she jolted at that. Just a little, hardly a whole flinch, but he saw it. In that second before she schooled her reaction—which was an interesting thing all on its own, and something he filed away—he saw it.

He expected her to say something, but she didn't. She only glared back at him, obviously prepared to stand there and scowl back at him for all eternity.

"Alonzo and Martie Hagan tried to sell that place for years. Martie had her heart set on getting out of the Alaskan winter and down to a beach somewhere south, where *cold* means the low seventies. But no one bit. Until you."

"Are you the only one who's allowed to open a business in Grizzly Harbor?"

"You bought the place sight unseen, paid cash, and showed up in early October. Which is not a time people generally decide to pick up stakes and move to Alaska from the Lower forty-eight."

Caradine shrugged. "I've never cared that much about what 'most people' do."

"I get itchy when fake people with fake names show up and start wandering around my hometown." And Isaac's voice was a little more terse than necessary. "Grizzly Harbor is supposed to be a safe, quiet, idyllic escape, far away from the rest of the world. And its problems. That's why people move there."

"Maybe you've missed what's been happening the past couple of years, then." She even laughed, right in his face, because Caradine was one of the few civilians who knew exactly how dangerous he was and taunted him anyway. "*Safe* is not the word I'd use to describe your hometown, what with all the dead bodies and bombs going off left and right."

"Five years ago it was perfectly safe, aside from the weather and the wildlife." Isaac studied the defiant way she tilted up her chin, like she'd welcome it if he swung at her. "And you're not the first person to turn up in the middle of nowhere and think that it would be better all around if you left your real name behind with whatever it is you're getting away from. I don't blame anyone who wants a new start."

"Are you sure? Because this sounds a whole lot like blame. Meanwhile, I guess we can keep pretending that Alaska Force isn't *your* version of a new start. Just with bigger guns than most and an exciting club name to go with it."

"The difference, Caradine, is that while a person might not choose to use their real name in casual conversation while they're living off-grid somewhere in the Last Frontier, it's always attached to them anyway. One way or another. But not you."

She didn't look cowed. Quite the opposite. He was sure she stood a little straighter and even smirked a little harder. "You sure seemed broken up about that. Each and every time you ended up naked in my bed, using the name I gave you."

Isaac let himself smile then and watched goose bumps break out down the distractingly elegant line of her neck.

They were in Maine tonight, not Alaska. And maybe they were both done hiding.

He knew he was. "I'm so glad you brought that up."

Isaac took a step closer to her, and she swallowed, hard. And for a moment, even though his pulse was racketing around and making noise, he let himself simply *look* at her.

This woman who worked so hard to pretend she wasn't as pretty as she was. All the scowling. The smirking. The rudeness, the belligerence, and enough armor to outfit the better part of the Middle Ages wrapped around her at all times. Especially with him.

When the truth of her was the delicate lines of her strong, sleek body. That dark hair she usually kept in a messy ponytail so no one would know it was this silky. Or that shampoo she used that made her smell like sweet drinks on a tropical night. That mouth that she was always curling into one sneer or another, so no one would notice how kissable it was. She was five nine and looked about 130 pounds, though he estimated she was a good ten to fifteen pounds heavier than that, all of it muscle. When she worked so hard to pretend she was lazy and soft and idle.

"I thought we were building up to a big, dramatic moment here." She sounded jaded and sarcastic, her specialty. "But apparently you chased me across a continent to bore me to death."

"I spend a lot of time thinking about that first night," Isaac told her, not letting her goad him.

She batted her eyelashes at him, not something she normally did. Likely because it would force a man to notice how thick and dark they were and how well they framed her eyes. "It's cute that the super scary head commando is obsessed with me. Really. If it's any consolation, I won't tell anyone. You can go on back to your little fraternity with your big, bad reputation intact. Hopefully soon."

"You were new in town," Isaac continued, ignoring her. "And maybe you were looking for a fun night, but you got me instead."

"I'm so glad to hear you say that. All this time it's been *so* awkward. I haven't known how to tell you that you're basically the opposite of fun. Always."

He wouldn't say he felt *goaded*, exactly, but there was an edginess in him. "What word do you want to use? Intense? Life-altering?"

Caradine sighed. "It's those puppy dog eyes of yours, Isaac. Every now and again, they're just too much, and I take pity on you. Do you really not understand that?"

But he only laughed. "Nice try. But I can see your pulse going wild in your neck. And your skin is flushed. How many times have we played this game? Remember what happened the last time?"

He did. In vivid detail.

"You're describing my uncontrollable physical reaction of complete disgust," she said loftily.

"I see that you do. But let me remind you anyway." He drifted even closer to her, almost entirely to see what she would do. Caradine didn't disappoint him. She moved back instantly, but then caught herself. And stood firm, tilting her head up to keep her eyes on his as he stood over her.

But he could see that her hands were in fists.

"It was late," he reminded her, remembering it himself. "You were in those hot springs you like to tell everybody you hate. You came out damp and hot and caught me on a patrol."

"Is that what we're calling episode 976,000 of you stalking me? 'Patrol'?"

"We had this exact same conversation, as I recall. But it was a relatively warm night, and you weren't wearing much. Just your bathing suit. So I figured I'd check to see if you were as disgusted as you claimed you were. To make sure we were still on the same page."

He did the same now, reaching over to the waistband of her cargo pants. She swatted at him with one of her fists, but not hard. Not like she meant it.

And having been on the receiving end of a punch from Caradine that she did mean, he could tell the difference.

"You wanted me pretty desperately then, as I recall."

"I'm never desperate," she lied.

Isaac ran the backs of his fingers this way, then that, over the soft skin just below her navel. He didn't have to point out that the jagged breath she let slip betrayed her completely. A lot like the way her nipples hardened beneath the fitted T-shirt she wore.

He knew. And she knew.

And this was one more way this same old game had always been played between them.

"You think I don't know how you work, but I do," he said, remembering that call again. Griffin's voice, completely lacking the icy calm the other man was known for. That helicopter ride. The smoke and the flames and no sign of her. "You spent five years pretending you don't feel anything. And it's Alaska. People are prickly. It's practically a requirement to cross the state border. But I know better. I've seen the real you."

This time when she swung at him, it was hard. He let the punch land. He even let his mouth curve. "Don't hurt yourself."

There was murder in her eyes then. But she pushed herself away from him instead of hitting him again, which he could admit was disappointing. Because he liked her hands on him. However that happened.

Isaac waited to see if she would throw herself toward the door and try to make a break for it when he was staring right at her and would run her down in two seconds flat.

But she could do the same math he could.

Her mouth flattened into a line. She moved until the corner of the bed was between them, crossed her arms again, and glared at him. Harder this time. "If you hear nothing else I say to you tonight, I need you to hear this. You don't know me. You don't know the real me at all. And that's not a challenge, Isaac. That's a gift."

"There's nobody here but me and you, four thousand miles away from Grizzly Harbor. You'll never have a better opportunity to tell me who you really are."

She laughed, and it was a hard, bitter sound. "I would rather die."

"You say that about everything, Caradine, and then do it anyway. You would rather die than open the café at whatever hour, but you do. You would rather die than admit you have friends. Or that they care about you. Or that you're a part of the community, except you are."

"You mean like you? The one who pretends to be a part of things when it suits him while living out there in his secret fortress in the woods?"

He didn't like that, but he held her gaze. "You would rather die than ever touch me again, until you do. And you always do."

"I'm dead inside, believe me, and this conversation isn't exactly bringing me back to life."

"Fine." Isaac folded his own arms over his chest and reminded himself that she wasn't the only one who'd been pretending to be something other than who she was. He'd been putting on the same approachable, harmless mask since he'd moved back to Alaska. "You want to act like this is an interrogation? We can do that, too."

"Oh, goody. Role-play."

"You wish." And he smiled a little when he saw her flush. "I haven't pushed too hard on the question of your real identity because I figured you probably had your reasons for keeping it private."

"Weird. I still do."

"But that was before your café took a bomb through the window and I thought you were dead."

Her shrug was too sharp to come off as indifference. "I didn't throw it."

"Someone's after you, and they found you. Your response was to run, then spend a week zigzagging around the country. Whatever secret you've been keeping all this time isn't yours any longer. It's in smoldering ruins in Grizzly Harbor, making it my business whether you like it or not."

"Because you're the self-appointed savior of Grizzly Harbor, who nobody actually wants racing in and saving them. Is that what you mean?"

"What it means is that I'm going to find out who you are. Whether you tell me or not."

Her blue eyes flashed. "Is that what we're going with? You're threatening to dig around in my private life when you know I don't want you to *because of the town*?"

"I should have done it a long time ago. Maybe if I had I could have stopped this from happening."

Caradine rolled her eyes. "I have no interest in being one of the reasons you martyr yourself, Isaac."

He glared at her, then reeled himself in. "I'm happy to say I have no idea what that means."

"It means you can climb on down from your cross, though we both know you like it up there. You didn't investigate me the way I'm sure you do everyone else because you're afraid to look. Afraid it might turn out that Captain America has been sleeping with the enemy." Caradine made a tsking sound. "What if I'm a criminal? One of the lowlifes you like to put away? Can you pretend to save the world when you might be in bed with the thing you hate?"

"Do you really think I don't have your fingerprints on file?" he asked, almost idly, though he could feel the tension in his body. And he didn't care if she could see it. "Or that Oz isn't sitting there at his computer, ready to turn all that genius on you the minute I give the order? He'll find out what you had for breakfast on the morning of your fifth birthday, and fast. I'm not afraid of who you are, Caradine. I've been waiting for you to tell me yourself."

He thought she looked a little shaken at that, but she hid it. The way she hid everything. She was the most frustrating woman he'd ever met in his life, and the only woman he would ever have spent a week tracking—to make sure she was safe and maybe find out what was going on with her, not to run her down.

If all he'd wanted was to catch her, he would have handled her in Juneau. Within minutes of her exiting that first ferry.

"Great," she said after a moment, her voice flat and her blue eyes glittering. "You're in total control of all things and the biggest and baddest there ever was, blah blah blah. Must be nice to have your very own collection of mercenaries to back up all these threats."

"That is not what Alaska Force is."

But if she heard his chilly tone, she certainly didn't heed it.

"My favorite part is that you came all this way and broke into my hotel room to tell me how you could know everything there is to know about me in two seconds *if you wanted*, but you thought a week of hard driving sounded like more fun somehow." He was familiar with the challenging look she threw his way. "Go ahead and dig up all my skeletons, Isaac. Knock yourself out. But you can do that back in Alaska. Why are you *here*?"

"You know why," he gritted out, but she gave him nothing. She only glared back at him like he was a stranger. And all the weapons he had at his disposal couldn't help him with that. They never had. "You don't want to tell me your story? I can't make you. But, Caradine. For God's sake. *I thought you were dead.* Tell me who's trying to kill you before they catch up and finish the job."

Four

And the crazy thing was that Caradine wanted to tell him.

She'd wanted to tell him for years. It had been there, on the tip of her tongue, too many times to count. Because in her few and far between moments of wild optimism—usually when he was grinning at her when they were alone and she was seduced by the *possibilities*—she couldn't help but think that if anyone could help her, it was Isaac.

But the moments always passed. Reality always reasserted itself.

Help wasn't coming. Ever. No matter how tough one ex-marine was.

And she'd made a promise.

More than a simple promise. She'd vowed that she would keep her word, and her silence, to the grave.

And she didn't get to change that now because, of all the islands in Southeast Alaska, she'd accidentally chosen to hide out on the one that was overrun with superhero commando types. This one in particular.

"You can't save me," she told him now, wishing there were something more substantial between them than the bed with its floral bedspread and a selection of her weapons laid out on one of the oversized flowers. Like a giant steel barricade, maybe. Anything but her own stubbornness, which he'd proven a little too talented at puncturing whenever he felt like it. "And you can't protect me. Do you want to know how I know that?"

Isaac only stared back at her, impassive and steady, as if he already knew what she was going to say. And would handle that, too, as effortlessly as he handled everything else.

Caradine told herself this would all have been a lot easier if he weren't so annoyingly gorgeous. All the time. Rain, fog, sleet, mud, snow. Genial or pissed, he was still beautiful. If he didn't always look the way he did now, carved from marble and sculpted to shine, maybe this would be easier.

But even if he'd been ugly, he still would have been Isaac. Less distracting, maybe, but just as lethal. And dangerous in every possible way. Especially to her.

Particularly when he looked at her the way he did now.

"Enlighten me," he said.

Daring her.

And the thought of what could happen to him if he insisted on sticking close to her made her wish that one of the bombs that had been lobbed her way over the years had actually gotten her, because that was the only surefire way she knew to make sure he was safe.

Too bad none of this is about him, she snapped at herself. *You need to get your head together.*

"If you were capable of saving me, you would have saved me already," she threw at him, as spitefully as possible. It should have come easily to be mean, after all these years of practice, but it didn't. It never did. It made her tongue taste like acid. "Aren't you the unofficial, un-elected, unwanted mayor of Grizzly Harbor? In addition to being the king of all the commandos?"

"I'm a local boy and a small-business owner. Does calling me names make you feel better?"

He wanted to shame her. She refused to be shamed. Or to show it, anyway. "Yes, actually. It makes me feel alive."

When nothing made her feel better. Nothing could.

"That's not what makes you feel alive, Caradine."

Her stomach flipped over, but she pushed on. "You can't save me, Isaac, because if you could? You would have. The Water's Edge Café wouldn't have a gaping hole where the restaurant used to be, we wouldn't be having this discussion, and neither one of us would have been traipsing around the Lower forty-eight for the past week. But that's not the situation, is it?"

"You don't have a lot of choices here," he said in a voice of quiet command, and she hated the way those eyes of his changed colors, like a storm. There was that dangerous silver from before, which heralded intensity. The usual unreadable gray, like Alaskan fog.

But right now they were a thunderous steel she'd never seen before. And the more she stared at him, the harder it was to breathe. Caradine understood, suddenly, that while she had always seen beneath that mask of his, he'd always been wearing it anyway.

He wasn't now.

A wild sensation shivered down the length of her spine, from the nape of her neck to her tailbone, as she realized she was looking at the real Isaac Gentry.

At last, a voice inside her whispered.

This was the Isaac who didn't grin and laugh and make people around him feel so comfortable they some-how forgot to look at the truth of him, which was packed into every lean, hard inch of his body. The Isaac who might have grown up in Grizzly Harbor but was certainly no *local boy*. He wasn't a boy at all.

This was the man who admitted to having been a Force Recon marine when it was unavoidable, but only smiled edgily when it was suggested he'd advanced to an even higher level of special forces than that. This was the man who ran teams of other dangerous operatives, because they all looked up to him. This man could change regimes, topple governments, carry the world on his broad shoulders, and turn her inside out with a single glance.

If she'd been smart, Caradine would have looked away that first night and never looked back.

You need to stop sniping at him, she snapped at herself. Because pretend as she might, she knew it showed passion. One of the friends in Grizzly Harbor, who she refused to call a friend—because she couldn't have friends at all and certainly not ones like Everly Campbell, who genuinely seemed to *like* her and would pay for it, if the people after Caradine got their hands on Everly one day when she wasn't with her ex-SEAL fiancé—had once called it her *love language*.

That was obviously unacceptable.

Try indifference, she ordered herself now.

"What exactly do you plan to do?" she asked him, keeping her voice flat. "There are other people staying in this bed-and-breakfast, you know. It's booked solid. All I have to do is scream."

His mouth curved. "You won't."

He was right, she wouldn't have. She didn't want that kind of attention. But it irritated her that he was so confident, so she pulled in a deep breath as if she planned to get operatic.

"If you do," Isaac said, very calmly, "I'll let you. And then you can explain to all the other guests that you were having a nightmare while fully dressed with a pile of weapons on your bed. Because there won't be anybody but you in this room when they get here."

"That sounds like . . . exactly what I want." She made a shooing motion with one hand. "Don't let me keep you from disappearing."

"And they'll remember you forever as the lunatic who woke up half of a tourist town at two in the morning. Not the best way to keep a low profile."

Caradine shrugged with elaborate unconcern. "They'll get sunburned and drunk tomorrow, overdose on lobster, and forget it ever happened."

"I tracked you for a week and you didn't notice," he pointed out, his bland voice at odds with all that thunder in his eyes and all over his face. "Just like you didn't notice me breaking into your room tonight. Do you really think a little scream is going to change anything?"

"It might make me feel better."

"If you wanted to feel better, Caradine, you would tell me who was chasing you. And let me do what I do best."

"It sounds like you're the one who's chasing me, Gentry." That steady gaze of his made her want to curl up into a ball, so she stood straighter instead. "You could try stopping."

"The two idiots who did the deed were hired help. Local talent, contacted in Juneau, and they didn't have much to say about the person who hired them. Another intermediary, if I had to guess." Isaac's voice was like steel now, to match the storm in his eyes. "But their orders weren't to kill you. They weren't even supposed to grab you, if you were worried about a kidnap attempt."

"I wasn't, actually. Until I woke up to find you looming over my bed."

He only gazed back at her until she felt that if she hadn't been focused on exuding indifference, she really would have flushed bright red. Averted her eyes. Curled into that ball, maybe, right there on the woven rug at the foot of her bed. Instead of glaring back at him like he didn't get to her at all.

"They were sent to find out if you were there and cause a little trouble while they did it. The job was to compare you to a photograph, which they did earlier in the day. Then they were supposed to take a new one and send it off to an anonymous e-mail address. They were asked specifically to scare you, Caradine. Not kill you, but scare you, even if you were the wrong person."

Caradine knew he wanted to see her reaction, so she just about burst a blood vessel keeping her expression blank. Like that information didn't creep her out or make the back of her neck itch.

"Who do you think would reach out that way?" Isaac asked. "Complete with a bonus fire regardless of whether or not you were who they were looking for?"

"Maybe it's my long-lost mother," Caradine replied dryly. "Sending a little love note, like last Christmas. In Grizzly Harbor, that idyllic escape from the world where an Alaska State Trooper's freaky relatives can blow stuff up and kidnap people to prove a point. Can any of the rest of us be safe?"

"What are the odds that your family and Kate's family would take the same approach?" Isaac asked mildly. His expression was not mild. "Were you also raised in a cult?"

"That really depends on your position on good old American family values." Caradine sounded like her usual self. Everything was such a joke. She was such a beacon of dark humor. But inside, she'd gone horribly cold. "Anyway," she said with more bravado than any real conviction, "the people after me didn't get in a Christmas kidnapping."

His gray gaze turned forbidding. "But someone will. Sooner or later. It's only a matter of time."

"Surely not with Alaska Force on the scene," she retorted, with a fake smile and too much edge. "Except—

oh, wait. I didn't hire you, you're not very good at your job, and I don't live there anymore."

"If I was trying to get my hands on you, I had a thousand opportunities over the past week." His voice was relentlessly even. "You never knew I was there. How would you know if anyone else was?"

"I don't have to know if someone's there." She nodded toward her weapons. "All I need to know is how to react when they turn up."

"That's the way a victim thinks, Caradine. The problem with relying on coffee and stubbornness to get you through is that both are going to fail. You're only one person. Sooner or later, the coffee's going to stop working, you're going to have to stop running, and, like tonight, you won't even wake up when someone comes into the room where you're sleeping. Then what?"

She scoffed to cover the coldness that swamped her then, because he was right. Of course he was right. "You weren't trying to hurt me."

"You don't know what I was trying to do, because I let myself in and hung around while you slept. Does that creep you out?" Isaac demanded when she made a face. "Good. Maybe you should listen to me for a change."

Caradine hugged herself tight and kept her gaze level on his. "I'm not going to tell you anything, Isaac. No matter how many times you break into my room and try to intimidate me."

He didn't actually crack a smile at that, but she had the impression of one. "Baby, I haven't begun to intimidate you."

She wanted to tell him not to call her *baby*, ever again. She also wanted to melt. And the truth about everything was right there on her tongue, again. Always.

But she'd promised.

"Listen," she said, with none of her trademark attitude this time. No edge, no slap. She found his gaze and held it, trying to show him that she was being as honest as she could. "I appreciate that you were worried enough about me to track me here."

"Don't patronize me."

She lifted her hands as if to surrender. "I mean it. I know you can't tell, because I'm normally all about the sarcasm, but I mean it. I do. You'll never know how much this means to me, Isaac. But I can't accept your help."

"I'm not offering my help. You're getting my help."

"Caradine Scott doesn't exist. You said it yourself."

"But *you* do."

That hit her. Hard. She had to blink back a sudden surge of emotion, and only hoped he couldn't see it.

"I'm going to disappear. Again." She shook her head when he started to say something else. "That's what I do. There are still a lot of places in this world where people don't ask questions. I got five years this time. Maybe next time it will be more."

"Caradine."

"But I can't take you with me, even if I wanted to. And you couldn't go anyway. You have an entire life in Grizzly Harbor."

"You going into hiding under another assumed name is not an acceptable outcome."

She actually smiled at that, a real smile. "You don't get a vote."

"Caradine—"

"Isaac. *Baby.*" She smirked a little when he narrowed his eyes at her, that emotional punch still echoing through her and making her want to shiver. She held it back. "It's late. I know you can summon a thousand military-grade vehicles to do your bidding with a single snap of your fingers, but some of us aim to be less conspicuous. If you're going to go, go."

"What part of this conversation makes you imagine I'm going somewhere?"

"If you want to stay, you have one option available to you," she said in the bossy, peremptory tone she'd used on him often in Grizzly Harbor. And just like all those times, usually late at night outside the Fairweather after pretending to ignore him, she watched his expression shift quickly from incredulity to something gleaming and silver that made her belly flip over. "Naked. And silent."

She hadn't meant to say that. She'd meant to throw him out again, the way she always did.

The way he always lets *you*, something in her whispered, and her belly somersaulted again.

She hadn't meant to say it, but she had. And she was already rationalizing that decision. If she wanted to say a long, involved good-bye to this man she never should have touched in the first place, she could do it here. Secure in the knowledge that he could keep them safe enough, at least for a little while.

And Caradine could think of a lot of ways to say good-bye, all a lot better than that adrenaline-fueled sprint up the side of a mountain in the summer almost-dark.

"Well?" she demanded, because she always pushed it with him. Harder and harder, because he never broke. "Are you going to stay? Or are you going to go? Because if you're going, go now. I need my sleep."

Something shifted on that gorgeous face of his that foolish people believed was friendly. Caradine knew better.

And even she shivered at the look he gave her.

Like he was some kind of wolf.

Isaac didn't speak. And the only thing she could hear was the thundering of her own heart. It pounded inside her chest. In her temples. In her wrists.

And deep between her legs.

He didn't say a word. He crooked his finger in a silent command, because she liked to shoot her mouth off and pretend she controlled this. Him. But they both knew better.

And this was her good-bye. This was her last chance. Her last taste.

Caradine didn't waste any more time. She moved around the foot of the bed, determined that she would make this night the kind of night that she could live on forever.

Because she would have to.

Isaac swept her up into his arms, making her feel light and sweet when she knew she was neither, and she loved that. God, did she love it. Then his mouth was on hers, ravishing her, and she loved that, too.

Fierce. Hot.

So greedy and wild that she thought she might scream after all.

He spun her around, throwing her down on the bed and sweeping her weapons aside with one arm. Then he came down on top of her, his body rock hard, pressing her deep into the mattress.

There wasn't any part of this she didn't love.

Isaac was like a fever. He always had been. Sensation streaked through her, flaring bright and hot wherever he touched her, and she gloried in it.

Because wherever she landed next, whatever happened to her, this would haunt her. He would haunt her, permanently. She already knew that.

He already did.

Caradine wrapped herself around him and kissed him with everything she had. He met that kiss, amped it up, and tossed it over the edge into something even darker, hotter, more out of control. Then he unpeeled her hands from his neck and stretched them up, over her head. She arched into him, reveling in the press of her breasts against his hard chest.

But when she tried to move her hands to dig them into his dark hair, her eyes snapped open.

Because her wrists were zip-tied together. Tightly.

Isaac was staring down at her, his face like granite.

And Caradine had the disorienting sensation that she'd actually never seen *this* version of him before, either.

"I'm done asking you questions," he said, his voice darker than she'd ever heard it. And she wasn't sure if that was fear or a thrill that shivered through her then. "And while we're on the subject, I'm done playing games."

"Untie me," she gritted out at him.

But she didn't have to see all the silver intensity glaring back at her to know he had no intention of doing anything of the kind. And while they both knew she could untie herself, given enough time, she doubted he was going to step back and let her do that just now.

Or maybe ever.

"New game," Isaac said quietly. "New rules."

Five

It was shockingly easy to hog-tie a person and cart them out of a cozy little inn in the middle of the night.

This wasn't news. Isaac had actually had ample opportunity to make this discovery, and practice it in various forms, in the cordoned-off parts of his past he didn't talk about.

But it occurred to him—when he wisely secured Caradine's ankles after she tried to kick him in a sensitive area, then popped in a little gag, too, because she had murder in her eyes and he wasn't sure she wouldn't scream for the fun of it—that he should have considered this approach with her a long time ago.

Or, more precisely, he should have acted on it.

Too bad there weren't any do-overs in this life, or that first night with Caradine would have ended a lot differently five years ago.

This is no time for nostalgia, Isaac told himself, almost entertained.

Only *almost*, because the fairy-tale version of Caradine

in his head wasn't real. The real Caradine had spent untold hours learning how to get out of situations like this one, always assuming she'd be in the hands of folks a lot less interested in her safety and well-being than he was. He'd watched her in class. He'd even taught her a few tricks himself.

He estimated he had about ten minutes before she freed her hands. Then used them.

But like most things in life, he knew he could get away with almost anything if he did it with a sense of purpose. If he looked confident enough, no one dared question what he did—something else he put to the test repeatedly. He gathered up her things, ignoring the furious sounds she was making from behind her gag. Then he tossed her bag over one shoulder, her over the other, and walked out.

Three minutes later, he was outside the inn right there on the harbor, hearing the lines on the moored boats dance against the masts. He belted her into the front seat of the SUV he'd used to track her across the country. He'd left it in a no-parking zone with a borrowed police shield on the dashboard, a little gift from some of his contacts in law enforcement.

Two minutes after that, they were mobile. Isaac took a roundabout way out of the sleepy little vacation town, driving away from the water to pick up the state road that would take him south to Portland. He would have removed her gag as soon as he started driving, but she'd handled that herself.

"This is a surprise," he said after, as he drove through the dark in a furious silence. "I figured the minute you could yell at me, you would."

"What's the point?" she asked in that flat voice that he'd always considered Caradine at her most emotional— a description he was pretty sure would make her head explode if he said it out loud. "I can plot your death silently."

"I gave you the opportunity to cooperate. You didn't take it."

"What's funny to me is that you honestly consider yourself one of the good guys." He glanced over at her to find her holding up her bound wrists as punctuation. "Maybe it's time you reconsidered your life, Isaac."

"Someday," he promised her, maybe a little more darkly than necessary, "you and I are going to sit down and have a nice, long discussion about life. Yours and mine."

"That sounds about as appealing as a spot of meningitis." She sniffed. "Or the average girls' night out."

"One of the things we can talk about is how you pretend you're not girlie. Even though you go to such trouble to keep your nails painted at all times. But black and chipped, of course, so no one can accuse you of any stray traces of femininity."

He didn't have to look at her to feel the way she glared at the side of his head. And when she made an anatomically impossible suggestion, he laughed.

And didn't release her wrists, the way he could have. And should have.

But then again, she could have done the same, and didn't.

So instead, he called in.

"Report, jackhole," answered Templeton, his big voice booming over the SUV's sound system. And then he laughed. "I'm not going to lie. I understand your power trip now."

"Pull it together," Isaac suggested. "You're supposed to be a professional."

"Ten-four, *Dad*," Templeton retorted, unrepentant as ever. "Is the target acquired?"

Caradine stiffened with outrage. "I'm not a *target*. I'm a hostage. And I want to come back to Grizzly Harbor and rebuild the café just so I can ban you for life, Templeton."

"Oh yeah." Isaac sighed. "Fully acquired."

Templeton laughed again. Caradine made some more improbable suggestions regarding anatomy. And select livestock.

Isaac was biting back his own smile when he turned onto Route 90, heading away from Camden, and realized that the car in his rearview mirror had taken the last three turns right along with him.

It could be a problem. Then again, it could be someone headed out of town toward Portland and points east and south like he was. He maintained his course.

"What's the situation in Juneau?" he asked Templeton.

"Nothing new or interesting." Templeton shifted back into seriousness seamlessly, one of his greatest skills. "We found the guy who hired those two idiots, but he's just some local wannabe big shot. He got a phone call from a guy who knows a guy, all blind. We tried to pull on the thread, but there's nothing there."

"My takeaway is that's a lot of layers and risk for a picture and some arson."

"Too much of both," Templeton agreed.

Isaac didn't like that, but there wasn't anything he could do about it. He and Templeton ran down the rest of Alaska Force's active missions in the abbreviated code they could use when civilians were listening, and when he was done, Isaac wasn't surprised to find Caradine scowling at him.

If one day he looked over and she was smiling at him, he'd probably have a heart attack.

"You sound suitably busy and important," she said after a moment. "I have to think you have better things to do than act as a glorified taxi service. For someone who didn't want a taxi in the first place."

Isaac shot her a glance, but his attention was in his rearview again. Fifteen minutes from Camden and the car behind him was maintaining a steady pace. Never catching up, never falling behind, no matter what he did with his own speed. He picked up Route 1 in Warren and then, for fun, looped around in a dramatic U-turn in the middle of the two-lane rural highway. Then headed back on the road to Camden.

Because anyone who'd been following him to get to Route 1, which stretched from north of Portland, up the coast of Maine, to the border of New Brunswick, certainly wouldn't do the same. It was two thirty in the morning.

And for a moment, speeding back down the dark, rural road toward Camden again, he thought he was being paranoid after all.

But then, as he went through the first stoplight, he picked up the same headlights in his rearview mirror again.

Interesting.

"Why are we headed back the way we came?" Caradine asked after a moment. "Have you had an attack of conscience? Or better yet, is this all some terrible nightmare? Will I wake up in my hotel bed at dawn and wonder if any of this even happened?"

"I'm pretty sure we have a tail. Maybe you find that more entertaining than I do."

"A laugh a minute." But she looked in the side mirror as she said it. Then turned to glare at him again. "Mind you, I've had a tail for the past week, so I'm probably used to it by now. I'm guessing big, bad Rambo types eat tails for breakfast or some such deeply boring—I mean, deeply *manly*—thing."

That sarcastic tone of hers could strip paint off a boat, and normally, Isaac liked it. Just then it dug at him. But he refused to give her the satisfaction of snapping at her—and besides, in fairness, he still had her restrained at the wrists and ankles.

Isaac took them on a long, lazy drive instead. It probably would have been scenic, had the sun been up. And romantic, even, had he been with a woman who didn't pretend to hate him. If he hadn't carried her out of an inn earlier, bound and gagged. And if whoever was chasing her wasn't staying tight on them the whole time.

He imagined suggesting that this was romantic to Caradine, and imagining her response to that kept him fully entertained while he drove around in circles that never dislodged the car behind them. He looped around, and when he got to Route 1 for the second time, he called in again.

This time, he spoke to Oz, who could do almost anything from behind his computer, and usually did. At dizzying speed.

"I have some company out here," he told Oz, who slept about as little as he did. "Find me a defensible safe house somewhere with minimal access so I can control whatever comes."

"On it," Oz replied.

And within a few minutes the navigation system of the SUV updated and led them north, deeper inland, toward one of the houses in their wide network. Some Isaac owned outright or had permission to use. Others were . . . available in one way or another.

Especially if they were put back the way they were found when Alaska Force was finished with them.

Beside him, Caradine had gone silent, which couldn't possibly be a good thing when one of her foremost weapons was her mouth. But silent or not, she was safe, so Isaac couldn't worry about it.

Their tail kept dropping out of sight but always returned—usually right about when Isaac was tempted to imagine that he'd either lost them or they'd disappeared because they were locals being idiots, not actual pursuers.

Finally, Isaac reached a dirt road that was the turnoff to the safe house Oz had found for them. As Isaac pulled off, he checked his mobile and saw more detailed instructions on the screen.

He followed them to the letter, bumping down a small

hill through thick woods. At the bottom of the hill, the woods opened up onto water. Some or other "long pond," according to the navigation system, which looked more to him like a large lake.

The dirt road turned into a narrow bridge that led to a house, set out in the water on a tiny island. The house took up most of the space on the island, save for some trees, rocks, and a yard. But it was exactly what he'd requested. There was only one road in or out and otherwise, dark water all around. Isaac sped up as he went over the bridge, driving them quickly to the house. He pulled the SUV around to the side, then got out.

The summer night was a wild, deep dark around him, broken up by the sound of water lapping against the shore. And as he stood there, the cry of a loon.

He found the key where Oz said it would be. He unlocked the side door and eased his way inside to sweep the house. He found nothing but a shut-up summer cottage, furniture draped in sheets and filled with the musty smell of forlorn, forgotten places. As expected. When he'd satisfied himself that no surprises lurked inside, he texted Oz that he was in. Then he returned to the SUV to find Caradine standing there, having gotten her ankles but not her hands untied.

"Inside," he ordered her. "Do not turn on any lights."

She gave him a glare he didn't need any light to see, but she did as he'd asked, taking her bag with her in the hands still bound before her. Isaac grabbed his own cache of weapons from the back of the SUV, then followed her in.

Inside, he locked the side door behind him and tossed his bag on the kitchen table. He moved toward the back of the house that faced the woods, aware that she was right behind him. He moved one of the heavy blinds that had been secured for winter and looked out, waiting.

"Do you think we lost them?" she asked quietly.

"That would be great, but I doubt it. Not when they've been on top of us for hours."

She stood there beside him, and together, they looked back at the woods they'd come through.

One beat. Another beat.

He tried to remember another time he and Caradine had ever simply stood somewhere together without having to engage in yet another round of their endless battle, and couldn't. He was tempted to find this a little more soothing than it should have been, given that this was a hunt and this time, he was on the wrong side of that equation.

Not to mention the fact he didn't have all the information. Or any information at all.

Still, he let himself enjoy the fact that she was standing there, a warm presence beside him. He could smell her shampoo and what he thought was body lotion, though he'd never seen her apply it. And he could hear her breathe.

He knew better than most that it was the little moments a person clung to, later, when they were gone.

A breath after that, sure enough, came the headlights in the trees.

Then stopped at the top of the hill, the light eerie in the midst of so much darkness.

"Well," Caradine said brightly. "*That's* creepy."

"I think we can assume that they're going to come all the way down the drive. Then the question is, Will they keep coming? Or will they stay there and wait us out?"

Caradine shifted around to stare at him, and he took her wrists in his hands, using the knife he kept on his belt to cut her free. She didn't jerk her wrists from his grasp, which he should have liked.

"Why didn't you take these off yourself?" he asked gruffly. "We both know you could have. I thought it would take you ten minutes, tops."

"Why would I do that when I can make you feel bad about it instead?" She didn't even smirk to take the sting out. "The way you should."

"News flash. Keeping you safe is what matters to me, Caradine. Not your feelings."

But despite what he said, the way she studied him made him feel guilty.

You mean guilti-er, something in him corrected him.

"Are we a team now?" she asked, her voice as dark as the thick Maine night outside. "I'm finding it hard to keep track. One minute you're bodily removing me from a bed-and-breakfast, against my will. Now you think we should work together like I'm one of your military buddies?"

"You tell me. Are those your friends out there?"

"Isaac. Please. You know I don't have friends."

He reached over and smoothed his hand over the hair she so rarely left down. It was as silky and soft as it ever was, and he expected her to swat his hand away. But it made his chest feel tight when she didn't.

"I guess it never occurred to me to ask a critical question," he said, his voice rougher than it should have been. "Are you running from something—or toward it?"

"That sounds like a philosophical dilemma." She smiled, though it wasn't a real smile. It was much too tight. "I don't do those, either."

"It's only a dilemma if you don't know the answer."

He studied her face in the gloom of the dark front room. That stubborn, pretty, clever face of hers, which had been keeping him guessing for years now. He was sure he could see something like regret. A kind of longing. And around and beneath it all, that stubbornness that might get them both killed. Possibly tonight.

"I'm not running to or from anything, Gentry. I *was* on a lovely New England vacation. I'm not sure why that led to kidnapping and careening around the countryside in the middle of the night, but here we are. I blame you."

"Here's what I don't get," Isaac replied, tracking the headlights as they bumped their way down the hill. "No one was tracking you for the entirety of the past week. I know, because I was there. Alone. How did they find you now?"

"Is this really a good time for a chat? The bad guys will be at the door any minute." She peered out the window, where the car had made it to the waterline. "Literally."

"Is that why you went to Camden in the first place? Were you planning to meet someone there?" He braced himself. "Please don't tell me that you really did blow up your own place."

"Of course I didn't blow up my own place. I was *in it*." She blew out a breath, but she kept her gaze on the car as the headlights winked out, there on the other side of the narrow bridge. "I'm not meeting anybody. Not the way you mean. Not exactly."

"Then what, exactly?"

He tilted his head in the direction of the dirt drive as the car began to move again, slow and dark, creeping closer every second. He eased the blinds back down into place, leaving him with no eyes on their visitor. But at the moment his attention was on the woman before him.

"I get it, Caradine. You have a deep, dark past. That's not exactly a secret. But if I'm about to get in a firefight, surely you can give me enough details to know whether or not I can expect you to shoot me in the back."

She looked as if he'd hit her. "I would never shoot you in the back."

The words came out so fiercely it took them both by surprise. He could see it on her face. He could feel it flare between them, surprise rolling into all the rest of it, in this battle of theirs that only got hotter and more dangerous with time.

Especially right now.

For a moment, a scant breath, they stared at each other. Almost—

But this was not the time. Isaac shoved everything ruthlessly aside, wishing he could compartmentalize her the way he did everything else in his life. God knew he'd tried, and that was before she'd been in trouble.

She had always been the one thing in his life he couldn't put in a box.

"How did they pick up your trail in Camden?" he demanded, low and urgent.

Outside, there was the sound of wheels crunching up the drive.

"They didn't pick it up," Caradine whispered back in that same fierce way. "I called them."

Of all the things she could have said, he hadn't been expecting that.

Isaac felt winded, as if she'd kicked him in the solar plexus. "You did what?"

"I called them." Her chin tilted up, and he was sure he could see her eyes glittering with the emotion she liked to deny. "I wanted to see who would show up. I needed to see which nightmare I should be having. The same one I've been having? Or a brand-new one?"

The sound of the wheels stopped. That was worse.

Isaac stared at Caradine, not sure if he wanted to strangle her or pull her into a hug she would claim she hated. Both, probably.

"Caradine," he began, quiet and furious, and more of the latter, "don't you think—"

But that was when the front doorknob, three feet away from them, began to turn.

Six

"Please tell me you checked that door," Caradine whispered, her heart pounding even as her stomach plummeted to the floor. And then stayed there, in a hard, ugly knot. "Please tell me it's locked."

It was the closest she'd come to prayer in a long, long while.

"Yes, I checked it," Isaac muttered in an undertone. "And yes, it's locked."

He sounded different, and that caught at her, yanking her out of the dizzy, nauseating spiral she was in. Memories of other terror-filled moments like this one, always scared and always in the dark and always sure that this was the end of it all—

But Isaac was here this time.

Deep inside, where she could be honest with herself, she acknowledged that what she felt was relief.

And when she glanced over at him, he no longer looked like any of the versions of him she'd been so sure she'd seen and known and cataloged. He was hewn from stone, as ever, but there was something different about him tonight. A crackling sort of *presence*.

He looks like a warrior, something in her whispered, from deep in that place where she kept her truths hidden.

He pulled her behind him as he headed back toward the kitchen, away from the front door and that doorknob that was rattling, just slightly. Just enough. Caradine squinted hard in the gloom, trying to keep her eyes on the dead bolt. As if she could actually see it.

As if she could make it hold with her will alone.

What was funny was that she'd planned this. She'd made that call from the phone beside her bed in the inn. She'd planned to do this all by herself. Accordingly, she'd made contingency plan after contingency plan. If they did this, she'd do that, and so on.

Caradine had been positive she'd worked out every angle. A hundred times over.

But she hadn't banked on the panic.

Because all of a sudden, it was like ten years ago all over again. Her head ringing. That pressure in her ears.

She had to keep checking to see if she was sprawled out on the ground. Bleeding, even.

But no. Isaac positioned her in the small hall between the front room and the kitchen, then left her there. Caradine stared at the walls that seemed to close in on her, covered in peeling paint and framed prints of wooden sailboats and bright red canoes. She felt something on her face and was sure she was bleeding again, there on the sidewalk—

Isaac was back, there in front of her and wider than the walls. Bigger and tougher than the world. He pressed a gun into her hand and then he grabbed her chin.

His grip was electric. It shocked her.

"Focus," he ordered her.

And Caradine had spent so many years making fun of

Alaska Force in general and Isaac in particular. But right now she was grateful for every scrap of experience that lent that unmistakable note of authority to his voice. For that uncompromising look in his gray eyes.

For every last choice he'd made in his life that had made him into who he was. This warrior before her.

She nodded, jerkily, despite that grip of his. She ignored the panicked ringing in her ears, held tight to the handgun, and found herself standing straighter.

"I'm focused," she told him. Or maybe herself.

He didn't argue with her. And there was something about his instant, automatic acceptance that made her believe in herself, too.

One more thing she would have to excavate—or ignore—if they survived this. *When* they survived this.

"Anyone walks through the door, take one second," Isaac told her. It was another order. "Inhale, see if it's me, then exhale. If it's not me, shoot. Got it?"

And suddenly, here in a lonely cottage on a remote lake deep in the Maine wilderness, when it was much too late, Caradine wanted to say . . . everything. All those things she'd refused to say when she had the chance. All those things that crowded in her throat and made her tongue taste bitter in her own mouth.

There was a man at the door, her past was coming at her too fast and too deadly, and Isaac looked like some kind of warrior god. And she wanted to tell him all the things she'd never dared. Now.

While she still could.

Instead, she swallowed it all down the way she always did. No matter what shade of gray his eyes were in the quiet darkness of the old house.

"Got it," she said.

And then she stayed there, rocked inside and out, as he melted off into the shadows. She could still feel where he'd gripped her chin, and she focused on that when her pulse picked up. She concentrated on the heat and strength his fingers had left behind and that controlled look he'd worn while his eyes had glittered—because it was better than spiraling into a panic attack she couldn't afford.

She thought she heard the faintest whisper of sound from the kitchen, but when she tensed—ready to aim and fire—nothing happened.

That was the back door, she told herself. *It was Isaac going outside.*

Straight toward the threat, the way she supposed he always did. That was what he'd spent his entire adult life doing. While she'd run, hidden, and panicked—

Focus, she ordered herself, the way he had. *Breathe.*

Everything was silent then. Dark.

As if the night were going to sit on her like this forever. Living in Alaska should have made her shrug off the dark, but not tonight. She tried to breathe more quietly. She tried to *listen.*

She tried to fight off the fear instead of surrendering to it.

But that was a lot easier when she was *doing* something. Climbing out her window, stealing a boat from a remote inlet, and so on. Even staying awake for days and driving crazy distances fueled only by caffeine. It was all *action.*

Sitting still like this—still and quiet and alone—reminded her a little too strongly of her childhood. Of hiding from her father's temper or worse, his business associates and so-called friends. And of the first five years after she'd run away from Boston, always crouched down somewhere, waiting to be discovered. Waiting to be hurt.

Waiting to see if this time, they would win.

If this time, they would finally get what they wanted.

Caradine hated waiting. She watched the front door, but the knob stopped moving back and forth.

She strained her ears, but there was nothing but the oppressive weight of the silence. Outside, the Maine night seemed to press down hard on this little cottage far away from anything. There had been no lights anywhere as they'd come down the hill, except the stars. That told her that even if there were neighbors, or other houses set around this same lake, none of them were awake at this hour.

Caradine was smack down in the middle of another dark night of the soul, and she could do nothing but flick off the safety, wait, and remind herself that she'd practiced—and practiced and practiced—for this.

The worst thing she could do was start imagining things.

Like what it would mean if Isaac wasn't the man who came to the door.

"Stop it," she hissed. Out loud.

An eternity passed. Then another.

She stayed where Isaac had left her, frozen solid, as if his command were some kind of spell she had no choice but to obey.

That notion was comforting. It was almost as good as his being here, with all that brooding intensity, strength, and power he wore so carelessly.

Another eternity rolled by.

Then she heard something.

Adrenaline and panic fused, then exploded inside of her. Her heart *hurt* and her stomach turned inside out, but all she did was straighten against the wall where he'd left her. It was possible she would see wooden boats and red canoes in her dreams for the rest of her life.

Assuming there was going to be a rest of her life.

The noise came again, from the back door off the

kitchen, and she shifted around to face it. She lifted the gun and waited.

The door flew open.

A man she didn't recognize stumbled in, bent in half, and she remembered what Isaac had said.

Inhale. She firmed her grip. She aimed.

But then Isaac stepped in behind the stranger and kicked the door shut behind him.

His gaze found hers, steel gray and intense.

Caradine exhaled. His gaze stayed on hers.

She lowered the gun.

She started to move, swaying toward him. But before she took a step out of the small hall, he stopped her. He didn't actually shake his head, but he stopped her as surely as if he'd thrust a hand out. He shoved the man before him into a chair at the kitchen table, putting his back at an angle to Caradine.

If she didn't come out of the hallway, he might not even know that she was standing there.

Isaac slapped on the kitchen light. Then stood there, unblinking, as the man before him screwed up his face against the sudden glare. Caradine felt a little teary herself.

It was the light, obviously. Not the fact that Isaac was safe and in control. Or that the man in that chair still wasn't someone she recognized. No matter how much she frowned at him in the overhead glare, when she'd been so sure she would know who he was.

Who did you expect it would be? a voice inside asked her, but she wasn't ready for that. Not yet.

Isaac widened his stance. He crossed his arms in a way that made his impressive chest seem even bigger, one hand still gripping his gun, which was far bigger and deadlier-looking than hers.

And then he smiled down at the man before him.

Not at all genially.

"I told you," the man said, with a thick Boston accent

that made Caradine's blood run cold. Because accents like that haunted her nightmares. "This was a misunderstanding."

"I don't think I misunderstood you trying to break into my house," Isaac said in his friendliest tone. It sent a shiver down Caradine's spine, but that wasn't where the sensation pooled. "Just like I didn't misunderstand you following me here, on back roads, through rural Maine in the middle of the night. You want to tell me why? Because I have to tell you, much as I like to be pursued, a girl does like to be asked to dance first."

"I thought you were someone else."

The man's voice was surly, and Caradine studied the parts of him that she could see now that he was glaring straight at Isaac. He had a flat buzz cut that showed off that extra, angry roll to his neck. It made her think of steroids. And of sitting in church, a thousand years ago, looking at the necks of the men who sat with her family as they rose around her like a red wall, angrily displayed above their Sunday collared shirts.

But this was no time for a trip down memory lane. Especially when, though she knew what *kind* of man this was, she really didn't know him personally.

Is that a relief or a letdown? she asked herself. And found she didn't have an answer for that, either.

"Who did you think I was?" Isaac asked, as if this were a casual chat with one of his buddies—which made her want to reevaluate every actual casual chat she'd ever seen him have. "Do I look like a friend of yours?"

"What you look like is a dead man," the man replied, with a snarl. "If I were you and I wanted to live, I'd back away from this situation."

"You're in my house, friend." Isaac sounded cheerful. "And I'm the one with the gun, remember? Yours took a swim."

The man growled. "You don't want the kind of trouble you're bringing on yourself, *friend*. You hear me?"

"Convince me," Isaac suggested. Cheerfully.

The man in the chair studied him, and Caradine could see his deep-set eyes narrow. He sat back in his chair, one hand on his thigh like he was in control. Like he was lounging there, holding court.

Not for the first time, she wondered how anyone could look at Isaac and imagine that he was something other than a predator. A warrior at the very top of his game.

The red-necked man was nothing but a garden-variety thug. She'd known dozens of him back in the day, but even if she hadn't, it was stamped all over him. How could a man like that, who had to be cunning enough to survive as long as he had—to his midforties, by the looks of it—actually look like he was relaxing when faced with an ex–special ops master of warfare? Isaac was so much more powerful and dangerous than a penny-ante thug from Boston that it was almost laughable.

But she'd seen it happen again and again. Isaac smiled, used that friendly voice, and everyone believed it.

She reminded herself that she never had.

"Let's just say that I represent certain interests," the thug told him grandly. "You had some moves out there, I grant you. You got the drop on me. Kudos. Then it turns out that you and me, we don't have the business I thought we did."

Isaac smiled again. "You mistook the rug I was transporting for a body."

The man nodded, his eyes still narrow. "A misunderstanding, like I said. It can end right here, or it can turn into a bigger problem. For you."

"From where I'm standing, I don't have any problems," Isaac said idly. "Can't say the same for you."

"How much of a problem you're going to have depends on what you do right now," the man said, his voice getting harder. "Shooting me would be a mistake. A huge mistake."

Isaac didn't look convinced. "Would it?"

"You're already skating on thin ice, buddy. And me, I'm a forgiving guy. I'd be inclined to let it go. But the people I work for?" The man shook his head. "They don't let anything go."

Isaac's head tilted slightly, very slightly, to one side. "What makes you think I let anything go?"

And Caradine watched, holding her breath, as it occurred to the guy in the chair that he was dealing with something a little more treacherous than a trained and unusually well-armed homeowner. He dropped that hand from his thigh. He went still.

"Who are the people you work for?" Isaac asked.

To Caradine's ear, he didn't change his tone of voice. He sounded the same as he had this whole time. But it was suddenly obvious who he really was, because the thug before him looked uneasy.

"You think you're a tough guy?" the man in the chair demanded, getting loud, no doubt to cover that unease. "You don't want to know what happens to tough guys."

"Let me guess," Isaac said. "You dispose of them. But that's not where this is going. *Buddy.*"

And then, the way he had when he'd taken her gun away from her, Isaac moved so fast that Caradine almost wasn't sure she'd seen him move at all.

She had the impression of explosive action. His hand reaching out.

Her brain told her that he'd hit the guy in the chair, but there was no sound of impact. And the man didn't shake, the chair didn't fly backward, or any of the other things she might expect to have happen if a man as strong as Isaac actually hit something.

It was only when Isaac shifted that gray gaze of his to

hers again that she realized that the man in the chair was unconscious.

"What did you do to him?" she asked, and was too unsettled to care that her voice was uneven.

Isaac wasn't smiling any longer. "I'm not in the mood to play twenty questions with a dirtbag."

He shoved his gun in the back waistband of his cargo pants, then set about fastening the man to the chair itself with more of the handy zip ties he apparently carried around with him. Something she felt she should have known about him. But hadn't.

When he straightened again, Caradine must have had some sort of look on her face, because his brows rose.

"Problem?"

"You have a lot of zip ties on hand," she pointed out. "I'm sure that's totally normal. For a psychopath."

His mouth curved into something that had nothing in common with that genial smile of his. "They have a lot of uses."

And to her horror, she felt the tug of that, everywhere. Worse, she felt herself flush.

She jerked her eyes away from his, back down to the gun in her hands. She kept staring at it as he made a call, muttering out instructions to what she assumed was yet another combat team, though he wanted this one for cleanup.

Caradine figured she knew what that meant.

And no matter that it was over and she was supposedly safe now, she could still feel the panic surging through her. The fear like a solid weight. Wooden boats and red canoes, and trying to fight off images of the worst-case scenario.

She hated how close she'd come to breaking here, and worse, how much of that he'd seen.

And he might have neutralized one guy in the middle of nowhere, but it wasn't over. It was never over.

"Trash collection is scheduled," Isaac told her when

he finished his call. He shoved his phone into his pocket. "But we're not going to wait around."

"Aren't we?" she heard herself ask.

And without meaning to, really, without fully understanding what she was doing—or maybe she understood all too well that it had always been coming to this—Caradine raised her gun and pointed it straight at him.

Again.

"This time, with feeling," she said quietly.

But Isaac only laughed.

Seven

"I don't know why you're laughing," Caradine snapped at him, her usual scowl on her face. And that gun aimed at his head. Her version of a love letter, Isaac thought—and that notion only made him laugh harder. "I'm not kidding around."

"Whatever you think is about to happen here," Isaac said when he could contain the laughter, "it's not."

"You think I won't shoot you, but I will."

"Okay," he said blandly. "Right in the face? Are you going to kill me, Caradine? Because if not—if you're thinking you'll wound me to slow me down—you should probably aim for a knee. And make sure you take it out with the first shot. Otherwise, chances are, you're only going to piss me off."

She dropped her gaze to his knee, and that scowl turned to more of a study. It should have curdled his blood, but it was Caradine. A big, loud, consistent bark, but no bite. Or not a deep bite, anyway.

Then again, she didn't lower the muzzle of the gun.

"You say that like I wouldn't happily wound you, Isaac." Her blue eyes gleamed. "With great pleasure. Joy, even. Maybe a song or two."

"Joy and singing are great, obviously," he pointed out, still not entirely finished laughing, but trying hard to keep it off his face. Unsuccessfully, if her expression was any guide. "But I'm a better shot than you, and I don't know that I'd be waving that gun around this tiny kitchen. Just throwing that out there."

"You don't know what kind of shot I am. Because I've always thought it was in my best interests to keep that to myself."

"It doesn't matter if your secret hobby is being an amateur marksman. You weren't a marine."

"I'm something far more dangerous than a marine, Isaac," she snapped. "I'm a determined woman who has no intention of being trussed up and carted around again."

"You telegraph your moves, baby." And he could see her temper and a hint of uncertainty flutter over her face, but she didn't lower her weapon. "That gives me about three seconds to react. And guess what? I only need one."

"Do you want to test that theory?"

"Go right ahead," he dared her.

And this was Caradine. So he wasn't surprised at all when her chin tipped up, stubborn and strong. Or when her shoulders squared.

He saw the exact moment she made her decision. Her eyes flashed a darker blue, she held her breath, and he was damned lucky she really did telegraph everything.

She aimed again, but he was already moving.

By the time the shot rang out, it was done.

Caradine was bent over, cradling her hand. Isaac had possession of her gun. And there was a nice bullet hole in the wall behind where he'd been standing. At thigh level.

"Do you feel better now?" he asked her, gruff and low. Deadly calm while she panted for breath.

"No, I don't feel better," she seethed at him. "I think you broke my wrist."

"I didn't break it. If it was broken, you would have heard it crack. And you'd be in a lot more pain. Meaning you wouldn't be whining about it."

"You hurt me." She straightened and glared at him, another thing she wouldn't have been doing if he'd really hurt her. "And now you're calling me a whiner?"

"You tried to shoot me, Caradine. Do you know what I normally do to people who shoot at me?" He grinned. Broadly. "I'll give you three guesses, and none of them involve hanging around talking about it afterward."

"Is that supposed to make my broken wrist feel better?"

And maybe it was because she'd made him feel like a giant rampaging stampede of bulls in all the china shops, *again*, when he'd done his best to disarm her without really hurting her. The way he could have, and easily, when there was a bullet with his name on it stuck in the wall behind them. And when he knew she was hardly the fine china in that analogy. Not his scrappy, forever-tough-talking Caradine.

Whatever it was, he wasn't as completely in control of himself or his emotions as he should have been when he reached over and hauled her toward him, with one hand wrapped around her upper arm.

"Are we pretending you feel something?" he bit out, his face in hers, his grin long gone. "Are you sure? Because I was under the impression that if a single emotion dared poke up its head around you, you'd implode."

Her gaze was much too dark. "Let me go, Isaac. Let me drive away and don't follow me."

"Not happening. Because I don't know if you noticed, but this has all gotten more intense. Who was that man?"

"I don't know." She tried to pull her arm away, but he

only tightened his grip. "I honestly don't know. I don't recognize him."

"But you know who he works for."

Caradine made a frustrated noise. "I have theories, that's all."

"I have theories, too," he retorted. "About you. Because I couldn't help noticing his accent, and that narrows it down nicely."

"Great. Theories upon theories and none of it matters. You still need to let me go. This has nothing to do with you."

"What exactly were you planning to do?" he demanded, and there was no getting around it then. He was definitely losing his cool. "Explain to me how you thought this was going to go. Whoever you called sent this guy. Did you think he was going to ask you out for coffee? Sit down, have a nice chat? Does he look to you like the kind of guy who could be reasoned with?"

Her blue eyes were filled with storms and fury. "I was perfectly happy to shoot you, Isaac. I don't know what makes you think I had a *coffee date* in mind for someone I like even less. I wanted to see who it was. I wanted to see if I recognized him. I wanted to see if it was my—"

She didn't finish her sentence. She gulped down whatever she'd been about to say.

"Your what?" he demanded. Edgily.

"Like I said. My nightmares. I have a lot of them. Some are more specific than others, and I wanted to know which this was."

"You've never struck me as an idiot before," he growled at her. "But now it's like you're going for the world record."

She yanked on her arm, and he finally released her. Grudgingly.

"I don't understand why you're doing this," she threw at him, and he was slightly gratified by how ragged she sounded. As long as it wasn't just him. "I don't want you here. I don't need you here. Your interference is not required."

"Do you want to get killed?" Isaac was almost loud then. He barely sounded like himself. And the part of him that wasn't much too close to losing it couldn't help but note that she was the only one who could do this to him. The only one who dug beneath his skin and drove him crazy. The only weakness he hadn't excised. "Is this some death wish you're acting out here?"

That vulnerable, uncertain expression moved over her face again, but her voice was cold. "I'm not an Alaska Force client, Isaac."

"No," he said. "You're really not."

And that electricity that was always between them flared, so hot he was surprised the cottage didn't ignite.

Finally, she looked away, which for Caradine was a major surrender.

"We're leaving now," he said shortly. "We're driving down to Portland, where there's a plane waiting. I'm taking you back to Alaska."

"I don't want to go back to Alaska."

"I didn't ask you what you want," he belted out at her, and took it as a minor victory when she jolted at the sound. "I told you what's going to happen."

"I'm not your client, and I'm certainly not one of your Alaska Force subordinates, ready and eager to do your bidding." She held his gaze, and whatever hint of vulnerability or surrender he'd thought he'd seen on her face was gone. "I'm not going to tell you anything, no matter where we go. I promise you that."

Isaac wanted to put his hands on her, desperately, so he didn't. He stepped back instead, before he lost it completely. He was too hot. Too *affected*.

But he had spent a lifetime controlling himself in far worse situations than this. Caradine might get to him in ways he wasn't exactly comfortable with, but it was still only the two of them and an incapacitated thug in a summer cottage. It wasn't a freaking war.

Handle your crap, he ordered himself sternly.

"You will," he told her, pitilessly. "Because you'll be locked up in a cabin in Fool's Cove under my command, whether you like it or not, until you do."

Most people fell apart when he used that tone. Caradine scoffed at him. "You're not putting me in your private jail, Isaac. Get a grip."

"You'll wish it was jail," he promised her. "This will be much worse. Because it won't be a cell, Caradine. It will be my cabin. With me. Until I'm satisfied that you've told me every last thing I want to know about your past."

And Isaac was smiling again as he ushered her out into the predawn darkness, because he'd known Caradine for five years now. But this was the first time he'd ever seen her without a single thing to say.

"Sulking?" he asked her after a solid forty-five minutes in the car, when her brooding silence in the passenger seat beside him was beginning to feel operatic.

"Only because I missed," she replied.

Isaac supposed that there was something wrong with him that he found that funny. Then again, the fact that he wasn't like other people had been a theme in his life for so long now, it hardly bore repeating. Even to himself.

You're not made in the same mold, his father had told him when Isaac had been an angry teenage boy, convinced the world was arrayed against him, so self-centered and awash in his adolescent misery that it had never crossed his mind they'd been living on borrowed time.

You're the one who isn't normal, Dad, he'd shot back. Because that was what he'd thought he'd wanted then, with all the righteous fury of a fifteen-year-old in the grips of hormone poisoning. To be like everyone else. *Or you'd move somewhere normal people live.*

His father had only laughed. That was what Isaac remembered most about him. That he'd somehow found a surly teenage kid entertaining. All these years later, it made Isaac wish he could have gotten to know his father as a man.

It's easy to move somewhere and pretend that's going to solve your problems, his father had told him. *But what's hard, no matter where you live, is figuring out the ways you're an individual. And then honoring those parts of you, whether that makes you normal or not.*

After his parents had died, Isaac had leaned in hard to that advice.

The last thing in the world Mom and Dad would want is you to go risk your life, Amy had argued with him when he'd started his officer training courses while still in college. *Don't you understand? All they'd ever want is you safe.*

Your job is to stay safe, he'd told his older sister, because she was the one with a collection of normal things. The husband. The house. The baby on the way. *My job is to keep you safe.*

The way he would have kept his parents safe, if he could have. If he'd had that chance.

Isaac had never regretted his choices. Sometimes he told himself that his parents would have been proud, the way his grandmother in Anchorage was. Even Amy had come around—especially when he'd finally come out of the service, more or less in one piece.

I'm glad you're home, she'd told him, fiercely, on his first Christmas as a civilian. She'd been making up his grandmother's pullout couch for him like he was still a kid, and he'd let her, because he figured she needed to feel useful. She'd taken a break from fluffing up the spare pillows—something he really didn't need, given some of the places he'd slept—to hug him. Hard. *But please, Isaac, whatever you do—don't end up like Uncle Theo.*

Admittedly, the fact that their uncle lived out there in his remote cabin, off the grid, like the wild-eyed mountain man he'd always been in Isaac's memory, weighed on him. Uncle Theo had been an army man, and he didn't like to talk about that part of his life. He didn't like to talk at all. If Isaac squinted, it wasn't hard to see that Uncle Theo might just be his future.

That was why Amy had gifted Isaac with a puppy he absolutely hadn't wanted when he'd settled down in Fool's Cove, corralled Templeton and Jonas into starting Alaska Force with him, and started repairing the old family fishing lodge.

It's great that you still want to save the world, she'd said. *But if you can't actually take care of another creature, maybe try that first.*

Isaac hadn't wanted to *take care* of anything, including himself. But Horatio as a puppy had been irresistible—and it helped that he was the smartest dog Isaac had ever encountered.

But taking all of that together, he thought on the drive to Portland and the long flight back to Alaska, it made sense that the woman who got under his skin was the one who had shot at him. *Merrily.* Because when had Isaac ever done anything the easy way?

A *normal* person would have washed his hands of Caradine a long time ago. Isaac had always liked an intelligent, smart-mouthed woman, because there was usually sweetness buried inside all that surliness and attitude. If he'd believed at any point that Caradine really meant the things she said to him, he would have bailed five years ago. After the first time she'd tossed him out of her bed.

Meaning, after that first night.

Instead, he persisted in believing that if he gave her enough time, she'd come around. She'd finally admit what was so obvious to him that there was no point even talking about it.

I had no idea you were such an optimist, Jonas had said in his stark way on one of the very few times he'd actually mentioned Isaac and Caradine's thing, which otherwise only Templeton dared to do. To his face. *I would have said we left all that crap behind when we left the service.*

Isaac would have thought so, too.

Optimism was imagining he could save anything in this world, including himself. Optimism was holding on to a person who'd repeatedly peeled his fingers off and shoved him away. There were other words for that kind of optimism, and one of them was *foolishness.*

And as the private jet hit cruising altitude and headed west, Isaac found himself staring out the window as the world slipped by beneath him. But he wasn't seeing the clouds, the sky, the hints of the earth far below him. He was thinking about her.

He was always thinking about her.

Caradine had marched on board the plane and wrapped herself in a pile of blankets that covered her from head to foot so she could hide all the way back to Alaska. He couldn't even see her beneath the lump of fabric that made her reclined seat into a cocoon.

He knew that if she had it her way, she would hide like that forever.

Maybe it was time to accept that the fact she'd unloaded her weapon *at him* meant exactly the same thing it would have meant if anyone else had done it. That the bullet hole he'd left in the wall of the cottage told him things he should pay attention to—things he should have been paying attention to all this time.

She wasn't going to tell him anything. Not of her own volition.

She wasn't going to wake up from her angry, pointed nap on this plane in a sharing mood.

She didn't do sharing moods.

When given the opportunity, she'd matched action to her intentions. If he hadn't moved, she would have shot him.

When people show you who they are, believe them, went the famous quote. His uncle Theo had carved it into the door of that hard-to-reach cabin of his.

But it wasn't until they switched planes in Juneau, going from the private jet that traveled long distances to the much smaller seaplane that would take them to Fool's Cove, that Isaac pulled a trigger of his own.

Or faced reality, at last.

"You ready to go home?" he asked Caradine as they walked across the tarmac.

"I don't have a home," Caradine replied stiffly, and maybe she really was forcing herself to sound that unfriendly, the way he thought she was. Like it was a mask she had to remind herself to wear. *Or maybe she's actually unfriendly,* he snapped at himself, *like when she* shot at you *without hesitation.* "You dragging me back to Grizzly Harbor isn't going to change that."

"Maybe it's time you started talking, then. The sooner you do, the sooner we'll figure out where your home is."

She glared at him, as always. "Hard pass."

"Caradine." He said her name like a warning. But he couldn't have said which one of them he was warning.

"You know full well that's not my name, Isaac."

"Whatever your name is, you're staying with me."

Her glare deepened into a scowl, its natural progression. "You mean in one of the little guest cabins? Rumor has it you have a lot of them out there."

"I mean, with me," he said. "Because you're not a client, remember?"

She stopped walking when they reached the smaller plane. And she stared at him, doing that thing that made her blue eyes seem remote. Even when she was right there in front of him.

"I know you're the mighty Isaac Gentry, lord of all you survey," she said, ice-cold all the way through. "But has it really never crossed your mind that I'm maybe . . . just not that into you?"

He studied her grimly. "No."

Her eyes flashed with something he couldn't read. "Maybe it should. At the very least it would cut down on all the kidnapping."

That was what stuck with him when she stalked away from him, climbing into the plane and strapping herself into her seat. It was a moody summer morning in Alaska. The mountains were draped in clouds, and the water looked dark and brooding.

Isaac kept thinking about that bullet. The look on her face when she'd taken aim. And her words echoed around and around inside of him, drowning out the activity on the tarmac and the kick of the wind.

He still didn't believe her. Or he didn't *want* to believe her. But there was only one way to end this game, and it wasn't waiting for her to see reason. Or to trust him. He'd already tried that.

He pulled out his phone and called Oz.

"Local law enforcement is already handling the situation in Maine," Oz reported when he picked up. "And when they run your new friend's prints, they're going to get all kinds of bells and whistles, so that should keep him occupied for a while."

Isaac knew it was only a matter of time before his buddy with the Boston accent reported back to his employers with information about Caradine, who he certainly hadn't believed was a rug. And information about him to go with it—like that he existed. That Maine officials had taken the man into custody meant the clock was already ticking toward that inevitable end. He needed to be ready.

But that wasn't why he'd called.

He needed something else first.

"Speaking of prints," he said, staring at the small plane Caradine had already boarded and wondering why this felt like a betrayal of her. When it shouldn't have. Surely it shouldn't have, when she was the one who'd denied him to his face, gleefully. And, more important, had tried to shoot him. "Run Caradine's. It's high time we knew what we were dealing with."

Eight

Caradine had never actually been to Fool's Cove.

She liked to refer to the hard-to-reach fishing camp as a secret hideout, or clubhouse—because she liked to minimize Alaska Force whenever possible. Particularly *to* anyone involved with Alaska Force. She'd seen pictures of the lodge that the Gentry family had run for several generations, because historical pictures of Grizzly Harbor and the rest of the island were impossible to avoid, hung up as they were in places like the post office and the general store.

But she'd never had occasion to poke around on the back side of the island. Not when there was absolutely no possibility that a person could wander that way without Alaska Force knowing it. She'd become Caradine Scott, moved in, and taken over the restaurant before she'd understood what was happening on the island. Or exactly what the men in fantastic shape with those calm—sometimes cold—eyes did for a living. If she'd known about them, she would never have come here.

By the time she understood, thanks to Isaac and the epic mistake of that first night, it was too late. It would have been much harder, and more conspicuous, to leave.

She had hunkered down and ridden out her first Alaskan winter. Then four more. And she could have tried to drive or hike over what all the locals called Hard Ass Pass—the only so-called road that went over the mountain and wound down and around into Fool's Cove, which was rarely passable—but she'd never done it. She'd never wanted to do it, because she wasn't suicidal.

And because the less she knew about Alaska Force—and Isaac—the better.

As the plane flew in that morning, the summer sun was kicking its way through the clouds, and Caradine hated that the hideaway she'd mocked all this time was . . . pretty.

Though that was a small word for so much Alaskan splendor.

She'd wanted it to look shoddy. Even though nothing Alaska Force did was anything but first-rate, she'd secretly hoped their headquarters would run more toward the dilapidated side of the scale. She'd envisioned a scary hunting cabin aesthetic, off-putting and dire.

The historic fishing lodge seemed promisingly decrepit from the air. But as the seaplane went in for a landing, skidding across the water of the cove, she could see all too well that while the lodge sprawled there along the rocky shore like many Alaskan waterfront dwellings, it wasn't ramshackle at all. It looked like what it was—the base of a private security firm that lacked for neither money nor clientele. There was a main part, two stories high there on the steep hill, and a lot of wooden walkways to connecting cabins. And there were hints of smoke in the trees, alerting her to the fact that other cabins sat farther back in the thick woods that climbed up the side of the steep mountainside. On the East Coast, people liked to build giant mansions on the waterline, but that wasn't the Alaskan way. The lodge here looked unpretentious and serviceable—until she looked closer.

Isaac led her down a dock, then up a steep set of stairs. It was impossible not to notice the quality of the wood, everywhere. At the top of the stairs, she saw that the walkways and many decks overlooking the water were in far better condition than the public boardwalks in Grizzly Harbor. The windows were clear, and the roofs all looked tight and snug. The attention to detail made what should have been a broken-down, gloomy sort of off-grid compound into something that exuded a quiet, rustic elegance.

Which should not have made her chest feel too tight, like a sob was building up in there and making it hard to breathe.

Isaac skirted the two-story main building, then led her down a walkway that led toward a large cabin set away from the rest.

Halfway along the cabin's walkway, she heard a sharp bark. Then Isaac's dog was bounding down the path, cavorting about with more energy and joy than she'd ever seen him display in Grizzly Harbor.

Everyone knew Horatio. He was usually Isaac's shadow in the village, waiting outside the Fairweather when it was warm and sitting next to his master's barstool when it was cold. He accepted some patting and the occasional treat, but mostly he watched. And judged, Caradine had always thought. Harshly.

She had to fight to keep her expression blank when Isaac broke into a smile as Horatio reached him. He bent over and took the dog's face in his hands, making low, crooning noises that spoke of love and companionship and a part of him that had nothing to do with sex or controlled violence or the battles they'd waged against each other for years.

It made her want to cry.

And not in the shower this time.

Caradine tried to tell herself she was tired, but she couldn't, because she was fine. Disconcertingly fine, in fact, when she really should have been riddled with anxiety and panic. Instead, she'd slept for most of the long flight here, because she felt, if not safe when Isaac was near—safer than she did at any other time.

Something she could seem to admit only to herself when she'd constructed an actual blanket fort, like a toddler, and then hid in it.

She'd had to bite his head off to regain her equilibrium, and her reward for that had been to watch his gray eyes get hard and dark. *Congratulations,* she'd snapped at herself. *You're the actual, literal worst.*

Watching the way he openly, happily lavished affection on his dog made her hurt.

She was so sick of herself in that moment that she felt weak with it. And *this close* to doing something she would regret forever, like telling this man exactly what it did to her to watch him love on something. This tough, dangerous man, whose face lit up when he saw his dog.

While all she ever seemed to do was make him go grim.

Which is exactly what you should do, she rationalized. *So he'll wash his hands of you the way he should.*

Isaac murmured something as he straightened, and Horatio sat down, then tilted his head and regarded Caradine with those odd eyes of his, one blue and one green. Isaac did much the same.

And she didn't get to do what she wanted. Forgetting that only hurt more, in the long run. How many times did she need to learn that lesson?

She glared at him. "I'm allergic to dogs."

"Then I guess you'll sneeze a lot," Isaac replied, and

indicated with the jut of his chin that she should move in front of him and carry on down the walkway.

Like walking the plank, though at this point she would have preferred to fling herself into the icy cold water of the sound. It would feel like a vacation.

Instead she walked forward as commanded, because her other alternative was throwing a temper tantrum. And she had the very distinct impression that just because she couldn't see anyone around this morning, that didn't mean they weren't all there. Watching Isaac escort her back to Alaska like she really was the person who'd blown up half a building in Grizzly Harbor.

They made it down to the cabin at last. Isaac reached from behind her to open the door, but Caradine made a noise of . . . protest, maybe.

A last-ditch effort.

"I can't decide what will be worse," she said, delaying the moment when she would have to cross this last barrier. When she would have to be in his space. His home. Something she'd made no effort to do, ever. And would have deliberately avoided if she'd ever thought it was a possibility. "What am I about to walk into here? What does the private soul of Isaac Gentry look like? Frat boy central? Or a whole lot of redneck?"

"You can call it whatever you want," Isaac replied, and she realized he was using that genial tone of his on her. A calm, pleasant lie. She hated it. "Just so long as you accept the fact that it's home sweet home from now on. Until we find out who's coming after you and make it stop. Okay?"

But that wasn't really a question, and he didn't wait for an answer. He threw the door open, and then his hand was on her back.

If she resisted at all, he would feel it. So she couldn't let herself. Caradine strode inside, shocked to find that her pulse was flipping out and her head felt light. Almost the way it had when she'd been standing in that dark room in Maine, staring at the doorknob on that locked front door while her past tried to break in.

Though she wasn't *afraid* now. There were no wooden boats and red canoes dancing before her eyes. There was only the looming horror of intimacy, which was worse. Caradine would have rather had to fight off more thugs with guns.

Isaac slammed the door behind her, and it felt like doom. It took every bit of self-control she had not to flinch as if she'd been electrocuted. Or as if she'd been tossed headlong into a prison cell.

She didn't want to look around. She didn't want to see his *things*. And she really didn't know if it was because she expected she would think less of him once she knew how he lived, or if she didn't want whatever extra information there was to be found about him here. The apartment she'd lived in on the other side of the island hadn't borne any signs of anything but the life Caradine Scott was meant to be living. But this was Isaac's actual home.

Was it that she didn't want to look? Or that she wanted, desperately, to look?

She forced herself to gaze around a bit theatrically then. And to keep a scornful, very nearly disdainful, expression on her face while she did.

Like that could make her pulse settle down.

"This is very disappointing," she said, finally. "I was led to expect a Batcave."

"Captain America doesn't have a Batcave," Isaac said from behind her. "If you're going to make comic book references, you should really get them right."

"Who reads comic books?" Caradine retorted. She sniffed. "I've watched a few movies, like a normal person."

Her neck itched, so she looked at him, and he was staring at her as if she'd kicked Horatio.

"You're everything that's wrong with the world," he said. "Pick up a comic sometime. Maybe you'll learn something."

And she needed to stop, because she wasn't here to banter with him. She certainly shouldn't have found herself biting back a grin.

This wasn't foreplay. She was fighting for her life.

And for his, too, though she doubted he would appreciate that if she told him.

He moved past her, and she let herself release a breath. The cabin was neither done up like a frat house nor a monument to his redneck roots, and she couldn't decide if that disappointed her or not. The room she stood in was large and airy, with a high ceiling that suited a big, tall man like him. There was a roomy fireplace on one wall, windows that overlooked the cove, and comfortable, masculine furnishings. She'd seen the satellite hardware on the roof and wasn't surprised that there was a study off the main room that looked to be entirely stocked with high-tech electronic equipment, monitors running and lights blinking even now. She could see the kitchen toward the back, through a wide rectangular opening.

Isaac walked across the main room and down a small hall, and she trailed after him, because it was that or stand in the front room staring at Horatio. Who was guarding the door. Literally guarding the door, like Cerberus, and she didn't care to test him.

Caradine followed Isaac to his bedroom, but stopped in the doorway, trying her best to ignore the way her chest ached. At the sight of the place he slept.

If Isaac Gentry actually slept.

He threw the bags he carried onto a bench at the end of the big bed. The bed was made but looked rumpled, and she knew two things instantly. He was still military enough to get up and make his bed every morning, which shouldn't have made her throat feel so tight. And the rumpled indentations on the dark quilt were Horatio's.

When Isaac didn't frown at those indentations or even seem to notice them, she understood in a flash that this man, this remarkably dangerous, lethal individual who as far as she could tell was afraid of nothing—including her—slept cuddled up with his dog.

Once again, there was no reason at all that should make her want to cry.

"I get it now," she forced herself to say, in that edgy, insinuating tone of voice that was starting to make her skin feel too tight, like she was poisoning herself. "This is a sex thing. You're pretending to save me, but actually, it's really all about your penis."

Isaac fixed her with that steady gray gaze that made her feel about half an inch tall.

And deeply, horribly ashamed of herself.

"You can sleep where you want," he said, with a quiet dignity that made her stomach knot up into something gnarled and hopelessly tangled. "You can lock yourself in the bathroom for all I care. But you're staying in this cabin."

"Kinky," she said, because she couldn't stop. Because she didn't know what would become of her if she stopped. "Everybody loves a captivity narrative."

He stalked toward her, and she wanted to run. But she didn't, of course, no matter what her pulse was doing. And then he was on her, crowding her where she stood in the doorway and sliding a hand around to grip her by the nape of her neck.

She was stuck between a rock and a hard place, as always with him, because if she wrenched herself away, that would tell him things she really didn't want to tell him. And if she stayed still, she had to suffer his touch.

Which wasn't suffering at all.

That was the problem.

"But to clarify," he said, his voice a rough silk, and

his eyes bright like silver, "you know where you're going to sleep. Because you can pretend all you want, but we both know what really happens when we're naked together. It isn't *me* begging *you*, Caradine. It never has been."

She thought he would kiss her again. She was ablaze with heat and that terrible longing, and she craved the taste of him. Better still, the way he claimed her so easily and made her forget she could never, ever be the woman she was pretending to be, who had nothing weightier on her mind than the ingredients for the next day's meals. . . .

But all he did was brush his thumb over her lips.

A different, more dangerous claiming.

Then he walked past her and out into the hall. And it took her a dizzy sort of moment to realize that he was headed for his own front door.

"You're not really leaving me here, are you?" she asked, and actually laughed, because she was so off-balance.

Her lips were tingling, and she wanted to press her fingers against them to make it stop. Or to better drown in the sensation, maybe.

But then he looked over his shoulder, and she knew that wasn't all she wanted.

She wanted him. She had always wanted him.

And remembering the numerous occasions that she'd been naked and at his mercy made everything in her heat up, then run through her veins like a sluggish gold.

"Miss me already?" he asked, that same dangerous light in his eyes.

Pull yourself together, she ordered herself sternly.

"Aren't you afraid I'm going to go through all your stuff?" she asked, in a decent approximation of her usual brash tone. "Learn all your secrets and use them against you?"

Isaac turned all the way around, then regarded her for

much too long. Caradine made herself stand straight. As if she were unbothered. She told herself she absolutely did not feel that swooping, fluttery sensation in her belly. Or that greedy ache between her legs.

"You're welcome to test the security measures in place in my office," he said, almost as if he were encouraging her to try. "And you can dig around all you want. I don't have secrets."

"Everyone has secrets."

"Everyone has stories that they might choose to tell, or not," he corrected her, a different, harder sort of light in his eyes. "But secrets are a whole different ballgame. Secrets make you sick, baby. They make you believe that you're all alone when you're not."

He needed to stop calling her that.

"That sounds very poignant, Isaac," she threw back at him. "Other people are just private."

He looked at her as if she disappointed him, and that was much worse than *baby*. She would never understand how she kept from crumpling into a sobbing mess right there on his thick rug.

Except that, as usual, she couldn't.

"There's food in the kitchen," he said instead. "Help yourself to whatever you want. I don't know when I'll be back."

She would not break. She would not sob. She would not lose herself here, in his home, where there were pictures in frames on the mantel that she didn't want in her head. "I don't know that I'll be here when you get back."

"What are you going to do?" And if she wasn't mistaken, the unflappable, quietly dignified leader of Alaska Force was taunting her. "You think you're going to swim somewhere? Have fun with that. The water *might* be above fifty degrees. Or, I know, you're going to hike Hard Ass Pass. It's all fun and games until you get to the part where the road's washed out and you might fall to your death, if the bears don't get you first. You can wander around the woods if you like, but it's steep and wet and rocky out there, and there's no other trail back to Grizzly Harbor. Also, again, bears. The only thing you're going to do is exhaust yourself, get eaten, or die. Be my guest."

"Your hospitality is overwhelming."

Isaac laughed at her, and then he walked out with Horatio at his side, and none of this was satisfying. She was left alone in this cabin that was entirely too comfortable and *nice*, and gave her nothing to use to ward him off. Worse, the minute the door closed behind him, his absence was like another living force.

Caradine didn't know what she was supposed to *do*.

She felt scraped out. Raw and hollow and wrecked.

It had been hard enough to leave Grizzly Harbor the first time, when she'd spent years preparing for that moment. It had been hard enough to leave *him*, she corrected herself.

She didn't know how she was going to do it again, and she knew she had to. It had been bad enough when he'd simply been a mistake she kept making.

Then he'd come after her.

She was hugging herself tight before she knew it. Still standing there, staring at the door, feeling broken in half in a way she would have vehemently denied if anyone had been there to see it.

Caradine forced herself to look away from the stupid door. She stared at her own feet, blinking furiously until her eyes were clear. She made herself breathe. She counted in, then out. Over and over again, until her pulse slowed down a little. Until she felt a little more like herself.

A little less brokenhearted.

"It's exhaustion," she told herself stoutly, her voice loud in the airy, empty room. "You're exhausted, that's all. Who knows what would have happened if you'd had to handle that man alone?"

She could still see that red, bulging neck of his. She could still hear his voice. That accent that brought back the worst of her memories.

She wheeled around and made her way to the back of the cabin, where his kitchen did not look as if it was the sort of efficiency bachelor setup in which he maybe made the odd cup of noodles. Evidence suggested that Isaac knew how to cook.

More intimate information about the man that she did not require.

She opened his refrigerator and found it stocked with staples. Again, in a manner that suggested that he actually prepared food, and ate it, with some degree of competence.

She helped herself to a banana, making herself eat it because she needed energy. And wondered who in Fool's Cove was responsible for restocking people's cabins while they were off having Alaska Force adventures, since as far as she knew they had no staff. She entertained herself imagining the various growly commandos on housekeeper duty. And when she was done, she threw the peel away and headed for the door.

Because everybody knew that Fool's Cove was inaccessible. Isaac had helpfully outlined all the reasons why. Still, everybody knowing something didn't make it true. Caradine's entire life was a monument to defying the accepted wisdom.

No point stopping now.

She threw open the door to the cabin, ready to go out and see for herself what *inaccessible* meant.

But there were people clustered on the wooden walkway, right there on the other side of the door. She stepped back, her hands up instantly as she went on the defensive, ready to fight—

Even as she shifted her weight to block whatever was coming her way, she stopped herself. She had a split second of recognition, and then Everly Campbell was hurtling herself through the doorway.

At Caradine.

Not to harm her, but to hug her.

Which was much, much worse.

Nine

"I can't believe you're here!" Everly was saying excitedly, holding Caradine.

Holding her. Tightly. She was *pressed against her.*

And Everly was still talking. "Blue kept telling me that Isaac found you, that you were fine, but I didn't believe it until now. I saw the restaurant! I was sure you were charred to a crisp somewhere!"

"Everly." Caradine was surprised she didn't actually scream the way she wanted to. The way she was inside. "For God's sake. *Why are you hugging me?*"

But Everly didn't respond. And the hug went on and on.

And that empty thing inside Caradine yawned open again, wider and deeper than before.

Because once upon a time, Caradine had been a different person. And that girl might have had few friends, but she'd been wildly affectionate with them. She hadn't needed all this armor.

Now she thought her armor might choke her.

Caradine looked past Everly's red hair and endless

embrace to the other two women in Isaac's doorway. "Oh my God. Please don't tell me this is some horrible *girlfriend* thing. I don't even like you people."

"Buckle up, sugar," drawled Mariah McKenna, cool and blond and Southern. "It's about to get obnoxiously feminine up in here."

"She does, too, like us," Everly said.

Mariah nudged Everly out of the way. And then, to Caradine's enduring horror, flung her arms around Caradine, too. And then, worse, rocked her a little bit from side to side.

While hugging her.

"You're doing that to be mean," she complained.

Mariah laughed. "And because it's fun."

Approximately seventeen ice ages later, when Caradine had died inside so many times she'd come back, haunted herself, and died again while still being hugged against her will, Mariah finally released her.

"I'm not going to hug you," Trooper Kate Holiday announced, standing behind Mariah. She looked faintly appalled at the very notion, which made Caradine like her more than she wanted to, given that Kate was a law enforcement officer and Caradine preferred to avoid the police in all their various forms. "Though it is nice to see you survived a Molotov cocktail in one piece."

"I don't understand what's happening," Caradine protested.

But then she was being borne backward on a tide of enthusiasm. None of it hers.

And the next thing she knew, she was sitting on one of Isaac's couches, glaring balefully at this pack of women, who were acting like she was one of them.

"Welcome home," Kate said with a smirk, as if she could read Caradine's mind.

"I knew you were going to come back," Everly said staunchly.

Caradine glowered at her. "You literally just said you thought I was dead."

Everly waved a hand. "At first, sure. Don't do that again."

"I didn't blow up my own café."

"No," Everly said, her gaze uncomfortably direct, "but you did go on the run without telling anyone you were okay." She smiled faintly. "I can actually tell you from personal experience that people who care about you don't love it when you do something like that."

"I can cosign that," Mariah said.

"When I went on the run, I was trying to get away from people who should have cared about me but didn't," Kate said in her mild cop's way. "My take on this involves less hugging."

"I don't want to be in this club," Caradine said, making a face. "And I didn't want to be found, either. I was running to get away from people, not find them."

"It sure is a hardship when you can't throw people out of your restaurant, isn't it?" Mariah asked, laughing. "You have to sit and talk to them."

Caradine didn't actually *say* that they couldn't *make* her talk. Not out loud. But she was pretty sure her body language conveyed the same message.

"I have a very important question to ask you, Caradine," Everly said after a moment. "Blue and I are getting married this summer, as I'm sure you know."

"I don't know," Caradine said desperately. "I don't know anything about anyone. Deliberately."

That wasn't true. Everly treated her like a friend, and sometimes Caradine forgot to police her boundaries the way she should have. This was her own fault.

Everly only rolled her eyes, because she'd appeared to find Caradine entertaining from their first meeting—no matter how rude Caradine was. It made Caradine like her, when she shouldn't have allowed herself to like anyone.

"We're doing it here." Everly sighed. "I mean, not *here*, obviously. In Grizzly Harbor. And you make the best food."

"I don't see how those two things are related," Caradine muttered.

"We want you to do it," Everly said, with exaggerated patience. "If you can stop acting like the Wicked Witch of the West for three seconds."

"*Do* it?" Caradine echoed, as if she had no idea what Everly meant.

Mariah laughed. Kate looked amused.

"The food, Caradine," Everly said. With less exaggeration and a whole lot less patience. "Blue and I want you to cook the food for our wedding. Whatever you want, as usual. That's part of the draw."

Caradine opened her mouth to say something suitably cranky and was horrified to find that her throat was tight. She had the terrible suspicion that if she tried to form words, she would sound squeaky and thick, and everyone in this room would know that she was capable of crying, after all.

Or worse, that she cared.

She waited a beat. She cleared her throat.

She firmly ignored that horrible, aching thing inside of her that wished she really were Caradine Scott. A curmudgeonly café owner but, deep down, the friend these women seemed to think she was.

When she knew better. And if she'd been tempted to forget, the way she had been these past five years, the past week was an excellent reminder of reality.

She stared at Everly, stone-faced. "I would rather die."

But that only made Everly laugh. "Of course you would. I'll take that as a yes."

And then they were all just . . . sitting there in Isaac's cabin. Staring at one another while in the other room, his five thousand computers whirred and chirped.

"Are we allowed to talk about you and Isaac now?"

Mariah asked after that dragged on awhile. "Since we're sitting here in his cabin. And not in one of the guest cabins."

Caradine eyed her, always elegant, though the self-defense course they'd taken together had showed her exactly how much steel lurked in this particular magnolia. "There is no me and Isaac."

"That sounds like a firm no on the talking about it," Kate said, with a smirk.

Mariah shifted her deceptively mild gaze to Kate. "What about you and Templeton, then?"

"I'm here in Fool's Cove in an official capacity," Kate said loftily. "Templeton is kind enough to play host. We're not shacked up in a house together like you and Griffin."

"Funny," Everly murmured. "I thought Blue told me you two had an apartment up in Anchorage?"

Caradine sat there, feeling like a fraud and a kind of ghost, as they all bickered good-naturedly amongst themselves.

About this life she'd already given up on.

This life she would have said, and had said—loudly—she didn't want.

But she couldn't seem to hold on to that quite as firmly as she should have. It was too easy to sit on Isaac's couch, surrounded by the scent of woodsmoke and leather, with a gorgeous Alaskan cove outside the windows and Isaac's bed in the other room. And these women she liked against her will, who had made her one of them, despite her best efforts.

Caradine had made a promise. But she still found herself slipping into what-ifs.

You know better than that, she told herself sternly. *You know where that leads.*

"You look like you're about to crawl out of your own skin," Mariah drawled. Then grinned. "Do y'all need another hug?"

"I would rather punch myself repeatedly in the face." Caradine couldn't seem to keep control of all the different aches and agonies inside of her any longer. They seemed to swell and hum, right there beneath her skin. She needed to sleep. She needed to run. She needed to get back in control of something or she was going to explode. "And I appreciate this . . . thing you're doing, but we can stop now."

"Do you mean caring about you?" Everly asked, and smiled innocently when Caradine glared at her. "That thing?"

"I'm not going to stay here," Caradine tossed out then, like a bomb. And she didn't scowl or stomp off, or any of the other things she wanted to do. She looked at each one of them in turn, though it was harder with Kate. Because she was too much a trooper. God only knew what she could see. "I enjoyed my time in Grizzly Harbor, but it's over now."

If she expected that to cause a commotion, she was in for disappointment, because none of the other women really reacted to that at all.

"You're here now," Mariah pointed out after a moment. Gently.

Caradine sighed. "Isaac has a hero complex. It's cute. But it's not reality."

"What exactly is your reality?" Kate asked, and again, there was no pretending she wasn't an Alaska State Trooper, used to interrogating suspects and talking down criminals in turn.

Caradine got the distinct sensation that Trooper Holiday knew more about her than she should. Or knew how little there was to know about Caradine Scott, anyway, which amounted to the same thing.

"People come to Alaska for all kinds of reasons," Caradine said, keeping her voice as even as she could. "For me it was an extended vacation. But all vacations must end."

The three women on Isaac's leather couches exchanged glances with one another.

"Where will you go?" Mariah asked.

"I don't know," Caradine said, trying to imagine what the character of Caradine Scott would say in a situation like this. "I don't like to be tied down."

"Right." Everly nodded sagely. "That's why you moved here in the first place, instead of living off-grid in the woods. And why you opened a restaurant in the center of town and made yourself a fixture in the community."

"Live and learn," Caradine said, and almost smiled, but she figured that would be a bridge too far. "I won't be doing that again."

Oddly enough, that was the most honest thing she'd said in ages.

Still, when a sharp knock came at the front door, she was pretty sure it was divine intervention.

Caradine shot to her feet and across the room, delighted to have a reason to stop . . . whatever this was.

When she opened Isaac's front door, Bethan Wilcox stood there. Her hair was pulled back into a neat bun at the nape of her neck. And she wore the same sleek, tactical attire that all the rest of Alaska Force wore, as if she woke up every morning ready to leap out of planes, scale buildings, save the world, and battle off scores of villains with her bare hands. Which, as the only female member of Alaska Force, she probably did.

Bethan took in the scene in Isaac's living room, a cool, swift assessment. Then her gaze rested on Caradine.

"You're wanted up in the lodge," she said.

"For what?"

Bethan only gazed back at her.

"Fine," Caradine muttered, as if she were disgruntled. When the truth was, she couldn't wait to leave.

"I had no idea you were so obedient," Everly said from behind her.

"That's me," Caradine said. "I live to obey."

And then she gleefully followed Bethan, letting the other women stay and do whatever they wanted to do in Isaac's cabin. Talk about their lives and their relationships. Hug more. All that stuff she hated.

All the stuff you tell yourself you hate, a voice in her contradicted. *When really, you wish you could sink into this life and make it yours for real.*

The what-ifs came for her hard. What if she stopped playing games with Isaac? What if she lived in that cabin and those were her friends and she didn't have to disappear? What if she could stay Caradine Scott forever?

But she couldn't break her promise. She wouldn't.

And even if she'd wanted to, it was too late now. It was only a matter of time before the man who'd tracked her down in Camden passed the information on.

It had all been borrowed time. Every second of the past five years.

"Is something the matter?" Bethan asked.

Caradine shot her a look, surprised that a member of the self-consciously stoic Alaska Force squad would bother to inquire about anyone's emotional well-being.

Bethan smiled slightly. "You made a strange noise."

"I stubbed my toe," Caradine said blandly.

That Bethan was aware she was lying was obvious. But all the other woman did was keep on smiling slightly as she led Caradine down the walkway and toward the main lodge. And everywhere she looked, all Caradine could see was Isaac. His imprint on the land here, the sprawling complex he'd made his own. All of the buildings here were beautifully maintained, which annoyed her. This was coastal Alaska, where the salt got into everything—peeling paint, warping wood, and mildewing everything.

But not here.

Any fantasy she'd had that Alaska Force was nothing more than a bunch of overgrown frat boys running around performing crazy high jinks to remind them of their glory days—something she'd said to Isaac's face more than once—disappeared when Bethan ushered her into the main room of the lodge. It wasn't quite a hotel lobby, though it had that feel. It also felt rustic and wholly Alaskan, but upscale enough that Isaac's more well-heeled clients would feel right at home.

Here again were the hints of state-of-the-art technology in and among the comfortable couches, polished wood floors, and the huge stone fireplace.

And the collection of grim-faced men who waited for her were definitely not frat boys. They were terrifying. Her stomach twisted and her heart kicked at her ribs, because this was clearly not a friendly meeting.

She knew everyone in the room. She'd served them all food, at one point or another, and could have reeled off a list of their dining preferences—whether or not she'd ever honored them. They usually greeted her with whatever their version of a grin was.

But none of them looked happy to see her today. Some looked suspicious. Others looked as if they were trying to take her apart with their gaze.

And over by the giant fireplace, looking scruffy, rumpled, and furious, was Isaac.

His gaze like gunmetal.

She thought she might choke, but she couldn't. As usual, she had to brazen her way on through.

"This looks like a business meeting," she said mildly, gazing around from one set, hard face to another. "Which means I shouldn't be here, because I didn't hire Alaska Force. I feel like I keep saying that."

"Why don't you take a seat?" Isaac suggested in that bossy way of his that was actually a direct order. He gestured to a chair that wasn't exactly set in the middle of the room, as if prepared for an interrogation—but it was close enough. "You can sit down and tell us your story."

That hard gray gaze slammed into hers from all the way across the lodge. Intense. Demanding.

It made her think of that bullet she'd shot at him. The way it had punched into the wall after the sting in her wrist that had reverberated all the way up her arm. And how long it had taken her to piece together what he'd done.

How easily he'd disarmed her.

A foreboding washed over her, bright like heat. Like a touch.

But Isaac didn't waver.

"You can start by telling us about your family," he said quietly. Too quietly. "Julia."

Ten

He thought she might try to bolt.

She didn't move, standing in her usual crossed-arm stance like she was prepared to fight, if necessary. But her gaze moved from his, coolly assessing the exits. And all the Alaska Force members she must have known would stop her. Easily.

When the door opened again and more people walked in—Everly, Mariah, and Kate—he thought he saw a flicker of something cross her face. But she didn't indulge it. She looked at the women she liked to swear up and down weren't her friends, and then looked back at Isaac.

Another time he would have smiled and told Kate she could stay in her professional capacity but asked the other two to go while they discussed Alaska Force business. But it wasn't Alaska Force business. It was Caradine business, and he knew no one would budge.

So he waited while they found seats, Everly communicating silently with Blue as she sat near him, Mariah smiling enigmatically and looking only at Caradine. Kate took a place near the main entrance, near Bethan.

But Caradine stood still. There in the center of the biggest room in the lodge with her head high, looking straight ahead. Straight at him.

She looked like the loneliest, most solitary woman in the world—but Isaac assured himself he was much too pissed to let that get to him.

"I haven't heard that name in a long time," she said finally. "I'd rather not hear it now, if I'm honest."

It was still her voice. A little raspy with an undercurrent of something he wanted to call fear, but likely wasn't, but otherwise Caradine all the way.

"Julia Colleen Sheeran," Isaac said. He didn't have to look at the files Oz had prepared. It was all burned into his brain. "Born outside of Boston thirty-two years ago in Massachusetts General. Grew up in Quincy. Went to Boston University, but never graduated."

"I'm especially pleased that I get to take this trip down memory lane in a crowd," Caradine said in that cool way of hers that he knew too well. It matched that murderous gleam in her eyes. "You know how much I love sharing. Particularly personal details."

Everly muttered something, but Isaac didn't ask her to repeat herself when it looked like Blue was handling it. It didn't matter anyway. Nothing mattered but the contents of that file—and whatever faint hope he might have had that Oz was wrong for once was gone. Because, clearly, this was her.

She was Julia Sheeran.

He finally knew everything about her, and it didn't make a single thing better. Not one thing.

It was that damned optimism, taking his knees out from under him. Making him imagine there were such things as happy endings. A person didn't disappear under a fake name without a reason. And they certainly didn't cling to the fake part when reality came crashing in. Or go on the run. Or do any of the other things Caradine had spent the last week doing.

Not Caradine. *Julia*.

"As interrogations go," she said now, glancing around the room and then shifting that narrow blue gaze back to him, "I have to tell you, this is a little bit lame. I don't like being stared at, sure, but it's not going to make me cry and tell you all my secrets."

"I don't need you to tell me your secrets." Isaac stared back at her, hoping he looked impassive. "I know them all now."

"Then I see even less reason for me to take part in this performance."

"You're Julia Sheeran," Isaac said again, as if saying it repeatedly could make her *Julia* to him.

He already regretted how he'd set this up, because now he wished he'd handled this privately. How many times was he going to learn the same lesson? When it came to this woman he wasn't Isaac Gentry, owner and cofounder of Alaska Force, a man with all kinds of medals and commendations to his name, trained in the battlefields of too many wars to count and consistently approached by the government to give his country a few more years. He was just a guy.

"Not for a while now," Caradine said, as if this were a game. "I have the ID to prove it."

His jaw felt like stone. "You're the oldest daughter of Mickey Sheeran, internationally renowned scumbag, arrested but never convicted of crimes ranging from gun-running to murder."

"He wasn't the greatest father in the world, either. Shocker."

"But the funny thing is that you're both supposed to be dead." Isaac's voice matched his jaw. Or maybe he'd simply turned to stone. "Blown up ten years ago, in that house in Quincy with the rest of the Sheeran family, pre-sumably by one of Mickey's enemies. And he had so many, I wouldn't know how to begin counting them."

"Before you say something flippant about Mickey Sheeran's enemies," Templeton said, his voice unusually grave, "you should know that most of the people in this room have put their lives on the line to clean up messes Mickey Sheeran caused. Indirectly or not."

"Your father is in prison," Caradine replied, moving her glare to Templeton. She glanced at Kate by the door. "So is Kate's. Are we blaming ourselves for our fathers' actions now? When did that change?"

"Ouch," Blue muttered, though Everly glared from beside him. At him.

But Isaac's attention was on Caradine.

"Are you enjoying this attempt at a public shaming, Isaac?" she asked. "I am. If nothing else, it tells me ex-actly who you are."

"You know exactly who I am. You always have. I've never lied to you or anyone else. I've never pretended to be someone I'm not."

"You do pretend to be a good man, though," she drawled, malice in every syllable though her voice was light. "Can't get past that one."

There was a kind of indrawn breath that shuddered throughout the room, and part of Isaac was almost amused, really. Everyone knew Caradine had a mouth on her. But it was almost entertaining for the rest of these people he called his friends and brothers to see the kind of wallop she packed into every swing she took.

Almost being the operative word.

"You weren't a kid when your father supposedly died," Isaac said, very calmly, because he wasn't im-mune to the low blows Caradine liked to dish out, but he could take them in stride. "You were twenty-two. About to graduate from college. That and the fact you're stand-ing here in Alaska ten years later, while your old life burns down buildings and chases you across Maine, suggests to me that unlike Templeton or Kate, you weren't exactly innocent."

Something shifted in her gaze, and he had the strangest idea that she'd gone hollow. "If you're expecting me to defend myself to you, you should probably let that go. I'm not going to."

"The explosion killed most of your family," Isaac continued, pitilessly, no matter if she was hollow or not. He wasn't the one who'd done this.

"I know," she said softly, her eyes glittering. "I was there."

Another kind of sigh went through the room, but Isaac kept his gaze trained on her. The biggest threat he'd ever met, and not because she was related to a notorious arms dealer.

He knew what to do with dictators and monsters. She was a whole other kind of problem.

"The hit on Mickey Sheeran was considered an act of revenge. One of Boston's crime families took credit, but despite their best efforts, the FBI could never prove they actually did it." Isaac waited for her to chime in, but she only stared back at him stonily. "The body count was only ever an estimation. Because the damage was so intense and the fire so hot it was impossible to be certain."

Again, no response. Though he thought he saw something glitter in her eyes.

"Complicating matters was the fact that no one knew exactly who was in the house that night," he said. "Your father liked to conduct business over Sunday dinner, so officials had to wait and see which dirtbags and relations stopped showing up. Over time, they landed on a particular group of ten. Your parents. All three of your brothers. You; your younger sister, Lindsay; and three lowlifes who worked either for or with your father. But here you are, Julia. All in one piece."

That name sat in his mouth and tasted sour.

"For all you know, I was resurrected," she replied, standing there looking cool and unbothered. "My mother was a devout Catholic. Her prayers alone should have delivered me straight into the life of the world to come. That's how it works, right?"

"You were an adult," Isaac said, trying to match her unbothered tone. Trying to pretend he could have been talking about any regular case. "Witness statements from your friends at college attest that you left your dorm that night and told at least two people you were going to your father's house. Were you going for dinner? Or did you always plan to blow up your entire family?"

"Oh, come on," Everly snapped.

Caradine didn't glance her way. She kept her gaze on Isaac, and there was no trace of vulnerability on her face now. No glimpse of anything like uncertainty, or hollowness. She lifted a dark brow. "You tell me, Isaac. I thought you knew everything."

"Do I think that it's possible that a twenty-two-year-old woman could meticulously plot to murder her entire family?" He shrugged. "Why not? Do I particularly think that Mickey Sheeran's daughter could or would do such a thing? Without question."

"Exactly how well did you know my father?" Caradine asked.

"Mickey made no secret of his feelings about women. The FBI takes it as fact he beat your mother, though she never pressed charges." He regretted that, too. But she looked only vaguely bored, not hurt in any way. "He treated all of his mistresses the same, and suspicious overdoses seemed to follow them around when he was done with them. I don't even know that I would blame a person for taking extreme measures to escape a man like that, because what must he have been like to his daughters?"

"I thought this was an ex-military tribunal, not a therapy session."

"Is that what you did?" He wanted her, just once, to

tell him something of her own accord. "Did you take the nuclear option?"

Caradine smirked, and something flashed in those cool blue eyes. "Do you really think that I'm a mass murderer, Isaac? Or are you mad that I won't date you?"

Isaac forced himself to keep his gaze on her, because the surprise wasn't that she'd said something like that. The surprise was that she hadn't started there. And he did not look around the room. He most especially did not look at Templeton or Jonas.

The studied nonreaction of every single person there was telling enough.

Great, he thought. But it was the least of his concerns.

"The Caradine Scott that I've known for five years was running from something," he said quietly. "I would have sworn that she didn't have murder in her. But you're not Caradine Scott, are you?"

"No." Her smirk took on an edge. "Caradine is a character I play. And when I leave here, I'll create another character. And next time, I won't be stupid enough to sleep with a clingy, dramatic stalker who doesn't know how to let go. If anyone needs therapy, Isaac, it's you."

Isaac smiled. "You can't embarrass me." That wasn't as true as he would have liked, but it was close enough. "I told you before, I don't have secrets. And that's not really the point, is it?"

"I don't know." Her eyes were glittering, and he braced himself, because he knew what that meant. She was taking a swipe. "I, personally, would find it difficult to take orders from a man who claims to be the biggest and the baddest around, yet found himself whipped by a woman he now thinks is a killer. But what do I know? I'm not a mercenary. Maybe it really is all about the money."

No one made any particular noises at that, egregious as it was. But then, they didn't need to. The tension in the room rose like a temperature.

"Does it give you pleasure to insult all these people?" Isaac asked.

Her head tilted slightly to one side. "Yes."

And Isaac shouldn't have been surprised to see Kate stifle a grin, back by the door, because that sounded not only honest, it sounded like Caradine.

"Okay," Jonas broke in, which was surprising. Since generally speaking, Jonas went out of his way to avoid talking whenever possible. "Let's try to keep this conversation productive."

"Is this a conversation?" Caradine asked, her voice acidic. "I was under the impression I didn't have any choice in the matter. Which makes it less a conversation and more of an interrogation, in my view. But then again, being kidnapped and forcibly restrained might have messed with my head."

"It must have," Isaac agreed. "Or you wouldn't have tried to shoot me."

There was another electric moment of silence. While all around him, Isaac was well aware, everyone was digesting that little tidbit.

Until Templeton laughed. Long, deep, and as infectious as ever.

It broke the taut, breathless thing that had Isaac and Caradine in its grip. Suddenly, there was a lot of shuffling. Shifting in chairs. And Isaac knew that his team didn't need to release their nervous energy in that manner.

This was different. This was Caradine.

And Isaac knew that he wasn't the only one who was already coming up with rationalizations for why she might have done this thing. Why it was okay. He could *see* Everly and Mariah looking at each other, working up a defense where they sat.

"I'm going to need to hear a whole lot more about you shooting at Isaac," Templeton said when he finished laughing. He tipped back in the chair he was sitting in, lounging as if he were settling in to watch a movie. "But first, I don't think it would kill you to give an accounting of what happened in Boston ten years ago."

Caradine didn't look like she'd released any tension. "Maybe I don't want to give an accounting of anything. Ten years ago or since."

Templeton shrugged. "It feels like we're past that. I know you want to keep poking at him, and I support that, but we need to know what we're dealing with here."

"You're not dealing with anything," Caradine gritted out. Maybe with the faintest hint of desperation. "I don't want your interference. Just because Isaac doesn't know how to take a hint, I shouldn't be forced to—"

"I get that you don't want to accept help from me," Isaac threw at her, louder than necessary. Louder than he could remember being. Ever. "But for God's sake. Accept help from *someone*. You've fed every single person in this room a thousand times. Not one of us wants to think you're capable of this. But even if you are, don't you get it? This is a family matter."

And that was the first time he saw a crack in her armor. She blinked and looked down. He thought he could see that softness to her lips that was the only sign he'd ever seen that Caradine, the real Caradine, was in there, no matter how she was acting or what stubborn, prickly thing she was saying.

"To clarify," Templeton drawled, "I'm not opposed to putting a family member in jail if warranted."

"Amen," Kate agreed, and they looked at each other with a little more heat than Isaac thought incarceration fantasies warranted.

Templeton continued, "But I would argue some extenuating circumstances for Mickey Sheeran's daughter."

"Caradine," Everly said quietly, "you're not alone any longer. No matter how badly you wish you were."

Isaac thought she might run then. He braced himself for it.

But Caradine took in a deep, visibly ragged breath, then

blew it out. She looked around as if she were only then noticing where she was, though Isaac doubted that. Then, instead of taking the chair he'd set aside for her, she moved to sit in the armchair where he usually sat, if he sat during a briefing. She lowered herself gingerly, making him wonder what it had cost her to stand so still and proud, despite everything. He knew grown men who wouldn't have been able to handle it.

Or maybe it was the fact they'd all basically excused a mass murder she might have committed—or said they would consider excusing it—that was getting to her. Or maybe the simple, obvious truth in what Everly had said.

Caradine pulled her legs up under her in the chair and gazed out at the gathering. At these people who'd called her *family*.

And were acting like one. Not the kind many of them had suffered through, but the kind they'd all wanted.

"You're asking me to break a promise," she said after a moment. With no trace of her trademark smirk. "And breaking that promise could be nothing short of catastrophic."

And Isaac couldn't very well demand that she make herself vulnerable when he wasn't willing to do the same thing himself. Could he?

He thought about the catastrophes he'd lived through already and figured one more couldn't hurt.

"Baby," Isaac said deliberately. Outing himself—and her. He didn't care that he was confirming whatever suspicions remained, and that half the people in this room had money riding on it. All he cared about was the woman sitting in that chair, looking, if not precisely vulnerable, something like bruised instead. He could do the same, if that made the difference. She didn't have to do it alone. "Catastrophic is what we do."

Caradine cleared her throat. She laced her fingers together in front of her, and for a long moment, stared at them.

Then she lifted her gaze. She looked at Isaac, then took in the rest of the room.

"I didn't kill my family," she said, her voice still quiet but sincere. "But I would have. If I'd thought of it, I would have done it happily." She pulled in another breath, another ragged sound. "Because there was no other way to survive in my father's house. One way or another, he was going to kill us all."

Eleven

Caradine felt hungover. There was a headache pushing at her temples, her mouth was alarmingly dry, and everywhere else she felt raw and heavy at the same time.

She was breaking her promise, when she'd always believed that was impossible. That it was a line she wouldn't cross. It was like a shattering inside her, sharp and painful, making every breath hurt.

But she'd started down this road, and she didn't think she could stop now.

Everly had said she wasn't alone, which almost canceled out the hugging. *Catastrophic is what we do*, Isaac had said, all that silver and steel in the gaze he'd leveled on her. The gaze that had held her up, even if it wasn't all that friendly.

He'd called her *baby*, in public, and what was she supposed to do with that?

The real truth was that she wasn't as upset about breaking her promise as she should have been. What had keeping it ever done for her except keep her alone and scared and on the run?

"I guess it never occurred to me that people would think I was capable of killing," she said now, slowly, carefully, because these were stories she didn't tell, and the words felt precarious against her tongue. "I don't know whether to feel insulted or complimented. But then, I've learned a lot about myself in the past ten years. Caradine Scott can and will do what she has to do. But Julia Sheeran?"

There was something deeply humbling in the way all these people hung on her every word, watching her solemnly, as if they'd been waiting a long time to hear what she had to say. Five years, maybe. "Julia was the worst kind of sheltered. *I* was. Because it didn't matter what books I read in college or what bright futures I imagined for myself. My father was never going to let me go off and live my own life. Never. I was the property of the family, and he ran the family. It was always going to end badly for me."

Isaac had used that word. He'd called her *family*, and he hadn't meant bruises and threats. He meant . . . this. This *thing* that had been happening all this time she'd been in Grizzly Harbor that she'd been denying and pretending wasn't there.

She'd had to sit down to keep from being knocked flat.

Caradine had defenses against everything else, and a thousand contingency plans. He could have interrogated her for hours. He could have tied her up again. He could have called her a murderer, everyone else could have agreed, and all of them could have arrayed themselves against her and flung accusations left and right. She had been prepared for all of that. She could have wisecracked for days.

But he'd called her *family*.

There wasn't a single attack she couldn't fight. Maybe

she'd win or maybe she wouldn't, but she would fight until she dropped.

She had no idea what to do with the opposite of an attack.

She had no idea what to do with *family*.

Or being claimed by Isaac Gentry in full view of all his friends and colleagues. All his *people*.

Your people, too, she dared to think, but it made her whole body clench down tight, in fear or longing or something else she couldn't name.

She concentrated on the task at hand. Telling the story so it wasn't a terrible secret any longer. So maybe she might have a shot at being a little less sick.

"I knew exactly who my father was," she said into the surprising quiet of so many usually big, loud personalities, all of them waiting for her to get there in her own time. "My brothers were a part of the business, but my sister and I were supposed to obey. Silently. I didn't always do that and I paid the price." She made herself meet Isaac's gaze. "He beat up everyone. Or he had someone else do it. Not only the women in his life."

"You knew what he did?" Blue asked.

He was sitting across the room, but the intensity of the way he studied her made it seem as if he were a lot closer. Caradine was having a hard time seeing these people who had joked with her, eaten her food, and even claimed to find her crankiness entertaining, for who they really were. She didn't know quite where to place it. Or the obvious reality that they'd all spent their entire adult lives dealing with situations like this—and men like her father.

Blue kept going when she didn't answer immediately. "What I mean is, did you know he was a dirtbag or did you know, specifically, that he was an arms dealer with links not only to crime syndicates in the U.S. but across the globe?"

"I always knew he was a very unpleasant man. The details of what he did were something I learned over time." She shifted in the armchair, resisting the urge to hug her knees to her chest. "I Googled him when I was twelve, and it was eye-opening. But also not entirely surprising."

"Did your mother know?" Bethan asked from the far door, and when Caradine looked over at her, she couldn't help noticing the way Jonas's dark gaze fixed on her, too.

"She must have," she said, forgetting about Jonas and the brooding way he always looked at the other woman. "My sister and I debated that for years. My mother was . . . I don't want to say weak. Because, yes, he beat her up, treated her like crap, and talked to her like she was either a child or an idiot. But there was a part of her that thrived with him."

Caradine considered the thorny, enduring problem of Donna Sheeran. "I've had a lot of time to think about it, and maybe it's as simple as she never expected any better. My grandfather wasn't that nice himself."

"Mario Iannucci," Oz contributed from behind his laptop. "Rumored to have been behind the hit on Freddy Marinelli that changed the power structure of the Zenato crime family in the mid-Atlantic region twenty years ago."

"Not everybody gets to use the FBI's most wanted list for genealogical research," Caradine said dryly.

"I prefer it, personally," Kate said in the same tone.

Caradine smiled despite herself. Then pushed on. "There's no getting around the fact that my mother took a deep pleasure in martyring herself. When my father would go off on one of his rages, she would provoke him further. Not to protect us, because she did nothing to prevent him from coming at us. In fact, when he was done, she liked to get her own hits in, too, and she was vicious." She looked at Blue. "Sometimes I think she knew. Sometimes I think she knew everything, and liked it. Other times I think she was another one of his victims. I don't know."

That sat there for a moment.

"What happened that night?" Griffin Cisneros asked.

She didn't ask which night. She cleared her throat, though it didn't make her throat any less dry. Then she told them all the story. How she'd been ignoring her father and knew there would be a reckoning. That she'd taken her time driving out to Quincy that night. That she'd been well aware that there would be a price to pay, and she'd been afraid she knew exactly what form this particular price would take.

Caradine told them about parking down the block out of habit. About standing outside in the dark, gearing herself up to go in. How panicked she'd been that her father would take her degree away from her and keep her from graduating, not because he really cared one way or the other if she was educated but because she'd defied him.

Then the explosion.

"I didn't know what it was at first," she said. "It's very disorienting." Then she remembered who she was talking to. "But I imagine you all know that."

No one smiled, exactly. But the mood in the room lightened a little anyway. And this wasn't the time to wonder what kind of person trained themselves to know how to react to explosions like that. Caradine had now been through two explosions, one significantly worse than the other, but both horrifying. She would be perfectly happy to never experience a firebomb or Molotov cocktail, or whatever other cutesy name people used to minimize the horror, ever again.

But whatever they were called, they were business as usual for Alaska Force.

She had to swallow past a sudden lump in her throat that she absolutely refused to name. Or analyze.

"I'd been dreaming about a way out," she told them,

pretending she couldn't hear the scratchiness in her own voice. "But there wasn't one. My father viewed his children as possessions. Currency, even. He told my brothers to jump, and they asked, *How high?* He was marrying my sister off because the best way he knew to control someone was to make them part of the family, and he deeply distrusted the man he wanted her to marry. He was really good at playing the long game."

"What game was he playing with you?" Jonas asked.

"It wouldn't only have been that he kept me from graduating," Caradine said. "There was no shortage of brutal, vicious men he could have handed me to, and he would have. And if he was really pissed, he would also have told them I needed a strong hand. Meaning he would turn a blind eye if I turned up bruised and battered."

Mariah hissed out a breath. "He really would have done that? Your own father?"

Caradine held her gaze. "In a heartbeat."

"Where did you go?" Griffin asked. "You survived the explosion. Then what?"

"You had five years between that night and when you came here," Isaac added. "Is this a five-year cycle? Did you spend that whole time somewhere else?"

It was always hard to look at him, particularly when she wasn't doing her little act. Being nasty *just because*. Spiteful and prickly, even when she didn't want to be either of those things. It was easier then, because she was constantly provoking a reaction from him. That was much better.

Because now, all she was doing was looking at him. And beneath all the fighting they'd done in the past five years, there was just Isaac.

The man who'd smiled at her when she'd walked into a strange bar, bought her a drink, and made her forget all of this. Why she'd come to Alaska in the first place. Why she should never, ever have let down her guard.

That was the worst thing about Isaac. And the best. He made her forget. And once she forgot, she began to hope.

Caradine had never been able to afford either.

"I had to figure out how I was going to survive once I ran," she said, to no one and everyone. She focused on Isaac because he was closest. And because he was Isaac. "But I had a few things going for me. My father had refused to pay for college, so I'd gotten myself a job. He took that as a personal affront, but I still did it. That meant I already knew that restaurants were a good way to make money and stay off the radar. It's not hard to find a place that will pay under the table. But the first thing I had to do was get out of Boston."

"One of the reasons it's assumed that you died in that fire is because there was no activity on any of the family's credit cards or banks after that night," Oz said then. Caradine thought, not for the first time, that he looked like no computer geek she'd ever known. It was disconcerting, even at a moment like this. "I would expect your father or your brothers to have access to all kinds of different unmarked accounts, and so on. But if what you're saying is true, you were legitimately a kid working her way through college. Did you have a secret stash somewhere?"

"I had nothing." Caradine had to be careful here to tell her part and no more. "All I had was what was in my pockets. I left my car where it was. Then I walked away from the scene, took the T into downtown Boston, and bought a bus ticket to the farthest distance I could go without bankrupting myself. Because one thing I've learned from a thousand movies is that if you think people are looking for you, trying to hide in the same place never works. Sooner or later, someone will see you, no matter how unlikely. So I went to Ohio."

"Ohio?" Templeton laughed. "I didn't see that coming."

"No one sees Ohio coming," Caradine said dryly. "Mostly because if they have any sense, they're leaving the state as quickly as possible." She lifted a hand and rubbed at the tension in her neck, though it didn't help. "Maybe I'm not being fair. I don't know what I expected from Cleveland. I had enough money for a motel room. I dyed my hair and got a job bartending the next day. Then waited to see what would happen. I watched the news and saw that I was dead. And since I was supposedly dead, but not, I couldn't assume anyone else in my family was dead, either. So I bought a car off one of the regulars for a couple hundred dollars, and as soon as I could, I moved on."

She could remember those strange weeks in Cleveland so vividly. They stayed relentlessly bright in her head when so much else since had blurred at the edges. Had she slept at all? She could remember doing nothing but watching the news round the clock, then working in the dive bar that had taken her, no questions asked. There was no part of her new, postdeath life that hadn't felt precarious and terrible, and it had still been better than life in the Sheeran family.

It had been sharp and cruel, but it was still freedom.

And even running for her life was living it, which was more than would have been allowed her if she'd stayed trapped in her father's clutches. Or if he really had died in that house, whoever rose to take his place.

Isaac studied her, and she bit back the near-overwhelming urge to snap at him the way she normally did. To divert his attention, because if she didn't, how long would it take him to realize that there was nothing underneath but the same sickness that ran through the rest of her family? Because what else could there be?

"It must have been hard to go from being Mickey Sheeran's daughter to living on tips and driving a two-hundred-dollar clunker," he said.

Caradine directed her attention toward her clasped hands and her knees, because that was less troubling than the way his gray gaze made her feel. "The first couple of years, I moved around a lot. The minute people started to greet me by name outside my job, I would go. After a while, I learned that it was easier to tell everyone that I was a recovering addict. Because that way when I disappeared, no one would look for me. Everyone thinks they know what happens to addicts, don't they? They're disposable. No one comes looking. It was easy enough to keep dyeing my hair, keep taking off in the middle of the night, and keep making money waiting tables, tending bar, whatever. The problem with moving around that much is that it provides a whole lot more opportunity to be recognized."

"Who did you think was chasing you?" Jonas asked.

"Somebody blew up my parents' house," Caradine said coolly. "On purpose. I didn't know if they knew whether or not I was in it at the time. And I also didn't know how the bomb detonated."

"It was C-4 with a cell phone activation," Templeton said, his voice a low rumble. "Someone called in the number and that was that."

"Yes," Caradine said, "but who made the call? And from where? If they were outside the house, did they see me?" She blew out a ragged breath. "I had to operate from the assumption that they saw me survive, then walk away. And then, after five years of moving around the way I had been from the start, I thought that maybe it might be better to construct an entire alternate identity. I figured that if I found a remote place and settled there, it would be more difficult, even if I was recognized, for anyone to connect the new me with that college girl who was supposed to be dead."

She was glossing over some details there, but the end result had been the same. So she told herself it really wasn't a lie. It was an omission. She was both breaking her promise and keeping it at the same time.

That should have made her feel better, not worse.

Especially because Isaac was looking at her as if he already knew what she wasn't telling him. "How did you find Grizzly Harbor?"

"I was looking at remote places. So obviously, I was looking at Alaska. I saw the ad for the Water's Edge Café in an online magazine. I had some money stashed away, so it seemed like a good match. And, of course, I was under the impression that Grizzly Harbor was a sleepy, remote fishing village where nothing ever happened."

She found she couldn't look away from Isaac then. No matter how much she wanted to, it was as if she were stuck.

Maybe the thing she didn't want to face was that she always had been.

"It occurs to me after telling this whole story that I'd like to hire you after all," she said, because that was probably the only way she could complicate this situation further. But as the words came out, seemingly of their own accord, she found they were true. "I'd really like to know how they found me."

"We'll be more than happy to answer that for you," Isaac said, mildly enough. Which was a clue, of course. It was always a clue. The milder his voice, the more dangerous he was. She braced herself. "But the first question I'm going to ask you as an Alaska Force client is *who*."

"That's what I'm hiring you to find out, Gentry," she said. Maybe with a little heat.

"Not who's after you."

The world narrowed down to his gorgeous face. The steady demand of his ruthless gray gaze. And how safe she always felt when she was near him. She knew better, and still, there was Isaac.

And he wasn't finished wrecking her.

"Who did you make a promise to? You said you were breaking a promise by talking about what happened to you." He was all steel then, head to toe. No give, and no matter that she couldn't breathe. He didn't soften at all. "Caradine, who else survived that bomb?"

Twelve

Isaac watched that question go through her like a body blow, and there was no part of him that liked delivering it.

But he didn't take it back. He didn't make it easier for her. They were way past that.

"I don't think that's relevant," she managed to say, with a clear attempt to lift that belligerent chin of hers.

"If you hire Alaska Force, the expectation is that we'll decide what's relevant, not you."

He threw that out there like it was another round in their endless punching match. But Caradine—he couldn't think of her as *Julia*—was sitting there, her legs pulled up and her arms tight around them, and he had the strangest notion that this was the soft underbelly she'd been hiding all this time. Behind all the sniping. Behind every sharp word.

Isaac wanted to tear apart the whole of Boston, and the world, to get her back to her usual cranky, smart-mouthed self. Even if the target of that mouth was him.

Especially then.

"I'm guessing it's your sister," Isaac continued in a low voice, sounding like who he was. The leader of the group who would solve her problems, as soon as she was honest about them. The way he sounded in every other meeting like this he'd ever held with a client. But who was he kidding? This wasn't any other meeting or any other client. This was Caradine. "I've never heard a single thing about one of your brothers or either of your parents, from you or anyone else, that suggests they'd be worth protecting."

Her face didn't crumple. Not exactly. He saw her lips tremble, slightly, before she flattened them into a line.

"I made . . ." But her voice cracked. She looked down at her hands for a moment, then out toward the cove. And in all this time, and all the many ways she'd put up walls, pushed him away, outright tossed him aside, he had never seen her look as remote as she did now. As lost. "I made a promise. And until today, I've kept that promise."

Isaac was so used to pretending nothing had ever happened with Caradine or ever would. Or changing the subject when someone brought her up. He was so used to the secrets, the too-short nights, that look she gave him that dared him to do something about it. It wasn't that he'd never dared. It was that he'd chosen to wait her out instead.

But then he'd gotten that call and thought she was dead for twenty hideous minutes. Even if she'd sat here and admitted that she'd burned down her parents' house with her family inside, he would still be relieved that *she* wasn't dead, and he didn't know where to put that. His career in the military had pretty much cured him of thinking in black-and-white terms, but Caradine felt far more complicated still.

He was done waiting.

Isaac crossed over and squatted down in front of her

chair and then, because he was a *go big or go home* kind of a guy, he took her hands in his.

Her blue gaze flew to his, startled. But she didn't pull her hands away.

"Let me keep your promise for you," he said. "I promise you, I'll protect it, and you, and whatever else needs protecting, as if it was my own."

He forgot that they weren't alone. All he could see was the conflict on her face. She squeezed her eyes shut, and her fingers tightened on his. If she were anyone else, he would have expected her to cry.

But she was still Caradine.

She opened her eyes and they were clear. And she nodded once, hard. Then she pulled her hands from his and Isaac shifted back onto his heels but stayed where he was, there beside her chair.

Caradine cleared her throat. "It was my sister, Lindsay, yes."

She outlined the differences between her sister and herself. While Caradine had been at college, Lindsay had been ransomed off to one of her father's business associates.

"He used to call Lindsay his princess. She was the youngest and she was very pretty, in that delicate, skinny, waifish sort of way he thought was the most feminine. Because she looked breakable. A certain kind of man likes that." And it was the Caradine he knew best who looked around then, that cool indictment in her gaze moving from one man to the next. Including him. "They like to break their toys. The man my father wanted her to marry could barely contain his excitement at getting his hands on *Mickey Sheeran's princess*. Still, Lindsay thought that was a better option. The other choice being defying my father. *That* always came at a price. Usually a very painful price."

"I take it you defied him, then." Blue didn't voice that as a question.

"You'd probably consider it a weak little attempt at defiance," Caradine replied. She made a face. "It's hard to remember, now, what a commotion there was when he said I couldn't go to college and I went anyway. I thought I was proving myself, but what I was actually doing was showing him that I was willing and able to go against his wishes. He killed men for that. He couldn't let it stand from *a girl*. Whatever he had planned for me that night was going to be a lot worse than a few bruises or broken bones. Lindsay was in the house. She told me it was weird."

"I know that there are tough fathers out there," Bethan said carefully. "My own wasn't exactly a joy to grow up with. But it's one thing to be hard-ass. And another to be . . ."

"Sadistic?" Kate asked brightly. "I'm familiar with that version."

Caradine smirked. "That. And also a raging, homicidal narcissist."

"It's like you've met my dad," Kate murmured.

"Lindsay was in the house that night?" Oz asked from his place at a desk in the corner, where he was dividing his attention between a laptop and a tablet.

"Lindsay was inside when I got there," Caradine said. "I texted her when I parked, and she came out to meet me. She warned me not to go inside."

Isaac watched the tension in the room shift, from whatever lingering suspicion of Caradine remained to a different sort of tightening altogether. The kind that usually cropped up when details came together to form bigger pictures. Everyone's second-favorite part, right after a decisive win.

"Now, why would she say that?" Templeton asked in a musing sort of way, though his gaze was hard.

"Before your imaginations run wild," Caradine said coolly, "the explosion knocked us both flat. Lindsay texted me from inside the house, then came outside, and was talking to me when it happened. My understanding of the particular ignition system on this bomb is that the lag time after making the call would be a second. Maybe two. Not enough time for Lindsay to sneak out of the house, then talk to me in the street, all without touching her phone."

For a moment, everyone processed that. Not only the information but the way Caradine had delivered it and what that meant.

"You considered your sister a suspect?" Isaac asked.

"Of course." There was a bleakness in her gaze then. "We all come from the same blood. The same dirty gene pool. We're all polluted by the same father. I knew that I'd dreamed about killing all of them. Why shouldn't she?"

"So the story you just told, about roaming around from town to town, getting work where and how you could, it was actually the two of you?"

Isaac didn't look over his shoulder to see the look on Griffin's face when he asked that question. He could hear it. Ice-cold.

"Yes." Caradine sat straighter in her chair but still didn't drop her knees down. As if she still wanted the barrier. "Lindsay was only twenty, and she'd never done anything but sit around in my father's house, waiting to be bartered off as it suited him. She had a harder time adjusting."

She considered her own words. "That's not entirely fair. My father also sent her out on dates, which she survived somehow, so she wasn't exactly a hothouse flower."

"How unpleasant were these dates?" Bethan asked.

"There's the kind of man who likes to break his toys, as we discussed. But without a go-ahead to use a strong hand, there's the risk of disrespecting my father. It's a very precise calculus, after all. How much will he care if you break something that's still his?"

Isaac didn't have it in him to think—to imagine—Mickey Sheeran's broken toys. It made his ribs ache. "So you both ran. You both got on a bus to Cleveland."

Caradine sighed. "Everything I told you is true, but I did it with Lindsay. Who I promised I'd never mention. Between the two of us, we could cover whatever our daily expenses were and stash some away. But after the second time we got robbed, because we had to keep it all in cash, and on us, I figured there had to be a better way."

"You took self-defense classes?" Blue asked. And sounded almost proud, since he was the one who taught the women's self-defense class here in town when he wasn't on an active mission. It had turned into a staple for the community.

And Caradine was always there, training herself into a lethal weapon.

"I couldn't afford a class," she said. "And I really didn't want to go to one where people would learn my name, because I was still having trouble keeping track at that point. We changed them all the time. Every time we got spooked and ran again." She dropped her knees then, and crossed her arms instead. "What I would generally do was find a scary-looking dude in the bar where I worked and beg him to teach me what he knew. That's how I learned to shoot. And do some nasty things with a knife. And a box cutter. A fine, upstanding gentleman in Daytona Beach, Florida, told me that you didn't need moves if you could open a vein. I took that to heart."

"You're not going to hear any complaints from me," Bethan said then, at the door. "We do what we have to do."

Caradine nodded. "That we do."

Neither one of them smiled, but Isaac thought it felt like a moment of communion. One he had to step in the middle of to get the conversation back on track.

"But you split up," he said.

"We thought they found us a few times," Caradine said. Carefully, he thought. "We'd see a familiar face, and even though it was almost always a stranger, the fear would get its teeth in us and we'd take off. Because it was better to run than to be wrong. We were pretty sure no one was looking for us, but again, Who would want to bet on that and be wrong? But then we had a real scare."

"Someone found you?" Isaac tried not to jump all over that. Or ask why she hadn't led with that. "Who was it?"

Caradine regarded him in that cool way that made his jaw flex. In case he'd forgotten who he was talking to.

"Walking away from a life is hard." She sounded almost philosophical, which got his hackles up. "We were young. Kids, really, and remarkably sheltered. In the sense that we only really knew what life was when my father was controlling it. Sometimes, especially if there was some drinking, we got . . . indiscreet."

"Since when are you indiscreet?" Isaac asked softly.

Caradine's mouth curved slightly, and once again, he wished they were alone. He wished he could fix whatever needed fixing so they could sit together, him and her, and talk about that curve awhile.

Even now, with everything that had already changed, that seemed impossible.

He shoved that aside, because she was still telling her story.

"Not me. But that didn't matter. We were a team." She shoved a hand through her hair, and maybe only Isaac could see how agitated she was beneath her cool exterior. How the faint tremor in her hand betrayed her. "We'd been in Phoenix for a while. Maybe eight months, which was an eternity for us. Lindsay had gotten close to this other bartender we worked with and thought she was our friend."

"Did you?" Everly asked.

Caradine's mouth curved again. "Whatever she was, she liked meth a whole lot more than us. So when she ran out of things to sell, she thought she'd tell some folks the story about a pair of sisters. Who escaped from back East after a bomb went off."

Again, the tension in the room ratcheted up as everyone filtered in that new detail.

"Sisters, a bomb, and back East." Templeton sounded disgusted. "Why not draw a map?"

"I had a similar response, and it's as unhelpful now as it was then," Caradine said crisply. "It happened. Our friend told us, which was the saving grace. She said her dealer knew a guy who knew a guy. And we all know what kind of guys those are. Lindsay and I took off in the middle of the night, as always. Possibly we also learned some valuable lessons about trusting people."

"When you say 'we,' I'm guessing you mean your sister," Mariah said then. "Because you trust people even less than I do, and I come from some notoriously suspicious country people."

"We'd gone to ground in Sioux City," Caradine said, without replying to Mariah. Though her gaze gleamed a little brighter. "Picked out new names, and were gearing up to do the usual dance. Bad bars, under-the-table tips, new temporary lives." Isaac watched her entire body tense. "But Lindsay was hung up on the betrayal aspect. She couldn't let it go. That was how she stumbled across a post on social media that our friend had died."

"Meth?" Jonas asked.

"Not meth." Caradine didn't get any less tense. "The news suggested she was a casualty in a drug deal gone wrong. Her dealer, his dealer, and two others. Plus her. All shot execution style. Some with evidence that there was strenuous questioning first."

"What did you do?" Kate asked, sounding all trooper.

Caradine stared right back at her. "We took off again.

But it was clear to both of us that staying together was a liability. I'm sure there are tons of girls who might shoot their mouths off or tell a friend in a bar about how they're connected back East. It's the sisters part that makes it more interesting. Clearly someone else agreed."

No one spoke. Oz typed in the corner, the keys making the only noise in the room.

"Jacinda Hall," Oz said after a moment. "Twenty-two years old. Her murder remains unsolved."

"No one's looking for her killer," Caradine said, her voice tinged with bitterness. "Remember what I told you about drug addicts. No one cares if they disappear. In most cases, whoever loved them said good-bye to them long ago."

Oz kept typing. Caradine was still too tense.

"Lindsay and I spent what was left of the summer figuring out what to do. How to split up, where we would go."

"Did she want to go off by herself?" Isaac asked.

Caradine did that thing that looked like a smile but was far too sharp. "We'd been living on top of each other for five years by then. And here's the funny thing about growing up with a sociopath. You're aligned against him when convenient, but that doesn't make you best friends. We were very different people." She blew out a breath. "I love my sister. I would die for her. But having almost died for her in Phoenix, I was also interested in a break. So was she. She got a fake ID and a plane ticket to Hawaii. I came to Alaska. That brings us to five years ago, when I arrived in Grizzly Harbor."

She didn't look at him, but Isaac felt it swell between them anyway. That first look. That first night. And everything that came after.

"You don't keep in touch?" Griffin asked.

"Too dangerous." Caradine glanced at Isaac. "But we do have a system."

"Let me guess," Isaac said. "You don't call her directly. You get a burner phone and call into a voice mail. That's what you were doing in Texas."

She glanced over at Oz. "We both memorized the number. I pay the bills online through a secure server. If necessary, I could probably access the messages online. But on the off chance that anyone's monitoring the account, we use burner phones and codes. I told her I was compromised when I was in Riverside, but we only check once a month. More, if we want to, but at least once a month. Which means it might be a full month before she checks again."

"And what will she do when she checks?" Isaac asked.

"She'll either tell me that she's also been compromised, or that she's fine. If she's been compromised, too, we might figure out how to have a conversation. Find a chat room, somewhere. Or something like that."

Caradine seemed to relax, slightly. Just slightly. "A couple of years ago she got in touch to tell me that she was moving from one Hawaiian island to another. We like to know where the other one is, at least generally. We like to remind ourselves that as long as we're alive, we're winning. Sometimes that's a direct message on social media somewhere. Other times it's a code word on an old voice mail."

She shrugged, and there was that ghost of a smile again. "Never let it be said I don't know how to make a mean lemonade out of whatever lemons come my way."

Isaac wanted to touch her but figured she might take off a limb. He stood instead.

"So here's the situation right now, as I see it," he said. "Somehow, somebody from your old life found you. Whether they've been tracking you since Phoenix or whether this is a separate situation, we don't know. What we do know is that whoever's coming after you doesn't care too much about collateral damage, and I don't like that."

"If that's the opening act, I'm worried about what comes next," Templeton agreed.

"Or it's a deliberate overreaction," Jonas countered. "Maybe the intended audience isn't Caradine."

Isaac considered that. Next to him, Caradine shifted position. "If I'm not the intended audience, who is?"

"Never underestimate your average scumbag's desire to impress the scumbag above him with his commitment," Jonas replied. "Speaking of boys who like to break their toys. The more toys, the better."

"Who did you call from Camden?" Isaac asked.

Caradine didn't smirk, exactly. But Isaac wouldn't call what she aimed at him a smile, either. "It wasn't a 'who.' There's a particular bar in Boston that you should really never walk into without a tetanus shot and a militia. I called and said Mickey Sheeran was alive and in Camden, Maine."

Isaac's eyes narrowed. "So if I hadn't carried you out of there, he wouldn't have followed us, because he would have seen you weren't an old man."

Now it was a smirk. "Even Captain America makes mistakes."

"I'm not convinced it was a mistake." Isaac rubbed a hand over his jaw. "It seems to me that we have several options. Option one, whoever blew up the house in the first place wants to finish the job. Option two, someone else survived and wants to clean up the mess. Or who knows? Maybe this is how the Sheeran family says hello. Option three, that person is one and the same. Whatever option we go with, we have to factor in Grizzly Harbor. Someone knew Caradine was here."

"On it," Oz said from his corner. "But if I had to guess, I'm going to say it's social media. It always is."

"I'm not on social media," Caradine said flatly. "I mean, I don't post anything. I have a few accounts I don't use, that's all. And I'm very, very strict about letting anyone take my picture. Meaning I take the camera and boil it, even if it's their phone. I'm not an idiot."

"You only have to be in the background of the wrong tourist's snapshot," Oz said, very calmly. "But don't worry. I'm going to find it."

"I want to know what option we're dealing with here," Isaac said then. "I wanted to know yesterday. Any questions?"

"Option four," Jonas said in that stark way of his. And standing so still it made the rest of them look like fidgeters on a sugar high. "The sister with the big mouth made a new friend."

Caradine tensed. Isaac was sure that she was about to flay Jonas alive, but all she did was nod, stiffly. "It's hard not to make that jump. Believe me, it's one of the first things I plan to ask her when and if she checks in."

"What's your fail-safe?" Blue asked. "She doesn't check in, what then?"

"She's my baby sister," she said quietly. "And as far as I know, my only living relative. What do you think the fail-safe is?"

"This time," Templeton said, and the chair he was rocked back in slammed into the floor like punctuation. "*This* time, if you go chasing after her, you're not going alone."

He threw a glance around the room, and Isaac saw everyone's version of a nod. Including from Everly and Mariah, the two civilians, who would be going nowhere.

"Oh, goody," Caradine said, without cracking even a hint of a smile, though her voice was still much too rough. "When I walked into this room you all thought that I was a murderous sociopath like dear old dad. Now you all have my back. Excuse me while I nurse my whiplash."

"I'm so pissed at you for lying about who you are," Isaac told her then, biting out the words before everyone else in the room could jump in. "That's not going away.

And as I said before, I would understand if you'd had to do something horrible because you had to get out of the situation you were in. But don't confuse that for what's really happening here."

He could see her *make* herself square her shoulders, like she was determined to start the fight again, no matter what. "You mean the interrogation?"

"No, jackass," Isaac replied gruffly, and he made it worse by reaching over and hauling her stiff, outraged body against his, side to side, with everyone watching. Her worst nightmare, he was sure, and that notion made him cheerful, despite everything. "This is your home. We're your people, like it or not. And you've been feeding us all for five whole years. Why don't you let us feed you a little in return, for a change?"

Thirteen

Caradine didn't have much to say after that.

And Isaac let her keep her silence because he knew that she might forgive him some of what had happened here, but if he made her break down and cry in front of a group of people—especially this group of people—she'd gut him in his sleep. Merrily.

She followed Oz back to his tech domain, deeper in the main building, to flesh out the file he'd compiled on her. Isaac made his way to the official command center, talking practicalities with Griffin and Rory as they walked. But once they hit command, he shifted away from this latest version of his Caradine problem and jumped back into the active operations that required his input and oversight.

It was late in the bright June evening when he was finally done handling a tricky extraction across the planet. He left the command center in capable hands and walked out of the lodge, buzzing with an energy he didn't know what to do with. He'd been so pissed off this morning that he'd skipped his usual workout, and that was always a mistake.

Or, anyway, he told himself that was why he was so restless tonight. The lack of decent exercise. It had nothing at all to do with the woman who was in his cabin, even now.

He knew she was in his cabin and not trying to hike up Hard Ass Pass with nothing but her stubbornness to get her over the washed-out parts. Or swimming for Juneau across the cold Inside Passage. Because he'd sent Horatio to guard her when she'd left the lodge hours earlier, and if she'd left the cabin, Horatio would have barked loud enough to bring him and most of Alaska Force running.

But his dog was nowhere to be found. He stood for a moment outside, there on the porch that overlooked the cove. It was one of those still-blue summer nights, this side of the June solstice. The sky hadn't even gotten into its eerie stage; it was just light. It bounced off the water in the cove and made the trees seem crisper, more defined.

He ordered himself to calm down.

And disobeyed his own order.

A few moments later, Isaac sensed the approach of two heavy individuals, not that they made any sounds as they exited the lodge. It was the faint creak from the door that gave them away. In the next moment, he recognized their tread against the wood. Or lack thereof.

When Templeton and Jonas flanked him there at the rail, he wasn't surprised. But he didn't look at either one of them, either.

"If you could hurry up with the mockery and smug remarks, I'd appreciate it," Isaac said mildly. "I have things to do."

"Where to start," Templeton drawled, sounding so entertained that an actual laugh would have put the whole thing right over the top. Not that such considerations had stopped him in the past. "Where to even begin parsing what happened today."

"You mean, when we gained a new client?"

"Alaska Force gained a client," Templeton said. "But I'm pretty sure you gained a girlfriend."

Jonas didn't make a noise on Isaac's other side. He certainly didn't laugh. But still, Isaac had the impression that he'd done his version of tossing back his head and roaring out his merriment, Templeton-style.

"Why don't you go tell Caradine that she's my girlfriend," Isaac suggested, still keeping his attention on the water out in front of him, because it would give Templeton too much satisfaction if he tried to get in his face. "Make sure you film it. I'd pay money to see how many veins she opens."

"It would be worth bleeding," Templeton retorted, unrepentant. "And besides, if it was untrue, she'd only smirk at me, so you're proving my point."

"I appreciate this conversation," Isaac said. "Really. I had no idea that you were a twelve-year-old girl, Templeton. I figured a sixteen- or seventeen-year-old girl, at the youngest. Good to know you can sink even lower."

He saw the one-fingered salute his friend made in his peripheral field of vision just fine.

"You're the kind of man who likes to hold on," Jonas said then, and both Isaac and Templeton fell silent at that. He flicked his dark gaze toward Isaac, no trace of laughter there now. "Or I wouldn't be standing here."

Neither Isaac nor Templeton jumped to dispute that, because it was true. All three of them had survived that last, horrific mission in a place they still weren't allowed to identify. In one form or another, they'd survived. But none of them spoke of it, and not only because what had happened there was classified at the highest levels.

But then, they didn't have to speak about it. They'd all left the service afterward, when the debriefings and the threats of court-martials gave way to the usual commendations, medals, and requests for further engagement from all three operatives.

They'd declined. The way they continued to decline every time the U.S. military reached out again. As much to make sure they weren't running around telling their story to any interested parties, Isaac often thought cynically, as to see whether or not they could get any of them back on board. They'd started Alaska Force instead.

But Jonas didn't mean any of that, or not directly. What Jonas meant was that trip Isaac and Templeton had taken, at Isaac's direction, deep into one of the most desolate stretches of Alaska's interior. Where Jonas had gone, not intending to come back.

Because it wasn't enough to *not die*. That didn't teach a man how to live. Not when he was used to fighting.

Like the man said himself, Isaac held on to the things he cared about.

He nodded now. Because he didn't trust what might come out of his mouth.

"You're trying to hold on to someone who doesn't want to stay," Jonas said. "Doesn't think she can. How long can you do that?"

"As long as I have to," Isaac said, his voice much darker than the night around them. "Which you know, because that's what I told you, too. Do I still have to prove it?"

"Sometimes," Jonas said quietly, into the soft stillness of the evening, as bright as day though it was coming up on ten o'clock, "it's better to miss them."

Isaac couldn't get that out of his head as he made his way down the wooden path to his cabin. He'd prefer Templeton poking at him all day, every day, to one of Jonas's seemingly offhanded remarks that always landed on him like some kind of prophecy.

He couldn't regret the things he'd done today that had made him and Caradine an open topic of conversation, instead of the usual whispers, innuendos, and *significant looks*. But that didn't mean he had to like it. Maybe he'd had this wrong the whole time. Maybe it would have been better to wait. To enjoy the stolen moments. To keep it theirs.

A secret everyone suspected was still a secret. It was different from everyone knowing.

Caradine was the only secret he'd chosen to keep after leaving his shadowy life in the service. The only secret that was his, not the government's.

But as he walked toward his cabin door, he couldn't help but imagine what it would be like if this were normal. If Caradine actually lived here. With him. If he solved her problem, slayed her dragons, and got to be with her. Just like this.

It was shockingly easy to imagine, when he would have said neither he nor Caradine were remotely domestic. He would come back to her from putting out fires all over the world, and he would always wonder exactly what he'd be walking into. Because one thing she never was, no matter what she called herself or where she stayed, was predictable.

Good thing he liked a storm.

Better still, she'd be here. Right here.

He couldn't decide if he was unsettled or filled with anticipation when he opened the door.

Inside, he could smell the remnants of whatever food she'd cooked. He glanced toward the kitchen, his stomach reminding him he hadn't eaten in a while, but he was more interested in finding her. He half expected her to be in his study, attempting to break into his computer system. But she wasn't there.

He walked farther into the house, down the small hallway, and stopped at his bedroom door.

And it wasn't until he saw her there, lying sprawled out across his bed, that he understood two things.

One, that he'd fully expected her to dramatically make herself a bed on his couch, clutching her pearls and denying him so much as a touch, just to be a pain. Just to prove that she could.

And two, that he had absolutely no defenses in place for what it did to him to see her lying there like that.

She stirred as if she sensed him and looked over toward the door, but didn't sit up. She looked scrubbed clean, her hair gleaming damply. He could smell his soap on her body, which struck him as almost unbearably intimate. And then, completing the picture, curled up next to her with his head on her belly while she scratched behind his ears, was Horatio.

His dog looked at him and whined. But didn't move.

"You're supposed to be guarding her," Isaac told him.

But all he got in response was the clearly unrepentant thump of Horatio's tail.

"I made food," Caradine said in a voice he hardly recognized. It took him a minute to realize she sounded relaxed. "You didn't have all the ingredients I wanted, but I did my best."

"I'm sure I'll love it," Isaac said, but he didn't make a move for the kitchen. He couldn't think of a reason he'd ever move again. "You know what I like."

She must have shifted then, because Horatio lifted his head. Caradine rolled up to a sitting position, letting her legs dangle over the side of his bed. And what could he do but look at her? She was here. It wasn't a few rushed hours after the Fairweather closed. She couldn't kick him out of his own home. He had a mind to look at her for a good long while.

Once again, she was dressed the way she often was in his head but rarely in reality. She wore a black T-shirt, another formfitting one. And what he was almost certain would be classified as yoga pants. Not that he could imagine Caradine doing yoga.

"What name do I call you?" he asked. "Have you picked a new one already? From a phone book in Maine, maybe?"

She studied him with those haunted eyes that made him think of long-lost summers, and that little half smile that made his chest ache.

"I don't want to talk," she said, still sounding relaxed, and her gaze changed. It got hotter, and he did, too. "I've done more talking today than I have in ten years."

Sometimes it's better to miss them, Jonas had said.

Isaac had felt the truth of that out on the porch by the lodge. But here it hit harder, looking at Caradine in his bed at last, but not the way he'd imagined her. Not naked and grinning wildly, with that wicked light in her eyes that drove him crazy. Because it was like this. With ghosts all around them, too many names to hide behind, and no clear way forward.

What he would give for a clear way forward.

Then again, he'd always been good at making paths in the wilderness, no matter what tried to stop him.

"Isaac," she said, a different edge to the way she said his name. "I'm in your bed. Surely you can think of something better to do with me than talk."

Without waiting for him to respond to that, she heaved a long-suffering sigh. She swung off the side of the bed, then started toward him as if she'd never been so put upon in all her life.

This Caradine he knew all too well.

When she reached him in the doorway, she tilted her head to one side so he could see nothing but the heat in her gaze, vanquishing any ghosts that might have been lingering there between them.

And in the next breath, she jumped him. Literally.

She jumped up and he caught her, and then he had her legs wrapped around his waist, her arms around his neck, and everything seemed to slide down hot and wild to the place where they were joined.

But not joined enough.

"Julia," he began.

But she bit him.

Nipped him on his jaw, to be more precise, just enough to make him hiss in a breath.

But not enough to make him let go.

"Caradine," she said against his mouth. "With you, no matter what, I'll always be Caradine."

And then she tightened her hold, angled her head, and slammed her mouth to his.

Fourteen

The best thing about kissing Isaac was that he always let her act like she was in charge.

For a moment or two.

Then, like now, he would make that hot sound in the back of his throat and take control.

And, God help her, but she loved it when he took control. She didn't want to think, she wanted to feel. She wanted to forget everything.

Everything but him.

Isaac, whom she never should have touched.

Isaac, whom she couldn't seem to stop touching.

Everything was heat and fire and that intense, electric connection that hummed so loud inside her she was sure he could hear it, too. And only when they were like this did they stop fighting each other, and start fighting together. Toward the same goal that felt more and more like magic every time.

Maybe he was the magic.

Isaac walked her backward and tipped them both onto

the bed, catching himself on one arm but still lowering her the rest of the way. And something about being pressed into a soft comforter that carried his scent while he kissed her like a lost, precious thing made her want to sob. Or scream.

Maybe she did. Caradine was vaguely aware of it when Horatio jumped off, then padded out of the room. But all she really cared about was the way Isaac kissed her, his mouth a slick, hot demand on hers.

She had left Grizzly Harbor never expecting to see him again. *Intending* never to see him again. Then he'd appeared in Maine. She'd thought she might get one last taste, but he'd tricked her.

In retrospect, she was angrier about that than being tied up and hauled off into the night.

But now she was here. At last. In his bed, which felt momentous in ways she refused to analyze. Not here. Not now.

Maybe not ever, if she could get away with it.

There were too many what-ifs. The day had been filled with broken promises and family, but not the family she was used to. And Caradine couldn't handle any of it in her usual ways.

She couldn't pick a fight. She couldn't order folks out of her restaurant. She couldn't issue bans, then close up early so she could head to the Fairweather, throw back too many shots, and cheat at pool.

She couldn't sneak up to the hot springs and indulge herself with a long soak sometime after midnight when no one would see her.

And she couldn't goad her favorite commando into slamming her up against a wall, because he was here already. Worse, he knew too much about her—like the fact she wasn't going anywhere, at least not tonight.

Not to mention a great many other truths.

But she could fight with him to get that T-shirt off. She could tip herself forward into the unending glory of his chest. She could taste him, reveling in those hard, lean muscles and that particular taste that was only and ever *Isaac*.

Salt. Man. Him.

Hers—but she shied away from that word, that thought, that possessiveness, because she knew better.

She was greedy enough without laying a claim. She was desperate, maybe, and she knew this was more than one of their spiked, temper-fueled tumbles. This was a reunion. A reminder.

A reckoning, she thought.

He wrapped the length of her hair around one hand and held it tight, and then he rolled them over, baring her neck to him so he could taste her. Tease her.

It was almost too much to bear.

When she sat back and looked down at him, she planted her hands on his ridged abdomen and marveled in the lean, hard muscles of his thighs. And she worried that he could see all the wonder inside of her that only he brought out in her.

But for once, she didn't try to hide it. They'd almost lost each other. They likely would again.

She could taste that, too, when he kissed her.

Isaac tugged her down again, setting his mouth against her collarbone, then moving, so slowly it made her worry she might *explode*, along the line of her neck. Caradine couldn't handle it. She wriggled against him, trying to remind him how much more fun it was when he was inside her.

But he only laughed.

"You're much sweeter after you come." His voice was a dirty little growl in the hollow of her throat, but it thudded through her like a series of blows, one right after the next. She couldn't catch her breath. "And I need you sweet, baby. Because this is going to take a while."

She meant to snap at him, she knew she did, but his

big, tough hand found its way beneath the wide waistband of the stretchy pants she wore, and her mouth didn't seem to work the way it should.

Isaac unerringly found his way to the place where she ached for him, scalding hot and needy. At the same time, he lifted himself, that terrible, wonderful mouth of his finding one stiff nipple through her shirt.

He sucked on her like she was candy, and his fingers were magic, and he knew her far too well. He knew her body. He knew *her*.

And almost before she knew what was happening, the twin sensations tangled together and fused into something brighter, wilder, hotter. Caradine could do nothing at all but arch herself against him, her head falling back, nothing but Isaac and the things he could make her feel washing through her.

Helpless, something in her whispered, but as if that were a gift, not a warning.

Because this was the only place on earth where she allowed herself to feel that way. Where Isaac made her feel that way and she exulted in it, to be more specific.

She was still shuddering when he moved, hauling her with him to stretch her out over his body.

Her hair fell around them. He smoothed it back from her face, then cupped her cheeks in his palms.

"Now we're going to take it slow," he said, and there was that challenging glint in his eyes. "Really, really slow."

She felt dizzy and giddy, her body was humming, and she would normally show him the door before she was tempted to indulge herself in him too much. But everything was different today. And for once she could settle herself over him. She could stretch herself out like a cat and rub herself all over him, and not because she was in a hurry.

But because she liked it. All of it, all of him.

Especially the part where she could move against the hard ridge of his desire and make them both shiver. And better still, make his eyes go silver.

"I don't like it slow," Caradine murmured, her mouth a scant inch from his.

Isaac's smile was darkly male, and if she bent her head, she could taste it. "Tough."

"You don't like it slow, either," she reminded him. "You never have."

His smile only got darker, if that was possible. Edgier.

"Wrong again. You don't like it slow, Caradine, because you want to get off without any pesky feelings getting in the way." His smile didn't take the sting of his words away. Instead, it spread into something a whole lot more, like a low, dull ache. Then again, maybe that was her heart. "My bed, my rules."

"You're suddenly a lot more interested in rules."

"It's not sudden." He shifted, his hand moving along her back, and she couldn't help but arch into it. "And it's not a surprise. You've met me."

"Yes, but—"

"Caradine." Her name was an order. His gaze was a command. "Shut up."

Then he kissed her, nice and slow.

And he did it for a good, long while.

She had always enjoyed the way Isaac took control. But she realized, some lifetime or two later, when they still had all their clothes on and she was *dying*, that she'd had no idea how much control he'd been displaying all this time.

It didn't matter what she did. When she tried to entice him. When she tried to hurry him. No matter how she tried to get her hands on him, he would laugh and then switch it up.

Every time.

Eventually, he got around to peeling off her clothes,

but that wasn't better. Or it wasn't *quicker*, because he decided to taste her.

Everywhere. Every inch.

Until she was writhing and panting and so outside herself she wasn't sure she'd ever find her way back in.

Ages and ages later, Isaac got around to removing his own clothes.

And then, Caradine thought he would break. Rush for the finish.

But instead, though it shouldn't have been humanly possible, he slowed down even more.

There was no part of her that he didn't taste, again. That he didn't touch, wringing out every last bit of sensation that he could find. Over and over and over again, while the light shone in on them from the Alaskan summer night outside.

And at a certain point, she stopped fighting it. Because it wasn't a fight she wanted to win. Because there was no pretending that things were the same now as they'd been over the past five years. Not with all that light cascading over them both, making it impossible to hide.

There was no forgetting here.

He knew her name now. He knew her story. He knew who she was.

She wasn't hiding anything anymore, and that made everything new.

Every touch. Every breath.

Every glorious shattering.

When he finally rolled over to his back and brought her above him, he handled the condom with his usual efficiency and then lowered her onto him at last.

And that was different, too.

Not the fit of him, big and hard and stretching her almost to the point of a wince, but not quite. Caradine loved that, every time. She loved having to adjust to him. She loved having to take a breath before moving.

For a long time, that little moment had felt like a simple truth in the middle of too many lies.

Tonight that deep, glorious slide that lodged him deep inside her, still with that same initial hitch, felt like a sacrament.

And she knew why he'd put her on top, because it was another kind of challenge. And this was Isaac, who never backed down.

He knew she wanted to go fast, set a blistering pace, and hurtle them into a wild finish.

But *she* knew he thought she would do exactly that, so she didn't.

Or maybe he knew what she'd do all along, but Caradine couldn't care about that. Not the way she normally would.

Not when his hands were wrapped around her hips, letting her know that if he wanted to, he could control this, too.

And maybe he was controlling it, with that steady gray gaze locked on to hers. As if he expected the best from her, and only the best. As if he expected her to do as he asked, simply because he'd asked.

The Caradine of years past would have defied him. She'd taken a great pleasure in that, always, because no one else dared.

But tonight she was someone else, someone new. Not Julia, who might as well have died in that house fire and had, really. And not the Caradine she'd been all these years, crafted from years of terror, running, and hiding.

Tonight she was a new version of herself. She wasn't hiding. She wasn't running. And she was with the only man alive—the only *person* alive—who knew her. All of her.

Intimately.

This, then, was intimacy. This taking that felt like giving. This celebration as she moved against him, rocking them both toward something far better than forgetting.

Caradine broke first, and she didn't try to hold herself back the way she usually did. She let herself cry out, her head falling back while wave after wave of the most intense sensation she'd ever felt gripped her.

She was still going when he flipped her over, brought her beneath him, and then, at last, let go of his own control.

Heat and driving need. Sheer male power.

He pounded into her. Caradine had barely finished shaking before she started again, falling over a cliff she hadn't known was there into something brighter, hotter, wilder.

Only then did Isaac join her.

They fell together like heat and light, wrapped around each other as if they'd been made that way. Their hearts pounding so hard she couldn't tell whether she felt his or hers. Tangled up together as if they could never possibly be torn apart.

A long time passed before either one of them moved. Isaac shifted the dense, heavy weight of his body off hers, but he still held her close. And surrounded by his warmth and strength, Caradine felt herself drifting off to sleep.

That, too, was a surrender, though she didn't fight it. She didn't force herself to leap up and *do* something, hoping that could break this spell between them. She just drifted off.

It was only when she woke up some indefinable time later to find herself with Isaac's arms around her, that gray gaze of his regarding her steadily, that the reality of what had happened hit her.

"Don't worry," Isaac said lazily, and she could feel his voice rumble in his chest. Something that struck her as so astonishingly *intimate* that she felt herself flush all over. It almost washed away the panic. "I told you. My bed, my rules. You can sleep here. I want you to sleep here. Notice I didn't throw you out while you were still gasping for breath, the way some people in this bed like to do."

Deep inside, Caradine could feel her usual prickliness surge at that, ready to do battle—

But she didn't have it in her. She was cuddled up next to this man she'd worked so terribly hard to keep at arm's length. And for once in her life, she felt . . . soft.

Not weak. Just not . . . weaponized.

She refused to analyze it. "I guess you're a much better person than me."

But even that came out wrong. Because she'd tried to sound arch and amused and, yes, a little bit prickly, but instead her voice sounded . . . sincere.

Isaac ran a hand down her back, and then held her even closer, his big, heavy arm making her feel cocooned against him. She loved the heat of him. It was why she'd never allowed herself to experience this before. She'd known that if she dipped her toe in this pool, she would dive straight in, then drown.

Because all she wanted to do was bury her face in his chest, let down her guard, and let him handle whatever happened next.

"Stop thinking at me," he rumbled at her. "You're fine. You're safe. I promise."

Caradine wanted that to be true more than she wanted her next breath. But she knew that wasn't the deal. That wasn't her life, no matter how tempting it was to imagine otherwise here in Fool's Cove, wrapped up in Isaac's arms. Because there wasn't only her life to consider.

And even though she knew better, she thought there couldn't be any harm in pretending. Just this once.

All these years of dire, endless pragmatism and punching herself in the face with reality, no matter how much it hurt. All the times she'd walked away from this man when she'd wanted to run to him instead. All the times she'd made herself sharp when she wanted to melt. Every time she'd pushed him out her door, then ached. Every time she'd slammed her door in his face, then stood on the other side, hating herself.

Surely she'd earned one night.

Caradine burrowed closer instead of rolling away, and thought she felt him release a breath. And she couldn't resist. She found her hands moving on his perfect chest, letting the last of the summer light lead her on a lazy exploration of every muscle, every indentation, every beautiful sinew. Every hour he spent maintaining his impressive physical condition translated to another fascinating inch on his body, and she tasted them all.

This time, she catapulted over the edge, sobbing the joy of it out into the crook of his neck. Isaac took his time following her, holding her there against him, locked in that embrace as if he felt all the same things she did.

The wonder of taking their time. The beauty of not having the inevitable limit of Caradine's need to cut it off before it meant more.

It already meant too much.

Something else she didn't want to look at straight on.

Caradine slept again. When she woke up, his heavy arm was draped over her. Her back was flush against the broad wall of his chest. He let off heat like a furnace, which made her wonder how she'd never taken advantage of that over the course of so many long Alaskan winters.

As she blinked the heavy sleep away, she realized she'd slept deeper than she could remember doing in at least ten years.

Outside, the sky was doing that deep blue thing it did to indicate it was a summer night. Farther north, there would still be daylight.

"Didn't you say something about food?" Isaac asked in her ear.

She could feel him smile at the goose bumps that shivered their way down from that point of contact to her wrists.

"Don't you ever sleep?"

"Everyone sleeps, Caradine." Another smile. Another shiver. "But I don't sleep much. And when I do I wake up instantly and fully alert. *Semper Fi*."

She would ordinarily make a snide remark about the marines, or the armed forces, or whatever she thought would irritate him the most. But tonight felt like it belonged to someone else, someone safer and softer, so she didn't. Caradine shifted around beneath the weight of his arm so she could face him.

Isaac Gentry, who had wedged his way into her life when she wasn't looking.

She reached over, then traced her way over the line of his mouth and the beard she'd felt all over her skin. His lips curved as she went, showing her that rare smile of his.

Not the one he shared like candy. The one he saved. For few and far between moments, when no one else could see it. Or him.

Mine, she thought, though it was dangerous.

And she didn't need light to see the way his gaze changed. Went from gray to silver in an instant and heated her up inside.

He pulled her closer and rested his forehead against hers, so they could breathe together. Until she thought she might cry.

If she were the sort of woman who cried, that was.

"Caradine . . ." he said, and she didn't know if he was going to say something else. Or if he was just saying her name, the name she associated so strongly with him that it hurt a little. The name that felt like her, even though it shouldn't.

But she couldn't risk it.

She pressed her fingers against his mouth and held

them there this time. "Come on," she said quietly. "I'll make you something to eat."

This time, she didn't wait for him to respond. She pulled out of his embrace and climbed out of the bed, grabbing her clothes as she went.

She dressed as she moved, ignoring the way her pulse pounded at her. And the choir of voices inside her she didn't want to hear, all of them calling her a coward.

Horatio met her at the end of the short hall, and she calmed herself by leaning over and kissing him on his furry forehead.

Then she went into the kitchen and did what she did best: She heated up the food she'd prepared earlier, because she hadn't known what else to do with herself after Oz was done extracting every detail of her life from her. An easy savory pie she'd thrown together from the ingredients in his refrigerator and freezer. Beef, vegetables, and a thick, creamy sauce that hinted at curry.

Cooking was better than breathing. Or feeling. Cooking filled all the ugly places inside her. It allowed her to pretend she was whole. Normal.

It let her imagine she could have things she knew she couldn't.

Isaac appeared in the kitchen. One moment she was alone and the next he was there, leaning against the counter, wearing nothing but a pair of cargo pants low on his hips.

He was enough to give her a heart attack.

And that was if she looked too long at the honed perfection of his abdomen alone. The rest of him was equally problematic.

"That's creepy." She threw him a glare, then served up two plates with the briskness she would have used in her café. If it still existed. Another thing she didn't want to think about, because it also hurt more than it should. "A man as big as you are shouldn't move so quietly. I'm going to put a bell around your neck."

She saw a hint of that dark smile. "You can try."

Caradine slid the plates on the table over by the windows. She wondered if the table, clearly handmade, was his work or if he'd inherited it from a family member. It had that sort of look about it. An heirloom or a piece of personal history.

"Where did you get this table?" she asked when he came and took a seat across from her. "Or did you make it?"

"My grandfather made it." The expression on his face altered as he looked down, running his hand over the surface, and there was a kind of familiar reverence in the way his palm moved over the wood. It wasn't unlike the way he'd moved that same hand over her skin. Caradine bit back a small sigh. "Grandpa Gentry was a fisherman, but when he had to wait out one of the sea's moods, he liked to work with wood. As he got older, he spent more time with it and made bigger projects. Like this table."

The table was a work of art, tucked away in the kitchen of this faraway cabin. It was an irregular shape, as if to honor the wood itself, the whorls and the knots. This was Isaac's legacy, Caradine couldn't help but think. Art. The work of careful hands, polished over time and set to gleam.

Meanwhile, she was a Sheeran. And the work of her family's hands was death. Blood and bullets. Bombs and guns.

The opposite of art in every way.

Isaac shifted across from her. When she looked up, she wasn't surprised to find that gaze of his on her face again. She braced herself, but all he did was pick up his fork and then take a long, deep breath. Of pleasure.

"How do you always know exactly what to cook? When I don't even know what I want?"

"Magic," she responded, once again without the edge she'd meant to put in her voice.

Isaac looked at her for a moment, and she expected

one of those killer questions of his. Something that would slam straight through her, rip her heart open, and force her to jump back into that prickly, armored space—

This is what you want from him, a voice in her whispered. *You like that he never lets you off the hook. That he would never let you run away.*

"So," Isaac said, settling back in his chair. She held her breath. "Looks like you have friends after all. That must have thrown you for a loop."

For a moment, they only stared at each other.

"I don't think you understand," Caradine said, in a baleful sort of outrage. "There was *hugging*."

Fifteen

Isaac chose not to point out that they'd never shared a meal before. He figured she might stab him with her fork.

When they were done, they actually sat there and talked. Like regular people.

He saw the exact moment that occurred to her.

And watched, fascinated, as she stiffened. He would have said he knew every expression that could possibly cross her pretty face, but it took him a moment to place the one that flashed there for a long, telling moment. Panic.

It was a relief when she scowled at him.

"You need to go away now," she said, sounding like herself again. Not the warm, pliable woman who'd been in his bed, but the sharp-edged, hot-eyed pain in his butt. Good thing he had a powerful need for both sides of her. "I need to clean this kitchen, to my satisfaction, not yours."

Her clear implication was that he, a career marine officer, could not maintain a kitchen to her standards.

"You remind me of my drill sergeant," he said. When her scowl deepened, he laughed. "That's a compliment."

She rolled her eyes as she stood, then swept up their plates. "Good-bye."

Cranky. Grouchy. That scowl in place. Just the way he liked her.

"You know I don't need you to cook and clean for me," he said as he got to his feet, watching her move with that efficient grace that had been getting to him for far too long now. "That's not a requirement."

She snorted. "If you needed me to, I wouldn't do it. And if it was a *requirement*, I'd burn your cabin down."

"Still."

Caradine dropped the plates and utensils with a great clatter into his sink. She did not turn to face him. "Isaac. If you say one word about my *true heart*, I will walk out of this cabin and drown myself in the cove."

"I think that's unlikely."

"I will take that cast-iron skillet off your wall and relieve you of your kneecap."

"You already tried to shoot me in the knee. You missed. I feel like the odds are in my favor."

She turned then, her scowl much deeper and her blue eyes a dark warning that bounced around inside him and felt a whole lot like joy.

"Don't you have work to do?" she demanded. "Wrongs to right and worlds to save?"

"Usually."

Her brows rose. "And here I thought that was who you were. In charge of every last thing every second of the day and night, so there isn't a single moment of downtime. Don't let me interrupt your long career of overcompensation and workaholic anxiety."

That punch landed, and he could tell she knew it, so he left her to her mutterings at his sink.

He went out to his study and checked in. And he didn't forget that Caradine was in his cabin. He was aware of her moving around in the kitchen, then stalking off to take a shower. He monitored what needed his attention, made sure no new information had come in while he was otherwise occupied, and sent out a raft of responses and new orders.

Normally he would keep that up for hours, but not tonight.

He took a minute, sitting there in his home office with Horatio at his side and Caradine in his shower, to consider the fact that everything was fine. Perfectly fine, as expected. No crises were unfolding. Nothing *required* his attention or interference at the moment.

That he'd set things up so that the whole operation could run while he was on an active mission himself always seemed to slip his mind when he was home—

But that wasn't true. It didn't slip his mind. He just . . . didn't let go.

His strength and weakness right there.

Overcompensation, Caradine had said. Because of course she had.

Because the question he really didn't want to ask himself was whether he was holding on because he thought Alaska Force and the whole freaking world would fall apart if he let go—or if he was worried he would.

Maybe, something deep inside him whispered, edgy like the woman who knew him too well and acted like that was an imposition, *you're afraid of what you might see if you stopped long enough to look.*

"Screw this," Isaac muttered.

He had no intention of wasting this night.

First he went and joined her in the shower, making sure to wipe that scowl off her face, just to prove he could. Then he set about enjoying her in every room of his cabin, because he knew her.

She had no intention of staying. He had no intention of letting her go.

But he preferred to state his case to the Caradine who sobbed in his arms. The one who moaned out his name. The one who fit so perfectly against his chest when she dropped her head there.

The Caradine who sank to her knees and grinned up at him, her blue eyes sparkling as she took him in deep in her mouth. The Caradine who covered her face with her hands when he returned the favor, and not to hide this time. But to muffle her own screams.

And in the morning, she was still there. Curled up with him in his bed, with Horatio at their feet, like a thousand dreams he'd never admitted he'd had.

As if she were home, at last.

He wasn't suicidal enough to say that last part out loud. It was too early, and he thrived on very little sleep, but she . . . did not. Caradine was even grumpy in her sleep. It made him smile as he nuzzled her neck.

"For God's sake, no morning sex," she muttered at him, burying her face in the pillow, but not before he'd seen that scowl. "I'm not an animal."

Obviously, he took that as a challenge.

One he won.

"I'm going out," he told her when she was panting helplessly beside him, her face soft again and a smile he would categorize as *dazed* on her face. She was beautiful when she scowled. But when she smiled, she rearranged the world all around him. Maybe he should have been glad she did it so rarely. He rubbed at his chest. "Only for a little while. I expect you to still be here when I get back."

"Yes, yes," she said grandly, still smiling. She waved a hand. "The famously revolting Alaska Force morning workout."

"You're welcome to join us. Get your sweat on. Learn some things about yourself."

"I would rather die," she said. She stopped smiling

and focused on him. Isaac was smug enough to enjoy how long it took her to do that. "And in this case, I actually, one hundred percent, mean that from the bottom of my heart."

Isaac was still grinning when he headed out with Horatio a little while later. He got in a quick, vicious trail run before he made his way to the cabin on the beach that he liked to call his *box of pain*. Particularly when everyone else complained about it.

Everyone not on active missions turned up in the mornings for the community workout, and Isaac enjoyed designing physical tests to challenge each and every one of them. Maybe a little too much. The grosser and more difficult the workout in Fool's Cove, the more prepared they all were for the kinds of things they had to cope with in the field.

And sure, on days like today when he found the way everyone was looking at him to be a little too smirky, he enjoyed making them pay.

In sweat and tears and unfortunate comments about his parentage.

"My parents were married, Blue," he said sternly at one point. "As I think you know. Let's do another round."

A solid hour later, he felt his honor had been sufficiently avenged when almost everyone was lying on the floor, groaning and spent.

Everyone except Bethan, who was capping off the workout with some blisteringly fast sprints down by the waterline. Isaac stood in the rolled-open door of the gym and watched her, not really surprised that she was pushing herself further and harder than everyone else. Wasn't that the story of women in her position? She'd spent her life preparing to fight but had been relegated to support positions until the ban on women in combat was lifted. He knew that was how she'd met Jonas, once upon a classified disaster neither one of them talked about. Bethan had gotten into Ranger School once it opened to female candidates. Then she'd distinguished herself even further as one of the few women who'd passed.

But the army didn't see her future the way she did, so she'd come to Alaska Force instead.

Where Isaac had no qualms whatsoever about assigning her to the active, dangerous missions she'd trained for.

No matter how curiously unsupportive Jonas seemed. When, asked directly, he'd had nothing but praise for her skills and abilities.

When everyone could breathe and walk again, more or less, they started heading out to do their various duties, or tend to their personal lives, before reporting to the lodge for the daily briefing.

Jonas hung back, likely to keep up his perpetual avoidance of Bethan. Isaac doubted his solitary friend would otherwise find himself seized with any sudden urge for Isaac's company. They took the beach route back toward the lodge through the cool summer morning, wreathed in a thick fog that would likely burn off before noon. Horatio ran in big loops around them, not quite herding them.

It was mornings like this that made Isaac the most nostalgic for his childhood here, even though everything had changed. He'd lost his parents. He'd spent those two years of black grief with his uncle Theo, who had never tried to comfort him. Isaac had learned to consider that a gift. Because instead, Uncle Theo had taught him how to become an unstoppable force in his own right. He'd given his grief-stricken nephew new tools and a new future to replace the kinder, gentler one that had been stolen from him.

And all the while, there had been this. The enduring grandeur of Alaska. The simple communion of sea and shore, mountain and sky. Whales in the sound and moose in the woods.

Home.

Though he admitted it felt more like home today than

usual, because Caradine was here. In Fool's Cove, where he'd never let himself believe she would ever come. Unwillingly or otherwise.

"I expected more fallout from that meeting yesterday," Isaac observed as he and Jonas walked. Before he did something unforgivable, like break into song. "All I got were a few smug looks and a handful of smirks. I must be more intimidating than I thought."

"You're the boss," Jonas replied. "Your personal life is your business. That's not intimidation, that's a professional courtesy."

Isaac grinned. "Surely I'm a *little* intimidating."

Jonas did something with his chin that made it clear that he, at least, was not remotely intimidated.

"You don't count," Isaac retorted.

They walked the rest of the way in a companionable silence, the crunch of their feet in the wet sand and the waves against the beach much better than any song he might be compelled to sing. Jonas melted off into the woods when they neared Isaac's cabin, and Isaac took the stairs that led up to his private walkway two at a time.

It was only when he hit the top step that he admitted to himself that he didn't expect Caradine to be there. He couldn't believe she'd stayed the night. He'd woken this morning fully expecting that she would have snuck out to one of the cabins set aside for clients, to prove a point.

When Isaac opened his cabin door, Horatio let out a happy bark. Isaac considered doing the same, because he could smell bacon.

She was still here.

She was still here.

He swung by his office, not because he was a control freak, but because he needed to see if there was anything urgent. And he also needed to get a grip.

When he'd checked in and taken a few calming breaths, he followed the sizzling sound of bacon back into the kitchen, where Caradine was moving around as if it were hers. One of his dish towels was tossed over her shoulder, like she was back in her café. She glanced over at him when he walked in, but she didn't say anything. She moved the cast-iron pan she'd threatened him with last night off the heat, walked over to the far counter, and poured him a cup of coffee. Then handed it to him in the extremely loud silence that had been their only form of communication for months at a time.

Then she returned to what she was doing. Isaac stood there, coffee, just the way he liked it, in his hands, his woman in his kitchen, and a pervasive sense of well-being that might have knocked him over if he'd had the slightest shred of hope that it could last.

But he didn't want to think about that, either.

He knew what happened to happiness. He'd lived through it once already.

More important, he knew Caradine.

The coffee was strong and nearly bitter, and he burned his tongue a little when he drank it. *Good*, he thought. Maybe pain would get his head on straight. When he regained his control, he moved over to the stove to see her pouring out what he suspected were the silver dollar pancakes she served him sometimes in her restaurant.

Just like his mom used to make. His favorite.

"Go shower," she ordered him, with more scowl than usual when he hadn't said anything. In case he was tempted to mention *her true heart* again, he figured. "It'll be ready when you're done."

He stole a piece of bacon, laughed at the even more ferocious scowl she aimed at him, and took himself off.

Then he stood in the water and braced himself against the wall, ordering himself not to want things he couldn't have.

"Pancakes are love," he announced when he walked back in, showered and dressed in his usual uniform of cargo pants and a T-shirt.

She was piling a stack of pancakes on a plate and only sniffed. "Not when I make them."

"I think you'll find they're always love, Caradine."

"My pancakes are made with spite and fury," she retorted, not bothering to look at him. "And don't kid yourself, Gentry. That's why you like them. You'd choke on love."

He sat in his chair as she brought the food to the table. She plunked his plate down with unnecessary force, then went to fix her own coffee. Isaac watched her pour cream into her cup, realizing that he'd had no idea how she took it until now. Because she was always the one who made the coffee and handed it out.

Knowing that she liked cream really shouldn't have made him feel like he'd won a war.

Her presence here shouldn't have felt like a victory. And yet.

"I've been thinking," she said in a rush when she finally sat down, poking at the pancakes she'd served herself.

He sighed. "That bodes well."

Her blue eyes narrowed, but she didn't snap at him for that. Which *really* didn't bode well.

"The plan my sister and I made never involved . . . well, you." She gave up pretending to eat and crossed her arms instead. "We agreed that we would never track each other down, because that would re-create the exact situation that we separated to avoid. The both of us in the same place, easy to follow, if someone was following us. And even easier to pick off. Or cart back to Boston."

He switched into work mode all too easily. "What do you think the goal is here? To kill you?"

She considered that. "Eventually, sure. I suppose it

depends. We walked away from a life people don't get to walk away from. It's not hard to imagine there might be a lot of reasons the people still in that life might like to use us as examples of why no one else should attempt such a thing."

"But you disappeared. As far as most people know, you died. Why go to the trouble to hunt you down and drag you back, when it would be easier to claim that you really did die? To put it out there that anyone pretending to be Julia or Lindsay Sheeran was full of it?"

Outside, the sun was starting to poke through the fog. A patch of light fell through the window, a wedge of a glare across the table his grandfather had made right here on mornings like this one, cool and bright in turn.

"People who sell illegal weapons, arming hateful groups who then take great pleasure in murdering each other, probably aren't rational." She shrugged. "My father was obsessed with respect. I have to think that anyone who would chase us down would think that's what this was. A matter of respect, that's all." Her mouth curved into something bitter. "Remember, Lindsay and I aren't *people* to them. Our lives only matter if they can be leveraged."

Isaac felt that muscle in his jaw twitch.

Caradine's eyes gleamed, as if that sign of his temper pleased her. "What I was thinking was that I wouldn't dare go by myself to see if Lindsay was okay. I'd be too afraid that someone could be following me, the way you were, and I'd never see it until it was too late, getting us both killed. Or worse. But *you* could go find her. You would know if anyone was tailing you."

Isaac actually laughed. "Was that a compliment? Wrapped up in there somewhere? Because it sounds a lot as if you're suggesting that we might actually be good at what we do here. That *I* might be more than a weird guy on an Alaskan island who plays Rambo games for fun."

"*Compliment* is a strong word." She pressed her lips together. "And I only said that a few times. In the early days."

He tried to imagine what she would do if he went over there and hauled her into a hug. And the imagining was almost as satisfying as the hug would have been, so he grinned at her instead. Especially when she frowned at him.

"Yes, Caradine, we can certainly go places without being followed. We know how to identify tails and, better still, how to dislodge them. That's part and parcel of the services we offer here. Speaking of which, we haven't gotten around to discussing your payment plan."

"Don't worry," she said, a little hotly. "I pay my bills."

"I'm not going to want your money, baby."

Isaac saw a flash of something on her face, but she looked down almost at once. He let it go, because he could see the way she was gripping her own arms as she sat across from him.

And because it probably wasn't the longing he'd wanted to see there.

Or even if it was, she had no intention of giving in to it.

"I think we should go find my sister," she said into the tension.

"*We?*" Isaac shook his head. "There's no *we*, Caradine. I get that you spent years keeping yourself hidden and preparing for an attack, and it's impressive. But it's not the same thing as military training."

"All the military training in the world won't make my sister talk to you when you find her," Caradine replied coolly. "Only I can do that."

His jaw hurt again. "It's out of the question."

Her gaze slammed into his, and all he could see was that blue, haunted straight through. Ghosts and secrets and too many lies across the years, even this morning after.

And that was the trouble, wasn't it? He didn't just want to help her.

He wanted to banish her ghosts, exorcise her demons. Fight her battles and win them all. And that was just for starters.

But she would punch him if he tried.

"I won't risk you," he said gruffly. "That's unacceptable."

"We have to go and find her, Isaac," Caradine said, with more urgency this time and what he realized was panic all over her face. "Before they do. Because they will. They found me. And Lindsay doesn't have Alaska Force, does she?"

Sixteen

Three days later, an Alaska Force team flew out for Hawaii.

Caradine went with them, fully aware that while everyone had agreed with her that she would be the key to any interactions with her sister, that didn't make her any less of a liability. It was something they'd all discussed right in front of her during the briefings Isaac had grudgingly allowed her to attend.

"That doesn't look like your game face," Bethan said in the middle of one briefing, while Isaac and Oz were called into a different room to handle an ongoing mission situation.

"Weird. It's my only face." But she relented when Bethan grinned, because it was possible Caradine had a weakness for people who weren't even remotely intimidated by her. Something she tucked away to look at . . . never. "I'm not exactly helpless."

"You're tough," Bethan replied with that same steady gaze they all seemed to have. And all knew how to use to make the unwary feel like they'd just been pulled over by flashing lights on the side of the road. "But you're not trained. And that means whoever's in the field with you has to make sure to protect you as well as do their job." She must have seen something on Caradine's face, because she laughed. "That's not a criticism, it's a fact."

Caradine hadn't been able to respond to that the way she'd wanted, because Isaac came back in, and it was back to contingency plans on a grand scale.

Her own contingency plans involved things like *run faster, use knife.*

Isaac's involved attempts to narrow down what name Lindsay might have been using these days, the satellite imagery of what parts of the island she might be staying in, and transport options with backup plans.

And, if all else failed, calling in the feds.

"How many missions do you run a year?" she asked Isaac when he arrived home late one night. Not that she should be allowing herself to think of his cabin as her *home*, but that was another problem she planned to avoid addressing forever. Or at least until this plan of theirs worked.

Or didn't.

God, she didn't want to think about the ways this plan could fail to work, or what that would mean, or the potential body count it could have. She'd glared down at the stovetop in front of her instead. Caradine found herself cooking a lot, because she'd fallen into the habit of feeding Isaac whenever she saw him. Because she didn't know what else to do.

Maybe she'd never known what else to do.

"We run as many missions as we want," Isaac replied. He grinned when she turned her scowl on him. "I'm not being funny. Every time we try to put a cap on it, a mission comes up that we can't refuse. So we make it work."

"But how do you—"

"Caradine."

He was still grinning when he came in closer and

hooked a hand around her neck, pulling her in for a kiss that made certain her food would get cold.

Caradine knew it was dangerous to give in. To let what had always had to explode between them simmer instead. To let it feel normal. Possible. Sex was one thing, or so she'd always told herself. But this was playing house. Pretending to have a life, when she knew that wasn't something that was on offer.

Because she knew better. She had ten years of experience in running away, and there was no reason to think that would change now that Alaska Force was involved. She *hoped*, but she knew better than to hope. She knew that hope led straight to hurt.

She resolved to lock up the hope inside her, where it couldn't poison anything, and proceed as normal. Because she knew that chances to run were split-second opportunities, never to be repeated, and she had to stay ready.

No matter what life she was leaving behind this time.

Having a life, she thought now from her seat on the Alaska Force jet, was something a person did when they didn't have to focus on staying alive.

She would do things differently next time. She wouldn't choose the *half-in, half-out* life she'd accidentally built for herself in Grizzly Harbor. It was too tempting to fall into routines. To become a character in other people's stories instead of leaving no trace. To make friends when she didn't intend to, no matter how she tried to pretend otherwise.

Friends who could get killed when the next bomb went off.

That was bad enough. But Caradine knew that the worst mistake she'd made by far was thinking that anything with Isaac Gentry could be casual.

You will be very different in your next life, she assured herself now. *You will call yourself something forgettable, and you will become beige in all things. You will be so boring and mousy you will be mistaken for wallpaper and will be able to hide in plain sight until you die of boredom in your old age.*

And she would never see Isaac again. Ever.

Assuming he lived through whatever happened now.

"We'll be landing soon," said the man himself, as if summoned.

He dropped into the seat across from her. And that dark, direct look he leveled on her made her feel in no way beige or mousy.

There was a little table between them in this part of the plane, and she found herself thinking of the wooden burls in the one his grandfather had made. She traced them on the tabletop before her, though they weren't there.

What a fool you are, she thought in despair. *Looking for connection when you should be looking for an escape route.*

"Good," she said out loud, hoping she sounded filled with a sober sense of purpose, the way everyone else on the plane seemed to be.

That had been the strangest part so far. These men she knew, and would even have said she knew fairly well, changed when they were in work mode. Or battle mode, she supposed she could call it. She'd seen glimpses of it before, but it was something else entirely to watch them plot out the details of their mission and then set off to undertake it. It made her realize that they'd been the ones hiding in plain sight all this time. Fooling the unwary—like her.

"I want to be very clear about what's going to happen." And the way Isaac was looking at her then, that gray gaze so steady, made her stomach quiver. "We're about to set down into an active mission."

"Is this the speech where you tell me you're in charge and blah blah blah mission parameters, mortal danger, do as you say and not as you do?"

"We don't know what we're walking into," Isaac said with a deep calm she would have thought was real had she not seen his eyes darken. Caradine congratulated herself on her tiny victory. "Everyone else is trained for this."

"I'm trained to survive really bad situations no matter the odds, so I like my chances."

"I expect you to follow instructions," he said in a voice that someone who didn't know him might have considered patient. "No matter how you feel about them. Your opinion has no weight against our experience. And I will not hesitate to personally incapacitate you if that's what it takes to keep you safe."

Steel in his gaze. Steel in his voice. Caradine found her lips curving despite herself. "That's the sweetest thing you've ever said to me, Gentry."

And suddenly he didn't look the least bit calm or patient. And once again, she felt in no way beige.

"I don't want you here," he said gruffly. "I don't want you anywhere near a situation that could harm you. Strategically speaking, it makes sense for you to be involved in this. I accept that. But I don't like it. Do you understand me?"

And once upon a time, she might have found a speech like that upsetting. She might have heard only the harshness and failed to notice that underneath it was the simple fact that he cared what happened to her.

He cared.

She pressed her fingertips hard against a tabletop that wasn't wood and had no history, and tried to pretend she wasn't too warm. That she hadn't walked into this situation step by step, year by year, with her eyes wide open, and could now blame no one but herself.

Hope. Caring. Isaac.

She was screwed.

"Everyone on this plane is invested in your safety," Isaac continued in that same low, rough voice that tugged at her despite her best attempts to wall herself off. "That investment puts us all at risk. And I know you take great pleasure in defiance, Caradine. But not today."

"I understand," she whispered.

Isaac held her gaze for a long, searching moment, then looked down at the tablet before him. He punched something into it, then lifted his gaze to hers again. "Are you prepared for any eventuality?"

"Probably not," she said, deadpan. "Does that take military training, too?"

She saw the ghost of a smile on his hard mouth. And she was used to being able to touch him now, so it felt painful to keep her hands to herself. Because even though no one appeared to be paying attention to them here, she would sooner chop off her own hands than engage in anything that could be confused for a public display of affection.

Especially if it was.

Because she needed to start preparing herself for disaster. She trusted that Alaska Force solved problems, but she knew this particular problem a little too well. She had no idea how to imagine that it could really, truly be solved.

"Families are weird when you see them all the time," Isaac pointed out, unhelpfully. "It's been five years."

Caradine made herself shrug carelessly. "Lindsay and I never fought. Not like that. We got a little pissy with each other here and there, but that was it. The benefit of growing up with actual monsters roaming around, I guess."

"Even when she almost got you both killed? Or worse?"

"Ouch." Caradine wanted to fidget. Rub her hands over her face, move her body, *something.* Anything but sit there taking the full brunt of that gaze of his. But she didn't move, because he didn't, and it added to that sense of power he toted around with him like another weapon. "Neither one of us knew how to fight. Not really. Because you didn't fight with my father. You took it. Maybe you tried to defend yourself a little, like curling into a ball if you were on the floor to protect your face, but you certainly didn't *fight*."

Isaac's jaw tightened in a way she knew meant he was furious. *For* her.

She still didn't know what to do with that, so she ignored it.

His gaze was a storm, but his voice stayed the same when he spoke. "Seems like you've put some time and attention into learning the ropes since then."

"I imagine Lindsay has, too." She considered. "I won't be surprised if she comes out swinging when she sees me. She was always the one with the temper."

Isaac actually laughed at that. "Really. *She* was."

"Really." Caradine smirked. "We both learned how to be meek in public as a survival tactic, obviously. But we shared a room growing up. And my sister took great pleasure in quietly destroying all her dolls. And mine. She was vicious."

Caradine could feel the plane begin its descent, as promised. But she felt buoyed by the way Isaac looked at her. She watched a silvery gleam break up some of that gray, and despite herself, she could feel that telltale, dangerous warmth spread throughout her body.

A feeling that only intensified when he smiled at her. That smile that almost felt like his hands on her.

That smile that she couldn't help thinking really was hers.

But a moment later it was like it had never been. He was up and moving. Talking in that voice of quiet command that made Caradine feel fluttery.

It made everyone else on board sit up straighter, too, and that was good, because it reminded her that there were any number of terrible things they could discover here. Lindsay could be dead. This could be a trap. Everyone could die, including her. Or everyone could die, except her. There were so many bloody, horrible possibilities, and she had to prepare herself for any and all of them, not moon after a man who might very well be one of the casualties, thanks to her.

A deeply depressing thought.

Caradine made herself stare out the window instead of at Isaac. There had been nothing there for hours but blue sky, but as the plane dropped down she saw clouds. Then a very different Pacific Ocean than the one she knew, blue and green instead of gray. And then the steep green slopes of Maui.

She almost thought she was dreaming, because who didn't grow up in the brutal Boston winters dreaming of Hawaiian islands? As the plane came in for its landing on a tiny airstrip that was very nearly in the sea itself, she saw water surging over black, volcanic rocks. Buildings with red roofs in a cluster she assumed was a town. Palm trees near the water, red earth, and the thick green jungle.

And as the wheels touched down, she acknowledged that she might not have been entirely honest with Isaac about her relationship with her sister. Or her feelings about it. Mostly because, if it were up to her, Caradine would dig out her feelings with a sharp implement and be done with them forever.

The truth was, she had no idea how Lindsay would react to seeing her, assuming she was alive and not the willing bait in a trap.

They had not parted on the best of terms. How could they have? They had been running for so long, and then everything that happened in Phoenix had been like a kick to the gut. Worse, actually. Caradine had felt restless and hunted and raw when they'd left each other, and she'd felt guilty about that for years now.

Because she loved her sister, there was no getting around that. But, God help her, she'd been relieved to finally be on her own.

What kind of person did that make her, that she'd been *relieved* to get rid of her only living family member?

She stared down at what remained of the black nail polish she had deliberately not touched up. Because Isaac had called her out on the fact she kept it black and chipped, so she was considering stepping out into a color scheme that he would find less predictable. French tips, maybe. Teal. Mustard yellow. Who knew?

Stop acting like you have a future with him, she ordered herself. *You might not have the rest of the day, for all you know.*

Nail polish seemed like a far safer thing to focus on than that awful thought. Or the way everyone was moving around her and exiting the plane, with that focus and intensity that made her feel a deep sense of regret at the way she'd poked at them all these years.

That was maybe overstating the case, she thought in the next moment, when Isaac's gaze found hers. He jerked his chin, ordering her to stand up and follow them out.

It was nice to see that they weren't a pack of overgrown frat brothers, sure. That added to the hopeful part of her. But that didn't mean that she had to treat them any differently the next time they were in her—

The sucker punch of that hit her hard. They wouldn't be in her café again. Because her café was gone, she wasn't going back, and all of this was likely nothing more than a very long, military-infused wake for the life she'd once had.

She was going to need to remember that.

"Caradine." Isaac's voice was crisp. No hint of that roughness that had warmed her earlier. "What did we talk about?"

"You didn't tell me it would be boot camp," Caradine said mildly, but she got to her feet. "I didn't realize that *exiting a plane* had to be accomplished in double time while singing a jaunty marching tune."

"The point is, you can either follow orders, or you can't."

"My mistake," she said breezily. "I expected you to actually give orders, not gesture with your chin like a—"

"Caradine."

By that point she'd reached him at the door and could feel the humid air outside, warm and ripe. And she would normally keep going. She would say something snarky to get a reaction, or touch him, or *do something*, because this man had always made her want to fidget, and she'd always channeled her restlessness around him into concrete things.

But this was a wake. She wasn't going back.

And she should never have pretended otherwise for those few days in Fool's Cove.

"Don't worry," she said, and she didn't smirk. She didn't scowl. She didn't pretend she was doing something other than what he'd asked her to do. "I understood you. I'll follow your orders, Isaac."

Another time, she might have enjoyed the way he blinked at that. But not today. Not when what had flared between them all these years belonged to a life she shouldn't have built and couldn't keep.

Not when the most probable outcome here was blood, terror, and Caradine running head-on into another life to hide away in.

Today she ducked her head because she didn't have anything sharp to say, or she had too many things to say. She moved around him without touching him and walked down the plane's folded-out stairs, toward her past.

Her real life, and her reckoning, whether she liked it or not.

Seventeen

They'd decided on a four-man team back in Fool's Cove. Templeton and Blue were talking about something in low voices when Caradine made it out of the plane onto the ground. And she told herself that what her heart did was her own business. No matter how much it hurt.

That's what happens when you let yourself hope for better, she reminded herself harshly. *How many times do you have to learn the same lesson?*

She stood by herself and waited. Jonas was off by himself, that flinty gaze of his scanning their surroundings, which consisted of little more than a tiny building with a soda machine out front. And when Isaac followed her down from the plane, he was on his phone again.

Caradine stood there and refused to hope for anything. Instead, she found herself wishing that she had worn something different in all this humidity.

It was like another unsolicited hug, long and close. The wet, warm press of the tropical air smelled of flowers and the sea, and an earthy, rich scent of wild growth. A bird called, somewhere in the thick, surrounding jungle, and it sounded like nothing she had ever heard before.

Goose bumps prickled down her neck and made her shiver, despite the warmth all around.

People always talked about how Alaska seemed like another planet. But Hawaii was more instantly, inarguably alien than anywhere else Caradine had ever been. Alaska might kill you, it was true. But at least it wouldn't smother you to death on contact—you'd have to go out and find an avalanche in the mountains for that.

Having never in her life understood the point of a sarong, Caradine would have killed for one now. Instead, she was dressed in what she knew Isaac would call tactical gear. A pair of tough hiking pants that were an approximation of the kind of battle-ready cargo pants the Alaska Force team members always wore. A pair of hardy hiking boots that could handle any terrain, but felt as if they were choking the life out of her feet and raising her temperature a good twenty degrees or so. And a black T-shirt in a fitted performance fabric that she figured she had to thank for not melting into a puddle where she stood.

She even had a gun strapped to her hip, which had been the topic of another debate.

Is she going to take a shot at all of us? Templeton had asked, in a voice that sounded like he was telling a joke when she could tell by his face that he wasn't.

I wouldn't miss if I was aiming at you, Templeton, she'd promised him.

But the debate had only truly ended when she'd pointed out that she didn't need their permission to carry her own weapon. Or to dictate where she could aim it, either.

Caradine is always carrying at least three weapons

at any time, Isaac had drawled, looking more amused than usual as he'd led the briefing yesterday morning. *I don't really see that changing.*

Are you flirting? Templeton had asked, grinning wide and unrepentant. Especially when Isaac had glared back at him.

"Okay," Isaac said now, shoving his phone into his pocket. "Oz thinks he's found her trail."

He cut his gaze to Caradine, so she nodded the way everyone else did. A bit stiffly, wondering if that was how Alaska Force recruits were expected to respond when the great leader spoke.

A question she had to bite her tongue to keep from asking.

"Remember what we talked about," he told her. Sternly. "This is neither the time nor the place for you to assert yourself."

Temper made her even warmer, suddenly. She opened her mouth to remind him that he'd already covered this same ground on the plane—barely three minutes ago, in fact—but he knew that.

Of course he knew that.

Caradine understood in a flash that this was not for him. This was for the team. All four men stood there, gazing at her intensely, and all she could think about was what Bethan had told her in Alaska.

You're not trained. And that means whoever's in the field with you has to make sure to protect you as well as do their job.

"I had no idea how much I intimidated you all," Caradine murmured, because she was still her, after all. And she might know better than to poke at Isaac when this could go so many different ways, but this was a group. Easier to poke without repercussions. "Way to give me all the power, guys."

"Is it out of your system now?" Isaac asked, with a

certain steady patience that would have been more of a slap if she didn't know this was a performance for him, too. That didn't make it *not* a slap. "You have thirty seconds. If you have something else to say that doesn't directly relate to this mission, now's the time."

Caradine allowed all the anxiety and tension inside her to bubble up. She even smirked for good measure. "This feels like a test. Let me think. Okay, lock and load. Five by five. I got your six, captain. Ten-four, good buddy. Yippee-ki-yay, mother—"

"Best Christmas movie ever made," Blue asserted.

"I think that's it," Caradine finished. "I definitely feel like I'm in an action movie now. That's good, right?"

"*Die Hard* is an action movie, not a Christmas movie, jackhole," Templeton said to Blue.

Blue snorted. "If you're dead inside."

"Terrific," Isaac said, and he might have sounded disapproving, but Caradine could see that gleam in his gaze, and she knew better. And hated that she could tell, because that was one more thing she was going to have to leave behind. "We have a little bit of a drive."

He started off across the small airfield, leading them around the tiny terminal building and out to a waiting SUV in the largely empty parking area. Caradine didn't ask who had delivered it. Just like she didn't complain when the four of them fell into formation around her, seemingly without needing to communicate with one another. They just did it. They fanned out around her, so she was in the center, and matched their strides to hers.

She almost thought it was automatic, and that settled in her like another flush of heat.

In the SUV, Templeton sat in front while Isaac drove, leaving Caradine to be sandwiched in the back between the tall, solidly muscled frames of Jonas and Blue.

She suddenly wanted to ask a thousand questions. Was this how they always traveled? What happened when they needed more people on a team? Did they carpool like this, shoved up against each other like kids in the back of a station wagon?

When she had to bite back an inappropriate giggle, Caradine understood that she was becoming hysterical.

She couldn't let that happen for any number of reasons, but most important because it would prove to Isaac that she couldn't handle this. And she would rather die than disappoint him or have him think less of her in any way.

Another time that her favorite phrase was completely true.

And another thing she needed to let go of now, or carry with her forever, out there in all that beige that waited for her.

Caradine gulped down the giggle, focused on *beige*, and sat as rigidly as possible between two large men with wide shoulders they couldn't do anything about as the SUV charged onto what passed for a main road in this remote part of a famous island.

Isaac drove the way he did everything. With skill and focus, which helped as they passed through a collection of buildings she thought was a town, then headed into the wilderness on a dirt track Caradine would never have called a road. Especially when the tangled green closed in around them like it was swallowing them whole.

At certain points she could see through the thick wall of jungle. There were sweeping views every now and again, while impossible flowers bloomed everywhere, offhandedly, down the length of the hill they were climbing. She saw the small town they'd driven through and, below it, a brooding sort of sea with rocky inlets at odds with the vision she'd always carried in her head of what Hawaiian beaches ought to look like.

"This is the windward side of the island," Blue said, almost as if he were commenting out the window. Caradine didn't know how to feel about the evidence that he was paying close attention to her. She kept having to re-evaluate all of these people she'd put into careful boxes a long time ago, and it was disconcerting, to say the least. "It gets battered by the wind, sees more rain above sea level than the leeward side, and is less populated. The kind of Hawaiian island beaches and resorts you might expect are on the other side, protected by the mountains and blessed by the trade winds."

"Hana-side is real upcountry Hawaii," Jonas said from her left, gruffly. "It's the difference between Anchorage and every other part of Alaska."

"I apologize, Caradine," Templeton drawled from the front seat. "You're stuck between two navy men. They think spending time on a couple of sailboats makes them experts on every island they find along the way."

"Better than an army man," Isaac said dryly. "Expert on nothing."

"Whatever, jarhead," Templeton retorted, sounding outraged, though he remained in his lazy, half-reclining slouch. "I'm the only person in this vehicle who is *actually* Hawaiian."

"Part Hawaiian," Jonas replied. "I'm sure that will impress the locals."

Everyone laughed. And it took Caradine a few more moments, jolting along the deeply rutted dirt track that climbed farther and farther up into the rain forest, to realize that all of this was affection.

There was absolutely no reason it should leave a lump in her throat.

Except, you know, that this could all end horribly any minute now, her usual harsh inner voice chimed in.

It only made the lump in her throat worse.

Isaac kept driving, seemingly into nowhere. The views disappeared, the lush green and riotous flowers on all sides so intense they blocked out the sky in places.

And about ten minutes up that road, right when Caradine was beginning to get concerned that she would succumb to the claustrophobia she'd never known she had, he stopped.

"Perimeter," he said shortly.

That meant nothing to Caradine, but Blue and Jonas opened their doors. Then they melted off into the jungle, disappearing with so little trace that she was watching them do it and had to blink. Because one moment they were there and the next it was as if they'd never been.

Caradine understood this meant they were close to the place Oz thought Lindsay was. She tried to take a deep breath. She tried telling herself to be calm. But her stomach was in knots, she felt vaguely nauseated, and she wasn't sure if it was because she wanted to see her sister, or didn't. She didn't know which was worse—or better.

That Lindsay would be here? Or that she wouldn't?

Or maybe you're afraid that she really is the reason the Water's Edge got hit, she told herself. *That she blew up your life all over again and will blow this up, too. And hurt people you like.*

That voice resonated deep inside, in that place she didn't like to admit was there. Because it was ugly.

Deep inside, she blamed Lindsay for what happened in Phoenix. And the lives on their hands because of it, even if those lives had been removed from them. From her. She wondered things she shouldn't, like how many seconds it had really been between the time Lindsay texted her outside the house in Boston and when it blew up. Ten years on, Caradine could no longer be sure what had actually happened versus what she'd decided must have happened, based on what came after.

Deep inside, where hope never dared penetrate, Caradine expected their father's sins to catch up with her, every day. And she suspected everyone—especially her little sister.

Deep inside, that she loved her sister was often an afterthought.

And what would she do if Lindsay could see that on her face?

The second Caradine saw the hint of a structure through the trees, and sucked in a breath, Isaac stopped again. Or almost stopped. The SUV slowed but never quite came to a halt. Isaac nodded. And Caradine watched Templeton, a huge man who should not have been the least bit graceful, roll out as if he didn't need to touch the ground to disappear into the jungle.

"Crawl up into the front seat," Isaac said to her with a quick glance in the rearview mirror. His voice was the same quiet command he'd used on the others.

Caradine was moving before she really thought about it, obeying him as if it were a reflex.

Social Isaac would have commented on it. Team leader Isaac didn't mention it.

"Is this her house?" Caradine asked, that lump in her throat making her voice scratchy.

"I think so." He threw a glance at her. "Oz is rarely wrong."

He navigated his way into a clearing where the house stood, and Caradine tried to take it in. It looked like all the other houses she'd seen so far in this part of Maui. A little bit ramshackle, with the living part of the house on the second floor. She realized she didn't know the cues here. She knew how to tell the difference between scary and weathered in an Alaskan context but not in this jungle, which seemed so different from anywhere else she'd been.

Or maybe what she was having trouble with was imagining her sister in a place like this.

Isaac pulled up in front of the house, but not directly in front of the doors on the ground floor or the stairs that led up on the sides. And he parked at an angle.

"There's movement on the second floor," he said gruffly. "Don't look."

Caradine blew out a breath, finding that the hardest order to follow so far.

"We're going to get out of the car," he told her in the same commanding tone. "I'm going to stand by the driver's door, looking unthreatening."

She made a noise and his brows rose, so she made herself nod. And reminded herself that a great many people seemed to have no trouble missing the fact that he was the most threatening man around—which in Grizzly Harbor was saying something.

And Caradine absolutely refused to allow herself to think about what might happen if whoever was in this house correctly identified him as the threat he was, when they could pick him off with a single shot. Her stomach hurt, but she did her best to ignore that, too.

"You're going to walk toward the house. Whatever happens, remember that I have eyes on you. And so does everyone else." He paused, his head angling slightly to one side, and it took her a second to realize he was listening to something on his comm unit. "Everyone's in position, and there's no sign of anyone else lurking around out there. Okay?"

Caradine nodded again, because she couldn't bring herself to speak. Because what could she say? *I hope you don't die for me because I don't know if I can bear it?*

And she was more grateful in that moment for the calm, steady way he looked at her than she would ever be able to express, because it took the clamoring, panicked racket inside her down to an almost-bearable roar.

"Then let's go," Isaac said.

Caradine pushed open her door. Isaac did the same, and she watched as he got out the way a normal man might. He hitched up his cargo pants, when they didn't need hitching. He stretched, the way a regular person might after driving such a treacherous road. He looked around like a bemused tourist.

In contrast, she threw herself out like a wild animal who expected to bolt.

Get it together, she ordered herself. Before he did.

Isaac had told her to walk toward the house, so she made herself do it. And she might not have looked to see what eyes were on her from the second floor of the house, but she felt them. Her skin prickled, like ants were marching all over her.

Caradine couldn't tell if it was a bad feeling, or just a feeling, and this probably wasn't the time to decide she needed to learn how to tell the difference.

Ants or no ants.

She kept walking until the door she was heading toward cracked open.

And then her legs stopped dead without bothering to consult with the rest of her.

Her heart was pounding so loud it was threatening to give her a headache. She tried to calculate angles, because she trusted Isaac but she was standing close enough to that door that if the person who came out wasn't Lindsay, but another thug like the one who'd found her in Maine, she would be dead. Instantly, if that was what he wanted.

I don't want to die, she thought, the way she had ten years ago when the world had ended, but she'd lived.

"You won't," Isaac gritted out from behind her.

And it was a welcome distraction to think about how she'd said that out loud when she hadn't realized it.

Then the door opened farther still, and there was no distracting herself from that.

She realized she had no idea what she expected to see, and that made her stomach cramp up all over again.

It was shadowy inside the house, so it took a moment for Caradine to decide that her eyes weren't playing tricks on her. There really was someone there.

Her trained, capable response was to hold her breath like a kid.

A woman stepped out of the doorway, into the shade cast by the upper level of the house, and Caradine felt her stomach drop.

Knots and all.

Because it was Lindsay . . . and it wasn't.

The girl from five years ago was gone. This Lindsay was rounded. Fleshed out. Gone were the sharp edges and angles, the waifish pixie with visible hip bones and razors for cheekbones whom she'd called her little sister.

This was a woman.

And not just any woman.

Caradine couldn't seem to do anything but stare.

"I know," Lindsay said, and her voice was familiar, even if the rest of her had changed. Sharp and wry, like the slap of home. "Can you believe it? Talk about adding insult to injury. I freaking look like Mom."

Eighteen

Lindsay didn't invite them in.

Caradine couldn't tell if that was an abundance of caution on her sister's part or that same dislocation she felt herself. Or, it occurred to her, it was possible Lindsay blamed her and suspected her in turn. Either way, Lindsay ushered them to the seating area there in the shade cast by the upper level, calling it a lanai, and the three of them sat there.

In what felt to Caradine like a tortured, fraught silence.

"Before we start this conversation," Isaac said, with that affable grin of his and the body language of a lazy good ol' boy, "are you going to invite your friend inside to come out and join us?"

It was difficult to find the Lindsay she recognized in the woman before her, but Caradine recognized the expression that moved over her sister's face then. The flicker of temper, then something darker.

"I don't know that I will." Lindsay nodded at Caradine. "You're not supposed to be here. And you came with a friend. I think I'll leave my friend where he is until I feel more comfortable with the situation. You understand."

Caradine understood completely.

"Of course." Isaac's grin widened. "But I'm sure you'll understand that I'm going to take a more strategic position while we wait to see whose friend is more trustworthy."

Lindsay smirked, another thing Caradine recognized. "You do you."

And Caradine took perhaps more satisfaction than she should have in the way Isaac moved. There one moment, gone the next, melting off into the tropics.

But then he was gone. And it was just Caradine and her sister, catching up.

"So," Lindsay said, after a long moment dragged by. Painfully.

"So," Caradine agreed.

"What are you doing here, Julia?" Lindsay asked softly, though her gaze was hard. "And who is that guy?"

"I've been compromised," Caradine said, ignoring the jolt it gave her to hear her sister say her name. When it no longer felt like a name that belonged to her anymore, much less uttered in a familiar voice.

It had been a long time since she'd felt like she had a sister. Or was one.

"You were compromised and you came *here*?" Lindsay's eyes widened. "We made a promise!"

"I know what we promised. But someone found me." Caradine searched her sister's face, but all she saw were too many unhappy Sheeran family memories wrapped up in the way Lindsay held her lips too tight. "I still don't know how. They firebombed my restaurant."

"I feel for you. I do." Lindsay clearly didn't, and she scowled to underscore that. "But you thought . . . what, exactly? You should bring that mess to my doorstep?"

"I ran, of course," Caradine said placidly, as if Lindsay hadn't spoken. "But my friend happens to be a man of many interesting skill sets. He tracked me down."

Lindsay's eyes widened. "That's . . . not better."

"I called Sharkey's," Caradine said.

Her sister paled a little, beneath the golden tan that likely came with living here. The way potential frostbite came with a move to Alaska. "Why the . . . why would you do that? Do you have a death wish?"

Sometimes Caradine asked herself the same question. "I wanted to see who would show up."

It was what she'd told Isaac. And it was true. But it was different, saying that to Lindsay, when they both knew what that could mean. She watched her sister flinch, then look away.

"Is that why you came?" Lindsay asked when she looked back again, and her scowl had disappeared. But her voice was harsher. "To tell me who came after you in person?"

"I wanted—" Caradine began.

"Was it Francis?"

And for the first time since she'd come here, Caradine fully recognized her sister. It was the way she asked that question, the terror so obvious in her voice. That sheen of panic in her eyes.

Caradine knew all of that, intimately. She'd been the one who'd woken up to Lindsay's screams after they'd left Boston. She'd been the one who'd soothed her sister's nightmares away with empty promises that Francis must have died that night.

Another hope that had hurt them both after Phoenix. Because maybe it hadn't been Lindsay's nasty, vicious ex-fiancé who had killed those people. But maybe it had.

"It wasn't Francis," Caradine assured her. "I didn't recognize the guy who showed up. I don't know who he worked for."

Lindsay blew out a ragged sort of breath, and when

she crossed her arms over her chest, Caradine realized she was looking at that same defensive gesture she made all the time herself.

Ouch.

"I still don't understand why you're breaking our promise," Lindsay said, traces of fear in her voice.

"Because I brought help. I didn't come all this way to tell you something I could have told you when you picked up my message. My friend—" And she remembered as she said that word, again, that though she hadn't been given a comm unit like the rest of the team, they'd put a recording device on her. Meaning they were all listening to her talk about Isaac. They were listening to her use the word *friend*, and of all the things that had happened, were happening, and were likely to happen still, it was ridiculous that she should get caught up on something like that. Still, it seemed to bang inside her chest like a gong. "My friend runs a business."

"He looks like a mercenary," Lindsay said flatly.

"His business is all about finding creative solutions for tricky problems." Caradine parroted something she'd heard any number of Alaska Force members say over the past five years, usually when they were meeting new clients in her café. "And they all have special ops experience, if you want to know the kind of solutions I'm talking about. Can you think of anyone who has a bigger problem than we do?"

Her sister's eyes darted around, as if she were looking for a way out. "What I'm not tracking is why you would bring our favorite problem directly to me."

"If they found me, they're going to find you. It's only a matter of time."

"A matter of time, sure. Or, you know, my sister coming straight for me, making a trail for them to follow to my front door."

Out of the corner of her eye, Caradine saw Isaac

again. He moved lazily around the SUV's front, then leaned against it, looking idle and vaguely bored when she knew he was anything but.

And the fact he'd put himself where she could see him warmed her all over again. It gave her a little more strength than she'd had a moment ago. Almost like—

But she shoved that aside, because there were miles upon treacherous miles yet to go.

"I live on a remote Alaskan island," Caradine said evenly. "Not on Maui. You have to work hard to get to Grizzly Harbor."

"Because it's a real picnic coming up the road here," Lindsay said sarcastically. "Tourists do it all the time."

Caradine ordered herself not to snap at her sister. "If they could find me there, Maui's got to be a walk in the park."

"Especially now you've drawn them a map to that park."

"I don't know what your life is like," Caradine said fiercely then. "But I know mine. Pretending to settle down but always having one foot out the door. Always knowing that at any moment it could all blow up. And then it did. I wanted to see you, Lindsay, not to make you a target. But to see if together, you and me and my friends, we could figure out a way to make this stop."

And as she said it, she almost believed it was possible. She almost believed they could do it.

The door to the house opened then and Lindsay turned, a look of wild panic on her face.

Caradine shot to her feet, but even as she started to back up, Isaac was there.

Thank God. Because the man who stepped out onto the porch looked like Isaac's kind of trouble. He was big, tall. He looked like possibly he played a defensive position in football in between bench-pressing cars for fun. He was Hawaiian, with visible tattoos all over his upper body and up his neck.

But it was what he was carrying that stopped Caradine dead.

Not the gun he held loosely in his right hand. But the tiny little girl he held in the crook of his other arm, who looked like a perfect, pretty little brown replica of Lindsay.

Caradine's heart . . . stopped.

Then slammed against her ribs like a train.

Lindsay had a child. A daughter. Her sister had a daughter.

Caradine was an aunt, and she would never have known that if she hadn't come here. Something washed over her then, a complicated mix of emotion and hope and determination for the future. Because there had to be a future.

And in the next beat came the fear.

Because she and Lindsay were one thing. They could run. They shouldn't have had to, but life was unfair, and running was still better than life in their father's house.

She couldn't bear the thought of passing that on to the little girl with big brown eyes who stared back at her, her middle two fingers tucked in her mouth.

The way Lindsay's always had been as a little girl, until their father had broken them when she wouldn't stop.

Caradine couldn't take that back. She couldn't change the past. She could never make it okay.

Nothing would make it okay.

But maybe, just maybe, they could make it *stop*.

And the surge of hope that bloomed inside her then made her feel nauseated and dizzy.

"You know my position on this," the man said, his gaze moving over Caradine, hard and quick. He lifted his chin in Isaac's direction, his black eyes glittering. "I'm tired of hiding. I want this over."

"And I keep telling you, that's a fantasy," Lindsay snapped. She moved over to the man and gathered the little girl into her arms. "It's never over. It's never going to be over." She glared at Caradine. "And I don't appreciate you coming here and trying to make the fact they found you into some kind of opportunity when we both know it's not. If they find us, we die."

"Unless they die," Isaac drawled.

"I like your sister's friend already," the man in the doorway said.

"It's not just you and me anymore, Jules," Lindsay threw out there. "And, to be honest, I care a lot more about my daughter than your restaurant."

Her man made a low noise. "Lindsay."

"That goes for you, too," Lindsay snapped at him.

He didn't look particularly bothered by that. "It's nice to meet you, Julia," he said in a friendly sort of tone, nodding at Caradine. "I didn't think that was going to happen in this lifetime. I'm Koa."

"Please," Caradine replied, still feeling dizzy and a little bit sick. She rubbed at her heart, hoping that would stop it kicking at her. "Call me Caradine. Julia was a very foolish girl who died a long time ago."

"While Lindsay has no intention of dying," Lindsay said wildly, her daughter against her chest. "Under any circumstances, using any name."

"Why don't you come inside," Koa said, with another look at Lindsay that made her flush but didn't make her back down. "After all, you're all *ohana*, more or less. My house is yours."

But he kept his eyes trained on Isaac, who grinned. Disarmingly. The two men moved inside the house together, warily, but Caradine waited for her sister.

Lindsay was breathing heavily. She caught Caradine's look over the top of her little girl's head, and Caradine couldn't have said what she saw on her sister's face. Grief. Panic. Resolve.

Caradine could hardly speak. "Lindsay . . ."

"I met him on the Big Island," Lindsay said, sounding

defiant and sad at once. "I told him I would never marry him, because I could never stay with him. He took that as a challenge."

"Linds. I don't—"

"And I didn't see the harm. Wives leave husbands all the time. I thought being married was an even better cover, to be honest, though I knew you'd freak out if I told you."

"Define *freak out*."

Lindsay shook her head. "But then I got pregnant. It was a mistake. Because I could never voluntarily bring a baby into this . . . this disaster." She coughed to clear her throat. "What kind of person would do that to an innocent child?"

Their eyes met. And neither one of them mentioned their own mother. But then, they didn't have to. Donna was the kind of ghost who lingered, even in the Hawaiian sun.

"I know I should have done the smart thing," Lindsay said in a small, anguished voice. "But I couldn't. I just couldn't."

"Lindsay," Caradine whispered. "She's *perfect*."

Lindsay looked down at her little girl, who buried her head in the crook of Lindsay's neck. There was no mistaking the proud, loving, worried smile on her sister's face. There was no mistaking the anguish and the determination.

"She's two," Lindsay said quietly. "Her name is Luana."

Caradine made a noise. A sigh, maybe. A sob. She couldn't tell. "That's beautiful. *She's* beautiful."

"Her name means 'happiness,'" Lindsay said. And her gaze was ferocious when she raised it to Caradine's. "And I might look like Mom, but I'm not her. There is nothing I won't do to protect my child. Absolutely nothing."

Nineteen

Isaac determined within a single sweep of the house that Koa was exactly what he appeared to be at first glance. A man who was willing to do whatever it took to protect his family, including letting an armed stranger look through his home to make sure it was safe.

But even if he was a better actor than he seemed, he was outnumbered. Isaac called in the rest of the team and tried to look friendly as Koa took in the information that said team had been out there all along.

"Not sure I would have invited you in if I'd known you came in a set," the other man said after a moment.

"Don't worry." Isaac tried to sound soothing. "They're all housebroken."

Meanwhile, Caradine and her sister were talking to each other warily out on the lanai. Through the screen, Isaac watched Lindsay put her daughter down to toddle around on her own feet. While she did, the two women stood next to each other. They both crossed their arms in the same way. They had the same nose. The same stubborn chin.

It was strange to think of Caradine as something other than singular.

"We keep the outside looking as down-market as possible," Lindsay said, sounding defensive.

"The Francis factor," Caradine said, nodding as if that made sense.

She noticed Isaac studying her from inside the screen door. "The man my sister was supposed to marry liked calling her *princess*. He liked her helpless, surrounded by luxuries, all of which he could take away whenever he felt like it."

"What he really liked," Lindsay added with a brittle laugh, "was making me pay for them."

Isaac watched as a very dark look passed between the sisters, while beside him, Koa looked murderous. The rest of the team came in from the jungle then, ambling across the clearing like they'd been out for a hike. And Isaac had been doing this a long time. But he still enjoyed the automatic look of alarm people got when they were wise enough to find an Alaska Force team intimidating.

Templeton broke the tension almost immediately as he strode onto the lanai, booming out an *aloha* to Koa and immediately lapsing into a mix of English, pidgin, and Hawaiian.

"My mother always said that leaving Oahu was the biggest mistake of her life," Templeton told Koa. He said something in Hawaiian that made the other man laugh. "From the islands to Mississippi, if you can believe it."

Koa mock-shuddered. "Sounds like death to me, brother."

"Good thing I resurrect well," Templeton replied blandly.

They both laughed and clapped each other on the back, lightening the mood considerably. It seemed almost natural for all of them to sit down on the lanai together, but this time more as guests than unwanted intruders.

As far as Koa was concerned, anyway. Isaac wasn't sure Lindsay was on board.

"The only question I'm really interested in," Koa said when they were all seated, "is how this ends. I want my family safe."

"I'm interested in that question, too," Isaac agreed.

"I'd like it to end," Caradine agreed. Too cautiously, Isaac thought. "But I'm also very interested in who's doing this."

She and Lindsay looked at each other then, and Isaac didn't like it.

"Is there something you two aren't telling us?" he asked.

Lindsay glanced at Caradine beside her, then frowned at Isaac. "There are probably a million things I'm not telling you. You're going to have to be more specific."

Caradine smirked. "Isaac is used to a greater level of deference, Linds. If you genuflected, that wouldn't go amiss. That's the level of reverence he prefers."

Her sister didn't grin, but the light in her eyes changed in a way that was too much like Caradine for Isaac's peace of mind. "Have you taken up genuflecting? That doesn't really sound like you."

"I don't know how I feel about this," Templeton said, looking back and forth between the two women.

"Two of them?" Blue laughed. "I know how I feel about it. Freaking terrified."

Even Jonas looked amused at that.

"If the two of you have thoughts about who's behind this," Isaac said, finding it harder than he should have to keep his voice level, "this is the time to share that."

Again, Caradine and her sister exchanged a look that clearly communicated all kinds of information they had no intention of sharing with everyone else.

"After Phoenix you must have started to think about who it could be," Isaac pushed.

Lindsay paled a bit at that, but Caradine only scowled. At Isaac.

"Of course," she said. "But then five years passed. As far as I know, that bomb through the front window of my restaurant was the first sighting we've had since then." She glanced at Lindsay, who nodded. "So the list remains the same. It has to be someone who would benefit from getting rid of my father in the first place. The question then is, Did the call come from inside or outside the house?"

Isaac waited for Templeton or Blue to make the requisite horror-movie joke, but neither one did. Possibly because the real horror was more than enough.

"Everyone thinks we died in that fire, too," Lindsay said after a moment. "It's never been much of a stretch to imagine that other people, who are supposedly dead, aren't."

"Who do you think would be most likely to hold a grudge that long?" Jonas asked from his place near the wall.

Caradine and Lindsay studied each other.

"It could always be Dad," Caradine said, almost tentatively. Almost as if she didn't want to put that out there.

"I don't think it is," Lindsay replied quickly. Too quickly. And she looked at her husband and Isaac, not her sister. "He was holding court the way he always did, sitting in his favorite chair in the den like it was a throne. And he didn't allow any cell phones in the den with him on Sundays, because he was talking business. So in order for him to set off that bomb, he would have had to get up, go out of the room, grab his phone, and then run out of the house."

She shook her head as if she'd proved something.

Caradine found Isaac's narrow gaze. "My father

didn't run anywhere. Ever. And when his cell phone wasn't on his body, he kept it locked up in the kitchen."

"Add to that the fact that if he got up and ran out, everyone else in the room would have gone with him like the little bootlickers they were," Lindsay said caustically. "They all would have gone outside, which would defeat the purpose of blowing up the house."

"Why?" Koa asked.

"Because if my father and all his lackeys were out of the house, only my mother and I would have stayed inside," Lindsay said, her eyes on her husband while their little girl sat on the floor at her feet, singing to herself. "And no one thought either one of us was important enough to take out like that, believe me."

Isaac looked to Caradine, who was nodding as if that weren't any kind of revolutionary statement.

And she sounded perfectly calm when she chimed in. "I have no doubt that if my father could have faked his death, he would have. What I don't see is him managing to keep under the radar for ten years. He loved his notoriety way too much. I can't see him hiding out anywhere."

Lindsay snorted. "Yeah. No. Our father didn't hide. He preferred to taunt the FBI openly, daring them to try to take him in."

"There were external factors," Caradine said, as if she were turning it over in her head. "There always were. People jostling for position. Trying to push Dad out of the business, or cut him off. And, you know, his clientele weren't exactly the most upright and honorable of people, so it could have been them, too."

"Irish mob. Italian mob. Street gangs. Creepy private collectors." Lindsay rolled her eyes. "And that's just in Boston."

"Do you think it was an external party?" Isaac asked.

"I don't," Caradine said, carefully, as if she were waiting for Lindsay to disagree with her. But her sister only shrugged. "I've been thinking about it. And the fact it's been ten years is the troubling part. Because, sure, let's say it was the people who took the credit for killing him. The Connollys have their own troubles. Local disputes, infighting, and that court case. Are they really going to waste time worrying about the possibility that two of the least important people in that house might still be alive? I don't see it."

"A year is a long time for your average dirtbag," Lindsay agreed. "Much less ten years."

"So that means you think it was family," Blue said.

"Inner circle?" Templeton asked.

"There was only inner circle in the house," Lindsay said. "Mom was in the kitchen. So was I, because that's where we waited for the men to be finished talking about important things. Like my life."

"Don't be silly, Linds," Caradine drawled. "Why would they waste time talking about your life in a big meeting like that?"

Lindsay actually laughed, and Caradine did, too, and Isaac felt like he'd sustained a blow. Because Caradine laughed so rarely. And Lindsay sounded just like her. And his chest hurt, when he was trying to think strategy and probabilities, because they sounded so amused. And it wasn't the least bit funny.

He was only slightly gratified when he saw that the rest of the team looked equally startled, something a person would notice only if they were looking for it. And it didn't do Isaac's chest any good to think about the fact that clearly, since Koa didn't look surprised at all, Lindsay must laugh a lot more than her sister did.

"I brought them drinks," Lindsay was saying, her voice a little soft as she conjured up her memories. "Whatever they were talking about, it was bad. Dad was pissed."

Caradine rolled her eyes. "Mickey Sheeran existed in

a state of perpetual rage. So when Lindsay says that he was pissed, that means he was much worse than usual."

"They obviously didn't say anything sensitive when I was in the room, but I did get the impression that they were specifically mad at someone." Lindsay looked over at Koa, and whatever she saw there made her straighten her shoulders a bit, then take a breath. "Sometimes something was wrong and you could tell that it was a deal gone bad or something like that. But Dad was wound up in a different way that night. It was weird."

Caradine nodded, sitting with her own shoulders squared next to her sister. "That's what you texted me."

"I didn't want her to come in," Lindsay said. Her gaze traveled from Isaac to Jonas, then over to Blue and Templeton. But then she went back to Isaac, and stayed there. "It was too tense, and she always made Dad worse."

"That's so hard to believe," Isaac said idly.

Caradine's eyes actually gleamed, which was the version of her laughter that he knew best. "It's hard to wrap your head around, I know."

"And sometimes, it was fine," Lindsay continued. "She would wind him up and he would freak out, but in a normal way."

"What does that mean?" Koa asked quietly, his dark gaze on his wife. "Because I don't think that what's normal to you is going to strike me as particularly normal."

The two women looked at each other again, as the toddler pulled herself up to cling to her mother's knees. Lindsay smoothed her hand over her daughter's hair, and when she looked up, she was somehow soft and made of steel at once.

"A normal amount of freaking out would be like a backhand." She looked at her sister. "Right?"

"The back of his hand, sure," Caradine confirmed. "Or he would throw something at you. Or grab the back of your head by your ponytail and slam your face into the table if you weren't paying proper attention."

"Little stuff," Lindsay agreed. "Just a couple of bruises to get your attention."

Isaac met each one of his friends' and colleagues' gazes, then Koa's, and saw the same stark, murderous gleam in each one of them.

The sisters didn't seem to notice how tense and furious their audience had become.

"If you were paying attention the way you should have been, you could ward off any glasses or plates he threw at you." Caradine lifted up her arms, moving her forearms as if she were batting away missiles with them. She and Lindsay even snickered. "Do you remember that time—?"

"Oh my God." Lindsay laughed again. Then remembered the men enough to explain. "He was yelling at Julia, about, I don't know, how ungrateful she was."

Caradine smirked. "A common theme."

"So he picked up his dinner plate, loaded with food, and threw it at her."

"Again," Caradine said dryly, "common."

"But, and she swore up and down this was an accident, she kind of caught it." Lindsay demonstrated, putting up her hands as if she were preparing to hit a volleyball. "Then winged it back at him."

They both laughed again, and even sank into each other a little while they did, touching shoulders.

And Isaac took another survey of the lanai, not surprised to find that everyone was as appalled as he was.

"Totally worth it," Caradine said after a moment, wiping at her eyes. "Really."

"What exactly did he do to you?" Isaac asked mildly.

He did not feel mild at all. More like lethal.

Caradine sobered. "That was less fun. That took a few days to recover from." She considered. "Maybe a couple of weeks, now that I think about it."

"I hate that you both lived through this," Koa said then, dark and furious. "It's sick. And that you think it's *funny* makes me want to break things."

"Cosign," Blue belted out.

"Tell us about that night," Templeton invited the women, even pulling out a grin—likely because he was the only one who could manage one just then. Isaac was with Koa. He wanted to raze a city or two. "It was weird in the room . . . ?"

"Right," Lindsay said, smiling down at her daughter. "What I keep coming back to, over time, is who was closest to the door. Just in terms of getting to the kitchen, getting their cell phone, and getting out of the house, they would have had to be close to the door. Because I left the den, Julia texted when I got to the kitchen, and I ran outside. The two of us talked for maybe a minute? Two minutes?"

"Not much more than that," Caradine agreed.

Lindsay shrugged. "So whoever did it had to be right behind me."

Isaac considered. "Do you think they followed you out? Meaning, whoever it is has known you were alive this whole time?"

"No one followed me out. I went out the front door, and if they'd gone to pick up their phone, it would make sense to go out the back and call in the ignition code more quickly." The look Lindsay aimed at Isaac was level. Steady. "And I would have known if someone was right behind me. You get attuned to that kind of thing, or you get hit."

"So you're out front with Caradine," Templeton said. Lindsay and Caradine nodded. "You think someone went out the back door."

On the coffee table, he set up a little scene, using the coffee that Koa had brought out when the whole team had appeared. One mug for the house. One mug for Lindsay and Caradine. Another for whomever they were talking about.

Templeton pointed to each mug in turn, then looked at the sisters. "Theoretically, could you have lived through the explosion and then walked away from it without someone coming out of the backyard to see you?"

The two women looked at each other.

"Absolutely," Lindsay said.

"The backyard wasn't accessible from the street," Caradine said. "I mean, there was this big, locked fence. And besides, it would have been on fire."

"Then who was closest to the door in that room?" Jonas asked.

"Two people." Lindsay cleared her throat. "Francis, because he liked to stand there so he could watch what I was doing. And then punish me for it later if he felt I was looking at anyone the wrong way. Or not looking at him the right way."

"I hope it's Francis," Koa said softly. "Because I don't think going up in a bomb is enough. Not for him."

"He hated Dad enough," Lindsay said, her gaze bleak. "That was part of why he liked to punish me."

"Who's the other one?" Isaac asked, though he agreed with Koa.

Again, the sisters looked at each other.

"Our brother," Lindsay said after a moment.

"Not Danny, the drug addict," Caradine said, in a way that made it clear this was something they'd discussed before. Or something so obvious they'd never had to discuss it. "Or Patrick, who was always in debt to someone or something, because he liked to gamble."

"It was Jimmy," Lindsay said flatly. "The oldest. And the meanest. And if I had to guess, the only one who was capable of going against Dad like that."

Twenty

"Let's say it is Jimmy," Isaac said, his voice so cold and focused that Caradine almost forgot that they were sitting on a Hawaiian island. "Does he think that you have some kind of information? Does he think that you being alive means that you'll blow his cover? Why would he come after you?"

"Don't be ridiculous." Lindsay laughed a little. "Jimmy was a pig. It would never occur to him in a million years that we could harm him in any way."

Her sister laughed a lot, Caradine thought, and she didn't quite know where to put that. It felt like an indictment of the way that Caradine had spent these past five years. Locked down. Hiding. Pushing anything that felt like a real life away while Lindsay had been out here . . . actually living.

What she couldn't figure out was if she was jealous—or if the very notion scared her half to death.

Or, more likely, both.

"Jimmy once told me that he thought Dad was too

lenient with me," Caradine said, trying to focus on the point instead of all the things she'd lost. Or made herself give up. "If it was up to him, he wanted me to know, he would have nipped my attitude in the bud long before I got so full of myself I actually went to college."

"Was college really such a bad thing?" Koa asked, sounding charmingly baffled. "Isn't it supposed to be a life goal?"

"Only if you believe women get to think for themselves." Caradine arched a brow. "Do you?"

"He'd better." Lindsay grinned at her husband. But her grin faded almost as quickly as it came. "And as I remember it, Jimmy didn't just talk about nipping things in the bud. He was happy to jump in and do it himself."

"The problem with Jimmy was that he was smart." Caradine remembered her oldest brother's mean, dead eyes, so much like their father's, and repressed a shudder. "He could wait. Our other two brothers, and freaking Francis, for that matter, had impulse-control issues. But not Jimmy. He was patient."

"He could hold a grudge forever," Lindsay agreed. "If you said something to him that he didn't like when he was ten, he would hold on to it and make you pay for it when he was thirty. You wouldn't even remember it, but he would. In detail."

"Jimmy was a psychopath," Caradine said flatly. "It makes my stomach hurt to think that he's still alive and coming after us, but if it's a member of our family, it would be him."

"Because he would take it as a personal insult that we dared to live through that explosion and then ran away on top of it." Lindsay made a face. "He never reacted to personal insults very well."

"If he wanted to kill his entire family, why would he care if a couple of them got away?" Blue asked. "Out of sight, out of mind, I would have thought."

"You're not thinking like a raging psychopath, obviously." Caradine settled into her seat. She glanced at her sister, then back at their audience. "If you were, you'd know that it's all about him. He decided to make a power move that he no doubt thought he richly deserved."

"Or he was mad at Dad for whatever reason," Lindsay chimed in. "Maybe Jimmy wanted the business. Maybe he just wanted to kill people. Hard to say."

Caradine nodded. "Obviously, once he made this decision, if his two sisters defied him in any way, they would need to be punished. Severely."

"What about this Francis?" Templeton asked. "We think he's less of a contender?"

Again, Caradine looked at Lindsay and saw the bruises, always on her abdomen and sides so no one could see them. And the fragile way she'd walked sometimes when she'd come in from a "date."

The way she'd stood in that dark street and looked at Caradine so bleakly. *I love that you think it matters what I say.*

"The bottom line is that if either of them are coming after us, it's for the same reason." Luana was babbling, standing between her mother's knees and drumming something on one leg. It seemed to take Lindsay extra time to look up, and when she did, her mouth was a flat line. "If it's Francis, he always thought that I was his property. And he hated Julia."

"I was a bad influence," Caradine agreed, almost cheerfully. Or possibly just manic. "Destined for a bad end."

"Either way, they thought they owned us." Lindsay's laugh was harsh then. "And whatever we like to tell ourselves now, they did."

That sat on Caradine wrong. It made her feel as if the world were spinning too fast. Like she'd had too much to drink and one false move might force her stomach to betray her.

"Well," Templeton said, drawing out one syllable to about three. "Looks like we're going to Boston."

Caradine glanced at her sister. Then looked around at these big, capable men arrayed around them in the shade of the lanai. And she knew the kinds of things that they could do. She'd seen a number of those things with her own eyes. But deep down, she wasn't sure she believed that they or anyone could save her from this.

"Do you really think that you can end this?" Lindsay asked. She was also sizing up the Alaska Force team, but she looked even less convinced than Caradine felt. "You look like you know how to get in a fight, sure. But can you actually end a war?"

"That's what we do," Jonas said quietly, his dark gaze level.

And by now, it was familiar to see the way they sprang into action once a decision was made. Isaac called Oz and put him on speaker. They started talking strategy and possibilities, producing tablets and batting around ideas.

All the while Caradine sat on the couch with her sister and the niece she hadn't known existed, and couldn't tell if the weight that felt trapped inside her chest was joy, a sob, or some heavy combination of both.

"Looks like they think they can do it," Lindsay observed in a low voice, eyeing her husband and the way he'd joined in the conversation. "But don't men always think they can do anything? Despite reality?"

"They have a good record," Caradine said, surprising herself.

"How did you end up tangled up with a militia? Or are they mercenaries?"

"Neither. They're actually good men." She caught her sister's sideways glance. "I know. Believe me, I know. But they are."

They both sat there a moment, listening to the two-year-old babble mostly incoherent words. As if she were singing herself the kind of song neither one of them would have dared sing in their silent, scared house growing up.

"I might look like Mom these days," Lindsay said in a low voice, her gaze on her daughter. "But I'm no martyr. And there's no way in hell I would sit by and watch someone brutalize my kids the way she did. I can't even get my head around it."

Caradine looked at the little girl, her own heart jarring unpleasantly in her chest. "No. I don't have to be a mother myself to feel the same way."

"Most days I forget," Lindsay said softly. "I live my life in one of the most beautiful places on earth. We don't have a lot, but we own everything we do have. And Koa's family is wonderful. They actually love each other, if you can imagine such a thing. That isn't to say they don't fight, but it's different. They don't . . ."

Caradine thought of that scene in the lodge, with all those people determined to learn the truth and love her anyway. Or before that, even, in Isaac's cabin. With the hugging.

Family, whether she liked it or not.

"They don't want to hurt each other," Caradine finished for her sister. "They disagree, but they don't try to take each other out when they do. I don't really understand it, either."

Lindsay looked at her a moment, then cut her gaze to Isaac. "You and him? Do you have . . . ?"

"We don't have—" But Caradine stopped herself. "I have a family," she said to her sister, and she felt a kind of riot inside. She couldn't tell if she wanted to rip her tongue out of her mouth, or give in to that sob, or maybe it was all joy, all along. Maybe she was still too unfamiliar with it to recognize it. She had to cough before it got too intense. "I have a kind of family, and yes, he's part of it."

And then, unsurprisingly, she wanted to die.

Lindsay's eyes got too bright, and Caradine was terribly afraid that hers did, too.

"So you know how it is," Lindsay said, though her

voice was now a whisper. "Some days you just forget. And then something happens and you're forced to remember, and that's worse. Because we're not safe. We'll never be safe. And I can run forever. If I had to, I could pick up and leave right now. But I don't want that for Luana. And if they find her—"

"They won't." Caradine knew that coughing wouldn't help the lump in her throat then. "*They won't*. No matter who's doing this, I can't think of anyone better to stop them than these men. I promise."

And she was surprised when her sister reached over and put a hand on her leg, because that wasn't like them. But then, Who were they now? Who knew what was *like them* after all this time?

Lindsay wasn't a princess anymore. Caradine wasn't a problem. Maybe they blamed each other, but they'd also always trusted each other more than anyone else, growing up. And their own family had always been treacherous and violent and sad, but they'd gone ahead and built new ones, anyway.

It felt simultaneously like some kind of betrayal and some kind of surrender to accept that she'd gone ahead and done exactly that in Alaska.

Built a life. Built a family. Built a place to live, and then lived there.

Despite her best efforts, she'd really *lived* there.

Deep inside, something shifted inside her. Something she was terribly afraid might be hope, or its untrustworthy companion, *what if*.

What if they really could stop this? *What if* she was finally free?

"Julia," Lindsay said then, fiercely, if quietly. "If they're good men, that might mean that when it comes to it, they'll make good choices. Proper choices. The way good people who believe in things do. Because good people don't know what to fear. Not like we do."

Caradine looked down at her sister's hand on her leg.

And had an almost overwhelming urge to cover it with her own. She didn't. She was still herself, after all.

Even if her heart felt like someone else's today. Someone softer. More sentimental.

Julia's heart, maybe.

And the truth was, Caradine kind of liked knowing that it was still in there. Still beating, still hoping, still what-iffing. After all this time.

"I can't leave Hawaii." Lindsay's gaze matched her voice, intense and serious. "Or I should say, I won't. Because I would go and do whatever had to be done if I could. But there's Luana, and she deserves better than this. Doesn't she?"

And Caradine knew what her sister was asking of her. She raised her gaze to Lindsay's, and for a moment, they just looked at each other, the way they had that night ten years ago. The way they had after Phoenix.

All that panic and terror. The bleakness. The rage. Their own kind of love mixed up in all of that, sure, dark and strained by the blood they carried in their veins. The bruises that would never heal. The running that never took them far enough away. The fear that they were just as bad as what they were hiding from.

And beneath it all, what had to happen next.

Caradine smiled. "It's so sad you died out there on the run."

"Not really that sad." Lindsay smiled back. "I was always the weak link."

"Less mouthy, anyway."

"Probably had it coming."

"You know you did." Caradine nodded once, sealing the vow. "I doubt anyone even misses you."

"Thank you," Lindsay whispered.

The day was spent in negotiations and planning. Caradine and Lindsay caught up, haltingly at first, but then with more deep, helpless laughter over the things only they found funny.

Then, as evening approached, it all turned into some-thing far more relaxed than a strategy session.

"This is Hawaii," Lindsay said, smiling, when Koa's family turned up. "You should have at least one night that's nothing more than that."

Koa's family had come prepared to get their barbecue on. If Caradine pretended not to notice the ex–special forces military men looming around, she might have been tempted to imagine it really was just a family gath-ering on a lovely Hawaiian evening.

A little slice of heaven in the middle of the thick, green jungle, with the tropical sky above and the sea in the distance. So far away from her memories of Boston—and her life in Alaska, which didn't involve all the soft, close, perfumed air that she'd gotten used to over the course of the day—it might as well have been a different world.

The different world she knew better than to let herself imagine. Even if that ribbon of hope deep inside her seemed to shimmer every time she breathed.

"Walk with me," Isaac said, appearing out of nowhere behind her, out in the yard. Caradine had been leaning against the SUV and staring up at the changing colors of the sky and the clouds that looked like sails.

"I'm not sure that I want to walk with you," Caradine replied.

It was Hawaii. Her sister was here, she had a niece, and tonight, everything felt okay in a way it never had. Tonight she was entertaining what-ifs without beating herself up for it. Maybe that was why she smiled at him. As if they were different people. "We're on a tropical island, Isaac. Surely you can come up with something more entertaining to do than *walk*."

His gray eyes warmed, and she did, too.

One of Koa's uncles was strumming a ukulele, an in-strument Caradine had always thought was a joke until she'd heard him sing and play. People had big plates of food, and they were talking. Laughing.

And even though most of the people here were dressed in summer clothes, or board shorts, or the colorful dresses that made sense here, somehow, it almost felt like one of Grizzly Harbor's festivals. The festivals were when everyone in town poured out into the streets, and no matter the temperature or the time of year, life felt bright for a while.

She didn't know what would happen in Boston. But one way or another, it would be over. And if she survived it, there were what-ifs on the other side.

For the first time in a long time, Caradine felt bright all the way through.

Maybe that was why, when Isaac reached out and took his life in his hands by lacing his fingers with hers, she let him. She didn't jerk away. She didn't even scowl. She curled her fingers around his and held on.

And for a moment, they were the only two people in the world.

She could feel the heat of him, and the sizzle from that same electric current that always flared between them. She felt as if she were free-falling from a great height, when she knew full well her feet were on the ground.

For once, she didn't pretend otherwise. She didn't want to analyze it. She *felt* it, from the lump in her throat to the tightness in her chest. It all seemed to swirl around inside her, then bloom into the molten heat between her legs.

When he tugged her hand, leading her away from the gathering, she went with him.

She would normally demand to know where they were going. What he wanted, and what he thought he was *doing*.

But not tonight. Tonight she followed him, as the sky

above them began to ready itself for sunset in lush shades of pink and orange.

He led her away from the house and into the waiting jungle. He found a path through the trees and followed it as it cut lazily down the side of a hill. The ground beneath their feet smelled rich and damp. Birds sang to one another. And the sky she could see through the jungle canopy only seemed brighter.

And then he ushered her out of the jungle and into a tiny little slice of paradise.

Caradine heard it before she saw it, but when she could finally see where he was taking her, she actually gasped.

A waterfall tumbled from above, cascading down the green, rocky hillside to collect into a pool at its base. The water splashed over the ledge that marked the boundaries of the pool and continued down the side of the mountain.

"I know you like your hot springs," Isaac said, his voice gruff. "I figured you might like this."

"That's a secret," she replied.

She didn't have to look at him to feel the impact of his gray gaze. "Maybe it's time to let go of secrets."

Caradine wasn't ready to let go of her remaining secrets or his hand, so she clenched his fingers a little bit tighter. She stared at the water tumbling down, the pool at its base, and then the stunning, impossible view. Far below, the Pacific Ocean stretched out to forever, and maybe beyond.

It was one of the most beautiful places she'd ever seen, but the man beside her was more beautiful still.

And her heart. Her poor heart.

Maybe, a voice in her suggested, *it isn't Julia's heart you have to worry about.*

"When I was a little girl," she said quietly, lost somewhere in the tumbling water and the waiting sea, "we sometimes went away in the summers. There were probably business reasons my father took us to the Hamptons, but all I cared about was the beach. I would play in the waves until my eyes stung from the salt, and there was sand everywhere. And sometimes I would swim out beyond the breakers and float there. And later, when there were no more beach vacations, and everything was tense and grim, I would remember floating like that." She looked up at him and wasn't surprised to find him looking at her with that unguarded heat on his face. "Held by the sea, staring at the sky. And the only other place I've ever felt like that was the hot springs in Grizzly Harbor."

"Caradine," Isaac said, his voice and his expression grave. "What were you and your sister whispering about on the couch? What are you planning?"

She laughed at that, though tears pricked behind her eyes, and she wasn't entirely sure that was really a laugh. How could she tell the difference any longer? She picked up the hand laced with hers and brought it to her mouth, kissing those tough, strong knuckles of his.

There was nothing to say to this man. There never had been. Because there was too much to say and no way to start. She'd never stop.

So she didn't speak. She dropped his hand, and then, holding his gaze, she began to take off her clothes. She kicked off her shoes and peeled off her socks. The volcanic rock that looked smooth and soft to the touch, but was so hard she was surprised it didn't cut her, reminded her who she was. Why she was here.

What she had to do.

She pulled off her shirt and the sports bra she wore because a girl never knew when she might have to run for her life.

Isaac's gaze went silver, then brighter still. She saw his chest move as though he were breathing hard as she tossed the sports bra aside.

But that was nothing compared to the way his face

changed when she unsnapped her pants and shoved them down over her hips.

"Caradine—" He shook his head. "You can't distract me."

She smiled at him then. Not a smirk. Not a scowl. Just . . . her smile.

She didn't actually *say,* Watch me.

Because he did. He always did.

She got rid of her pants, kicked off her panties, and then, still smiling, headed for the pool and eased her way in. The water was cooler than the air, but it still felt more like a hug than anything else.

She didn't look behind her.

She moved to the center of the pool, feeling the water beneath her palms as she eased her way over the rocks beneath her feet. When the water was up past her waist she sank down, submerging herself completely.

And when she came up out of the water, he was there.

"You drive me crazy," Isaac said against her mouth as he swept her up into his arms.

Her smile widened, there against his mouth, as she wrapped her legs around his waist. "I know."

And she spent the time they had left proving it, again and again, as if they were the reason the sun lit up the sky with so many bright, wild colors as it put itself to bed and ushered them into the dark.

Twenty-one

It was an overcast summer day in Boston, humid and occasionally rainy.

They had left Maui around ten o'clock island time so they could arrive here midday. And Isaac expected Caradine to be on edge. The way she had been in Maine. After all, they were closing a very long circle. Instead, she was disconcertingly calm.

Which meant Isaac was on edge instead.

They'd gone over various schematics and had plotted out different strategies during the flight, but the only sure information they had to go on was the call Caradine had made to Sharkey's from that bed-and-breakfast in Maine.

And, once again, though Isaac would have preferred not to involve Caradine in this directly, he had no choice.

"Go over the plan with me one more time," he ordered her now.

They were sitting in the front seat of yet another interchangeable SUV that had been waiting per his orders when they'd landed. Caradine looked serene, which had alarms going off in him like air raid sirens.

She even smiled at him. Almost. "We literally discussed the plan for eight hours straight on a small plane. In exhaustive and exhausting detail."

"Walk me through it anyway."

She let out a long-suffering sigh and shifted around in the seat so she could look at him straight on.

"Are you nervous, Gentry?" she asked.

He had parked a few blocks down from the bar in question in a busy section of a street where no one was likely to notice an idling vehicle. Everyone else was already in place. Jonas and Templeton were inside the bar already. Blue was on the roof across the street. Isaac would take command, but that didn't make him any happier about the fact that he had to use Caradine as bait.

Anyone could wander in and say that they were Julia Sheeran, Caradine had pointed out on the plane.

If anyone can pretend to be you, then why should you go in at all? Isaac had retorted. *We can send a decoy.*

Because I look like my dad, Caradine had replied, with a matter-of-factness that made Isaac's jaw hurt. *He lives on forever in my face. And I have to live with that in the mirror every day, but in this case, why not use it?*

He didn't like it. He more than didn't like it.

"This is not a scenario in which you're bait in a trap," he said now. "I want to make sure you're clear on that."

"So your answer is yes, you're riddled with anxiety."

"You're wired. Templeton and Jonas are already in the bar, blending in."

"I find that very difficult to believe." She smirked when he glared at her. "What? They don't blend. Anywhere."

"You might find yourself surprised."

Because the truth was, all three of them had made a career out of blending in. They could disappear while they were standing right in front of someone, if necessary. But this was no time to get into the kind of work he, Templeton, and Jonas had done—and continued to do in missions like this.

Not when she was the one at risk.

"You're going to go into the bar and do your thing," Isaac said tersely. "No editorializing. Just stick to the script we agreed on and everything will be fine."

She gazed at him for a moment, something almost rueful on her face. It was making his neck itch. He would have expected her to be extra cutting at a time like this. Sharp, furious. The Caradine he knew best.

This version of Caradine he didn't recognize, and while he might have liked to imagine it was because of what had happened between them at that waterfall, or even her reunion with her sister, that didn't quite land. He didn't believe it.

Because he'd been watching her whisper with her sister over on the couch while the rest of them had been talking with Oz about how to track people who were supposedly already dead. He'd seen the grave looks on both their faces. And more tellingly, given the Sheeran sisters, the fact that there had been touching.

"What is it you're not telling me?" he asked.

"I go out of my way to tell you as little as possible," she replied, with that curve to her mouth that would normally turn into a full-blown smirk. But not today. "You know this."

"You're running out of secrets, baby," he said.

And his heart lurched in his chest when instead of smirking at him, razor-sharp as usual, she smiled.

An honest-to-goodness smile. Much brighter than the one she'd aimed at him on the island last night, which he'd chalked up to a family reunion and a tropical sunset.

This smile was on a South Boston street where gentrification was slowly taking over, pushing out the seedy liquor stores, check-cashing places, and occasional strips of boarded-up buildings in favor of swanky condo developments. There were threatening clouds overhead and set-faced strangers trudging from the nearby T stop.

He'd always thought he wanted her to smile at him like this.

"You were right," she said, alarming him even more.

"Have you ever actually uttered that sentence before?"

Her smile widened. "You told me a while ago that I walked into the Fairweather expecting a good time, but not being at all prepared for you. And you were right. It never occurred to me that I would find any of this. I didn't know what to do with it then. I still don't."

Isaac tried to keep his cool, but he couldn't. He scowled at her. "Is this your good-bye speech?"

Another smile. Damn her. "Isaac. I want you to know—"

His hand shot out before he could communicate that intention to the rest of his body. He gripped her behind the neck and pulled her close. "If you say one more terrifyingly nice thing to me, Caradine, I'm going to lose it."

And it was better when that smile faded. When her typical scowl replaced it. He felt actual relief.

"I'm trying to say that I appreciate—"

"I will lose it." His jaw was so tight he was surprised he could form words. "And when I do, I can't promise I won't take it out on you in ways I doubt very much you will enjoy."

Her scowl deepened and that was better, too. Not that it solved his problem here, but it helped. It was better than Caradine being *nice*.

"It might be time for you to pay some attention to your parade of psychological problems, Isaac."

"Do not make speeches before you go into battle," he growled, right against her mouth. "They become self-fulfilling prophecies. I don't want your good-byes, Caradine. I never did."

And he wanted to kiss her, but he didn't. Because kissing clouded his judgment. Obviously. He thrust her away from him instead. Then they were in their respective seats, staring at each other while they both breathed too heavily.

"You go into the bar," he said, more darkly this time. "You do your thing. Are we in agreement on what that thing is?"

"A very long parade of very severe psychological problems. You may have to surrender your numerous arsenals for public-safety reasons."

"I'll take that as a yes. You shake the tree, that's all. We'll be there to handle what comes loose. Do you have any questions?"

Another smile, but this one was acidic. Be still his heart. "Only one. Do you see a fully licensed psychiatrist? It might be time to consider having one on staff."

"Okay," he muttered. "We're done here."

He switched on his comm unit, made sure her wire was operational, and then checked in over his car speakers while he made sure her wire lay flat along her spine. His preferred place to tape one on, because everyone had seen too many movies and looked at the chest.

"Report," he bit out.

"In position," Blue said at once. "I'm on the roof across the street with eyes on the front door. And halfway down the alley next to it."

"I'll take the back," Isaac confirmed.

"The thing of it is," Jonas said, sounding garrulous and drunk, "you have to think about *offense*, my man."

Isaac flicked a look over to Caradine, who was staring at the car radio as if it had sprouted tentacles.

"We're going in," Isaac said, and switched off his comm unit.

"Was that Jonas?" Caradine asked.

Isaac didn't touch her. He didn't yell at her about the things she wasn't telling him, because he didn't yell. And she wouldn't tell him anyway.

"One of Jonas's best characters is a drunken sports fan," he said instead. "Nobody pays any attention to a drunken sports fan. He can be in any bar at any time, ranting and belligerent, and when he leaves people will describe his team spirit, never him."

Caradine shifted against her seat, probably because her wire was making her back itchy and not because she felt anything. No matter what he might have preferred. "I had no idea Jonas could string that many words together."

"He sings, too," Isaac informed her as he put the SUV into gear. "With perfect pitch or egregiously off-key, depending on the situation."

He let her sit with that visual as he drove through the streets of South Boston and acknowledged that he was pissed at her. Pissed, but also still fighting those persistent alarms inside him. The ones that had saved his life more times than he could count.

What worried him was that he couldn't tell the difference today. Were they personal? Or did they have to do with this particular mission?

This was why he had never let anything get personal before.

He pulled over again a couple of blocks away from Sharkey's, where they'd all agreed Caradine would get out and walk.

"Caradine—"

Her eye roll was more implied than actual, but it still packed a punch. "Don't you dare say anything *nice* to me. The world could end."

"I haven't forgotten," he told her, pinning her there for a moment with his gaze alone. "You and I are overdue for a discussion about our lives."

Once again, there was that flash of something on her face that he really didn't like. "Can't wait."

In her usual, snarky, *I would rather die* tone, which should have comforted him. But it didn't. Not today.

Then she swung out of the car, slammed the door, and walked off.

She didn't look back.

Isaac found himself rubbing at his chest as if he could calm those alarms still kicking up a fuss inside him.

He tried to tell himself it was anticipation, the way it usually was as a mission commenced. But he couldn't fool himself.

"She's walking," he said into the comm unit.

Isaac watched Caradine walk down one block, then into the next. He would know her walk anywhere. No matter what name she used. Or how she colored her hair. He would know that lazy amble that hinted at the toughness underneath. The long, muscled legs that had been wrapped around his waist last night. And the way she tipped her chin up as she walked, daring the people passing by to look at her.

Some did. Some didn't. But Isaac confirmed that he was the only one on the street who didn't look away.

Inside the bar, Jonas was drunkenly overexplaining the intricacies of football in a belligerent tone, growing ever more agitated. Isaac had seen this show before. Jonas, usually so still and watchful, vibrated with wild, erratic gestures, and he never stood still. He rocked this way and that, as if at any moment he might tip himself off his feet altogether.

People who'd stood next to him in his drunken state usually failed to recognize him when he came around later, no longer in character, and asked them questions about what had occurred in his usual stark, cold way.

"I have eyes on the prize," Blue said. "She'll be at the door in approximately two minutes."

Templeton laughed uproariously, which was his affirmative.

"Moving into position," Isaac replied.

He pulled away from the curb, headed around to the back of the bar. Despite the flashes of gentrification he'd seen during their initial canvas, this particular block might as well have been stuck in the '70s. This was a stretch of chain-link fences and cracked sidewalks, not a place where tourists came to wax rhapsodic about the rich tapestry of American history. There were the typical Beantown bricks here, too, but they were old and weathered and crumbling in places. No one had bothered to restore them.

Sharkey's stood like a beacon to a very specific Southie past. Back when this neighborhood had been nothing but working-class Irish Catholics and the people who preyed upon them. The myth of Sharkey's was that it was a safe space for Boston's tough guys to interact, though the truth had usually been far more bloody.

Isaac had studied city-planning drawings of the bar itself and knew its layout backward and forward. Thanks to several stings over the years, and Oz's ability to help himself to all kinds of files that shouldn't have been accessible, he even knew a great many of the regulars without having to set foot inside. The current owner was an innocuous man called Peter Mullen, who was almost certainly a front. Or a patsy.

When Caradine had done no more than call this place, there'd been a thug tailing her within hours. Now she was walking inside and announcing her true identity.

His gut didn't like any part of this. If he'd had all these alarms going off in him at any other time, Isaac would have called a stop to this op before it started.

But for the first time in as long as he could remember, he wasn't certain about what call to make here. He honestly couldn't tell if it was emotion or experience that was causing the commotion inside him.

He figured he could blame her for that, too. And would, once they survived this.

"She's walking through the door," Blue reported.

Isaac found his vantage spot exactly where he'd expected it, again thanks to Oz's preliminary work from Fool's Cove. He pulled the SUV in behind a Dumpster and left the engine running. He switched the comm unit from the car speakers to his headset and then held his phone up to his ear in case anyone happened by. Since a dodgy alley behind a notorious bar was really not the place a random, well-intentioned person was likely to sit around in for the hell of it, he should probably look like he had a reason to have pulled over here.

He didn't hold his breath, because he was a freaking professional, but part of him expected something terrible to happen. Right now. Caradine to disappear, maybe, somewhere between the street and the door to the bar.

Jonas was halfway through a dissertation on the Patriots, slurring wildly.

"She's in," Templeton said in a low voice.

Isaac knew he would have done that while lifting his drink to his mouth. If anyone was watching him, it would look like he was muttering at his drunk friend.

"Hi there," Caradine said brightly into her own mic, and everything in Isaac tensed further. Because she sounded different again. Not as edgy. As if she were trying to sound brave when she wasn't. *Julia*, something in him whispered. She was trying to sound like Julia. "I'm hoping you can help me."

"I think you walked in the wrong bar, girl," came a thick, rough, unfriendly voice that sounded like too many cigarettes and the worst of South Boston. "I was you, I'd walk back out."

"This is definitely the right bar," she replied, sounding wholly unfazed. And Isaac could almost see the way he knew she would be standing. Her hands on her hips, her head tilted to the angle that made her look the most unbothered, her blue eyes bright with amusement. "I'm Julia Sheeran. And I have a message for whoever came after my father in Maine a couple of weeks ago."

There was a snort. "Do I look like your voice mail?"

"Maybe you've heard of my father," she said brightly. "Mickey Sheeran."

"I heard of Mickey Sheeran," the bartender replied. He coughed. "Mostly I heard that he was dead."

"I was dead, too," Caradine said. "But look at that. Here I am anyway."

"Are you going to buy a drink or not?" came the belligerent response.

Caradine ordered whiskey. Neat.

And they waited.

Templeton muttered updates. Jonas moved on from football to baseball. Blue told stories purely to irritate the rest of the team—like the time Templeton had gone to rescue Kate and she'd announced, very audibly over his comm unit, that she'd had to rescue herself *again*— and Caradine sat at the bar.

No one came near her.

After a while, the bartender pulled out his phone and typed into it.

Everyone got ready, assuming whatever text he'd sent would bring the people they were waiting for into play. But nothing happened.

And Isaac, who had made stillness an art form and himself a master, found it almost impossible to keep his agitation at bay.

Jonas was soundly abusing the Yankees, and anyone listening to him would have been surprised to learn that when in New York, he could be just as comprehensively insulting about the Red Sox. Templeton was joining in now and again, mostly to laugh and plant a few seeds about how maybe the two of them were construction workers.

Blue was making note of any cars that slowed down out front.

Isaac was going slowly insane.

"She's hitting the head," Templeton reported in a mutter.

And the agitation inside Isaac—all those alarms and gut-level warnings—exploded.

He thought about Caradine, who had trained herself to climb out of a second-story window in Grizzly Harbor, steal a boat, and change her appearance to get out of Alaska. Caradine, who carried three tiers of weapons on her at all times.

Would she really wander off in the middle of this thing to use the bathroom?

He heard an odd, scraping sound.

It all flashed through him then. The schematics of the bar he'd studied. This was Boston, an old, historic city, where history asserted itself by building on top of what had come before. Especially in this part of town, where no one was overly concerned with the historic register, because it usually had something to do with Old World criminal organizations.

He thought of that look on her face from the passenger seat, the speech she'd tried to make.

And he knew.

"She's not going to the bathroom," he bit out. "She's making a move."

But he was already out of the SUV. At a dead run toward the back door no one had tried to go in or out of. No one would, he understood then.

If this was happening, it wasn't happening here. Not as planned.

Four flat-out seconds later he threw open the back door to Sharkey's and found himself in a small, shabby hallway that smelled like stale cigarettes and old beer. He scanned it, finding two empty bathrooms, one utility closet, and two locked reinforced steel doors that didn't budge when he tried them.

The only other thing in the hallway, tossed to one side, was the wire he'd carefully attached to Caradine's back.

The one he'd heard her scrape off her back only seconds ago.

"There's no one outside," Blue reported, his voice terse. "No one's gone in or out in over fifteen minutes. There are minimal pedestrians, and cars haven't even slowed down out front."

"Put the bar on lockdown," Isaac gritted out.

In the hall, he bent and picked up the wire with the tape still attached. He could see the plans Oz had sent them in his head. More than that, he could see Caradine on the plane next to him, pointing at the buildings across the street and across the alley. He could hear her talking about that long two-block walk she would have to take, and what if there were spies in all the windows?

She'd been diverting his attention.

Something he should have recognized, but she'd planned for that, hadn't she? She'd softened him up at that waterfall.

Deliberately.

And he'd fallen for it. Hook, line, and sinker.

The way he always did with her. Only with her.

The comm unit was quiet. Jonas had stopped performing, and the profound silence suggested that he and Templeton had already completed their task. There were two of them, after all—meaning it wasn't a fair fight for the rest of the patrons. Anyone who tried to go against them would find that out, and fast.

"There's nothing written on her napkin," Templeton said over the comm unit, but in his normal speaking voice. Confirming that he and Jonas had silently taken control of Sharkey's. "There is, however, the impression of a key."

Isaac shoved the wire in his pocket, then pushed into the main part of the bar. He took in the situation with a glance. Jonas stood near the front door, still and deadly again. He had a gun in his hand, though it pointed down to the floor. The three regulars Templeton had counted earlier were lying down on the ground, faces pressed against the sticky floor. They weren't even grumbling, suggesting that any tough-guy fronting had already been dealt with.

Brutally.

Templeton stood behind the bar. The bartender stood in front of him, with his hands resting on the top of his head. The 9 mm on the sticky, scarred wood in front of them wasn't Templeton's, indicating that he'd relieved the bartender of it.

Painfully, Isaac hoped.

"Where did she go?" Isaac asked the bartender softly.

Very, very softly.

The bartender bared his teeth. "Wouldn't you like to know?"

Templeton laughed in that booming, unsettling way of his. "Oh, buddy. You're reading this situation the wrong way."

"Who did he text?" Isaac asked.

Templeton tossed the bartender's phone onto the bar, letting it clatter as it slid, then stop in a puddle. "A number. No name. All it says is, *Package in the hall.*"

Isaac got good and still.

She'd been saying good-bye to him. She'd known exactly what was going to happen, set it up, and she'd been trying to clear her slate before she did it.

Caradine had played him. Deliberately.

He was going to find her, save her if necessary, and then kill her himself.

But right now he concentrated on the smirking bartender with every bit of temper and adrenaline inside him.

"You're making a mistake," the bartender snarled.

"Good," Isaac told the man, doing absolutely nothing to contain the rage inside of him. He didn't even keep it out of his voice, and he ignored Templeton's startled look. "Then let's make sure it's a big one."

Twenty-two

The last time Caradine had been in these tunnels she'd been about twenty. She and Lindsay had been sent here by their mother on a summer's night because their brother Danny had needed collecting. Again. He'd been passed out after a spot of belligerence, embarrassing the family the way he always did.

You don't want your father having to deal with him, their mother had said sharply when they'd been slow to get up from the television to do her bidding. *Or your brother Jimmy.*

That had been back in the days when her mother had still believed that Danny could be saved.

Or maybe not, Caradine reflected as she made it to the bottom of the stairs that led down to the cellar. She heard a slam from up above and winced, certain she knew exactly who that was. Isaac, slamming his way into the building. She pushed on, moving more quickly than she might have otherwise down the dim hallway that opened up in front of her.

And as she moved, she thought about her mother and that long-ago night. Maybe Donna hadn't thought she could save anyone. Maybe she'd used Danny as a way to poke at her husband—not wanting to save him so much as wanting to keep Mickey from handling him the way he liked.

Either way, Caradine and Lindsay had been met at the back door by the usual flat-eyed goon, shoved roughly down these same stairs, and told to drag their wasted brother out to the car they'd parked on the next block before someone took him out with the trash.

For good, was the implication.

Neither one of them had wanted that on their conscience, no matter how unpleasant Danny was when he'd gotten himself into this state.

The place still smelled the same. It was dank and shadowy. There was the scent of decay in the air and the creepy echoing sound of leaking pipes.

It was easier to walk down this hall—this narrow tunnel—without dragging the dead weight of a fully grown man between her and her frail sister, but that didn't make what Caradine was doing any easier.

There was not one part of her that wanted to do this. She preferred Isaac's plan to this, a thousand times over.

But this time she intended to keep the promise she'd made to her sister. Not the old promise, but the new one. That Lindsay had died out there on the run. That she was out of this, no matter what.

She wanted to make it clear to whomever waited for her that she was the only survivor of that bomb ten years ago. So no one would bother looking for anyone else.

And if no one was looking for Lindsay, no one here would discover Luana's existence. Ever.

She wanted to run again. She'd trained to defend herself when attacked, not throw herself into a fight she might not win. She wanted to find a way out of this—or a way out of Boston again. She could turn beige before she got west of Worcester, then disappear for good.

But she kept going, because she was done running. There was more to think about here than her feelings. Or her panic. Or what she might lose.

And besides, she knew—she hoped—she only had limited time. If she knew anything about Isaac, it was that he'd come after her. And soon.

She had work to do first.

It was a long walk even without dragging Danny, who had stunk of booze and uglier things and had kept insisting he was fine and should be left alone. The walls were uneven and too close. Nothing smelled good or clean.

Caradine didn't really want to think about all the terrible things that had happened down here over the years. The things her father and men like him had done here. The deals they'd cut, the betrayals they'd enacted, the revenges they'd indulged. She was afraid that if she breathed in too deep, she would get all that violence, all that despair, into her own lungs. Like some kind of tuberculosis.

She couldn't afford to get sick.

But who was she kidding? She already had all that mess in her blood. She couldn't outsmart her own genes. Or outrun them, either. God knew, she'd tried, and here she was again. Not just in Boston but *underneath* it. Walking toward the destiny she'd escaped a decade ago.

Maybe the lesson here was, there was no escaping. Not really.

Escaping would have meant living a real life. Not hiding, walling herself off, pretending not to connect with anyone or anything. . . .

She tried to shake that off. It was too late now.

Eventually she came to the door on the far end of the subterranean hall that crossed the main street Sharkey's sat on and veered south, taking her down to the corner she'd crossed aboveground. She paused there, refusing to let herself shake.

She could be still. She could breathe. She could make herself do it.

Caradine had watched Isaac and the rest of them turn to stone at will, though as she tried it now, she quickly realized it was another thing they must have trained hard to do. Because every part of her felt alive and electric and buzzing with what she was choosing to call *anticipation*.

Not panic. Not terror.

She put her hand on the door and tried to prepare herself.

Because she still didn't know who she expected to see on the other side. Nasty, vicious Francis, who would probably have become far worse than her father if he'd had the time? Or a member of her own family—her own blood—who had always been pretty horrible on his own?

Nothing can possibly be worse than drawing this out any longer, she snapped at herself. *You need to get out there and do what you came here to do.*

One way or another.

Because she might have a new family in Alaska, but she needed to do what she could to protect the only part of her real family she had left.

I would go and do whatever had to be done if I could, Lindsay had said in Hawaii. *But there's Luana.*

And Luana deserved to be free of the Sheeran family in a way Caradine and Lindsay never had been.

But when Caradine cracked open the door and stuck her head through, there was nothing but another basement. There were boxes piled against one wall and enough dust in the corners to make her nose tickle, but mostly there was nothing but a latticework of pipes above and a concrete floor below.

And the clatter of her own heart, thick and hard, in places like her thumbs. Her ears. Her throat.

She wiped her suddenly damp palms against her thighs and kept walking, crossing the room and skirting the ominous drain in the middle of it. She made it to the other side and opened another door to find herself in a stairwell. She vaguely remembered it, mostly because Danny had been so boneless. And obnoxious. Calling her and Lindsay names as they'd tried to rouse him enough to help them get him up the stairs.

It had never occurred to her then that she might look back on another dark and squalid Sheeran family night as if it had been innocent. Fun, almost. But compared to her other family memories, dragging her wasted brother around with Lindsay felt like a happy, bonding, nostalgic experience.

Something worth laughing about on a porch in Hawaii.

Caradine really, really wanted to get back to that porch someday.

She walked quietly and carefully up the stairs to the first floor and tested the reinforced steel door she found there. The handle moved when she tried it, so she pulled it open—

And then everything happened too fast.

There was a hand on her throat, and it hurt. But even as she processed that she was hauled forward, then slammed back against the wall so hard she lost what little breath she had left. Especially with her feet just off the ground, letting gravity do the work of choking her out.

Caradine knew what to do. She knew how to fight choke holds. She'd worked on this with Everly, Mariah, and others in Grizzly Harbor. Blue had taught them how to duck their chins and raise their hands, and she did both now. But she didn't let herself enact the rest of her actual training because she didn't want to show her hand.

Even when the hand at her throat tightened.

She couldn't help but move her chin a little more then,

and tug with her hands to free up her airway. She tried to focus on the man before her.

And for a long moment, she stared at him while he sneered. While her vision narrowed.

But no matter how much or how hard she stared, despite losing her air, she couldn't make the face in front of her make any sense. It wasn't Francis. It wasn't Jimmy. It wasn't anyone she knew.

"Who are you?" she managed to wheeze out.

The hand around her neck loosened slightly. Caradine could already feel where the bruises would come in, but she told herself getting to worry about bruises was winning. The alternative was death.

But he didn't tighten his grip again. He lowered her instead. Her toes found the ground, and that was better.

It was even better when he took his hand off her throat.

And watched, his eyes glittering, while she coughed and fought to breathe freely.

Caradine wiped the moisture from her eyes, swallowed a few times and ignored how raw her throat felt, then straightened.

He was still sneering.

"You should've stayed out there in the middle of nowhere, Julia." His voice was half a sneer, half a growl. It shocked her. "You should never have come back home."

The shock reverberated through her as she took him in, this man with a stranger's face. A different nose. A different chin. A shiny bald head.

At a glance she would have sworn she didn't know him.

But she did.

Those terrible, dead eyes alight with a certain malicious satisfaction. The middle-aged paunch he hadn't had ten years ago, but reminded her a little too strongly of another ghost. And that telltale red roll on the back of his neck that she'd spent far too much time staring at in places like the parish church.

She bet if she lifted his handprint from her face, she'd recognize that, too.

"It's nice to see you, too," she said, though her mouth felt swollen and talking hurt. "You look a little bit different, Jimmy."

Far behind her brother with his new face, two other men in ominous suits stood near a set of glass doors that Caradine knew led out to the street. It couldn't have been more than ten yards, but it might as well have been ten thousand miles. She had a sudden, irresistible image of herself running for it, crashing through the glass, rolling out into the street . . .

But that wouldn't do much besides hurt her.

Ten years ago this had been the lobby of a down-market office building that opened up into a dead-end alley, not a main street. It looked even shabbier than she remembered, which suggested it was unlikely any offices would empty out and accidentally help her. And there would be no one out in that alleyway. No pedestrians cutting through to get somewhere else.

No one and nothing but her, which was what she'd planned.

But that didn't make it feel any better now that it was happening.

"I haven't heard that name in a long time," her brother said, and it was weird and creepy to hear his voice come out of the wrong face. Like a horrific puppet show.

Caradine had always hated puppet shows.

"I don't want to hear it again," Jimmy warned her. "Jimmy Sheeran died with the rest of his family, including you, ten years ago. Best you let him lie." He smirked. "Caradine."

She wanted to claw that name out of his mouth. Instead, she concentrated on the pain in her face and kept herself from reacting.

It helped that he clearly wanted her reaction.

"What name do you use these days?" she asked him, as if he hadn't threatened her.

"Brian," he said, with that malicious edge to his voice that made everything inside her curdle. "Brian Jones."

"How creative," she said, and got another smack for it.

This time she tasted copper, but she was glad. It helped her focus.

"There are supposed to be two of you," Jimmy said. "You think I don't know you've been traveling together?"

"Lindsay's dead," Caradine said flatly.

Because that was the most important part of this. That was the gift she could give her sister, and it was why she'd left Alaska Force behind, because she knew Isaac would never have okayed this. And no matter what else happened, if Jimmy believed Lindsay was dead, he would stop looking for her. Luana would be safe. This madness would stop here.

Caradine was not her mother. She had no intention of sacrificing herself needlessly the way Donna had always liked to do. But if it had to happen, this was as good a reason as she could come up with.

A thought that made her stomach cramp, but she ignored it.

"Bullshit," Jimmy snarled.

Caradine glared at him. "What's the matter? You don't think bad things can happen unless you do them yourself?"

She'd expected him to hit her again, but it still hurt. A hit was a hit. The force of it took her by surprise, but she rolled with it as best she could. She let the tears spring into her eyes, and did nothing to wipe them away when she looked back at him.

"Lindsay picked up some bad habits over the past ten years," she said, and let the tears spill over. "It was horrible. She kept saying she would quit, but she never did."

She'd spent a lot of time on the plane ride crafting the appropriate death for Lindsay. She figured linking it to Phoenix was her best bet. Whoever was responsible for what had happened there would have known that the people he'd killed—or had ordered killed—were junkies and dealers. It made sense to loop it in now and tie it all up in a bow.

"She overdosed," Caradine said flatly. "It was awful."

Jimmy didn't react to the news of his sister's death. He studied Caradine instead, until she couldn't tell if her skin crawled from the pain or that look in his eyes. "You don't look like a junkie, Jules. Just the same dumb bitch."

"I'm tired of running," she told him, still letting the tears drip down her cheeks. "I don't know how you found me, but it felt like a sign."

"The freaking Internet," Jimmy told her with entirely too much satisfaction. "There was a picture of someone who looked like you in a restaurant in the middle of nowhere, thanks to some old friends of Mom's on a stupid cruise. It got around and it eventually got to me. Figured I'd light it up and see what came out, just to be sure. And here you are."

Caradine had always hated social media on principle and this didn't help. But she tried to look tremulous and hopeful, not revolted. "I want to come home."

"Home." Jimmy hooted. "What home do you think there is to come back to? You're a ghost. You died a decade ago and you should have stayed dead."

"Come on," Caradine whined. Actually whined, which made her want to hit herself in the face a few times. She would never know how she didn't make a fist. "You don't know what it's like. Always looking over your shoulder. Always waiting for something to burst into flames like it did. It was almost a relief, if I'm honest, that you found me. I always knew you would."

She thought that was laying it on a little thick, but then again, it wasn't entirely untrue. Having her past catch up to her after all this time was like tearing off a scab. It hurt, but there was a relief in it, because it justified all that running.

And if she remembered her brother right, it would please him to imagine she'd spent ten years scared he, personally, would find her.

"You always thought you were so smart," Jimmy sneered at her now. "But you're not. A smart girl would never have come back, throwing Dad's name around. Because Dad died. And so did I. And the last thing I need is for too many people to connect the individual I am now with any member of the long-lost Sheeran family."

"The bartender—"

"Donnie is well paid to call me anytime someone turns up asking after people. It doesn't matter who. Because who asks for people in a place like Sharkey's? It's not an information booth."

"But—"

"A smart girl wouldn't have shouted out a long-dead name in a public place, encouraging people to remember things I'd rather they forgot. I'm a businessman. I can't do business if people are hung up on ancient history."

"You killed your entire family," Caradine whispered. "What kind of business is that?"

"Not yours," Jimmy said with soft menace. Caradine couldn't entirely hide her shudder of revulsion. "Did you really think you could come back here and weasel your way into my good graces? You were a liability back then." His flat eyes narrowed into suspicious slits. "Are you wired?"

"What?" Her voice cracked on the word, which was only partially feigned. Because she kept trying to see Jimmy in the bald head or the curled lip he wore, and she couldn't, and she suspected all of her nightmares would wear this face. "What? No! Of course I'm not—"

Jimmy threw her back against the wall. And he gripped her throat again while he pawed at her. Not gently. Not lasciviously, for which she supposed she ought to have been grateful. But still, he made it very clear that he didn't care if he hurt her.

At all.

Caradine could feel a murderous haze washing over her. Fury. Shame. And that dark ugliness inside that she'd always known was there. The part of her that was like him. Like the rest of her family. The thing in her blood that she'd never indulged, because she never wanted to turn out like the rest of them.

She didn't much care if she let it loose here. With Jimmy.

But she couldn't let herself give in to it. Not now. Not yet. She told herself, over and over, that she was choosing to subject herself to this. She was choosing to let him manhandle her, because it was expedient.

Because she knew that a clock was ticking, even if he didn't.

And because she'd rid herself of the Alaska Force comm unit before she'd gone down into the tunnel, so there was nothing for him to find.

"I told you I wasn't wired," she managed to say through her damaged throat when he was done. And she wasn't acting when one hand rose to touch her own throat gently, or when she tried to swallow and winced. "I don't know what you think is happening here, but all I'm trying to do is come back home."

"There's nothing I hate worse than a rat, Julia." Jimmy's nostrils flared. "You remember that."

She didn't point out that if he killed her, which seemed to be the direction they were heading in, she wouldn't need to remember anything.

"Are you why Dad was so weird that night?" she

asked him, even though it hurt to speak. "Is that what was going on in that room?"

"Did Lindsay tell you that before she kicked it?" He looked disgusted. "I told them it was a mistake to let her in there. The eye candy wasn't worth it."

"She was your sister," Caradine managed to say. "Not eye candy."

"She was a piece of ass," Jimmy said, with a horrible coldness and distance that probably left their own bruises all over her. "The only difference between you and her was that she knew her place."

"Nice," Caradine couldn't seem to help herself from saying.

She expected him to hit her again. Instead, he smiled.

And she shuddered again, not sure she cared if he saw it.

"Here's a reality check for you, Jules," Jimmy told her, with obvious relish. "Dad was going to let you graduate. He was going to let you go through the whole rigmarole, especially since you paid for it yourself. Why not? Then he was going to sell you off to Vincent Campari down in Jersey. You remember Vincent?"

"The name doesn't ring a bell," Caradine said, though it did.

Too many bells. All of them horrendous.

"Let me remind you." And Jimmy was actually grinning now, with his fake face and his same old dead eyes. "His first wife killed herself. His second wife is locked up in a psychiatric hospital in Hackensack. You would have been number three. How do you think you would have fared with an old-school type like Vincent, with the mouth on you?"

Vincent Campari was a very bad man. A known murderer who had also been old, ugly, and lecherous. He'd given Caradine the creeps, something she'd been foolish enough to let her father see when she'd been all of thirteen.

She'd known better by then. Never give her father or men like him weapons when they already had so many of their own.

"If he puts all his wives into early graves or mental institutions, how could marrying me to him possibly have benefited Dad?" she asked now.

As if they weren't discussing, almost casually, what would have been repeated rapes, other abuses, and God knew what else. She would have been silent and enduring within six months, or dead.

This was what her father and brother had wanted for her.

In case she was tempted to forget why she was here.

"It was a win-win situation," her older brother told her, sounding as happy as she'd ever heard him. "If he sold you off, he would get that in with Vincent's friends and family down there. When Vincent messed you up, he'd get to be gracious when he excused it. Points all around. If Vincent killed you or incapacitated you, even better. He got to hold that in reserve, an ace to play. You're lucky Vincent's dead or I might consider making the same deal myself for the same reason."

She felt torn in two then. There was the part of her that had lived in Grizzly Harbor for five years. The part that had cooked food and thrown back drinks in the Fairweather. The part of her that had breathed in that crisp, cold Alaskan air and looked forward to days filled with nothing more worrying or upsetting than the occasional moose at large in the village.

The other part was Julia Sheeran, daughter of a sociopathic, violent criminal and sister to this literal psychopath. The one who had known that her future was dark but had been convinced she could, at the very least, smuggle a night-light in. But light or no light, she would have been expected to suck it up and take what was given to her. Whether it was Vincent Campari or any of the other equally sociopathic and violent criminals her father associated with.

She tried to imagine discussing these things with her regulars at the Water's Edge Café, and couldn't. Even though they'd burned it down, it was still hers. *Hers*, not Julia's. It was a place none of this touched.

"This all sounds insane," Caradine pointed out, though she knew better than to antagonize Jimmy. Then again, he was going to hurt her either way, so why not? "You know that, right? You're talking about my life, not a movie. My actual life, where I would have been the one who died. Me. Your sister."

"This is where you always went wrong, Jules," Jimmy said, in that soft way that made her spine want to curl up into a ball. Maybe it did. "Who cares about your life? Whatever made you think you had a say in anything? Your job was to shut your mouth and do what you were told, but you sucked at it. All that fancy education and you still don't know how to be what you are. A frickin' pawn."

Caradine smirked. She couldn't help herself. "Like you know how to play chess, Jimmy."

She braced herself for a blow. Wanted it, even, which gave her some insight into her mother that she didn't want.

What she didn't expect was for him to smile at her.

It was more than just creepy. It literally made her blood run cold.

Especially because he wasn't wearing the right face.

"I'm going to hurt you for that," he promised her, and it took her a second to register what that odd note in his voice was. *Delight*. "I'm going to hurt you a lot, Julia. And I'm going to enjoy it. I never liked you. I don't have any use for your kind of uppity."

"It's called intelligence, Jimmy," she said, because she was in for a penny, a pound, and the whole rest of it, too. "Lindsay had it, too, but she was a junkie. At least she had it. I can't say the same for you."

"You never did know your place." He sounded sorrowful, but she could still see that delight flickering in his gaze. "Mom and Lindsay, it caused me pain, thinking I'd killed them. Their only crime was being part of the family. But you. Patrick with the gambling and Danny high all the time. You were all useless embarrassments. Dad couldn't control you, so I handled it."

And the worst part was that he didn't look or sound rabid. Or crazy. He sounded perfectly sane. Conversational, even. There was no doubt in her mind that he would kill them all again without a single qualm. He would feel badly for Donna and Lindsay—had she died when she was supposed to—and never question what he'd done.

"Some people prefer therapy," Caradine said dryly. "But sure. Firebomb the whole house. A random restaurant on the other side of the continent. Why not?"

That one got her another slap. She needed to watch herself, because she wasn't entirely sure he hadn't loosened a few teeth with that last one.

"A man who can't control his house can't control his business, either," her brother told her, leaning in close. "I don't have that problem."

He grabbed her by the arm, a painful, awful grip that made her bones ache, deep and wrong. Then he started across that long lobby, his fingers digging even deeper into her arm as he dragged her with him.

"It doesn't have to be like this," Caradine said desperately, the way she imagined the Julia she'd been ten years ago might have. *Beg*, she ordered herself. "I have a temper, but it runs in the family. You don't need to hurt me, Jimmy. I can be useful. I promise."

Any minute now, she told herself. All she had to do now was make sure she didn't let Jimmy take her to a second location. She couldn't let him put her in a car. Or knock her out and throw her in a trunk, which was his more likely move.

She dug her heels into the lobby floor, ignoring that painful grip he had on her arm. And was grateful it was a sticky linoleum, not marble, so she got a little purchase.

He turned on her again, shaking her so hard her teeth really did rattle. "So help me God, Julia, if you give me any more trouble—"

But that was when the world exploded again.

Only this time, it wasn't the crackle of flames.

It was Isaac.

Twenty-three

Isaac had this nightmare all the time.

It was one of the reasons he rarely slept.

Caradine in peril and him playing catch-up. Running and running and never quite making it. He'd watched her die a thousand times in those nightmares. Over and over and over again, he was too late.

He was always too late.

The only difference today was that it wasn't happening only in his head.

It had taken ten minutes to get a spare key from the bartender, which had seemed like an eternity or two to Isaac. He could have gotten the answer he needed a whole lot faster, but he'd made a bargain with himself a long time ago to stay on the right side of certain lines.

A man who did the things he had, and would again, had to make very sure he didn't let himself become a monster.

In all the years since he'd made himself that vow on

his first tour, Isaac had never come close to breaking it. Until today.

But he hadn't. Somehow, he hadn't. He'd had to take the time to convince a bartender in a place like Sharkey's that he needed to be more afraid of the men in front of him than the men in the neighborhood. A delicate proposition, but they'd gotten there.

Eventually.

"How did we miss the tunnels?" Templeton demanded when the bartender finally gave up his key to one of the reinforced-steel doors leading to the basement.

"We didn't miss them," Isaac gritted out. "We were directed away from them by a woman who acted like she'd never in a million years go into one."

He could see the face she'd made. The way she hadn't actually *said* she wouldn't go into a tunnel but had let him assume it.

"If she's really a Sheeran, what do you expect?" the bartender chimed in, displaying more of that talent for failing to read a room that had already cost Isaac too much time. "Scum, all of them. There's a reason the whole family was wiped out, buddy."

Isaac took approximately four seconds to think about how little he liked it when men he would never speak to in normal circumstances called him *buddy* or any variation of it.

But then he was moving. He signaled to Jonas to come with him, Templeton to handle the bartender and the patrons on the floor, and headed for the shabby little hallway.

Down the stairs at a run. Down the hallway like it was a race—and he'd always been good at a sprint.

The clock in him ticked the way it always did in the dreams he had. The ones where Caradine merged with his parents and the plane was going down, but he was there, and he had to watch them all die.

Again and again and again, and now it was happening. And he didn't know if he was prepared after all of this or if it had all been one long, tortured premonition.

"Ready?" he asked Jonas when they made it through a basement that was obviously used for wet work, then up another flight of stairs. He estimated they'd crossed the street, then headed south, and said so into the comm unit.

"On it," Blue replied.

"I'm going to keep babysitting," Templeton said, sounding irritated that he wasn't in the middle of the action.

At the door, Jonas nodded toward Isaac, indicating that he was ready.

They were a well-oiled machine after all these years. Isaac threw open the door and went in at a dead run, Jonas right behind him, because that made them a harder target to hit.

Isaac went low, knowing Jonas would stay high. That let Isaac scan the scene, make his determination in a split second, and then throw himself at the knees of the goon with his hands on Caradine.

As he moved, Jonas shot twice.

Isaac hit the goon as the two thugs at the far door went down, howling in pain.

But Isaac's focus was on the tangle of bodies on the ground. And the only part of the tangle he cared about. He saw bruises and blood, but her blue gaze was the same. Sharp and furiously lucid and focused on him.

If he wasn't mistaken, she looked annoyed. With him.

As if he'd taken too long when she'd deliberately—

Not the time, he snapped at himself, rolling to his feet and instinctively going into a fighting stance.

"I knew it," the man bellowed.

He scrabbled backward, heaving himself back against the lobby wall to help him find his feet the way tough guys who relied on their size but not any skill often did. Caradine dived forward to crawl away from him, but he hauled her toward him with what looked like a painful grip on one ankle.

Isaac took aim.

And had to wait while Caradine fought. And while the man with his hands on her wrestled her around into a choke hold.

Isaac was tense and ready and looking for *just enough* space to blow his freaking head off—

Then the idiot made it even worse by sticking his gun to her temple.

Not gently.

There was a pause full of labored breathing, mostly coming from the dirtbag.

"Hey, Isaac," Caradine said mildly, though her blue eyes gleamed with a cold, hard fury, and she was panting a little, too.

They were in a stalemate for the moment, so Isaac let his gaze track over her. He didn't like what he saw. Marks on her face. A swollen mouth. And if he wasn't mistaken, bruising around her neck.

All of which he intended to make this animal pay for.

"This is my brother Jimmy," she continued, and then made a choking sound when the man tightened his grip. And ground the muzzle of his gun against her head.

"You're going to want to tell your buddy back there to drop his gun," Jimmy growled.

Isaac studied the man before him. He was unrecognizable as Jimmy Sheeran, having clearly undergone intensive plastic surgery to hide his identity. But he still looked like a Grade A scumbag.

He didn't bother glancing around to see who Jimmy was referring to. He knew Jonas had his gun pointed directly at the threat, on the extreme off chance Isaac missed.

"I don't control him," Isaac said. "You can always try."

Behind him, he could feel Jonas's deadly intent and stone-cold focus. He personally found it intimidating and he was used to it. Being on the receiving end of that glare often ended situations like this before they got going.

"Don't bother," Jonas said with a certain quiet ferocity. "I'm not in the habit of taking orders from men who rough up women."

Isaac enjoyed watching Jimmy's expression change. He cherished the dawning realization on Jimmy's part that Isaac and Jonas weren't the typical Boston lowlifes this man was likely used to dealing with. It might have made him smile if there weren't a gun at Caradine's head.

"You can point your guns all you want," Jimmy said after a moment, his gaze darker and flatter than before. "But my sister and I are walking out of here. You try to stop me? I'll shoot her."

"He's going to shoot me anyway," Caradine said with a blandness Isaac would have found amusing if it had been someone else. Anyone else. "And if I'm honest, I'd prefer he shoot me here. I'm not really jonesing for all the hurt he promised to deliver my way once we leave."

Jimmy laughed. It was an unpleasant sound. "You stupid, stupid bitch."

Isaac hissed out a breath. "Keep tightening that arm around her neck, Jimmy, and I'll return the favor. And rip your head off."

"One car waiting outside," Blue reported on the comm unit. "Driver neutralized."

Templeton sighed. "Babysitting continuing to be boring."

"Initiate phase two," Isaac replied.

Then he shifted his attention back to the deadly family drama unfolding in front of him.

The one that kept flickering into his own family drama, somehow, when he knew he couldn't let that happen. This wasn't the day he'd lost his parents—and one crucial distinction was that he was right here. Not haplessly sitting in school with no idea his world was ending.

Focus, he barked at himself.

Caradine was whistling theatrically. "Oh, Jimmy. Bad news, big brother. Phase two is the feds. Won't they be surprised to learn that you're not dead?"

"You can call the feds all you want," Jimmy snarled, and shook her, like a rag doll. Isaac kept his aim steady, because he knew it was a distraction technique. Not that knowing it made him less homicidal. "They can't help you, Julia. You should have died ten years ago. You're *supposed* to be dead."

"You're looking pretty spry for a ghost yourself," Caradine said airily.

Isaac wondered what it cost her to sound like that. So carefree when a monster had her in a tight, hard grip.

"You never could do what you're supposed to," Jimmy growled. "Why couldn't you be like Lindsay?"

"She ran away, too," Caradine pointed out. One eyebrow arched as she looked at Isaac. "Even if she did end up dying. I'm not sure she's the angel you think she is."

"Then you can tell her all about it in hell, bitch."

And everything seemed to slow down to a deadly crawl.

A flattening Isaac knew all too well.

Caradine's gaze was locked on to his, that eyebrow high and a smirk on her face, looking bruised and battered but still the woman he knew so well. Still the only woman who had ever lodged herself beneath his skin.

The only woman who mattered to him like this.

Her brother shifted his weight, then slammed that gun against her temple again, intent and resolve all over his fake face.

Isaac wished he'd let her say what she was going to say in the SUV. He wished he'd allowed that good-bye speech.

He wished a thousand things, all of them in an instant—

Then he was lunging forward, but it was already too late—

Once again, he was much too late—

And all he could see was her face. That determined chin. That light in her blue gaze, locked on to his.

I can't lose another person I love, he thought, very distinctly, as her brother's finger moved on the trigger. *I won't live through this if she doesn't—*

And then everything sped up.

Jonas roared from behind him.

Something slammed into the floor where he'd been standing.

He heard the crack of a bullet a split second later, and he was still midlunge, suspended in the air, but Caradine was moving, too.

She was moving.

Her head was tucked and her hands were in a position he'd seen her practice in Grizzly Harbor. A duck of the head and the thrust of her hands and the muzzle of the gun was pointed somewhere it couldn't hit her.

She moved.

Isaac let his fist lead, slamming it into Jimmy Sheeran's plastic face. Jimmy was still holding on to Caradine, so they both moved as Isaac slammed Jimmy back into the wall.

Maybe Isaac ordered him to let her go. Maybe he only thought it.

But Caradine did something else, using her hip and a vicious twist. Then she had the gun, and she propped herself up against the wall while her older brother lurched for the far door, slipping and sliding over the lobby floor.

"This is really just embarrassing," Jonas said, almost lazily, still standing back by the door to the stairs. He didn't even raise his weapon.

Caradine was flat against the wall, the gun hanging at

her side. But she was looking at Isaac, not tracking her brother.

"I told you I missed you on purpose," she told him, her voice hoarse. "In Maine."

Isaac saw something he recognized in her gaze then. A certain bleakness he knew all too well, each and every contour.

And he didn't want that for her. He'd spent so much time in that desolate place it was like a second home. He didn't want her to add that particular darkness to the things she already carried around.

He didn't want her to touch it, because once she did, there would be no taking it back.

There was never any taking it back.

"If you do it, you become it," he told her softly. "That's how it works."

"You do it all the time."

"Not all the time. And never lightly." He saw her hand twitch at her side. "And I've never pretended I wasn't what my choices made me. You can't take a life without paying for it, one way or another."

He understood the misery on her face then. Too well.

"Caradine—"

But another shot rang out across the lobby before he could finish his sentence.

And this time, her brother went down in a heap. But he made a lot of noise while he did it, which made Isaac's chest feel slightly less frozen solid.

Because Caradine had shot her own brother, but she hadn't killed him.

"Right to the knee," Jonas said like a sports announcer. "Ouch. That's going to sting."

And later, maybe, Isaac would think about the fact that she really might have missed on purpose in that little house in Maine.

But not now. He was there before her, his hand aching

from the punch he'd delivered, and she was staring back at him with that familiar mix of longing and defiance all over her.

Everything was different. And yet this was the same. They were the same.

"Report, for God's sake," Templeton snapped over the comm unit. "Some of us are stuck in the bar time forgot."

"Threat neutralized," Isaac replied, but his gaze was still on the woman who stood there propped up against the wall, her ten-year nightmare in a heap on the floor of this dank lobby. But his nightmare remained the same. And would be worse, now, with this scene etched on it. "Caradine is fine."

Jonas took over then, listing potential injuries and requesting medical attention as well as law enforcement to clean up the mess.

Isaac shut off his comm unit because his attention was on Caradine, who didn't look fine, no matter what he'd said. Bruises seemed to multiply the longer he looked at her throat. Her pretty face was swollen, cut, and battered. And still, she was glaring at him like she was daring him to do something about any of this.

It took him a moment to recognize the sensation that soared through him at the sight of that glare.

Pure joy.

"Are you?" he asked her, quietly. "Fine, I mean."

She smirked, though it must have hurt. And there was a glaze over her eyes, which made him want to shoot things himself.

"Of course I'm fine. I'm always fine. It's my defining characteristic."

"I can think of other definitions." He shook his head at her, fighting to keep his fury at bay. "What would you call someone who deliberately put herself in danger the way you did today?"

"Determined," Caradine said, and the smirk faded. Leaving only bruises and scrapes and too many ghosts in her eyes. "Desperate."

And all he could think about was running through that long tunnel, in that same frozen state he'd been in when he'd gotten that call weeks back. When he'd taken that helicopter flight into Grizzly Harbor to find her restaurant charred.

"I thought you were dead," he gritted out. "Again."

"Then you'd really know what to do," she said, and her voice was thicker then. Her words slurred. Adrenaline was draining away and turning into shock, he could tell. She tried to smile. To stand up straighter. "You do like your suffering, Gentry."

This time, when he lunged forward, he caught her in his arms before she crumpled into a heap on the floor.

"I'm not *swooning*," she said, sounding disgruntled and faintly horrified. "If you tell anyone I fainted, I'll kill you. As soon as I can stand up again."

"Noted," Isaac said gruffly. "Now shut up."

Her lips curved as her eyes fluttered shut. And Isaac stayed where he was, cradling her in his arms in a way she would never have allowed him to do if she were in complete control. He smoothed her dark hair back from her face, taking care not to touch any of the cuts or bruises or red, angry swelling that made him want to storm across the lobby and finish the job she'd started.

She let out a breath as if she'd been holding it in a long time.

Isaac stayed where he was while time flattened out and lost all meaning again. The way it had when he'd been in that tunnel, running to find her. The way it had when he'd been sixteen and had been pulled out of school to discover everything he knew was changed forever. Grief and love, panic and joy, all of them fused together and hummed in him like so many sides of the same coin.

And all the while, this woman who lied to his face

with glee, deliberately misled him, and was affronted when he helped her turned her face toward him and snuggled in closer, breathing him in like he was the only thing that had ever mattered to her or ever would.

Isaac knew he would pay for that, too.

But not right now. Not here.

"Incoming," Jonas said, tapping his comm unit. "Sirens blaring."

Soon enough, too soon, Isaac had to tear his eyes away from his woman yet again. He had to hand her over to the paramedics, though she looked fragile and vulnerable and it made him want to break things with his hands, because she would hate to think anyone saw her like that.

And then, though he had no interest in any of it the way he normally did, he had to suck up and surrender himself to official business in the form of the deeply unimpressed federal government. Because he was the head of Alaska Force, not the former Julia Sheeran's boyfriend, and it was high time he remembered that.

Or better yet, acted like it.

Twenty-four

It took days.

Isaac had spent most of his career building his relationships with officials for use in situations like this. Often, he worked magic in tight spots, thanks to those relationships. But even he couldn't wave away a decade-old mass murder, the five-year-old murders in Phoenix, Jimmy Sheeran's new face and rise to criminal prominence after his supposed death, or the ten years Caradine and her sister had spent on the run.

Much less Caradine's obvious preference that Lindsay be officially declared dead—and therefore free, he understood.

He sat in briefing after briefing, up and down the food chain. He called in favors. He played games he'd always been good at but that seemed little more than hollow now. He did his best to control his impatience and focus on the end game—that being Caradine and Lindsay free and clear and no longer forced to run or hide, unless that was what they wanted—when all *he* wanted was three seconds alone with her.

Because he wanted to know what the hell she'd meant. *You do like your suffering, Gentry.*

It ate at him.

Four days later, after he'd debriefed and bargained, declined the usual employment offers, and reminded himself why he was glad he was out of government work these days, he was finally released from custody.

Not that anyone had called it *custody*, of course, even when they'd issued him an invitation to fly south to the Pentagon and had thoughtfully provided him with armed transport to hurry him along.

He walked out of the building and squinted in the summer swelter of Arlington, Virginia, still happy to have left his former life behind. He liked his life less classified and with less bureaucracy. He fished out the phone that had been confiscated for two days and monitored for the next two, and called into Fool's Cove.

"The rest of the team got released yesterday," Griffin told him once the line was secured. "They kept them all in Boston, so I'll send you the coordinates to the safe house they're staying in while they wait for you to finish doing the dance."

"I hate dancing."

"You can dance until the music stops," Griffin replied. "Everything here is under control."

"The music ended a while ago," Isaac said shortly as he walked toward the Metro station, some ten minutes away. "Give me the highlights."

Griffin launched into a breakdown of active missions, including a developing situation in Brazil that everyone was hoping wouldn't blow up.

It occurred to Isaac then, walking away from the Pentagon with as little interest in looking back as he'd had when he'd left the service, that of all the things he'd worried about over the past four days, Alaska Force wasn't one of them.

He'd offered explanations to men who required salutes. He'd explained himself to men who'd declined to introduce themselves. Mostly, he'd worried about Caradine. And throughout the process he'd had absolutely no doubt that his business was in safe hands. That the people he'd hired could take care of it themselves.

Meaning that, after all this time, this overcompensating workaholic could maybe let go a little.

A notion that might have felt revolutionary if he'd known where Caradine was.

"Do we think Brazil is going to heat up?" he asked. And rubbed at the back of his neck, because he had the feeling he already knew the answer.

Griffin sighed. "Oz thinks we should send a team, but there's no way of telling how long we'll have to be there if we do. Typical quagmire."

"Okay." Isaac moved swiftly to get around a group of tourists. "Let me think about who we can send down there on an open-ended op." It was a different math these days, now that the better part of his first string had personal lives back in Alaska to consider. He still wasn't used to it. "No fires to put out?"

"None whatsoever."

Isaac didn't want to ask, but he'd scrolled through all the messages on his phone. He'd checked all his voice mails. She hadn't contacted him, which wasn't a surprise.

It was another kick in the gut, but it wasn't a *surprise*.

"Where is she?" he made himself ask.

He thought of the way she'd closed her eyes and put her battered face in the crook of his neck. He figured he'd carry that with him.

Griffin paused. "She didn't tell you?"

"How would she do that? With telepathy? They don't allow that in the Pentagon."

And when the icy, emotionless sniper laughed, Isaac gritted his teeth.

"She's still in Boston, though not in the safe house," Griffin told him. "She's giving press conferences from the Four Seasons."

It was entirely too easy to slip past Caradine's security, such as it was. And even easier to break into her hotel room.

The same way he had in that little bed-and-breakfast in Maine.

Isaac had attempted to cool off his temper by flying commercial up to Boston. It was good to remind himself that not everything was private jets and the most restricted halls of the Pentagon. It was even better to spend time around all the regular people who didn't know what evil lurked in the world, who had no idea what he did to combat it, and to remember that there were good reasons he did what he did.

Better still, the hours of inconvenience and overcrowding had allowed him to catch up on what he'd missed over the past few days. He'd read all the headlines in the *Boston Globe* about Jimmy Sheeran's arrest ten years after his death, Julia Sheeran's escape all those years ago, and her sister's subsequent death, and flicked through all the old articles they referenced from back then.

But he was most interested in now.

In Julia Sheeran herself, notably blond and pale in all the coverage of her, which the cynic in him couldn't help but note made the beating she'd taken all the more noticeable. She'd stood outside the FBI building in Chelsea, leaning on the arm of an attorney as if she were too weak to stand. She'd been wearing pastels, as she spoke in a trembling voice about how scared, yet determined, she was.

Caradine in pastels. Caradine making public statements in a soft, shaking voice. Caradine weak and trembling or *scared*.

He had a lot of follow-up questions.

Isaac made his way into the hotel suite, silently. He took a moment to let his eyes adjust to the dark, then he made his way to the foot of yet another bed where she slept, hard.

With one hand under her pillow where he felt certain she still kept her gun.

He couldn't have said how long he watched her. Or when her breathing changed.

She woke in a rush in the next moment and sat up straight—one telltale hand sliding beneath her pillows, confirming his suspicions.

He took his time wandering over to the far side of the bed, then switched on the bedside light.

"This is like déjà vu," she drawled, without the hint of any shake. Or any softness, either. "Or, wait a minute. Is this a dream? If I pinch myself, you blow away like smoke?"

"I can pinch you if you want."

He enjoyed, maybe more than he should have, the way her eyes widened as she took in his expression. "I believe I'll pass on that."

She sat in the center of the king-sized bed, cross-legged and looking the sort of *calm* that would normally require medication. He knew she was faking it. Just like he knew she'd stolen that T-shirt she was wearing from his cabin in Alaska. The blond hair made her blue eyes look different, but it was still her face. The face that had haunted him for years now.

The face that would always haunt him.

And he knew that while he would remember each and every moment he'd gazed at her when she was nothing short of perfect, he would catalog how she looked tonight, too, and wear it like some kind of talisman. Every bruise on her that had bloomed into deep purple and black. The scrapes that looked sore and angry. The mottled patches of abrasions that stood out against the skin of her throat.

He would add each and every one to his nightmares.

"Press conferences?" he asked, keeping his voice as quiet and almost-friendly as possible. And enjoying it when she tensed. "Is that smart?"

"I think it's very smart, actually, thank you for asking." She rubbed at her eyes, taking care not to touch any of the tender parts of her face. "Why not accuse my brother of his crimes on as grand a stage as possible? I tried hiding for ten years and I ended up getting beat on in the lobby of a crappy building in Southie. Figured I'd try a different way this time."

"Blond."

She held his gaze, as challenging as ever. And slowly, deliberately twirled a piece of blond hair around her finger. "Not a wig, this time. Just to give it that extra dose of reality."

"What's your actual, natural hair color?"

"What does *natural* even mean? It will be gray soon enough, now that I have a life expectancy longer than the average carton of milk."

"So this is like your name. Do you pick out dyes while you come up with new identities?"

"One-stop shopping is everyone's favorite, Gentry."

He knew she liked to call him *Gentry* to keep him at a distance. He should have heeded that years ago. "Do you really think you can taunt him into leaving you alone?"

Caradine studied him, and Isaac had the lowering notion that while some of the military's finest interrogators couldn't get him to say a single thing he didn't want to say, she could. And probably would. All it took were bright blue eyes he couldn't resist and her attention.

He could take apart the world with his bare hands, easily.

But this woman had him in the palm of one of hers, and worse, he suspected she knew it.

"What I think is that he's going to go to jail," she said after a moment. "He might not have killed all the people in that house, but I'm pretty sure the difference between seven and ten bodies is more or less academic at this point."

"What if he sends some more of his lackeys to handle you?"

"He's not a Mafia don. He just knows Mafia dons. A crucial distinction."

"They're all splashing around in the same sewer, as far as I can tell."

"It doesn't matter." Whatever she saw on his face made her sigh. "It really doesn't. Lindsay gets to stay dead as far as Jimmy knows, and that will keep her safe. What would he gain by sending people after me?"

"You'll be dead. That's the gain. And bonus, you won't be able to testify."

"Maybe," she said. "But I'm not running anymore. I'm done."

"*Maybe* is not acceptable. We're talking about your death, Caradine."

"You're talking about my death. I'm talking about my *life*." And when he'd dreamed of her smiling at him, it wasn't like this. As if he made her sad. "I survived my homecoming when I was sure, for ten years, that coming back here would kill me. I'm not scared anymore. Jimmy's in custody, and I don't see him getting out anytime soon. Even if he did, he's compromised. He lied about who he was to people who take that kind of thing very, very seriously. I'm the least of his problems." She shrugged. "And the more press conferences I give, the more attention I draw to myself, the more he would have to lose by coming after me with so many other problems to worry about."

There was a certain logic to that. If he were a better man, Isaac wouldn't resent that, surely. "You played me. Deliberately."

She didn't look away. "I did."

He wanted to rage at her about how she'd put herself at risk. He wanted to pick apart the decisions she'd made. To plan good-bye speeches in the car, then walk into Sharkey's knowing he might not make it to her in time.

He wanted to ask her what she thought would happen to him—and the whole world—if he'd burst into that lobby to find her gone. Or worse, in pieces. What did she think he would do? How did she think he would survive that?

"Is there ever a time when you're not playing games with me?" he demanded.

Caradine blew out a breath. "Really, Isaac? Have you noticed that we're in a fancy hotel room?" She stretched out in her bed. "Is an interrogation the only thing you can think of to do?"

And something in him snapped.

"Not everything is about sex!" he roared at her.

He couldn't remember the last time he'd yelled outside the job. Not once. He'd made it his art and calling to exude calm no matter what. To be friendly and approachable and— Too bad. He was done.

Isaac had watched her get manhandled because she'd thrown herself headfirst into yet another situation that could have killed her. She could have died, and he was trained to be the exact person she should run *to* when she found herself in trouble.

He was not supposed to be the guy she ran away from, again and again and again.

Almost like she knows, too, he told himself.

She blinked at him, and he saw her pulse in the undamaged part of her neck. He saw her glance at the hands he'd curled into fists at his side, then up to his face, and he heard her pull in a steadying sort of breath. He couldn't deny it was gratifying that maybe, for three seconds, she might not see him as a freaking teddy bear.

But he didn't like it when she smiled again, as sadly as before. "I've been thinking about it a lot," she said. "Nonstop, actually, since I woke up in the hospital and you weren't there to confuse me."

"I was in federal custody at the Pentagon," he bit out. "And I wasn't aware that I *confused* you. Or that anything could."

"We've had this connection since the beginning." She was meeting his gaze in a way that made the back of his neck itch. Foreboding. "We've had a lot of sex. We tried a few days of domestic harmony in Fool's Cove—"

"Domestic harmony? Is that what you call it? I had to kidnap you and take you there against your will."

"Fine, then call it Stockholm syndrome," she snapped. She shut her eyes a moment, then took another one of her steadying breaths. And when she opened her eyes again, he hardly recognized the expression he saw there. A beat or so later, he realized she was being *kind*. "That isn't any better. We fight. We have sex. We fight some more. I spent five years telling myself that it had to be that way, but it doesn't now. But maybe that's all you and I have."

You'd choke on love, he remembered her saying over pancakes.

"I've been waiting for you to admit we actually have something since the night we met," he growled at her. "Why am I not surprised that you want to make it into another game?"

"See? Even now, you want to fight. It's the only thing you know how to do."

"Caradine." He raked his hands through his hair. "I can't fight you by myself. You know that, right?"

"I fought because I had to. Because I had no other choice if I wanted to survive. You fight because you like it. It's your job and you're good at it." Her blue eyes seemed too bright, or maybe that was him. Maybe something terrible was happening inside him. "But I did it. I survived. And I don't want to fight anymore."

"Then don't fight." He managed to get the words out, even though it felt as if he were the one who'd been choked. "Tell me what this is. What you want, since you had all this unconfusing time over the past couple of days to change your appearance, play a character for the press, and in your spare time while receiving medical attention, figure out our entire relationship."

The Caradine he knew glared at him, then winced, because that must have hurt.

"Are you offering me something?" she asked. "Because I can't help noticing that we're out of your comfort zone now."

He let out a laugh. "Do I have a comfort zone where you're involved? That's news to me."

Her head tipped slightly to one side, which he took as the warning it was. "I don't need saving any longer. I'm not reeling around, lost and in need of Captain America to swoop in and save me with his magic hammer."

"Shield," Isaac growled at her. "Captain America has a shield, not a hammer. Thor has a hammer, and what did they teach you in that college of yours?"

She ignored that. "What all that means, no matter what superhero we reference, is that you don't get to mope around, pining all over Alaska, waiting for my past to catch up with me. I'm over it. I'm moving on. Can you?"

"Marines do not *pine* or *mope*, Caradine."

"We both know why I acted the way I have for the past five years." Her eyebrows arched. "But you don't have the excuse of being chased by homicidal maniacs and having to hide out to save your own life and protect your sister. What have *you* been doing?"

"Right. Of course. I must be the bad guy, because I like you. Because I've always liked you. And haven't made a secret of it."

"Who do you like, Isaac?" she asked softly. "Who *is* Caradine Scott?"

He wanted to reach for her, but he didn't. "I'm not the right person to play this game with. I've spent years pretending to be people I wasn't. It's never the differences that haunt you, in the end. It's the similarities. The way it bleeds together until what hurts about an extraction isn't what you leave behind, but what you take with you."

It was the most he could recall saying about his career to a civilian . . . maybe ever. Caradine looked almost dumbstruck for a moment.

Isaac kept going. "Is that what you're trying to tell me? You think I'm going to believe that I was just something you did to keep your cover?"

"No," she whispered. "You were the one thing I did that I thought would blow my cover, and you know it. But that's the problem. You don't like *me*, Isaac. You like what you can't have."

He wanted to roll his eyes. He wanted to shout at her, because once again, she had to be playing some angle. . . . But there was something devastatingly honest about the way she was looking at him. Not smirking. Not challenging him. Not stripping off her clothes to redirect his attention.

If she was playing him again, she was doing it by being so raw it hurt.

"You like to prostrate yourself to the impossible, because that's the only kind of love you understand," she told him, every word like a stone hurled from a great height. He could feel each one of them hit. And the damage each one inflicted. "The kind you lose."

Something roared in him, a wild kind of howl. He wanted it to be temper, fury, outrage—but he had the distinct sensation that it was really more like grief.

"You don't know how to love anything," he told her, and he wanted to shout. To make noise. When instead, he was so quiet it was like he was the one who'd died. "You've been running so long that you don't know how to stop. You asked me to help you and then you manipulated me anyway. You don't trust anything or anyone, and I don't think you could if you tried."

She swayed a little, as if he were the animal in that lobby, pummeling her. As if he'd landed a much harder hit than her brother ever had.

And Isaac was always surprised that it was possible to hate himself more. To find a new depth to it.

But he detested himself tonight.

"Your response to your parents' death was to turn yourself into the patron saint of lost causes," Caradine told him, almost gently. Almost as if it hurt her to say these things to him, and that only made it worse. "The marines weren't enough. Delta Force wasn't enough. When you left the service, you had to set up your own thing so you could keep on fighting the good fight, knowing you could never, ever win."

"Or possibly to do good in the world."

"You don't want to win, Isaac," she said, very distinctly, her blue gaze on his like a revelation. "You want to suffer."

He thought he was reeling, but the wall was at his back. "You keep telling me that, but it doesn't make it true."

"Okay, then let's test it." She crawled to the side of the bed, in nothing but the T-shirt she was wearing. His T-shirt, and his chest felt tight enough to blow. Then she knelt up and laid her palms on his chest, still looking at him. Through him. "I love you, Isaac. We don't have to date, let's jump right in to the real stuff. You want to move in with me? Or should I move in with you? It's been five years, why wait?"

He felt numb, everywhere. "Do you think this is funny?"

"I've never been more serious in my life. You want me?" And that look on her face wasn't the usual challenge. If anything, she looked sad. But resolute. Something in him . . . broke. "Here I am. I've been fighting for years, but I'm done. I'm not running anymore."

Isaac wanted to wrap her in his arms. He wanted to tell her she was wrong about him, and about this. He wanted to prove it. He wanted to fight.

The truth of what she was saying might as well have been another pipe bomb. He felt his foundations go up in flames. He thought about the choices he'd made after high school, in college. Officer training, then the corps. And every choice since then.

Always to fight.

He always, always wanted to fight.

Isaac had no idea what waited for him on the other side of the fight, and he didn't want to know. If he thought about it at all, he'd imagined he'd live out his days doing what he did now until he couldn't do it any longer. And he'd never imagined himself growing old.

He'd figured he'd die in battle first.

His heart thudded at him. Time flattened out again, and there was nothing but Caradine's hands on his chest. Her blue eyes seeing far too much.

"Caradine . . ." he whispered.

She nodded as if it hurt her, and not because of the injuries she'd sustained.

"That's what I thought," she said, her voice rough.

And when she dropped her hands and sat back on her heels, he felt grief plow into him again, black and bright and blinding.

"Caradine," he said again, like her name could make the difference here.

Like it was still her name. Or had ever been.

"Isaac." She said it in that same rough way that sounded like a sob. That felt like one inside of him. That he knew he would carry with him, always, like too many other things he didn't want to look at. She shook her head, her blue eyes filling. "I already said good-bye to you."

And later, he had no idea how he left, only that he did.

He staggered out into the hallway and alerted her security detail that they sucked. Hard.

"I didn't *try* to get past you," he growled. "I walked right up to her door and let myself in."

He called Blue in the safe house and ordered him to find and manage a far better security force to keep her safe.

"You got it, boss," Blue said. "Are you—?"

But Isaac hung up before he could ask the question. And he didn't call Templeton or Jonas, who wouldn't accept that kind of nonresponse.

He found himself in the Public Garden in the dark. There was music coming from somewhere, and he was vaguely aware of people moving on the dark paths, but all he saw was Caradine.

That's the only kind of love you understand. The kind you lose.

God, he wanted to fight . . . something. Anything.

Everything.

I love you, Isaac.

He took a breath, and then he called Griffin.

"I'm going to take the Brazil job myself," he said. "And I'm leaving tonight. Now. I want to be in Manaus by morning."

"We're talking about a month down there, potentially," Griffin argued, sounding less than his usual icy self. "Maybe two."

"I'm headed for the jet," Isaac told him shortly, because there was no room for debate. There was only the next fight, the longer and more complicated, the better. Because what he loved most died, and so he saved what he could. The things he didn't love but could help. As if that could make up for it. As if somehow, that might make him whole. "Make sure it's ready."

Twenty-five

It was getting toward the end of August when Isaac finally returned to Grizzly Harbor.

Though summer in Alaska after almost two months in the Amazon felt a whole lot like the dead of winter. He actually almost shivered while walking across the tarmac in Juneau. As a native-born Alaskan, he was appalled.

He'd immersed himself completely in the tricky situation he'd had to monitor and guide toward a fruitful resolution down there, relying on texts and the occasional e-mail to keep him updated about what was happening at the office. That was the only takeaway he cared to acknowledge from earlier in the summer—that Alaska Force ran smoothly.

Whether he was obsessively monitoring it or not.

And if relying on infrequent texts cut down on his friends' and colleagues' ability to ask him extraneous questions about his personal life, that was more than all right with him.

The seaplane he took from Juneau delivered him into Fool's Cove with a showy jump or two on the water, letting him get a good look at the place he'd called home for years now. The home he'd built for himself and had made into a haven for men like him who didn't fit anywhere else. The cabins set into the rocky hillside, which was already starting to look like the coming fall. The fog draped over the mountain and dancing through the trees.

That was the thing about Alaska. No matter how roughed up he was, no matter what he'd lost, it always felt like home.

When he jumped down to the dock, the cool air smelled like woodsmoke and salt, and the slap of it against his face made him think about smiling—which was more than the humidity in Brazil had done. He slung his bag over his shoulder and climbed up the stairs to the lodge, happy to see that everywhere he looked, everything seemed to be just as he'd left it.

And it was a strange thing to acknowledge that he didn't know if he should feel pleased that it turned out he wasn't indispensable after all, or if he should indulge the raw thing inside him instead. Probably both.

He didn't head to his cabin, because it was one thing to be largely unreachable while in the Amazonian jungle. Now that he was back, it was time to go to work.

Another good thing, to his way of thinking, was that he felt a kind of relief when he walked into the lodge.

"I don't believe it," came Templeton's booming voice from down the length of the lobby-like great room. He was sitting oh-so-casually on one of the couches with his tablet in one hand, as if he hadn't seen the seaplane come in. "Do my eyes deceive me? Or is this the ghost of Gentrys past?"

"Do I look like a ghost?" Isaac grinned. Blandly. "And here I thought it was a successful mission."

"I guess that depends on how you measure your successes," Templeton drawled, stretching out his legs. "Me,

I have a different metric than running off to the jungle to avoid—"

"The end of the world?" Isaac interjected with an edge in his voice, daring his friend to come back at him. "Because that's what I was doing. And I didn't realize that we were back in middle school."

"Never left," came Jonas's voice from the opposite side of the big lobby.

Where he was leaning in a doorway like he, too, was casually wandering around the lodge in the middle of the day for no particular reason. Or like he ever *leaned*.

Isaac decided he didn't want to deal with either one of them, so he headed for his office. And he didn't have to turn around to see them following him. He could hear them. They stuck with him as he pushed through the doors, then headed down the hallway toward his main office. The one he took clients to when they came here, not the one he kept in his home.

The home he hadn't gone to yet, because the last time he'd been there, she'd been there, too.

Isaac would have ordered himself to stop thinking about Caradine, but what was the point? It hadn't worked in almost two months. What made him think it would work now?

He expected to find Horatio waiting for him in his office, curled up on the sofa with a baleful glare, ready to punish him for being gone so long. But his dog wasn't there. He tossed his bag on the spot Horatio normally claimed and caught a glimpse of himself in the mirror on the wall. A little too wild man and not enough easygoing boy next door, but he didn't have it in him to care. Not enough to do something about it.

There were stacks of papers on his desk. The light on his desk phone blinked wildly. Ordinarily he would dive right in.

But instead, he eyed his unwanted entourage as they loomed about in his doorway.

There were a thousand things he could have asked them. He went with, "Where's my dog?"

Templeton whistled in that way he had that put Isaac's teeth on edge. The way it was meant to, he knew.

"Cold as ice," Templeton said.

"Your first question is about your dog," Jonas said carefully, as if he were giving Isaac the opportunity to change his answer.

"Normally I don't have to ask about Horatio, because he's right here. I assume that if something happened to him, someone would have informed me." He lifted a brow. "Or am I supposed to interpret your dog and pony show another way?"

"Cranky," Templeton observed, apparently still narrating. "And this from the individual who once lectured us all on how breathing into the solar plexus could cure jet lag."

Jonas, who normally did not engage in such shenanigans, actually cracked a smile. Or a faint curl in the corner of his mouth, which was the same thing when it came to Jonas. "All I wanted to do was punch him in the solar plexus."

"Good talk, thank you," Isaac said impatiently. "If that's all, I have two months to catch up on."

"The thing about Isaac," Templeton said conversationally, as if he had nothing better to do than lounge in the doorway, looking as boneless and lazy as those eyes of his were sharp, "is that he sure does love to dish it out. Taking it?"

"That, he doesn't like," Jonas answered.

Templeton shook his head. "No indeed."

Isaac sighed. "What is it that you would like me to take?"

"Your dog is fine," Templeton told him. "He's in town."

That was strange, but Isaac didn't pursue it. Because he could see there was no point. If Templeton had wanted to give him more information—like why Horatio, who normally hung out at the lodge while Isaac was away so he could be fawned over by everyone, would go to town in the first place—he would have given it. If Templeton didn't want to give out the information, Isaac certainly wasn't going to beg for it.

"Great," he said. "Thank you."

He waited for them to go away, but neither one of them moved.

"Jimmy Sheeran, on the other hand, is not fine," Jonas said. He and Templeton were staring at Isaac like this was the opening gambit in a tough interview, so Isaac kept his expression locked down. "Someone took him out in police custody."

That thudded in him. A direct hit. "What?"

"It turns out that your average dirtbag doesn't really like it when another dirtbag lies about who he is for almost ten years." Templeton shrugged. "They found him in a cell. Whoever did it didn't even bother to dress it up like it was a suicide."

Isaac thought of that look on Caradine's face, back in Boston. In that cursed lobby. The gun in her hand and that bleak acceptance on her face, because she'd been prepared to do what had to be done.

What he'd wanted to do, too.

He was fiercely, deeply glad she hadn't had to do it.

And maybe a little sad that he hadn't had the opportunity to do it for her. Maybe all he knew how to do was fight. But he was really, really good at it.

"I can't really work up any particular sadness about that," he said now.

"The two idiots he had with him have been throwing everyone and everything under any bus they can find," Templeton continued. "Just like the one you left up in Maine. They can't accuse each other fast enough."

"Good," Isaac said. Maybe a little gruffly. "I like it when they eat each other alive."

"Julia Sheeran did a media tour," Jonas said, and it didn't matter what name they used. It was her, and thinking about her . . . hurt. Though that was a tame word to describe the raw thing in him. And Isaac couldn't really place the expression on his friend's normally stark, unreadable face then. His dark eyes actually gleamed. "All the talk shows. All those news programs."

Isaac had a lot to say about that but settled for a curt nod.

"The level of stupidity it would take to go after her when she made herself such a public figure . . ." Jonas shook his head. "I don't think anyone would be dumb enough to do it."

"And if there was someone dumb enough to do it," Templeton chimed in, "there would be no point now. Not with Jimmy dead. There's no one to curry favor with anymore."

"She's always been smart." Isaac meant that. He did.

"And then," Jonas said, his gaze still gleaming, "she announced that she was retreating to Europe to write her memoirs."

Isaac let that land. "I'll admit I didn't see that coming."

"She boarded a plane to Germany, then disappeared," Templeton said, with great satisfaction.

"What do you mean, she disappeared?"

Templeton nodded sagely. "There were heated calls from the feds. You know what they're like when they can't find someone."

Isaac thought about the wigs. About Caradine in Texas, all those curls and a drawl to match. He thought about how she'd played him, ruthlessly and unapologetically, and would again, no doubt, if necessary.

He wondered what kind of woman she would be next. What kind of life she would arrange around herself this time. If she was truly free, who would she become?

Who do you like, Isaac? she'd asked him. *Who* is *Caradine Scott?*

And he hated how that question bounced around inside him the way it had been doing for almost two months, making it all too clear that he was far emptier than he ought to have been.

He'd had all these weeks to get used to it, but it still snuck up on him.

Or maybe, that voice inside him, sharp like hers, chimed in, *it's always there. You just can't drown it out with machine gun fire every second of the day.*

"I appreciate the update," he said now, and managed not to sound as stiff as he felt.

He nodded at his friends, both of whom he currently wanted to cause physical harm to. But didn't, because he was in control of himself and not a complete animal, thank you. Then he moved toward his desk, indicating that the conversation was over. That he had work to do.

When he looked up again, Templeton had vanished. But Jonas was still there, still standing in the doorway.

And he was watching Isaac with a certain hooded focus that boded ill.

Isaac sighed. "You, too?"

Jonas didn't smile. Not exactly. "Time was, I dug myself a hole. You came and dragged me out of it."

"I'm not in a hole."

"And I promised you that someday, I would do the same for you."

Isaac tried to control his impatience. And all the rest of it. "I'm not in a hole, Jonas."

"I'll tell you now what you told me then," Jonas said in that same calm voice of his. "You do no honor to the people you've lost by wasting your life. No honor at all."

Isaac said things like that all the time. But very rarely did people say it *to him.* He couldn't say he liked the reversal.

"I appreciate what you're trying to do here," Isaac said, and it cost him more than he planned to acknowledge to sound that even. That unbothered. "But the situation isn't what you think it is."

"I'm pretty sure the situation is exactly what I think it is."

"Not everything works out," Isaac said. Another thing he'd been telling himself a lot. "What did you expect? Wedding bells? Have you met either one of us?"

"Have you?" Jonas's dark eyes gleamed again. Possibly more intensely. "Because it seems to me that you're so busy not looking at yourself in the mirror that you don't know who the hell you are."

"You're confusing me with someone else. Maybe you?"

"I'm fully conversant on this particular mess," Jonas said quietly, indicating himself. "Men like us, we know too well how to lose. We know how quickly, how easily, things are taken from us. But we also know, better than anyone, that you can't live your life waiting for accidents to happen. That's why we train. That's why we fight. Not to keep them from happening, but so we can respond to them when they do."

"I know why I fight, Jonas."

His gaze was much too direct. "Then stop fighting for the wrong thing."

And if this had been Templeton, Isaac would have rolled his eyes. Argued. Dismissed it, one way or another. But Jonas was not Templeton.

Jonas never put on a show. He never talked that much, either.

Which meant Isaac had no choice but to take what he said on board. Even though he really, truly didn't want to do anything of the kind.

Jonas didn't stick around after that, no doubt having gotten in his daily quota of words. Isaac was grateful for the work on his desk. The messages on his phone. He lost himself in both. And had long, involved meetings with Oz, then Bethan, who was running command on the current ongoing missions.

When he'd done as much as he could do in this time zone, he swung by his office again, grabbed his bag, and headed to his cabin.

He didn't like that Horatio was "in town." And he really didn't like the fact that when he walked inside, he was struck by the memory of those few days Caradine had spent here. Those few days that had allowed him to imagine things he'd never dared imagine before. Not in such detail.

"Because you're an idiot," he muttered at himself.

He changed, then headed out for a brutal, near-vertical trail run, like he was trying to break himself on Hard Ass Pass.

But he was hard to break. That was part of what made him who he was.

Only when he'd made it back to his cabin in one piece, more or less, did he shower, then attempt to work on the wild man he might bring home from a mission but didn't like to show in town. He didn't need to give Otis Taggert any more ammunition.

"I know exactly who's in the mirror," he growled at his reflection.

He headed into town as the August sun began to put on a show, announcing the end of another one of the too-few remaining days of summer. Most of which he'd missed this year. That would catch up with him when the winter dark settled in.

Isaac liked all the toys that came with Alaska Force. The boats, the helicopters, the jet. But at heart, he was still the Alaskan boy who'd learned how to pilot pretty much anything that could float, thanks to his father. He took one of the smaller boats now, sticking close to the rocky shore as he made his way around to Grizzly Harbor.

He felt closer to the kid he'd been when he was out in

a small boat. Closer to the father who'd loved him even when he was at his teenage worst.

Closer to that life he might have had, had his parents lived.

He docked his boat and took a deep breath as he walked toward land. Grizzly Harbor hadn't been his home in years, but it still felt like it was. He liked seeing the lights go on in the houses and cabins as folks prepared for the coming dark. He liked knowing that if he showed his face in the Bait & Tackle, the way he liked to do sometimes, Otis Taggert would snipe at him. If he walked into the Blue Bear Inn, he would find Madeleine Yazzie there, her red beehive trembling and her face pressed to one of those paperbacks she got from her sister in Anchorage. He liked knowing almost everybody he saw on the street, especially in winter, when there were never any tourists around.

He wished that he could go back in time and tell his father that he got it now. That he understood that a town like this wrapped itself around a person, then sunk in deep, so it wasn't about whether it was *normal* or not. It wasn't even about whether or not Isaac liked it here. Grizzly Harbor was part of him. He was part of it.

Whether Caradine was here or not, he was. The way Gentrys had been for generations, no matter the tragedies that had befallen them.

That was the thing about belonging. You couldn't decide on it. It pretty much decided on you.

It was still summer, so even though it already looked like fall up on the mountain, with the clouds coming in low and that bite in the air, people were still out in what bit of daylight there was left. He nodded to Chris Tanaka, who was sitting down by the beach with a bottle of whiskey, and local fisherman Ben McCreedie, who was never sober on dry land. He smiled at the constantly shifting cluster of romantic drama that was Maria, Luz, the men they traded back and forth, and their babies of uncertain paternity, who were gathered together outside the general store having one of their intense conversations.

Isaac assumed that Horatio had jumped in a boat with Griffin one night and headed to the house Griffin and Mariah kept here in town, so he walked in that direction. But halfway up the hill, right when he should have turned to climb up toward Griffin's house, he stopped.

Because where he expected to see the burned-out husk of what had once been the Water's Edge Café, he saw instead . . . something else. Something new.

Brand-new construction, in fact. And where the old sign had once been, painted by Alonzo and Martie Hagan all those years ago and ignored entirely by Caradine, there was a bright new one.

THE NEW WATER'S EDGE CAFÉ, it shouted, in a big and bold graphic that Isaac knew instantly had been designed by Everly. COME FOR THE FIRE, STAY FOR THE FOOD.

Isaac's heart did something funny in his chest, but he was good at ignoring that by now. Instead of heading for Griffin's, he walked up the street toward the café, his boots making a familiar sound as they hit the wood of the boardwalk beneath him.

And he didn't choose to acknowledge what his pulse was doing when he drew close.

The restaurant was completely rebuilt. There had been one big room, but now there were two. There were more windows in front, letting in the view. He could see that the kitchen had been seriously upgraded. Not only upgraded. It was open and visible—so whoever cooked there wouldn't be hidden away, banging pots and pans as a communication device instead of talking.

"Isn't that something?"

Isaac didn't jump, because he was too well trained, but it wasn't lost on him that old Ernie Tatlelik had wandered up to him without his noticing.

Get it together, Gentry, he snapped at himself.

Isaac shook his head. "How did this happen?"

The old man gave him a look. "You know how it is around here. We don't like it when outsiders mess up our stuff. And nobody wants to spend the winter living off burgers from the Fairweather."

Ernie howled at that, as if he'd made a joke, then tottered off in that particular bowlegged walk of his.

Isaac couldn't seem to move.

It was good for everyone, of course, that the Water's Edge Café continued to exist. Grizzly Harbor didn't have much in the way of restaurants, so losing this one would be a blow. He hadn't even gotten around to thinking what winter would be like without it. Everybody in town relied on this place. On it opening early when folks had to get their boats out. On the holiday meals Caradine cooked, creating a festive atmosphere that it occurred to him now, looking back, was as much for her as it had been for the rest of them. Not that she'd ever admit it.

But he didn't know how he was going to act like it was the same now. How he was going to walk in and see someone else back there in the kitchen, cooking food that would never be as good as Caradine's.

The new owner might even have a menu, like a regular restaurant. Everything in him rebelled at the thought.

For someone who'd lost almost everyone he'd ever loved, Isaac thought darkly, he sure was bad at it.

Against his will, he found his gaze moving up the hill in the direction of that blue house where he'd grown up. The house that Amy had always wanted to sell, let others live in, or *something.* But Isaac had insisted they leave it as it was. A dedicated museum to loss and grief. And the life he'd thought he was going to live when he was sixteen.

The things Caradine had said to him in that hotel room seemed to hum inside him then.

Your response to your parents' death was to turn yourself into the patron saint of lost causes, she'd said. And worse still, *You don't want to win, Isaac. You want to suffer.*

It was hard to argue with the truth of that when he was staring at a house he'd made into a gravestone.

He turned and headed down the hill, but instead of going to Griffin's, he headed for the Fairweather. Because it seemed he was going to need a little whiskey to handle being home.

The sky was turning pink when he reached the bar, reminding him unpleasantly of the tropical sunset he'd shared with Caradine in that damned waterfall. He didn't think he was ever going to get that out of his head.

He pushed through the heavy door, certain that a long pour from his favorite bartender would get his head on straight. Things would get back to normal soon enough. He would do his job. Life would go on.

Because that was always the hardest part. Life went on whether he was finished mourning or not. Life went on no matter how he grieved, no matter what he'd lost, no matter how broken he felt.

Life went on. All Isaac had to do was live it.

He stepped into the familiar, dim embrace of the best dive bar on the planet, and his gaze went almost instantly to the bar.

More specifically, to the once again dark-haired woman who sat at the bar with his dog at her feet. The woman who looked like she'd been engaged in conversation with the man to her left, who bore an uncanny resemblance to Isaac's hermit of an uncle.

But even as he thought that, she turned. As if his entrance had been magnetic and her eyes were pulled straight to him, against her will.

The way it had been five years ago.

Caradine.

Here.

And this time, Isaac was the one who walked to the bar, his gaze locked on to hers.

When he got there, she turned around on her bar seat and leaned back lazily. It was a fair representation of how he had greeted her all those years back.

Horatio whined at him, but as he'd clearly chosen sides, Isaac did, too.

Caradine. Here.

He couldn't look at anything or anyone but her.

"Good Lord, Gentry," she drawled, sharp and spiky, the way he liked her best. "What took you so long?"

Twenty-six

Caradine had never been normal.

Deciding she was going to live like a normal person now that she wasn't dead, and might in fact live a long and happy life, was easy in theory. In practice, however, it was . . . harder.

There had been the publicity she'd thrown herself into, theorizing that the best defense was a calculated offense—and the more noise she made about being the last remaining Sheeran, the less anyone would even think of looking for Lindsay. Or be tempted to come after her.

But all that had come to a screeching halt when Jimmy died.

She'd been surprised to find that his death made her more emotional than she would have imagined. Not because she mourned him, specifically. She didn't. But because, with his death, she could finally mourn what had happened ten years ago. Because she didn't have to run anymore.

We're free, she'd told Lindsay when she'd gone ahead

and called her. On a regular phone, no codes or protocols. *You don't have to be dead if you don't want to.*

Like we know how to be alive, Lindsay had replied, sounding shell-shocked and possibly happy and, like Caradine, maybe swamped with too many conflicting feelings about all the things they'd been too busy surviving to process.

Julia had laid down one last trail, just in case.

Then Caradine had taken all her conflicted feelings home. Where she belonged.

"What are you doing here?" Isaac asked, looking brooding and beautiful, and maddening, all at once.

And he was still the only thing she could see when he walked into a room.

"I've decided to stay here," she said, the way she'd imagined saying it to him approximately nine million times. Casually. Not coldly, but not warmly, either. Just a simple statement of fact. "Turns out, I like it here. I like being Caradine Scott."

"Does that mean you like hiding from the FBI?"

"The FBI didn't know where I was for maybe twenty-four hours. But they're the FBI. They found me." She saw his jaw tighten, but she was getting to the main point. "In exchange for Julia Sheeran's testimony when necessary, they're going to issue me documents making me . . . me. Legally."

When he only gazed back at her in the same impassive manner, she sighed. "I'm going to be Caradine forever, Isaac."

His reaction was underwhelming. If it weren't for that hard jaw of his looking more like marble by the second, she might have thought he didn't hear her.

"Caradine forever," he repeated. "Is this a joke?"

The man beside her, whom she'd forgotten about, let out a raspy laugh. "You never were any good at taking on information you didn't want, boy, were you?"

Caradine watched, with perhaps too much satisfaction, as Isaac turned his head and finally looked at the person she was having a drink with tonight.

"Uncle Theo," he said, his tone forbidding. "I thought that was you. But why would my famously antisocial uncle be out here in civilization when he could be tucked away in his off-grid, nearly unreachable cabin? Far out of reach of the government?"

"A man likes an invitation," Theo replied, through his acres of beard. He nodded at Caradine. "She came all the way up the mountain and *asked me*."

"Besides," Caradine said after a moment, when Isaac's gray gaze pinned her again, "it turns out that your uncle can build pretty much anything. Like a new restaurant, for example."

"I saw that." Isaac's eyes narrowed. "Looks like you expanded."

"This is the new, improved Caradine Scott," she said loftily. "Who knows what I'll do? Maybe I'll make up a menu, or one of those adorable daily chalkboards. Or start dispensing hugs at the front door."

She didn't see Isaac's gaze so much as flicker, but he reached out and picked up her hand. Not to hold it. But if she was reading that expression on his face correctly, as an accusation.

Caradine tilted up her chin. "That's right. That's a bright pink nail polish. Not chipped, but glossy and perfect. Do you know how hard it is to keep shiny magenta nail polish from chipping, Isaac? Well, it doesn't matter. I'm doing it. That's the level of commitment I'm prepared to deliver."

And for a moment there was nothing but his hand touching hers. The weight of his gaze, all gray and no hint of silver. Distantly, it occurred to her that he might have taken her comment on commitment to mean something else entirely.

Her head felt light. As if she were drunk when she'd been nursing the same beer since she'd gotten here.

How had she forgotten that he could do that? When he wasn't even looking at her as if he wanted to tear her clothes off?

"Are you trying to steal my dog?" he asked her, quietly.

He shifted his gaze to Horatio, whose tail battered the floor. But the dog didn't move until Isaac nodded, and then, once again, Caradine could only stare while Isaac smiled at the dog, took his furry head in his hands, and *crooned*.

Her heart exploded into a million pieces, so the good news was, she'd already gotten used to living without it the past couple of months.

"Horatio's been my best friend this summer," she told the man who'd taken her heart with him when he'd left. On a mission no one here would give her any details about, not even when he might come back. Jerks. "Dependable. Loyal. Always here, and always happy to see me. Really, the perfect man."

She didn't know which jerk had transported Horatio over from Fool's Cove. But a few days after she'd arrived back in Grizzly Harbor to see what was left of this life of hers, the only life she'd liked so far, Horatio had appeared. He'd been her shadow ever since.

And if she'd fallen asleep cuddling him a little too tight, that was no one's business but hers. Also, she would deny it.

"That dog has more sense than you," Theo chimed in.

Isaac glared at his uncle. A look that would have made even Caradine shake a little and rethink some things.

But Theo Gentry only laughed. "It's good to see you, too, Nephew. You should come by sometime. Remember you're not alone out here. It might do you some good."

"You told me not to visit you," Isaac pointed out. "With a shotgun in hand."

Theo laughed again. "When you were a self-righteous,

sanctimonious lieutenant fresh out of OCS. Never let it be said a Gentry doesn't know how to nurse a grudge."

And then he hefted up his drink, nodded at Caradine, and wandered over in the vague direction of the pool tables.

Isaac took his time turning all of his considerable attention back on her. "I'll ask you again. What are you doing here?"

"Do you really want to have this conversation here?"

Isaac studied her, and she hated that she couldn't read him. "I'm not the one who usually likes an audience."

Of all the things he'd said to her, that struck her as perhaps the most unjust.

Caradine stood up in a rush. She was tired of glaring at him. Of scowling and sniping endlessly. She wanted to hit him, but then, she always did. That chest of his looked like sculpted marble beneath the henley he wore, and some months, that was the only way she got to touch it.

But she'd told him she was tired of fighting. Now she needed to show him.

"If I wanted to fight with you, sure," she said, striving to sound serene. Or at least even-keeled. "We're not doing that."

"Aren't we?"

With a tremendous dignity she only wished she'd had with this man in the past, she turned and walked toward the door. Horatio looped around her as she pushed her way outside, letting the dog run in front of her. Out in the street it was getting on to full darkness, though a hint of indigo still remained.

The crisp Alaskan air filled her lungs, and she still wasn't finished marveling at it. Not when she'd taken a tour of so many other places this summer, none of which got to her like this. She loved the quiet that hung all around the town, as if it poured out of the mountain itself. No traffic, no crowds, no oppressive heat or humidity. She could hear the music from inside the bar. There were people wandering around, talking in the mild evening. Somewhere in the trees, she could hear a guitar and some singing.

But in and around all of that, there was Alaska.

It felt like peace, no matter how far from that she might have been feeling inside. It made her imagine that if she stayed here long enough, breathed deep enough, she would get there, too.

And the man who she knew was behind her, though she couldn't hear him and didn't look, was the same kind of presence. That huge. That intense.

That perfect.

She didn't wait for him. She headed down toward the beach. Before she reached the docks, she took a turn and climbed up a set of rocks that were almost like stairs. She navigated out to the large, flat boulder that jutted out toward the water.

He didn't make any noise, but she knew when he climbed up and stood beside her, there on the edge.

Below them, the tide was coming in. The dark water surged against the stone, retreating but always returning. Five years ago she'd stood right here and identified with the water. Always fighting, always failing.

Tonight, she was thinking about the rock. Still here. Still solid.

No matter what the water threw at it.

"Do you remember?" she asked him. She turned then, as the stars got bright above them and the inky night seemed to grip them, hard.

"Caradine." He ran a hand over his face, which made her pulse kick at her, because this was Isaac. He didn't do things like that. He didn't fidget. *Unless,* something in her whispered hopefully, because she let herself do that now, *he's just as agitated as you are.* "I remember everything."

And his voice was so raw it hurt.

It actually *hurt.*

She even lifted her hands as though she were going to put them on him, but he gave her a look that was so intense she dropped them to her sides.

"Why did you come back here?" he demanded, and he wasn't loud this time. He didn't shout. But his voice was ragged. Uneven. And somehow, that was worse. "After all the things you said in Boston?"

She wanted to do what she normally did. Scowl. Glare. Say something mean and storm off.

But if she kept doing the same things with him, she would end up in the same place with him. You couldn't expect things to change if you weren't willing to change, too. The fact that motivational quotes made her feel dead inside didn't make them untrue. And she didn't have to festoon them around her restaurant on cheerful plaques, decorated with butterflies, to take them on board.

That was a performance. Here in the dark, on a cold rock above a pitiless sea, she could do the hard work.

All she had to do was let herself be vulnerable.

She thought she really did die then. But that didn't change what she needed to do here.

After all, she'd basically died at least once already.

"What is it you want from me?" he asked, still in that rough, un-Isaac voice.

Maybe, just maybe, she wasn't the only one feeling vulnerable tonight. She clung to that.

"Everything," she told him, and she didn't look away. She didn't hide. She held his gaze, and she let him see whatever he wanted to see. She let herself . . . open. "I want absolutely everything, Isaac."

He looked away, down toward the rock, but this time, it wasn't to tighten that jaw she was afraid might shatter one day. It wasn't to look over to where Horatio waited on land, as if he were guarding them. This time, Isaac was breathing too hard.

As if he were running when he was standing still.

Tears pricked at her eyes, another thing that she would

normally dive into the cold water rather than let someone else see, but this was Isaac. And she was *doing this*, so she did nothing. She didn't blink them away. She didn't wipe at her face.

"The first night I saw you," she said quietly, "we walked down here after we left the Fairweather. We stood on this rock, just like this." Her throat was dry, and swallowing didn't help, so she pushed on. "I said I couldn't imagine coming from a place like this. And you said, it's not the winter that ruins you. It's the summer. Because you can resign yourself to winter, but summer reminds you how to hope for better. And then there you are when fall blows in, left to pick up the pieces and start all over again."

He made a low noise. "I know what I said."

"You made it sound like you were joking when you said it. I'm pretty sure I laughed. But you weren't joking, were you?"

"It was something my father used to say. He thought it was funny." He cut his gaze to hers. "We're really going to talk about the weather?"

"It's not really about the weather, is it?" She tilted her head as she looked up at him, and if there was vulnerability in him, he was hiding it well. "It's the way you see the world. It's all *endurance*. Struggle and pain and hopelessness. And any little sliver you have of something better you treat like the enemy."

"It takes real guts for you, of all people, to stand here and say something like that."

"I had to act that way. You didn't."

"You concealed your identity from me for *five years*," he belted out at her.

So loud that back on shore, Horatio whined.

But Caradine had to bite back a smile. Because Isaac Gentry had just shouted at her. Right out here in the open, displaying a shocking lack of his much-vaunted control for anyone to hear and see.

What had happened in her hotel room in Boston wasn't a fluke.

"You're the only person I ever wanted to tell," she told him, solemnly, because it was true. "I came close to telling you a thousand times."

"But you didn't. And then you ran. You let me think you were dead. You *wanted me* to think you were dead."

She studied his face as he said that. The wildness in his eyes, like a storm.

"You can endure anything, can't you?" she said softly. "Except the possibility that you might be happy."

Isaac muttered something under his breath.

Caradine decided to take that as encouragement. "All my worst fears came true this summer, Isaac. They found me. And worse, you discovered who I really was."

"How could that be worse?"

"Because, Captain America, I've spent my whole life thinking it was only a matter of time before the ugliness in me spilled over. And then corroded everything around me. I'd already watched it happen. That was what being a member of my family did to people."

He looked astonished then, and it was gratifying. "That's ridiculous."

"For years I've been sure that at any moment, that switch could flip. That when I least expected it, I could just . . . turn into a murderous sociopath. Burn down houses filled with people I knew. Commit unspeakable acts of violence. That was the other reason Lindsay and I split up after Phoenix. We were responsible for what happened to those people. We had to live with that—and with the worry that one false step and we'd sink even further, and maybe start doing hideous things like that ourselves."

"I don't think it works like that."

"You *hope* it doesn't work like that. So did I, but I went off on my own anyway, just in case." She smiled when he looked like he was going to argue with her. "But then I went to Hawaii. And I discovered that my baby sister—the one who I'd always thought was more likely to turn bad, because she was the one who'd given in to Dad—hadn't just *survived* our time apart. She'd *thrived*. Made a life. Lindsay got married and had a baby."

Caradine shook her head, aware that there was moisture on her cheeks but doing nothing to hide it. "All that time that she's spent living, I've been hiding away up here. Because I thought that at any second, *boom*. I would turn into my father."

Isaac was staring at her now. There on that rock that, despite herself, she had always considered theirs.

Because it was the first place he'd kissed her.

Back when she'd imagined she could kiss a man like Isaac and then let him go.

"Caradine," he said, very deliberately. "There isn't a single part of you that is anything like your father."

But she couldn't stop, or she'd never keep going. "Then we went to Boston. And I saw what it really looks like to be made in my father's image. Head to toe, no matter what face he bought to hide behind." She shook her head, tasting salt on her lips. "And that wasn't something that *happened* to Jimmy. He was like that from the start. As long as I can remember, he was openly, happily psychotic."

"You're nothing like him, either. You couldn't be if you tried."

And she loved how fierce he sounded then. Like he would go back in time and punch Jimmy in the face all over again if he could.

"I wanted to kill him, but you wouldn't let me," she said. "And at first I didn't understand that. Why wouldn't you let me do what had to be done? But then I got it. You knew what that would make me. The exact thing I didn't want to become."

"There are things you can't take back," he said gruffly.

This time, she reached over and took his hand in hers.

And she could tell that he wanted to pull it back, but he didn't. It was another victory.

So she held his hand between her palms, feeling all of his strength. And heat. And the sheer *Isaacness* that fueled the fire in her, the electricity, and that beautiful spark that lit up even the darkest night. Here and always.

"Isaac," she whispered. "Baby. You can't take things back, but some things don't need taking back. That you've had to make hard choices doesn't mean you're responsible for the losses you suffered. You're no more of a monster than I am."

She felt the jolt go through him, a full-body affair. His hand tightened in hers, but he didn't jerk away.

"I know exactly what I'm responsible for," he said in that low, uneven voice.

"You know what you blame yourself for," she corrected him. "That's not the same thing."

Caradine reached over and took his other hand, and she wanted to laugh at that startled look on his face, as if he couldn't believe this was happening. She laced her fingers with his, and she tipped her head back to look at him.

"I'm not going to argue with you," she said. "We could argue forever. We already have."

"Caradine."

And she realized, belatedly, that her name was a full sentence as far as he was concerned. She could hear the exasperation. The resignation. The affection and the longing. All of their history, all of that need and denial, wrapped up in three syllables.

She was definitely going to be Caradine forever.

"You need to listen to me," he said, and he sounded like himself again. The commander of the universe. "For a change."

"You're in charge of everything," she reminded him. "But not me. We're not on one of your missions."

"Let's talk about that. The part where you *took off*

your wire and walked into a situation when you *knew* you could—"

She put her hand over his mouth.

His eyes darkened with astonishment. And the promise of retribution.

"I told you I was done fighting, so let's cut to the chase before you have another temper tantrum and disappear into the jungle for another two months." She ignored his sound of protest. "You are head over heels in love with me, Isaac."

His mouth was firm and hard beneath her hand, but he went still. Very. Very still.

"And that was easier to take when you thought it was a lost cause, because surrendering yourself to something you can never have requires nothing of you. You know it." She dropped her hand, but she kept her gaze glued to his. "I ran away from you, yes, and you thought I was dead. For maybe ten minutes."

"Twenty, Caradine. *Twenty.*"

"But you ran away from me, too, and I knew perfectly well that you were alive. I don't think you can convince me that what you went through was worse."

She could see everything in him tighten. That gunmetal gaze, so dark tonight. All the strong, tough muscles in his body, which was always a weapon, but could also hold her so tenderly she'd actually slept like that. In his arms. So tenderly it had hurt to wake up and remember that she couldn't have him.

Caradine pushed on. "Deep down, you think you could have done something to keep your parents alive. Sometimes I think I could have done something to keep my whole family alive. You think you're a monster. I know, given the chance, I could be, too." That muscle was flexing in his cheek. His mouth was a hard line. So she smiled, big and bright, and watched his pupils dilate. "Don't you see? You're not going to scare me, Isaac. Because I love you, too. I think it started right here on this rock that very first night. Or why else would I have been so scared to let you in?"

He let out a breath then, long, hard, ragged. As if he'd just finished one of his revolting workouts.

"When I was hopeless," she whispered, "the only hope I had was you. I tried so hard to hate you for that. But all I could ever seem to do was love you instead."

"Baby." And his voice came out of him like it belonged to someone else, tortured and wild. "Caradine. You're killing me."

"When I went to Germany, I had every intention of wandering off into the wilds of Europe and losing myself forever. Because that was what I always thought I wanted to do. But, Isaac. When I was finally free, when Jimmy was dead and no one was coming after me and I could finally do anything I wanted, the only thing I wanted was you."

"Listen to me." He grabbed her shoulders then, in a grip that might have been uncomfortable if she didn't long for it the way she did. If it didn't thrill her. "You weren't wrong. Those things you said to me in Boston . . . I wanted to dismiss it all out of hand, but I couldn't. Because you were right."

"This isn't about who's right and who's wrong," she said, sounding as wild as he did. As if the Alaskan sea all around them was in them, too. "This is about what has always been between us. Always, Isaac."

"From day one. I know."

Caradine smiled, and there were tears everywhere. But she truly didn't care. She slid her hands onto his chest. "What if, once in our lives, we got to do it over? The right way, this time. What if we got to make this one thing right?"

She watched this man, this beautiful, remarkably tough man, crumble.

She watched that storm break in his gray gaze. She watched the thunder, the rain, and then everything was silver.

Isaac dropped his forehead down to hers, and then they were both gasping for air together, as if they might never breathe normally again.

Then he was kissing her, or she was kissing him.

And it was so hot it burned, but it was more than heat.

It had always been more than heat. Even that very first night, when he'd kissed her here and changed them both. Forever.

"We don't have to do it over," Isaac said against her mouth. "I don't regret a single moment of the past five years. Not if it brought us here."

"We were always coming here," Caradine said right back. "Always. If it wasn't worth it, we wouldn't have fought it so hard."

Isaac lifted her up, wrapping her in his arms and grinning when her legs went around his waist.

"No more running," he said. "No more hiding."

"I won't if you won't," she vowed, wrapped around him at last.

And this time, she never planned to stop. This time, she could fall asleep in his arms and wake up with him, only to do it all over again. This time, maybe he would sleep, too.

This time, they could love each other the way they should have from the start. Openly. Happily.

"The only place I'm running," Caradine promised him, "is straight to you."

The way she always had, even when she hadn't wanted to admit it. Even when she'd run all the way to Maine, she'd known he would come after her. She hadn't believed that anyone could save her, but deep down, that part of her she'd pretended wasn't there had hoped that he would.

Because he already had.

The same way, she thought, she'd saved him. One hope, one smile, one winter made of stolen bits of happiness woven into the darkness, one at a time.

That was how they'd made it here.

That was how they'd go on.

Nothing beige about it.

Isaac kissed her again, deep and long, right there on the spot where he'd kissed her the first time. Horatio, too smart by far, barked his approval from the shore.

She would push him, but he wouldn't break, because he was tough and strong and the kind of man who held on to the things he loved. And she would hold him tight right back, no matter how he challenged her, because she'd been waiting all her life for someone to truly love her—and five long years to allow herself to love him.

And it wasn't a do-over. They didn't need one.

But starting now, they were going to do it right. They were going to love each other forever, openly and honestly and always.

At last.

Caradine couldn't wait to see how they saved each other next.

Twenty-seven

Blue married Everly while it was still technically summer. Alaska had other ideas, dressing up Grizzly Harbor in fine fall colors with the requisite cold, foggy mornings, rainy days that sometimes yielded to the moody sun, and deep, thick nights that hinted of the dark winter to come.

It was Isaac's favorite time of year.

On the wedding day itself, all the friends and family who'd made the trek from the Lower 48 to celebrate the tough ex-SEAL and the woman who had been his neighbor as a child were treated to a little bit of the kind of Alaskan splendor that made Isaac prouder than usual to be born and bred right here, where he stood.

The bride was gorgeous, of course. Her smile was so big and wide as she walked down the aisle they'd made on the hill overlooking the water that it made everybody else smile, too.

Especially Blue, waiting for her in his dress blues.

And Isaac thought that the rest of his Alaska Force friends and colleagues stood a little taller, because one of their own was taking this step none of them could have imagined possible a few years ago. Not for Blue—and not for any of them, either.

Because when an individual had seen as much as they all had, sometimes it was tempting to imagine they'd never see anything else. Isaac knew that all too well.

But everything was different now.

Isaac stood at attention while Blue and Everly said their vows, high above the waters of the harbor. And Alaska put on a show for them, with whales spouting in the distance and a sunset so magnificent it made everyone gasp.

Still, his eyes were for the caterer of this wedding, who stood at the back of the gathered assembly.

Scowling, naturally.

And Isaac was an expert on those scowls. This one was Caradine pretending not to be moved by the ceremony taking place—or the jaw-dropping sunset, for that matter. And if he wasn't mistaken, and he very rarely was on this subject, she was also ever so slightly stressed out about the fact that she was going to be feeding all these people.

Something she would rather die than admit.

And when her eyes met his and her scowl deepened, he knew that one was all for him.

They were figuring it out, one step at a time. The first thing Isaac had done, that night on the rock, was take Caradine back to her apartment. Where they both reacquainted themselves with each other on her bed, the way they had the first night they'd met.

And all those nights afterward.

Are you going to throw me out? he'd asked lazily, a long while later, when they were both sprawled out and breathless.

I'm thinking about it, she'd replied, grinning at him. *Just for the sake of historical accuracy, you understand.*

He'd done his best to convince her that history was best when it was revisited but conscientiously updated to fit the modern era.

And that was the first night that he allowed himself to fall asleep while he was lying next to her. Then stay asleep, with his arms wrapped around her and his head near hers, for the whole of the night.

He hadn't actually known that was possible.

Good God, Gentry, she'd said the following morning when she'd woken him up, which had to be the first time in as long as he could remember that he'd had to be *woken up* by another person. *I thought you were dead.*

But the truth was, Isaac felt fully alive.

Alive and kicking for the first time since that plane had gone down so many years ago.

In that vein, he'd called up his sister. Amy had come out to Grizzly Harbor, and the two of them had made the trek out to Uncle Theo's cabin, where they'd spent a surprisingly pleasant night. And then all three of them had gone to the blue house there on the hill and cleaned it out at last. Until it was a house again, a potential home, not a sad grave marker to two people who would never, ever have wanted to be stuck in stone.

Mom and Dad would love this for you, Amy said fiercely after a breakfast in the Water's Edge Café the morning she left. She was headed north to the house she kept up in Fairbanks, but only in the summer. During the winters, she and her husband left Fairbanks to the snow and subzero temperatures and poked around the Lower 48 in their fifth wheel, visiting her kids at college and usually finding their way to a selection of beaches. *They would love Caradine.*

Isaac had looked back at the café, standing tall and shiny and new. And its owner, who wasn't as cheerful as the colors she'd used on her walls—but wasn't exactly the grumpy black cloud she'd pretended to be for five years, either. Especially with her new addiction to screamingly bright nail polish.

They would, he'd agreed. *They really would.*

I can tell you as a parent, Isaac. Amy had smiled when she'd hugged him. *They just wanted us happy.*

He thought about that a lot, particularly today. Because a man he would have said had no more acquaintance with real happiness than he did looked . . . swamped with it. Blue was grinning ear to ear, especially once Everly became his wife.

"That's forever, baby," Blue said, though that wasn't in his vows.

"That sounds like a good start," Everly replied.

And it was hard to say who kissed whom, only that it sure looked a lot like forever from where Isaac was standing.

After the ceremony, everyone gathered in the big tent Isaac and the others had helped put up behind the wedding site. The whole village was invited, because that was how they did it here in Grizzly Harbor. A wedding was like another one of their beloved festivals. A local band played, everyone wandered around and got acquainted while Everly and Blue took pictures, and Caradine bustled here and there with her usual fierce energy and smart mouth, feeding all of them appetizers.

Her food had always been love. Isaac knew that now.

But tonight it was something even better than that.

Because she was happy, too, and he was pretty sure everyone could taste it. He knew he could.

Once the blue house had been cleaned, repainted, and taken care of the way it should have been years ago, Isaac had moved in.

You have a cabin in Fool's Cove, Caradine had said, glaring at him from the fancy new kitchen of the Water's

Edge Café while she made lunch for a few tables. *Why do you need two residences on one island?*

Because sometimes I'll need to be in Fool's Cove, and sometimes I'll need to be here, he said. He raised a brow at her. *Won't I?*

I thought we were all in, she'd said, frowning at him. *Or is this one of your cute little games? The ones you pretend you're not playing when we all know you are. And then we end up going round and round and—*

I want you to live in it with me, jackass. He'd cut her off. *I thought that was the plan. Isn't that what you asked me in Boston? You can stay in both places, too, unless you'd rather have your own place you can throw me out of. Are we doing that again?*

She'd scowled at him. And burned a grilled cheese.

No, she'd said, grinning down at the ruined sandwich as she scraped it out of the pan. *We're definitely not doing that.*

And that was how, almost five years exactly after their first night together, Isaac and Caradine not only stopped hiding their relationship, they solidified it by shacking up together. In the blue house on the hill that she'd christened with a strange painting of sailboats and red canoes.

Now, can we talk about you and Isaac? Mariah had asked Caradine a few moments later from a nearby table, grinning over the top of her laptop, where she was working on her various accounting spreadsheets.

Sure, Caradine had replied serenely. *If you want a lifetime ban from the café.*

Because she was still Caradine. She didn't magically transform into a Disney princess overnight, thank God.

The truth was, Isaac liked her a little surly. He liked her grumpy, he loved that scowl, and he would have had to beat someone up if there had ever been menus in the Water's Edge Café. Or the artistic chalkboards detailing specials, complete with smiley faces, that she showed him on her phone at night while she laughed like a lunatic.

Over the course of that first month, they both learned how to be all the things they were with each other for the first time, instead of just feeling them. Because it was one thing to make grand, sweeping announcements about how no one was hiding anymore. And it was something else to turn those statements into actual intimacy.

Waking up together. Sleeping together. Simple negotiations about things like counter space in a bathroom. There was roommate stuff, relationship stuff, and, for them, the fascinating shift from knowing each other for a long time, plus sex, into building something that was about both of them. Together.

It was like the tables his grandfather had made. It wasn't enough to choose the right piece of wood. The wood had to reveal itself to the maker, too. Art only happened when those two things were aligned.

And if you're lucky, his gruff grandpa had told Isaac when he was small, *you figure out how to make it beautiful.*

As goals went, Isaac liked that one the most.

"Ladies and gentlemen," Everly said now, clapping her hands together to get the crowd's attention and direct it to where she and Blue stood. "Dinner is served."

She looked over her shoulder at the long tables where Caradine had set up her offerings and was now standing off to the side, looking mulish and put out.

Everly grinned. "For those of you who aren't lucky enough to know my friend Caradine, she's famous here in Grizzly Harbor."

"I wasn't told there would be speeches," Caradine muttered.

"Suck it up," Isaac suggested from beside her, winning a scowl for his trouble.

Everly was addressing the crowd again. "When I first

arrived in Grizzly Harbor, looking for Blue, I made the mistake of trying to order something from Caradine's café." All the locals groaned at that, and Everly laughed. "The thing about the Water's Edge Café is that you don't order. Caradine gives you what you want, whether you want it or not, and you accept that. Because it's usually the best food you've ever had in your life."

Caradine's brows rose. "Usually?"

Isaac only grinned.

"When Blue and I decided to get married here," Everly said, pausing for a moment to smile up at her brand-new husband, who gripped her hand like he had no intention of ever letting go, "we knew that no celebration could possibly be complete without Caradine's food. In true Caradine style, there have been no tastings, no consultations, and Blue and I have absolutely no idea what we're about to feed you."

Everly looked over at Caradine then, her eyes full.

And, if Isaac wasn't mistaken, Caradine's eyes were suspiciously bright as well. Though if he pointed it out, she'd deny it. And probably hit him.

"But I already know one thing," Everly said, her voice a little thick. "If you could put love on a plate, that's what Caradine does, every single day, as long as I've known her. This is going to be the best food you've ever had at a wedding. Maybe in your whole life."

And it was.

Later, after the crowd had stopped cheering at all the speeches, the ones that made everyone laugh, and the ones that made them cry, Isaac found his favorite caterer standing by herself, her arms crossed, biting back a smile while Blue and Everly had their first dance.

"If you came over here to say nice things to me," Caradine told him, scowling ferociously to hide the hectic glitter in her blue eyes, "you can stop right there. Mariah hugged me extensively and without my consent.

Kate *almost* did, which was worse. And then *Bethan* got emotional about my salmon. I'm full up, Isaac."

"Too bad, baby," he replied.

He took her hand, still amazed that he got to do that. Right here in public, where everyone could see. He *wanted* them to see.

He drew her out with him as other couples joined Blue and Everly on the dance floor. Mariah and Griffin. Templeton and Kate. Blue's mom and stepfather. Everly's parents.

Isaac pulled his woman into his arms, where she still fit. Perfectly.

"I don't dance," Caradine told him.

He grinned down at her. "You do with me."

And the Alaskan winter would come in hard, the way it always did. Life would do the same, throwing up obstacles and testing them to see what they were made of. To show them who they were.

Luckily, they already knew.

He spun Caradine out and she laughed, tossing back her head and letting out a sound of pure delight. He couldn't get enough of it. And when Isaac glanced around the tent, he could see the startled looks on the faces of all these people here who loved her, too. From the bride and the groom right on down to crotchety old Otis Taggert.

Because this was family. And Caradine was theirs.

And Isaac planned to dedicate his life to making her happy, but these were the people, and this was the place, that would help keep the both of them whole.

"I love you, Gentry," she said when he spun her back to him.

"You used to call me that when you wanted to keep me in my place. Now you do it when you're holding me close. You can see how that's confusing."

"Isaac," she said, her face open and bright and all his.

Just as she was all his. "I don't ever want to be predictable."

"You say that like you could be if you tried."

Her smile widened. "I don't think we have to jump through any hoops to get a happy ever after, by the way. I'm pretty sure it's already started."

"Five years ago," he agreed. "I was there."

And there were so many things they were going to do together. Go back to Hawaii and stay there awhile. Take vacations in pretty parts of the world where neither of them had to fight a thing. Isaac was going to sleep more and obsess less. Caradine was going to accept that people loved her, she could love them back, and figure out how to live when she didn't have to hide.

Someday soon, he was going to make her his wife, and he could already see the kind of mother she was going to be to his kids. One a lot like his, if he had to guess, so he already knew those kids were going to be lucky. He would raise them right here in that same blue house and then laugh at them when they complained about living in the middle of nowhere, the way his father had before him.

At some point he was going to retire from Alaska Force, too. Or at least from active missions, and she would help him figure that out. And she would cook when she felt like it, ban people when she didn't, and he would build her whatever life she wanted.

Wherever and however she wanted it.

And all of those things seemed to hover there in the air around them while they danced, gazing at each other, under a tent they'd helped put up to celebrate two people they loved.

They danced all night. They ate Caradine's food, they celebrated with their friends and family, and it was dark and chilly when Isaac finally took her home.

Where they danced some more.

Just the two of them, up in the bedroom where they would make their babies, patch up their differences, and make their life together sing.

And the love that had always burned so bright between them was the only light they would need to illuminate those beautiful, endless Alaska nights.

Then, now, and forever.

Acknowledgments

My thanks, as ever, to Kerry Donovan and everyone at Berkley!

And to Holly Root, for all the things.

But above all, thanks to the readers who've loved this series along with me!

Thank you for taking Alaska Force into your hearts!

Continue reading for a preview
of the newest Alaska Force book

SPECIAL OPS
Seduction

Coming in early 2021!

The sudden explosion wasn't the first clue that all was not as it should be in this supposedly abandoned saltpeter mining town in the Atacama Desert at high elevation west of the Chilean Andes, but it was the most emphatic.

And it almost knocked her over.

Bethan Wilcox—former Army Intelligence, PSYOPS, technically an Army Ranger, and currently a member of Alaska Force—had already had the sinking feeling this particular op was heading south. That queasy little twist, down in her gut, that she'd learned to trust implicitly in a different desert long ago.

But inklings and gut feelings were one thing. A bone-rattling C4 blast was another.

"Who knows we're here?" came a pissed-off growl over her comm unit. Even with her ears ringing, Bethan knew the speaker without him having to identify himself. Jonas Crow, who was a great many things—all of them complicated. But most importantly for her purposes at the moment, he was in charge of this operation. "Report."

"Holding steady," Bethan replied.

She scanned the open, arid square ringed with decrepit buildings, trying to see *who* had found them here so she could work on *how*. But there was nothing to see. It had taken them three days to climb the three thousand feet from sea level, moving only under the cover of night in almost complete radio silence as they picked their way through the distant gunfire of drug lord and mafia-controlled territories to access the town.

Bethan could have sworn they hadn't been seen. Much less followed.

That likely meant the threat had been waiting for them here, not stalking them across the desert.

Bethan turned that over in her head as the rest of the team checked in.

"Could be a coincidence," Griffin Cisneros, former Marine sniper, bit out in that cold voice of his. "There are landmines all over this area."

"Do you still have that line of sight, Bethan?" Jonas asked in that same low growl of his, though, as always, there was the way he said her name.

Bethan was a professional and keenly aware that she was the only female member of Alaska Force. It meant she worked out harder and longer and with more intensity and determination, back in Alaska at headquarters and everywhere else. It meant she always had to be conscious that she couldn't be only herself, she had to represent all the women who fought so hard to win coveted combat assignments, in the military and out. It meant she could never, ever lose her cool, no matter the situation.

It certainly meant that she was not about to admit to herself or anyone else that there was something about Jonas that got to her.

The way it always had.

"I can see just fine," she replied matter-of-factly. "The question is, was that blast for us personally or was it a little perimeter gift for anyone dumb enough to come out here? Is it supposed to put us off our game?"

"Do you feel off your game?" Jonas asked.

Because of course he did.

He didn't actively disapprove of her. Not Jonas. The man barely spoke of his own accord off mission, so it wasn't as if he'd made any speeches about how he didn't want her here. Still, he got that across. It was the distance, even when he was standing in front of her. The total silence that greeted any remark of hers that didn't require an operational response.

"Negative," she replied.

"Proceed," Jonas ordered her.

"I have you covered," Griffin said, cold and precise.

Bethan's gut was working overtime, but courage wasn't the absence of fear. It was using fear as fuel. She eased out of her protected position, squinting past the billowing smoke from what they'd had down as a meaningless outbuilding in this creepy, abandoned place. She could feel eyes on her, no doubt friend and foe alike, and wished she was in full combat gear—but that wasn't how they were playing this.

She quickly considered her options. The inhabited ruined building was directly across the square from where she was. The original plan had been for her to take the long way, skulking around the back of what was left of the row of houses where she'd been squatting. Then find a way in through a window that was almost certainly alarmed, if not actively guarded.

Bethan hadn't seen any guards yet. And it was always possible that someone was blowing stuff up on the outskirts of this crumbling ruin of a mining town for reasons that had nothing to do with why she was here. Anything was *possible*.

But the more likely scenario was that there were guards, and those guards knew Alaska Force was here. And that they'd expressed themselves with a little C4 as a welcoming gift, so there was no point sneaking around anymore.

Bethan stood. Then she sauntered around the corner of the ruined house like she was out for a stroll somewhere civilized. She headed across the arid dirt square, in the kind of broad desert daylight that made her lungs hurt, to go knock on what passed for the front door opposite.

"I like it," Rory Lockwood, former Green Beret, said with a quiet laugh from his position around the far flank of the building she was approaching. "A frontal assault always confuses them."

"Shock and awe, baby," August Vaz, former Army Night Stalker, agreed.

Jonas, naturally, was completely silent.

Bethan knocked. The sound echoed strangely out here, with the Andes towering in the distance and that profound, if deceptive, emptiness all around. She knew how American she was, because she wanted to see a tumbleweed roll by, or a creaking saloon door, or the beginning twangs of a Wild West theme. But there was nothing.

Bethan knocked again. Louder.

She could feel all the targets up and down her back as she stood there. As if the eyes on her were punching into the light, everyday tactical gear she wore and, worse, directly into the back of her deliberately uncovered head.

Look how friendly and approachable I am, her clothes were meant to proclaim across the desert, to all the various bad guys lurking around. *No need to shoot.*

Every single alarm inside her body was screaming bloody murder, and she wanted nothing more than to duck, cover, and hide. Instead, she stood tall. Because she knew the fact she wasn't visibly cowed was as much of a statement as a blast of C4. A bigger one, maybe.

"I know you're in there," Bethan said in a very specific dialect of a language that very few of her own countrymen knew existed. She aimed her voice through the makeshift door, leaning against the gutted wall beside it as if she felt nothing but casual, here in the middle of a creepy, abandoned desert village in a place even the few, hardy locals avoided. "The trouble is, everyone knows you're in there. And sooner or later, they're going to come. All of them. And they won't knock at the door, as I think you know. They'll come right in—if they haven't already."

She waited as the pitiless sun beat down on her. She had that same sort of split focus she often did in situations like this. There was a part of her that was all here, right now. She was aware of everything, from the faint sounds of life from the other falling-down structures around the square, to the wind from the far-off mountains, to that skin-crawling sensation of being in the crosshairs of too many targets. And on the other hand, she found herself thinking of her home of a year and a half now. In faraway Alaska, where a March afternoon like this one would almost certainly be gray. And wet. It might even be snowing.

"All I want to do is ask you a question," she said to the door. Conversationally. "What will the rest of them do, I wonder?"

Another eternity passed while the sun blazed down on her, lighting her up and giving every sniper in the village ample opportunity to take her out.

But no one did.

Far in the distance, she heard what sounded like a foot dragging. Faintly.

"There were three guards around the perimeter," Rory said into the comm unit a few beats later. "Neutralized."

Griffin's voice came like a knife. "Three seems like a low number."

Bethan knew their best sniper was up high on one of the buildings around this square, but she didn't bother looking for him. She knew she wouldn't be able to find him unless he wanted to be found.

"A little house to house turned up some more," August said quietly. "Bringing the total to an even eight, which is still low for an asset like this."

"I don't like this," Jonas said, in that stern, considering way that he had.

Bethan was sure he was about to recall her—order her to fall back and find defensive position—but that was when the door cracked open.

She waited, aware that she looked relaxed when she was anything but. Her weapons were holstered, so she simply stood there with her arms loosely at her sides, looking as unobtrusive as any of them did in their tactical gear. Her cargo pants and a combat-ready shirt weren't as dramatic as Army fatigues, but she doubted very much that the slender woman who stood there in the sliver between the board masquerading as a door and the questionable wall would confuse Bethan for anything but what she was.

For a moment, the two women eyed each other. Bethan smiled. The woman did not.

"Hi, Iyara," Bethan said quietly. Warmly, as if she knew the woman personally instead of from photographs. "Do you want to tell me where your brother is?"

"How do you speak the language of my childhood?" Iyara Sowande asked softly in return. "How do you know a single word?"

"I'm only looking for your brother," Bethan repeated in the same steady tone. "I don't mean you any harm."

"What is harm?" Iyara asked bitterly. "You're too late for that."

The door was wrenched open wider then.

And suddenly there were guns in Bethan's face.

"What are you saying? What does she want?" a male voice was yelling, in a completely different language than the one Bethan had just been speaking.

Hands grabbed her roughly. She let them drag her inside, protesting ineffectually. Mostly so they would yell louder as they slammed the door behind her, trapping her in the boarded-up ruin of a row house. Then they shoved her toward the ground.

Bethan went down on her knees and lifted her hands in the air, slightly cowering while she did it. Because they expected her to cower. And likely wanted her to so they could feel big and bad. That made it an excellent opportunity for her to take a quick sweep of her surroundings.

"I don't know what you want!" she cried out, making herself sound shrill and scared. "I'm only here to deliver a message. Why does that take three guys? With rifles? What did I do?"

"Received," Jonas clipped out in her ear.

"Shut up," one of the men with a rifle aimed at her face snarled. He shoved the other woman down on the ground next to Bethan, and from the corner of her eye, Bethan could see that Iyara really was cowering. "Tell me what you said to each other or I'll start shooting."

"I have a message for my old friend," Bethan protested. "How could I know she wasn't here alone, the way I expected?"

The man before her bared his teeth at her. "What is this message?"

Bethan glanced at the woman beside her then grinned widely and incongruously at the man towering over her. "Well. It's our high school reunion. I take my duties as a reunion chair very seriously, and insisted that someone come out this way to see if everybody's favorite prom queen could make the trip."

She heard someone on the comm unit laugh. The man in front of her, however, did not so much as crack a smile.

"Do you think I'm a fool?" he snarled at her. And then, less amusingly, the barrel of his rifle was there against her forehead. But that was a tactical mistake on his part. "You think I don't know exactly why you're here?"

"I already told you why I'm here," Bethan argued, and the barrel of the rifle dug deeper into her forehead. Hard enough she knew it would leave a mark.

"Understand that he will hurt you," Iyara murmured next to her, in the language the man did not understand. "Badly."

"Tell me what she's saying!" the man screamed at Bethan. "Tell me where her brother is!"

Bethan risked another glance at the woman kneeling beside her. Iyara was shrinking there where she knelt, but there was a certain set expression on her face.

She understood in a flash that these men had gotten no information out of Iyara, sister to the scientist they were all after. And that the only reason they hadn't shot Bethan on sight was because she appeared to speak the same language that the woman did and they'd figured they'd use Bethan to get what they wanted.

Too bad for them that wasn't how this was going to go.

"Why can't you understand her?" Bethan asked the man holding the gun at her head, and cowered a little bit more, on the off-chance he might think she really was scared. "Out of the three of you, not one of you knows how to communicate with her? Why would you come all this way, then?"

"In position," Jonas said intercom unit.

"You have ten seconds," the man with the rifle to her head snarled at her. "Then I'll shoot your head off."

"Is that smart?" Bethan asked him. "You don't know what she told me. And it sounds like you can't ask her."

The barrel jammed into her forehead. Harder. "Then you both die, bitch."

Bethan blew out a breath.

"Ten," the man said. "Nine. Eight."

"On his three count," Jonas said.

Bethan had the stray thought that she liked his voice in her ear.

"Seven. Six, *puta*. Five."

Beside her, Iyara began to murmur what sounded like a prayer. Or a very long curse.

Bethan shrunk, there on her knees, trying to make herself as small as possible. And in so doing, angled herself even closer to the long muzzle of the gun.

"Four," the man snarled.

"No, no, no," she cried, the way a victim might. "Please don't hurt me—"

"Three," he said.

And then Jonas burst in through the front door like a reckoning.

Ready to find
your next great read?

Let us help.

Visit prh.com/nextread

Penguin
Random
House